DIVINE BLUEPRINT

Echoes of Tomorrow
Book 3

ALEXANDER TITUS

SEAN PLATT

DIVINE BLUEPRINT

Chapter One

JIANNA MAKINDE HAD NEVER SEEN the lake at the top of Mount Buratti.

But she'd seen the pictures. Jagged peaks cradled a wide basin of shallow water that looked black under the violet sky. All gone now. Some colonist, driven insane by a prion plague, had vaporized part of the lake bed five hundred years ago, unwittingly triggering the Reunion. The council chambers sat at the largest mountain's base, set outside the boundary of Vitruvian City because Councilors needed an outside perspective to make the best decisions for the citizens they governed.

So said her father, and Soren had served as Councilor for longer than Jianna had been alive.

But even though she'd never climbed up to the lake, she'd spent plenty of time exploring the caves beneath the mountains, hunting for extremophiles to study. If her father knew how deep she'd gone, far past the mining complex and the reinforced tunnels they'd dug to prospect for rarer minerals, he would've cut her spelunking expeditions short.

The council building looked like someone had crossbred a greenhouse with a courthouse: marble curves, green terraces, translucent roof panels letting plants flourish everywhere. Pretty, sure. Also ridiculously impractical, as it needed to be cleaned after every sporestorm.

She made her way through the entrance and down the hallway, passing through bands of sunshine filtering through the branches overhead, until she reached the doors to the inner chamber.

It was now or never.

She pushed the doors open.

The Council was already in session: twelve members seated at the oval table, most of whom she'd known since she was a child. Harold Thane picked at something under his fingernail. Xanthe Vohl had angled her tablet so no one could see what she was reading. Next to Xanthe, Willow Evans, the token Naturalist who'd inherited her mother's seat on the Council at the same time she'd stepped up to be cult leader, made a show of dipping her fountain pen into the open ink pot before her and writing something in a handmade notebook.

She looked up at Jianna and smirked.

Jianna tightened her trembling grip on the tablet until it steadied, pressing the heel of her other palm to her thigh. No doubt Willow would do the same thing she always did: ask ignorant questions, jump to an unfounded conclusion, then make an impassioned speech about how Jianna's next experiment would destroy them all, as prophesied by her holy ancestor, Mother Basu.

Then the Council would vote five-to-one in favor of approving Jianna's proposal. Because even though the rest of them didn't understand the science either, they did understand that the only reason humans existed on this planet was because her ancestor, Samara Makinde, had proven Mother Basu wrong.

"Welcome, Jianna," her father said, using his Councilor Soren Makinde voice. The one she'd grown up fearing, because he pulled it out whenever she'd ditched school or broken something or refused to do her chores.

"Thank you." But it came out a squeak. She cleared her throat, ignoring the patronizing looks from the older Councilors and the smug smile on Willow's face, which somehow steadied her. No matter what else changed, the Naturalist leader's disdain remained constant.

"I appreciate you hearing my proposal," Jianna added.

Her father gestured to the speaker's chair, and she claimed it, hoping they couldn't see the trembling in her hands.

No matter how many times she came to the Council for approval on her research, she couldn't shake the feeling of being called to the headmaster's office, unsure what she'd done to warrant the summons and stuttering through her defense once the accusation was finally uttered. She was an adult, for Chytrid's sake. But having to justify her research to people who had no hope of grasping it took her back to those school days where no one had understood why she couldn't sit still and focus on a tedious lecture that built slowly to a conclusion she'd already reached five minutes in.

The only cure for that feeling was to jump right in, so she didn't bother waiting for the go-ahead. She just launched into her presentation, triggering the projection from her tablet.

A second later, strands of blue light assembled into a 3D protein model above her desk: two helices twisting around each other, with protrusions marking the side chains. Green indicators blinked at each binding site, highlighting the points of interaction.

"This is the defensive enzyme I told you about," she said. "The one produced by the lichen from the cave systems beyond the mines."

The display broke the structure down step by step. It unspooled the amino acid chain first, listing all three hundred forty-two residues by their single-letter codes, then folded the alpha helices counterclockwise and aligned the beta sheets using standard hydrogen bonding patterns. It drew disulfide bridges between distant cysteines, locking sections of the chain together.

The display built the final structure piece by piece. Hydrophobic bits folded inward. Polar residues faced outward, where they could make friends with $H2O$. The zinc-binding site positioned itself exactly three-point-seven angstroms from the catalytic center. Close enough to work, far enough not to interfere.

"It survives in conditions that kill most lifeforms and has evolved a resistance to *Necrotrophia pastoralis*, the parasite that's infected nearly fifteen percent of our livestock this quarter."

She rotated the model forty-three degrees along the vertical axis. The active sites illuminated in sequence: first the recognition domain, then the cleavage site, finally the molecular lock that trapped the fungal invasion machinery.

"This enzyme prevents cellular breach by targeting the chitin synthase pathway. If we can transfer the gene responsible, we won't need to keep dosing our livestock with synthetic antifungals every quarter. We'll have higher survival rates, less chemical load, and—"

Xanthe held up her hand. "A word, Jianna?"

"If you could hold off on questions until the end—"

"You misunderstand," Xanthe said. "We haven't asked you here to review your proposal."

Thank Phoebe, she wasn't going to have to answer a million questions this time. "You've already approved it?"

"No, I'm sorry. It's the opposite. We're shutting this project down."

Jianna stared at her.

She opened her mouth. Then closed it again.

They weren't even giving her a chance?

She looked up at the hologram still turning above her. Pointless now. Just light and spin, light and spin.

Her hands were shaking again. She didn't care. She looked over at her father, who refused to meet her eyes.

Coward.

"We don't know what this gene will do once it's inside a modified animal," Xanthe said. "Today everything seems fine, but seven generations from now, we've got glow-in-the-dark cows. If we're lucky, and they survive."

"There's no way this gene could mutate to cause bioluminescence—"

"The Fourth Law exists for a reason. As Samara so wisely said, off-target effects ripple outward. And, as we know from the past, that ripple can become a tsunami that drowns everyone."

Jianna's jaw clenched, the pressure radiating upward until her temples throbbed. "You're quoting the Fourth Law to justify inaction. The very inaction that is killing our herds."

Her father shot her a warning glance. But he should've warned her before she came that they were going to pull this on her.

Since he'd let her walk into an ambush, he had no right to complain if she fought back.

"We talk about seven-generation trials like we have

seventy years, but we don't. These microbes, these genes that come from them, have survived for thousands of years in conditions harsher than anything our livestock will ever endure. We can use it to protect them. Samara wrote the Fourth Law when she had the luxury of time. But she didn't always follow it. When the Bloom attacked Generation One, she acted."

Leyna's mouth turned down. "The council believes fifteen percent is a manageable loss. We've held stable herd numbers for decades with current treatments. What you're proposing risks total collapse."

"With respect—"

Xanthe held up her hand again. "You say Samara acted fast. She did. She also made mistakes. And those off-target effects still run our bloodlines. She proposed the Law because she learned what happens when you don't wait long enough to know better. A parasite that we can treat with inoculations is not a death sentence for our cattle. A gene you can't take back could be."

Great. Another day, another committee of people who thought PhD stood for Please Don't.

At least they'd told her right away, instead of making her push through her presentation while they pretended to consider her proposal. "You're choosing death over progress."

Xanthe didn't blink. "That's your theory."

Silence settled over the chamber.

Jianna's gaze swept the council table. Councilor Thane was back to picking at his fingernail. Xanthe had already returned to her tablet. The others studied their hands, the ceiling, anything but her face. Her father sat rigid in his chair, jaw muscles working like he was chewing words he couldn't swallow.

"So, you're not going to fund me."

It wasn't a question.

Xanthe shook her head. "No."

"And you all agree?"

"It's unanimous," Leyna said.

What else was there to say?

Thank you for choosing ignorance over science.

Jianna switched off her tablet, picked it up, then turned and walked out of the chamber. She should have seen this coming. Getting funding for phase one had been like pulling teeth from a particularly stubborn corpse. But she'd stupidly thought that solid data might change their minds.

She heard footsteps behind her. "Jianna."

She blew out a breath, turning to see her father. Why couldn't he just let her be miserable in peace?

"What, Councilor Makinde?"

He grimaced. "I'm sorry."

Jianna's voice pitched higher. "You couldn't have given me a heads-up?"

"The council voted on it minutes before your arrival. I had no idea they were going to reject it."

"You voted against it."

Jianna's father rubbed the back of his neck. "They had valid points."

"I spent three months preparing my data, and I didn't even get to share it."

"I know how hard you worked on this."

A bitter laugh burst from her lips. "But it didn't make a difference."

Silence fell between them. Soren glanced over his shoulder, then sighed. "I need to get back to the chambers. I'll see you this afternoon."

"For what?"

"The ceremony."

Was he serious? "I'm not going."

Soren's eyes hardened. "You're a direct descendant of Samara and Renata. If Phoebe had lived, she would've been half-sister to your ever-so-great grandmother. What will people think if you're not there?"

Jianna tightened her hold on the tablet. "I don't care."

"I know you're disappointed about your research. But this isn't about you. It's about coming together to celebrate our heritage of survival. You're a symbol of that heritage."

She snorted. "Well, I'm tired of living my life for everyone else."

"It matters that you are there, Jianna. That tree—"

"Is not Samara. It's not Phoebe. And just because I'm related to her doesn't make me the keeper of her legacy."

"You've never appreciated the honor it is to be a daughter of her germline."

"I'm honoring Samara more by crawling through caves looking for extremophiles than I ever could by standing next to you while you pretend to mourn her in front of the whole planet."

"I do not pretend to mourn her," he said.

"Dad. She died over five hundred years ago. For all we know, she was a terrible human being. So many of the greats back on Earth were."

He said nothing.

"The parasite is adapting faster than we can find new treatments. At some point, we won't be able to catch up, and then what?"

"You're not the only person researching—"

"I just showed you a solution that's been tested by evolution for thousands of years in conditions harsher than anything our livestock face. But you'd rather watch our herds die than take a calculated risk." She held out her tablet, jabbing at the screen. "Every quarter, we lose more animals. Every quarter, the treatments get less effective. How long before fifteen percent becomes thirty? Fifty?"

Soren sighed, rubbing the back of his neck again. "Your curiosity has always been stronger than your sense of caution. It is both your greatest asset and your most dangerous flaw."

"It's only a flaw when I don't agree with you."

He studied her face for a moment, then he brought out the official voice again. "The ceremony starts at four."

"Have fun watering the tree of your ancestors. I'm going to work." Her hand betrayed her with a violent tremor. She clenched it into a fist and stormed off, boots striking the stone floor like hammer blows.

The moment she was out of sight, she yanked the pill case from her coat. Her fingers fumbled with the lid, nearly dropping the whole thing. One pill rattled into her palm. She threw it back and swallowed hard, tasting the bitterness of alkaloids and defeat.

Which pretty much summed up her whole morning.

One of the downsides of being a direct descendant of Samara. The ancient geneticist had tested the first version of the gene therapy on herself before refining it and treating the rest of Generation One. Everyone in their germline shared a unique set of off-target effects similar to the ones that Phoebe had, because Samara's first version had been based on the modifications Samara had made to Phoebe.

And that made her father's reverence for their ancient ancestor even more galling. Because if he'd defended her research with half the passion he reserved for a woman who'd doomed her to a life of dependence on anti-seizure meds, painkillers, and other drugs as she got older…

Her ancestry wasn't an honor. It was a curse.

Chapter Two

WILLOW EVANS YAWNED, and her jaw cracked like old wood. Three hours of sleep wasn't enough for anyone, especially when those three hours came after her Brother Theo pounded on her door at midnight, babbling about mysterious lights in the sky.

But it was her job to comfort the members of her flock, even when they took Mother Basu's teachings much too seriously, like Theo did.

"I was praying for a new home, a place where we can live in accordance with the Divine without the contamination of Vitruvian science." Theo leaned forward, white-knuckling the mug of herbal tea she'd brewed for him. The herbs were supposed to be calming, but they seemed to have no effect on his enthusiasm. "Then I saw it, flaming through the sky—"

"A meteorite?"

"A sign from the Divine, headed toward Mother Basu's final resting place".

Willow reined in her impatience, thinking of her warm

bed upstairs and the fluffy down pillow that had been cradling her head a few minutes ago.

"My parents believed we should reclaim the settlement she chose centuries ago, and so did their parents before them," Theo continued, gesturing emphatically with his mug and slopping tea on Willow's table. "It's time for us to separate completely from wickedness and found a pure society. Mother Basu knew best, and Cira said at prayers yesterday that it was only Atlas' weakness that forced our people to accept their heresy. She said we've compromised too much in the name of spreading the truth to the Contaminated."

No surprise to find that Willow's younger sister was the instigator of Theo's new outburst of pious zeal. She'd never quite settled with the fact that the firstborn inherited the position of Guide, along with the Naturalist seat on the Council.

"I applaud your piety, Theo." Although she genuinely wished he'd direct it somewhere else. "But we know from Mother Basu's only records that the site she chose wasn't sufficient to support a hundred colonists, even after nearly two decades of cultivation. I've seen the reports on the soil myself. We could never grow enough food to support a few hundred thousand of us."

"Are you going to believe a sign in the heavens, or the lies of Vitruvian scientists?"

Sometimes Willow wished that her people didn't take the scriptures so literally. Mother Basu hadn't been against science altogether. She'd been against the misuse of science. That distinction was clear in her journals but often ignored by the firmest of believers.

"The Divine blessed us with the ability to understand our world, Theo."

"But the sign!" He nearly jumped out of his chair.

"How do you explain that it appeared just as I was praying for a new colony?"

Mother Basu, grant me patience.

"We've seen signs in the heavens before, and they usually turn out to be meteorites." Willow laid a hand over Theo's while allowing a touch of condescension to slip into her smile. "Or a piece of a decaying satellite, burning up through the atmosphere. At some point, the colony ship's going to start breaking apart, too."

"How long must we suffer the contempt of the Impure?" Theo lamented.

"Let's pray on it," Willow said. "If it really is a sign, it won't be the only one."

Theo left twenty minutes later, unconvinced that his sign could be explained through mortal logic but finally taking the hint that the Guide had other Brothers and Sisters to pray for.

With a sigh, Willow washed his mug before returning upstairs to lie in bed, staring at the ceiling. Sleep wasn't happening.

So she got up, walked downstairs, and went outside, following the stone path between the raised beds to the center of her yard, where the wooden trellises wouldn't block her view.

She craned her neck back, scanning the northern sky. Same constellations that had been there for five hundred years. Atlas, Mama, and Baby Pipkin, the Great Lanternfruit, the Three Spoons, exactly where they should be. The sibling moons hung low in the west, the smaller one nearly brushing the mountaintops. Somewhere up there, the *Borlaug* orbited unseen, as did Vitruvian City's one and only communications satellite, launched from the *Borlaug* by Generation One.

As far as she could tell, everything was normal. No

signs in the heavens. Not even the glint of a communications satellite in synchronous low orbit.

Willow wrapped her arms around herself; her nightgown was useless against the chill seeping up through the stone path and into her bare feet. She stood there until her toes went numb and her neck ached from craning backward, scanning the void for any flicker of movement.

It was the same sky it always was.

She'd have to get up soon for the ceremony, where she'd have a chance to lobby for her measure to make Mother Basu's birthday a legal holiday for anyone of the Naturalist faith. If she could get Soren to support it, the rest would likely fall in line. And Soren loved it when Willow owed him a favor.

She forced herself to go back in, but only as dawn was breaking did she finally manage to drift off. And two hours later, Cira had woken her to solve the first of the day's little dramas: a ham missing from the Collective's larder, discovered by the breakfast crew.

Willow slogged through her morning's duties, barely making it to the memorial grove by the time the ceremony started. She hated this political theater, but as her people's Guide, it was her duty to protest the Vitruvians' ritual of devotion, reminding them that the legends they idolized had been flawed people, just like everyone alive today. No one knew that better than her. She was the keeper of Mother Basu's journals. She knew the truth of who Samara and Phoebe had been.

And that truth had been ugly.

As she stood at the edge of the grove, the afternoon sun warmed her face, making her sleepy. She curled her lip at the Remembrance Tree, genetically engineered by the temptress Phoebe, daughter of Samara, who'd stolen the Divine Blueprint from them all.

The massive tree loomed over the celebrants like a six-foot-wide middle finger to nature itself. The trunk spiraled upward in mathematical precision: golden ratio spirals, Fibonacci sequences sculpted to create a genetically engineered temple shading the resting place of its creator and her wicked mother. Phoebe and Samara.

The Vitruvians called it beautiful. A symbol of how science could enhance nature.

Willow called it what it was: a symbol of hubris, a desecration of natural wisdom.

She didn't know what the Hyperionites thought of it. Samara had urged the Generation One colonists to tolerate those abominations, and Phoebe had even befriended one. Several dozen of the filthy beasts clustered at the far edge of the crowd, waiting their turn to leave offerings among the roots of the Remembrance Trees. Sunlight gleamed off their scaly skin, flashing bright colors, glimmering iridescent, while their huge black eyes showed no emotion at all. They carried grass dolls, bunches of flowers, strings of wooden beads: gifts for the dead heroes who'd championed coexistence between human and abomination.

Their offerings weren't so different from the ones left by humans, except that the humans paired theirs with whispered prayers and requests for blessings, as if an arrogant scientist and her headstrong daughter might somehow be able to influence the Divine.

The Vitruvians accused Naturalists of clinging to superstition. But here they were, conducting their own ceremonies, their own rituals, their own acts of faith. Only theirs were dressed up in scientific language.

Hypocrites.

They loved Phoebe, of course. She was twice a martyr, first to undergo the genetic modification that had allowed them all to survive, carrier of the off-target effects that everyone after her had inherited, including the Naturalists who'd been coerced into accepting that first vaccine. Phoebe was the reason that Willow and her people lived shorter lives, forcing down herbal concoctions designed to soften the side effects of the immunosuppressants and antifungals that allowed them to survive the Bloom.

But the Vitruvians villainized Mother Basu instead, believing that she'd deserved to be murdered when she'd done everything she could to protect her people from Vitruvian lies and the Buratti dynasty's tyranny.

No one built monuments to Mother Basu's martyrdom. No one poured ceremonial water over her grave or spoke her name with reverence.

That was the hardest part of this ceremony, watching them all worship the lie.

Willow felt tears prick her eyes, blinking them away as a familiar purple scarf caught her attention. Cira. What was her sister doing here?

The last thing Willow needed was Cira spotting her talking to Soren. Always on the lookout for gossip, Willow's sister could turn a conversation about the weather into evidence of a political conspiracy. "Collaborator" was Cira's favorite accusation against worshippers who failed to live up to her standards of faith, and that accusation always hit its target.

Cira would expect Willow to treat Soren like the enemy; if she spoke to him at all, it could only be a confrontation. Willow understood that relentlessly defending their way of life in Council sessions sometimes meant compromise, but Cira only understood black and white.

Thankfully, Soren would play along, pandering to his own constituency while offering a worthy opponent to spar with so she could show her own people how hard she fought for them. As long as neither of them truly lost, they could each go home and declare victory.

Despite the fact that their ancestors had been nemeses, she secretly liked the old man.

She fiddled with the locket at her throat as he approached the tree, carrying a crystal vessel filled with water. Stopping among the twisted roots at the base of its trunk, he looked out at the crowd as he poured out a libation.

"From root to shoot, we rise."

Three hundred voices answered as one:

"Let the past nourish us. Let the future sustain us."

Willow stayed silent.

Around her, maybe two dozen others joined her in silence: the woman in the faded blue dress, the old man with the walking stick, the teenager whose parents kept shooting him disapproving looks, and others farther away. Last year, she'd counted maybe fifteen holdouts. This year felt closer to thirty.

They were here to hear her speak out against the lie. In the past year, the Naturalist movement had grown, fed by a hunger for something real in a world that seemed increasingly artificial. Willow's outreach program had started to gain steam.

The ceremony concluded with the usual platitudes about unity and progress. After the formal portion ended, people dispersed into smaller groups. Willow headed straight for Soren.

"Guide Willow." The journalist's voice made her spine stiffen. She turned to find Omira, her tablet already recording, her smile sharp enough to cut glass. "Would you like to give your usual statement?"

Willow straightened her shoulders. This was part of

her duty as Guide. It didn't matter that all she wanted was to quietly ask Soren for his support, then head home for a nap.

"It's important that someone tells the truth at these celebrations."

"And what truth are you referring to?"

Willow's gaze fixed on the tree. "The glorification of Samara and Phoebe as secular saints. It's a lie we've been telling ourselves for generations."

"Strong words," Omira said. "Care to elaborate?"

Willow clenched her teeth. "If you'd read Mother Basu's journals, you'd know that Samara wasn't some noble scientist saving humanity. She was drunk on her own power, convinced she could improve on divine design."

Omira leaned forward. "And Phoebe?"

"What about her?" Willow asked.

"Atlas chose to be with her."

"Love makes people stupid." Willow's voice cracked. "After Phoebe died, Atlas could've had children and shared his gift the way nature intended. Instead, he wandered off into the wilderness to die, taking the Divine Blueprint."

She gestured toward the crowd around her. "Every single one of you could be healthy right now, instead of addicted to drugs that only compensate for the genetic impurities that Samara Makinde forced on us all."

"So you're saying the off-target effects are Atlas' fault. He could have saved us, but he chose to abandon us instead." Omira held the tablet closer, clearly thinking that she'd caught Willow in her trap and was about to force her to admit that her doctrine was faulty. "It's convenient that all samples of his DNA were destroyed, so we can never verify that the Divine Blueprint existed."

"Phoebe destroyed them because she wanted the

Divine Blueprint for herself. Mother Basu's daughter, Hyacinth, forced Samara to admit that."

"Then why don't we have any rec—"

"Willow." Soren's voice cut through her speech like a blade. She spun around to find him three feet away, jaw tight. Swooping in to ensure there were good soundbites for both sides. "That's enough twisting history to serve your ideology."

She let her features drop into a scowl. "Mother Basu was there, Soren. She watched Samara inject children with experimental genes, watched her splice DNA from one species into another, watched her turn human reproduction into a manufacturing process."

"Your cult's founder was a religious extremist who would prefer her people die rather than accept scientific help. She kept meticulous notes on everything she did in the lab to save a dying colony, despite Ayesha Basu's efforts to destroy us all. And Phoebe—" his voice caught perfectly, "—Phoebe was a young woman who died because of the kind of intolerance you're peddling right now."

Omira's head swiveled between them like she was watching a tennis match. Willow focused on Soren's face, refusing to give the reporter the satisfaction of acknowledging her presence.

"I'm trying to preserve what makes us human. Humanity is not some rough draft to be edited. You've convinced people that survival requires abandoning their divine design." She gestured toward the Hypers who were chatting in the corner. "Look around you. Look at what genetic manipulation has created. Monsters."

Soren stiffened. "Councilor Evans, show some respect for the Descendants. Don't spread hatred for them because you've chosen to remain ignorant."

Had she gone too far? Or had she fed him a straight

line that would rocket him up the polls for weeks? The Vitruvians did love to make a show of tolerance for the Hyperionites, even though they themselves barely tolerated the creatures who ventured into their city.

Maybe she should shift to one of their safer standing arguments.

"You're so quick to accuse Mother Basu of ignorance, when you know her objections to Samara's legacy were rooted in the very off-target effects that we all suffer. She understood the science all too well, and she wasn't afraid to face the facts that Vitruvians choose to ignore." She scanned the crowd around them. "Who among you isn't dependent on at least two drugs to soften your symptoms?"

Some reddened, others refused to meet her gaze or looked down in shame. But Soren looked pleased. She'd shown him the opening for his next volley.

As Soren ramped up his own speech about the importance of genomic diversity and the value of advancing humanity's wisdom, Willow realized she'd lost track of Cira, but while searching for her sister, she saw Camilla Lombardi's son across the grove. Nearly two meters tall, perfect proportions, gorgeous features. His perfection was clearly unnatural, and some whispered that he wasn't merely modified, that he was a synthetic, designed completely from scratch according to some template his mother had created in her black-market laboratory.

Yet the Council looked the other way at his mother's offenses because the wealthiest Vitruvians wanted their own children to have advantages that no one else could afford, and Camilla was a genius at minimizing off-target effects. Camilla and her son were living symbols of Vitruvian corruption. Willow couldn't count the number of times she'd proposed an investigation into the rumors, only to have the rest of the Council shut it down, threatening to vote her out if she took matters into her own hands.

But that didn't mean she couldn't inspire others to speak up. As soon as Soren finished his own soundbite with a call to keep progress on course by installing the guardrails of wisdom, Willow replied:

"Despite those guardrails, we have black market geneticists who skirt the rules because their rich clients protect them. Every week, more people come to our Sanctum. They're angry that we live in a society built around genetic privilege. They sense what we've lost and they want to reclaim their humanity." Willow looked straight into the camera. "We Naturalists have devoted our lives to contemplating what it means to be human. We might not be able to save your genome, but we can save your soul."

Willow made her way through the dispersing crowd, head high despite the weight pressing down on her shoulders. Several faces turned toward her, their expressions curious, some even admiring. The movement was growing. That should have filled her with satisfaction, but all she felt was bone-deep exhaustion.

Three hours of sleep. A missing ham. Theo's midnight ravings about objects in the sky. Cira's suspicions. Soren's practiced indignation. Omira's sharp questions. Each one, a stone added to her burden.

The thought of her bed, of blessed unconsciousness, pulled at her like gravity. But gravity was just another force to resist. She straightened her spine and quickened her pace. The Divine had chosen her path.

Sleep could wait.

Chapter Three

MICHELANGELO LOMBARDI'S fingers found the pill bottle in his jacket pocket, sugar pills that he rattled comfortingly against glass as he watched Councilwoman Evans stride out of the grove. He'd bowed his head with the rest of the crowd when she'd asked them to deny they were taking medications, but his face flushed with shame for a completely different reason: he didn't need them.

Before she'd been fired from her university position, Michel's mother had figured out how to eliminate off-target effects completely, but because her techniques opened the door to the creation of synthetic humans, she'd been fired, her research confiscated, and her techniques banned.

Rather than surrender, she'd made him a living protest against the government that had rejected the truth she'd uncovered. But the hypocrites still let her work as a basic gene tech, looking the other way when she applied her forbidden skills to their children under the guise of fixing basic defects.

Because the rules were different when you were rich.

Councilwoman Evans was wrong to oppose all genetic modifications on principle, but the rest of them weren't any better. They opposed anything that threatened their ancient laws, no matter how outdated those laws might be.

Michel glanced at Apprentice Glint, the only Descendant in his entire department, but one of their best engineers. Better than him, when it came to coaxing a balky harvesting combine back into action or tracing shorts in a mining robot's convoluted circuitry.

"She hates us, but her people still use our medical treatments when they're sick." The words emerged from the sleek band around Glint's throat, a collar that read micro-vibrations from Glint's larynx—muscle contractions, airflow patterns, vocal cord tension—and translated them into language.

"Who are you talking about?" Michel asked.

A woman in a purple scarf nearby glanced at Glint with disdain, then said to her companion: "If the Divine intended for that abomination to talk, it would have been born with proper vocal cords."

Glint stepped forward, voice dropping to a dangerous whisper. "Call me 'it' again and see what happens."

The woman stepped back, putting distance between herself and Glint, then turned on Michel. "You've endangered everyone here by bringing that dangerous animal into the city."

"Glint is legally a person. They have just as much right to be here as you do."

"Only because the Hypers bribed our corrupt Council to let them in. We chose to give those creatures a pass on even more dangerous technology just so they could play at being people. We banned AI for a reason."

Michel wasn't sure what grated on him more, that he agreed with her about the Council being corrupt or that her reasons for believing it bordered on conspiracy theory. Because if the people around them knew what he was, they'd have considered his very existence to be conspiracy theory fodder.

But at least he could correct her misconceptions. Even if it didn't change her mind, he might get through to the growing crowd of people watching their exchange.

"Glint's collar isn't artificial intelligence. It's actually fairly basic tech. Generation One had most of it. There are sensors that pick up subvocal muscle contractions and translate them into words. A lot like the throat mics we issue to security officers."

Except that Michel had helped Glint trick theirs out with minicams and a cloud backup, so that if anything ever happened to them off-shift, it couldn't be covered up.

Legal rights didn't always translate to physical safety.

The woman scoffed. "All that fancy tech so an animal can pretend to be human."

Glint trilled, which their collar echoed as a laugh.

"What's so funny?" the woman asked.

"That you think any Descendant would want to downgrade to baseline human."

The woman's mouth opened and closed before she turned and walked away, her purple scarf trailing behind her.

Michel watched her go, then turned back to Glint. "I'm sorry."

"I'm used to it." They shrugged, then trilled again. "Her face, when I called her a baseline human."

"That was a good one." But he remained uneasy.

If Jianna had been here, she'd have treated the woman to a lecture that would've started with the unethical foundations of genetic discrimination and slowly morphed into a dissection of the woman's ignorance about her own genome. She was fearless about speaking up when she saw an injustice, no matter who was being mistreated.

She'd even argue for a Naturalist's right to refuse medical treatment, while simultaneously explaining to said Naturalist that they were an idiot for doing so.

Jianna was her father's daughter, through and through.

He checked his comm again. No message from her since she'd told him she was skipping the ceremony to go hunting in the caves, then promised to see him tonight.

"Did Jianna get her grant?" Glint asked.

"No idea." But he was pretty sure she hadn't, and that her absence was designed to protest the Council's decision. For a Makinde to skip the Remembrance Tree ceremony was almost unheard of.

A selfish part of him was looking forward to comforting her.

After she was done ranting about the foolishness of letting people without a scientific education make scientific decisions.

As Michel returned the device to his pocket, his fingers brushed the pill bottle yet again. If the woman with the purple scarf knew what he really was, she'd have called him an abomination, too. That slight tremor in his hand? He'd learned how to fake it. Along with the periodic headaches that he complained about but never actually felt.

All while trying to remember not to overdo it, because then he'd be told to see the doctor, who might uncover his secret.

It was exhausting. Not even Jianna knew.

But Michel's mother had warned him: the performance was everything. One slip and questions would follow. Questions that could land both mother and son in prison, if they were allowed to live at all.

Glint had way more courage than he did. And was more human than the woman with the purple scarf, in his opinion. Baseline humans, as Glint had put it, could be monsters in their own right; having twenty-three chromosome pairs in the right order didn't prevent that.

Every hair on his body lifted as a faint electrical hum tickled the insides of his ears. It reminded him of the time he'd been working in the guts of the magnetic particle imager at the hospital and someone had mistakenly powered the machine on. He shivered as the hum grew louder.

Glint nudged him, pointing upward.

Michel followed their trembling finger. His muscles locked, and his mouth went dry.

Ripples of green, gold, and magenta light overhead, an impossible aurora that was somehow visible against the lavender-blue sky, casting luminous hues through the cirrus clouds that hadn't been there a minute ago. Even a class Z solar flare wouldn't be strong enough to cause visible aurora in the middle of the day. Lightning cracked from cloud to cloud in a dozen directions.

"What is that?" someone asked.

Now, everyone was staring upward.

Michel felt a sudden heat against his thigh. His comm unit. He pulled it out and dropped it immediately as the plastic casing burned his fingers. The air was heavy with the acrid tang of burning plastic and ozone as others discarded their own devices. Sparks popped out of the center speaker in Glint's collar. She ripped it off and held it away from her as wisps of smoke bled through the cracks in the casing.

"Inside," Glint signed.

"Everybody take shelter." Michelangelo grabbed the arm of the man beside him and started herding him toward the gathering hall at the other end of the grove. "Get inside, before it gets bad."

Once he'd managed to get a few of them moving, the exodus began in earnest, the uneasy crowd shuffling toward the hall, then moving faster as the crackling and popping of energized plasma overhead was followed by a deafening roar, as if the sky was protesting against the intrusion of this strange aurora.

Michel hung back with Glint, urging stragglers to hurry as arcs of energized plasma spread sideways through the sky. The ionosphere lit up in patterns that made no sense, visible waves rushing outward from a point almost directly overhead. Each wave came faster than the last.

"Electromagnetic pulse, but not solar." At least, not any solar phenomenon that he'd been trained for. "But what could set off a pulse this big?"

Even the city's biggest power plant exploding wouldn't release an electromagnetic pulse strong enough to cause something like this. A bomb might, but who would be attacking them? The Naturalists avoided technology whenever possible, and they lived near enough to the city that they'd be hit, too.

Glint signed, "The wave patterns aren't following normal magnetic field lines."

They stood transfixed near the entrance of the gathering hall beneath the storm's eruption of impossible color. Bright bolts of lightning darted between the clouds, illuminating the terrified faces of those scrambling for safety.

Then something snapped, a soundless, invisible break, like the pop of a bubble the size of the sky.

The transformer across the park exploded in a cascade of blue-white sparks, ceramic insulators shattering like gunshots. Then another blew fifty meters down the block.

Then a third. The ground trembled beneath Michelangelo's feet, followed by the boom of a distant explosion. More shaking, more explosions.

He wasn't sure what would be worse, if it were an attack, or if those were the sounds of the city's infrastructure being overloaded by some natural phenomenon they'd never seen before.

The city's lights dimmed, flickered, and died. Systems failed, one by one. The distant thrum of Vitruvia City faded away to nothing.

The silence felt unnatural.

Then the sirens began.

"We should get to the water plant," Glint suggested.

Michel nodded. Then he remembered: "Jianna. She's in the caves right now."

And she wouldn't be in the upper levels, where miners might notice a collapsed tunnel or hear the cries of a trapped spelunker. Jianna went deep into the mountains, mapping new tunnels as she hunted for exotic microorganisms to study.

If the earthquake had trapped her down there…

"Come on," Glint signed. "Let's go find her."

Chapter Four

THE TUNNEL WANTED to crush her.

Jianna wriggled forward on her belly, ignoring the scrape of stone through her jacket. A jagged edge bit into her elbow, and she cursed, twisting right. Her headlamp beam jerked across wet walls, illuminating water droplets that hung like tiny stalactites inches from her nose.

Damp air clogged her sinuses. She wiped her nose on her sleeve and squeezed deeper into the passage.

Water had spent centuries carving this route to the chambers she'd been mapping for months. Down here in the perpetual dark, extremophiles thrived in conditions that would kill a surface dweller. The Council could keep their funding. She'd prove them wrong with or without their blessing.

She wiggled around a cluster of flowstone formations, dragging her sample kit behind her. Then she stopped and marked her map. The formations were beautiful, twisting spirals of calcium carbonate built layer by layer over millennia. She paused to scrape a sample from one of the moisture-darkened crevices where bacterial colonies might thrive. Then she pulled a numbered tag from her sample kit and adhered it to the rock face.

The silence was profound here. Just the occasional drip of water and her own controlled breathing. No wind. No insects. No committee meetings. Preferrable to the noise of crowded Vitruvia City.

Down here in the dark, life evolved without committees.

Or seven-generation impact studies.

A rumble rolled through the rock.

Jianna froze. The vibration traveled up through her ribs, rattling her teeth. What the hell was that?

Silence.

Equipment failure? Michel had told her that the mining crews in the upper levels had been having problems all week: an excavator gone haywire that had to be shut down for emergency repairs.

She waited, counting her heartbeats. Ten. Twenty. Thirty. Nothing but the steady drip of water.

Then the cave shuddered. A tremor rolled through the stone like a freight train having a seizure. She crouched next to a stalagmite, covering her head as pebbles rained down. Then rocks. Then chunks that could definitely ruin her day if they connected with her skull. Or if one of the tunnels above her caved in.

The sound of massive stone slabs dragging against each other somewhere deep in the mountain's belly rang out, a grinding that built and built until—

Crack.

Sharp as breaking bone. The cave floor beneath her dropped an inch.

She scrambled forward, elbows scraping, knees banging, headlamp beam jerking, scrambling out into the tunnel, back the way she'd come. A larger cavern opened ahead just as another slab gave way with a sound like the world splitting open. The air pressure changed, and her ears popped as tons of rock shifted behind her.

Dust exploded from somewhere up ahead. It filled her lungs, her eyes, turning her headlamp beam into a useless halo of choking gray. She couldn't see. Couldn't breathe. Couldn't tell which way led out and which way led deeper into the collapse.

Jianna threw herself flat against the cavern wall, arms protecting her head. Pebbles rattled across her back like hail. Something larger, maybe the size of her fist, bounced off her shoulder, sending a jolt of pain all the way down her arm. A second crack rang out, closer this time, sharper, followed by the creak of settling stone.

Then silence, broken only by her ragged breathing and the soft patter of dust still sifting from above.

She stayed frozen, every muscle locked.

But the cave was still again.

She turned, her headlamp beam dancing in the dark.

There hadn't been seismic activity in these mountains like this for as long as she'd been alive.

She remained crouched next to the wall. She had no idea if her path back to the surface was now blocked. And even if she had a clear path now, aftershocks could collapse more of the tunnels, trapping her so deep in the ground that she'd die of dehydration before anyone could find her.

At least she knew they'd look, as soon as she failed to come home that night. Her father knew where she'd gone, and so did Michel.

Dust settled like snow in her headlamp beam. She pushed herself upright and grabbed her sample kit, boots crunching on debris as she picked her way across the cavern.

The collapse had punched a hole clean through what

used to be a solid wall. Rock that had been one piece for millennia had split apart, revealing a passage just wide enough for her to squeeze through.

The earthquake hadn't sealed her in. It had opened a door.

A door to what?

The smart move would be to head back. Mark the location, get to the surface as quickly as possible, then return with backup.

But her feet were already moving toward the gap.

Your curiosity has always been stronger than your sense of caution.

She marked the location on her map, then set her sample kit beside the opening. She'd go in, no more than a few steps. Just to see if it went anywhere.

Jianna squeezed forward, her shoulders brushing rough stone as she stopped, examining the tunnel beyond the new fissure.

This wasn't natural.

There were chisel marks on the stone. Deep parallel grooves cut into the stone. Someone had carved this tunnel. She shivered. Who else would've gotten this far down? Not the miners. Not anyone she knew of. At least, not anyone who'd come back to talk about it.

Another tremor rolled through the passage. She stilled, dust drifting down from overhead.

And somewhere in the darkness…

The sound of something humming.

The passage ended in a wall of rubble. Massive boulders had tumbled down from above, blocking the way forward. She should turn back. The smart thing would be to turn back.

Instead, she started climbing.

The humming grew louder. It was definitely mechanical, coming from somewhere beyond the rockfall.

She reached the top of the pile and found a crack in the stone wall, narrow but deep. She pressed her ear to the opening.

The pulsing hum vibrated through the rock and into her skull, a mechanical heartbeat that had no business existing this far underground.

She peered inside.

And spotted a small white-blue light.

She adjusted her headlamp, angling the beam to cut through the darkness beyond the crack.

And blinked.

Holy shit. It was a lab. Genetic synthesizer, thermal cycler, centrifuge, stuff she recognized mixed with equipment that looked like it belonged in a museum. Or a really expensive garage sale. The designs were centuries out of date, boxy and utilitarian compared to the sleek interfaces she worked with today. Everything wore a fine coating of dust, like the chamber had been sealed for some time.

And in the center of the room sat a man.

Jianna jerked back hard. Her helmet cracked against stone, the sound like breaking bone. Pain exploded through her skull, and her headlamp beam careened across the walls before cutting to black.

Darkness swallowed her whole.

Except for the light from the lab that bled out through the opening. Her heart hammered against her ribs so hard she could hear it echoing off the cave walls.

Breathe. Just breathe.

Panic made you careless. Carelessness can get you killed.

She fumbled for the headlamp, picked it up, and switched it back on.

The man sat perfectly still against the wall, head tilted forward as if asleep. What looked like a clunky-looking cryobox rested in his hands, which rested palm up on his lap. The device hummed steadily; that was the sound she'd been hearing.

The man looked familiar, and so did the cryobox.

Jianna angled her headlamp to get a better look at the man who couldn't possibly have survived down here for more than a few days. His clothes were dirty and worn, with dark stains spattered up his sleeves. But the crazy thing was, he was dressed in a style that she'd only seen in the Museum: a Generation One work uniform.

Which meant that either he was a nut case who'd dressed up in historical wear to come spelunking and got trapped down here so recently that he hadn't died of thirst yet, or…

That seemed even more impossible.

But it was the only explanation.

She sniffed. Not even a hint of decay, despite the fact that he remained so unnaturally still, he had to be dead.

She ran the beam from her headlamp over the man, freezing as the weak light illuminated a thin cord emerging from the collar of his shirt and trailing down to connect to the cryobox.

It *had* to be him.

The android who'd disappeared after murdering the first Naturalist leader. Jianna had watched the video in ancient history class, sickened like all of her classmates by his violence as their instructor droned on about the dangers of artificial intelligence gone rogue.

He was the bogeyman that her father, like all Vitruvian

parents, had threatened Jianna with when she'd come home late or snuck out at night for another adventure.

He was the reason for the A.I. ban that Michel regularly lamented as he built and rebuilt the robots that tended their fields and repaired their roads.

He was the betrayer whom Samara had never forgiven for failing to protect Phoebe.

Lucas.

Who else could have built a secret lab so deep in the bowels of the mountains that it had gone undiscovered for more than five centuries?

And the cryobox on his lap looked exactly like the one in the video that had caught him extracting what legend said was the fertilized embryo of Phoebe's child with Atlas, who had disappeared shortly after the Reunion.

She didn't know how long she stared as her mind kept reaching for another explanation and finding none.

The impossible made more sense.

Lucas had run off with the embryo after murdering the first Naturalist leader, which he wasn't supposed to be able to do.

Then he'd returned to this impossible secret laboratory with a mythical embryo in a cryobox, where he'd been trapped, possibly by the same explosion that had flooded the fanatics' settlement and forced the Reunion.

Which would mean that the cryobox in his lap contained the mythical Divine Blueprint, the sacred combination of genes that had supposedly given Atlas his legendary ability to tolerate the Bloom without drugs or gene therapy, and which had been lost when he'd wandered off into the wilderness to die of grief.

She'd hit her head more than once during the earthquake as bits of the cave ceiling had collapsed.

Maybe she was back in that cavern, unconscious and

dreaming. Or in a coma, never to wake up again. This might all be a hallucination.

But of all the things she could hallucinate, why this?

She pulled back from the crack, fingers already reaching for her comm unit before logic kicked in.

No signal this deep. Obviously.

But even if she could call someone, what then?

Hey Dad, remember that bedtime story about the killer robot that used to give me nightmares? Well, a funny thing happened during that spelunking expedition you told me not to take…

Yeah. That conversation would go great.

But if this was real, the implications were staggering. Generation One had tolerated Lucas' presence even after they'd discovered what he was, because they'd had no way to contain him, and he'd been their only link to the ship. Only something drastic, like being buried under more than a mile of mountain by an explosion that had altered the landscape above, could've restrained him.

Thank goodness he wasn't still alive.

No, *alive* wasn't right. Powered on.

Robot, remember?

It was creepy how human he looked.

If she reported him, the Council would order him destroyed. Or maybe they'd just close the gap in his natural prison that the quake had created, for fear that they'd accidentally reactivate him. He was more dangerous than any other threat on the planet.

She peered through the gap again. The android still sat motionless, bathed in the blue-white glow of the cryobox in his lap. His hands were curved around it almost tenderly. But machines weren't capable of tenderness.

Her instructor had explained that too, how Lucas had been programmed to mimic human behavior so closely that he seemed to be having emotions, but it was all a manipulation. He'd manipulated Phoebe and the other colonists into trusting him. Even Samara had been fooled, and she'd worked more closely with him than anyone.

Jianna was assuming that the android's power source was dead, but what if it wasn't?

What if she woke him up by accident?

Because if she was right about the device he held, it was the most important historical artifact in existence.

Possibly also the most important religious artifact, too, although Jianna didn't believe in any of that superstitious nonsense.

But it might also be proof that everything the Naturalists preached was founded on a lie, including their phobia of genetic engineering, which had been slowing down every generation's scientific progress since the first.

And how could she leave that alone?

She sat back on her heels. If she went in there, she could wake up the biggest threat to civilization that had ever existed on this planet, aside from the Bloom.

But if she walked away, she could be abandoning the most important scientific discovery that anyone had ever made, except for Samara's cure for the Bloom.

She had to know what was in that box.

Chapter Five

MICHELANGELO PUMPED HARD, pedaling his borrowed bicycle as fast as he could toward the edge of the city, Glint right beside him, seeming to keep up with minimal effort. The storm had taken out the electronics in every vehicle at the grove, and probably every vehicle in the city, from cars and trucks to fire engines and ambulances.

The city was in chaos. Stunned people watched buildings burn; with the city's pumps out, there was no water to put out the fires. Other buildings featured new cracks in the walls; a few had even collapsed as the quake rolled through, and clusters of people dug through the rubble with crowbars, shovels, or bare hands. Michel noted more than one charred communications tower, still smoking from the burst of power that had fried it.

Without his comm unit to mark time, he guessed they'd been riding for forty-five minutes by the time they reached the city's edge. Maybe twenty or so up the path to the mining operation's base camp, where Michel skidded to a stop and let the bike drop to the ground, racing toward the small prefab building that served as the foreman's office and mess hall for the crew.

Several miners clustered near the mouth of the nearest mineshaft, connecting themselves with a line of rope through carabiners on harnesses. The emergency lighting in the tunnel remained dark. The first miner tried his headlamp, but it didn't turn on either. Placing one hand against the right wall, he entered the tunnel.

Hopefully, all the stone surrounding Jianna had protected her equipment from the storm. Michel couldn't imagine how terrified he would be down there, alone in the dark, without even a working headlamp.

Michel went straight to Radha, the foreman who'd been on duty the last time he'd been called up here to fix an air compressor in their ventilation system. "Status?"

"Cave-in. A few of the crew are trapped down there." She gave him an odd look. "I'm surprised they sent you out so fast."

A chill ran down his back. "What's the damage?"

"The excavator tore through a load-bearing limestone shelf like it was tissue paper. Brought down half of Section C and tore right through a structural shelf. We felt the rumble as far down as Level Seven. Then everything went dead at once. Power, communications, even the backup systems."

"What about the auxiliary shafts?" Michel asked.

The supervisor looked puzzled. "We're not mining those. Why?"

Michel didn't answer. He sprinted toward the equipment locker near the mine entrance, Glint keeping pace beside him. Michel grabbed two hard hats with LED arrays, testing the battery packs. Twelve hours of life on each, assuming the EMP hadn't fried the circuitry. None of them worked.

He grabbed a handful of glowsticks, handed half of them to Glint, and cracked the first one, then shook it. The bioluminescent algae inside slowly came to life as glucose and other nutrients flooded into the compartment where they'd been hibernating, emanating a warm magenta glow.

He slung a coil of rope over his shoulder while Glint grabbed water, ration bars, and a first aid kit.

Then they headed toward the auxiliary tunnel entrance, where Jianna often started her expeditions. The auxiliary entrance was partially blocked by five decades of scrub growth. Warning signs hung askew: *DANGER - UNSTABLE GEOLOGY and NO UNAUTHORIZED ACCESS.* As much as he wished Jianna didn't feel drawn to go spelunking on her own, at least she always told him where she'd be. And she always marked her trail clearly, so as long as they could pick up the first mark and their glow sticks didn't run out, they had a shot at finding her.

He paused at the dark opening, feeling the cool air flowing out from the mountain. "You don't have to come. This could be dangerous."

Glint gave him a look that was both amused and slightly offended. Then they gestured toward the dark tunnel: *after you.*

Michel nodded, entering the cave. As much as he wished Jianna wouldn't go alone, at least she always told him where she'd be exploring. And he'd gone down with her plenty of times, although she was the one who was certified Advanced, while he was barely qualified for an Intermediate rating.

Michel swept the glowstick back and forth, but it only illuminated about a meter ahead, so he was forced to walk the perimeter, looking for Jianna's breadcrumbs. There. A flash of orange plastic. One of her sample tags zip-tied to a flowstone formation near two tunnels, both leading downward.

Jianna had written today's date on the flag, along with a note saying she'd taken the right-hand tunnel leading down. "This way."

Each marker led to the next, breadcrumbs through the darkness. It wasn't long before the passageway narrowed, then the ceiling dipped to less than a meter high, and broken stone littered the ground. Shaken loose from the ceiling by the tremors?

Forced to a crouch, then to crawl on all fours with the glowstick in his mouth. Sweat trickled down Michel's back despite the increasingly cool air. Every time they approached another split, he couldn't help holding his breath until he located Jianna's next marker. As they rounded each turn, he sighed with relief that the way forward wasn't blocked with debris.

The tunnel narrowed further, and he had to scrabble forward on his elbows to fit.

"You okay back there?" he called to Glint, more to reassure himself than because he was worried about them. "One is yes, two is no."

One tap on his ankle. So he pushed forward.

Eventually, they came out into a large chamber. To his left, what was once a solid rock wall had partially collapsed, bringing down chunks of ceiling with it. Jagged slabs of limestone formed a chaotic pile, some pieces as large as Michel's torso.

Jianna's sampling kit lay abandoned beside the rockfall, its metal case dented but intact. She'd been here when it collapsed.

No.

Michel darted over. Looking for blood. Or any sign she might be trapped beneath the fallen stone.

"Jianna!" His voice echoed off the stone, bouncing back unanswered. "Jianna, are you down here?"

Silence.

Glint grabbed his arm, pulled him toward an opening in the wall, and stuck her glowstick inside. Not just an opening, but a passage carved into the living rock, the chisel marks still visible after centuries. And it was just wide enough for someone Jianna's size to squeeze through.

Smoke billowed over the Naturalist Quarter wall as Willow ran toward the gate, lungs burning with each ragged breath. Three columns of black smoke climbed into the periwinkle sky above the city. Buildings showed jagged fissures up their facades, power lines dangled and sparked where they'd torn free, and broken glass glittered on the streets.

The attack had come without warning. First, those impossible aurorae, then transformers blowing one after another, and finally, the tremors that had shaken loose everything not properly secured.

A Vitruvian security officer directed panicked citizens away from a burning storefront with a manual bullhorn. His electronic amplifiers lay useless at his feet. Willow pushed past the crowd and ducked under a concrete barricade.

The walls of the Naturalist Quarter stood three meters high, built from the same gray concrete as the rest of Vitruvian City, though trailing vines and native flowers cascaded down the sides.

Two of her people frantically waved others through the open gate.

"Guide Willow!" Bram jogged over, soot smudging his beard and cheek. "Thank the Divine you're safe."

"Report," she said, fingers finding the comfort of the locket at her throat.

Bram scratched his cheek, leaving another streak of soot. "The electromagnetic pulse cooked every circuit board in the Quarter. The Hendersons' main panel caught fire, took out half the house, before our bucket brigade was able to put it out with greywater. The pumps are dead."

"How much water do we have right now?"

"Rooftop tanks hold maybe two thousand liters total. Personal storage in clay vessels, another five hundred. We've already started rationing."

Cira appeared beside them, purple scarf askew. "The fire on Devotion Street is spreading to the archives. We need water now."

"No," Willow said.

"What?"

Willow looked toward the fire, where smoke rose from three different locations. "We can't use our water to put out flames. We need it to drink."

"And if the power comes on in an hour?"

"I'll take responsibility. Houses can be rebuilt."

"Easy to say when it's not your house burning."

"Anyone who needs shelter can stay in the Sanctum," Willow said. "Rescue the people and bring whatever blankets and provisions you can. But don't endanger anyone trying to save structures."

"We need to ask the Vitruvians for water," Bram said.

"The whole city has lost power. They have less than we do, because they're dependent on their treatment facilities."

She pushed herself up. "Let the fires burn themselves out. We need to preserve our water."

Her lungs felt raw, but she couldn't rest, not with so many people depending on her. There were still others to save.

Mother Basu had not faltered in the face of crisis. Neither would she.

Hours later, water dripped from Willow's face as she sat at the edge of the reflecting pool, the cold shock momentarily dulling the raw pain in her throat. The Sanctum rose behind her, its stone walls draped with native vines that had only this morning been dotted with tiny white flowers. Now the stone was scorched black in places and covered in ash; the vines had caught fire as sparks drifted up from the southern end of the Quarter on a breeze that would've been idyllic any other day, and the thick sap that nourished their tiny blossoms had ignited spectacularly but burned out almost as fast.

Generations of Naturalists had cultivated those vines, coaxing them into a living tapestry of graceful, interwoven patterns. They could be started again from cuttings but would take decades of tending to.

Fading daylight filtered through the hand-blown glass of the Sanctum's arched window, fracturing into rainbows that danced across the courtyard where hundreds of her people now gathered. Mothers nursed infants, elders shared water rations from clay cups, and children huddled together, their eyes wide with unspoken fears. Inside the temple's main hall, more families had claimed spaces on the stone floor, marking territory with salvaged blankets and meager belongings.

Some of those people, she'd helped pull out of burning or collapsed buildings alongside Bram and the more able-bodied, passing the rescues off to Cira and Theo for care. Others had managed to save themselves or their neighbors, and Willow couldn't have been more proud. When disaster struck, her people came together without needing to be asked, offering comfort to whoever needed it. Some had even volunteered to help their Vitruvian neighbors, once the fires in the Quarter had largely burned themselves out, leaving behind blackened shells of homes and gardens of ashes and embers.

"Willow." Cira's voice cut through the murmuring crowd. "I need to speak with you."

Willow rose, her legs still unsteady, and followed her sister into a meditation room off the main hall. Dried bundles of sage, lavender, and fennel hung from the rafters, their scent a pleasant counterpoint to the smoke embedded in her clothing. A shallow basin of water captured the last light from a small window, sending ripples across the ceiling.

Cira closed the door. "Half the greenhouses are gone. The northern gardens, too."

Willow's stomach tightened. Their food supply.

"How bad?"

"Sixty percent of our crop, gone." Cira's voice remained flat. "The stone walls protected some, but not enough."

In the silence that followed, distant coughing echoed from the main hall.

"The people need to hear from you. They're waiting."

"I don't have any more information than they do."

"They don't need information, they need inspiration." Cira stepped closer. "You're the Guide. Sometimes I think you enjoy playing Councilor so much, you forget that."

A soft knock interrupted them. Theo stood in the doorway, face stripped of color beneath the soot that marked him. "Guide Willow. I need to speak with you. Privately."

"Can it wait?" Cira asked. "We're in the middle of—"

"It's about the sign." Theo kept his gaze on Willow. "Please."

This needed to be managed. If Theo started going on about how his sign in the heavens had been a warning of this crisis, he'd gain plenty of listeners for the theory that this was a punishment for their complacency, and he'd start pushing for a new colony as a solution. Cira would back him, and Willow would have yet another crisis to deal with.

"Of course, Brother Theo." She turned to Cira. "Would you mind getting the service started?"

Cira looked like she wanted to object, but then she nodded and left. Before she'd even closed the door behind her, Theo blurted: "The new colony. We don't have to leave, we can start it right here."

What was he babbling about? "I'm not sure what you—"

"The sign wasn't telling us to leave, it was heralding a gift. The Divine has taken their precious technology away from the Vitruvians." Theo raised his hands above his head. "It's time to witness in the streets, warn them that worse is coming if they choose to disobey. Send everyone out to spread the message."

That would go over well, adding to the chaos while the city's workers struggled to restore order during a disaster. Her people would be arrested in droves, and even Soren would refuse to cooperate with her.

But Theo had never heard about catching flies with honey, whatever that was. Mother Basu had alluded to the old Earth practice more than once in her private journals. Which someone like Theo would never read, because he wasn't capable of understanding the philosophical nuance that drew Willow back to their founder's writings again and again.

"The best thing we can do right now is offer kindness," she said. "Show the Vitruvians that the Divine is there to aid them by pitching in to help with repairs and sharing our bounty."

He glared at her. "A Guide who refuses the gifts of the Divine doesn't deserve her position."

"If the Divine wishes to replace me, I will accept its judgment gladly," Willow replied.

But had her sister's machinations cast doubt on her leadership?

Those, she'd fight to her very last breath.

Chapter Six

THE SMART MOVE would have been to turn around, mark the location, and return with backup.

Instead, Jianna pulled off her headlamp and set it down on a nearby rock. Five centuries of Samara's genes had apparently programmed her for spectacularly bad decisions.

She studied the android through the gap in the rock. It had been trapped down here for centuries, motionless. Its power cells had to be depleted by now. Just an ancient machine frozen in place, clutching a historical artifact in its lap.

An artifact so important that the android had held it for more than five hundred years.

She could slip in, retrieve the cryobox, and be gone before it knew she was there. It seemed to be completely dead. But every nerve in her body screamed at her to stay where she was.

She was alone in a cave with an android that had killed despite the programming that should've stopped it. What if

Lucas wasn't powerless at all? What if it was just waiting, playing dead to lure her closer?

This could be the most dangerous thing on the planet. The android had been trapped down here for five hundred years, where it couldn't hurt anyone. Could she really risk releasing it?

She should crawl back the way she'd come and get Michelangelo to help her block up the entrance to this passage. Make sure no one else could ever discover it.

But the scientist in her couldn't turn away. Not before she'd had a chance to examine that small box in its hands.

Jianna squeezed through the jagged opening, scraping her shoulder against rough limestone. The air here felt different against her skin, and she wasn't sure if there was an actual difference or if it was just fear ramping up her perceptions. She crept forward, keeping her headlamp beam trained on the floor to avoid tripping over debris.

Her elbow knocked loose a chunk of limestone. It tumbled down the rubble slope, the sound multiplying in the confined space. *Click-clatter-click.* The echo bounced off the walls like gunshots.

She froze, her heart pounding. For one terrible moment, her muscles locked as she waited for the grinding roar of shifting stone, for the ceiling to come down on her head.

Silence.

Just the rock she'd knocked loose. Nothing more.

Jianna exhaled slowly and continued her approach. The android remained motionless. It seemed completely dead. Its hands still cradled the cryobox in its lap, fingers curved around it with an almost protective posture.

Up close, its synthetic skin looked unnervingly real. Whoever had built it had paid attention to the smallest details. Pores. Fine lines around the eyes. Even a hint of stubble. If not for the cable running from his neck to the cryobox, he could have easily passed for human.

But it was definitely the figure in the surveillance footage of Dr. Basu's secret fertility clinic. Now that she was this close, there was no denying it.

She reached for the box. The metal surface looked scratched but intact, its digital readout dark. This could be it. The mythical Divine Blueprint. The genetic code that would prove once and for all whether the Naturalists' beliefs had any basis in scientific reality.

The android's eyes snapped open.

Jianna stumbled backward, nearly falling over the debris behind her. Her heart leapt into her throat as adrenaline flooded her system. She had no weapon, nothing to defend herself with. Stupid, stupid, stupid.

"Hello," the android said. His voice sounded strangely normal despite centuries of disuse. "I'm sorry to startle you."

Jianna pressed herself against the wall, hand fumbling for something to use as a weapon. "Stay where you are."

"May I ask your name?"

The question was so mundane that it caught her off guard. "Jianna Makinde."

A slight smile crossed its face.

It could smile?

"My luck appears to be holding," the android said. "Do you know who I am?"

"You're the robot that murdered Dr. Basu, then disappeared."

"That is true," it said, smile fading. "But you can call me Lucas."

Jianna stared. Had it just attempted humor?

"I couldn't hurt you if I wanted to," it said.

But she knew that wasn't true, because the android had

hurt Dr. Basu. She'd seen the proof in ancient surveillance video.

"The last thing I remember is the cave-in," it continued. "I was forced to power down all non-essential functions to conserve power."

Lucas blinked, and she wondered if it needed to, or if the android was choosing to expend power to trick her into treating it like a person. Probably the latter, and if that wasn't a reason to run out of here as fast as she could, she didn't know what was.

But it hadn't done anything to her yet. Because it was gathering information? Or because it couldn't?

"How long have I been down here?" it asked.

"About five hundred years."

"Then I need your help more urgently than I thought. My power cells are nearly depleted. I've been diverting most of my energy to maintain the cryobox."

"You killed Dr. Basu?" The words burst from her mouth before she could stop them.

"Because she killed my daughter." No hesitation. No remorse.

And just like that, she couldn't think of the android as "it" anymore. Even though there was no way a machine could have been Phoebe Makinde's father, he'd said it like he'd actually cared about Jianna's distant ancestor.

"You mean Samara's daughter."

Lucas shrugged, a surprisingly human gesture. "Phoebe considered us both her parents."

Watching him, Jianna could almost forget what he was. His expressions, mannerisms, and speech patterns were all perfectly calibrated to mimic humanity. No wonder the early colonists had been fooled. With this level of sophistication, and without any reason to look for inconsistencies...

Her ancestors' ban on AI suddenly made perfect sense.

"Will you help me find a power source for the cryobox?" Lucas asked.

"What's in it?" She edged closer despite herself. "Does it really contain the Divine Blueprint?"

"It contains the embryo of Phoebe's daughter with Atlas."

Jianna felt lightheaded, and the room seemed to tilt around her. "Are you saying that the Divine Blueprint actually exists?"

"Atlas possessed a unique set of mutations that allowed him to survive exposure to the fungal Bloom without genetic modification."

This was monumental. Not some religious superstition, but actual science. Proving this meant she could settle the centuries-old debate once and for all. Rewrite the entire history of their planet.

Would the Council make it public? Or would they bury it to maintain peace with the Naturalists? Her father had already shown that he valued stability over scientific advancement. She wasn't sure he would champion the truth when the stakes were this high.

She could take the cryobox herself. Verify its contents, isolate the genes responsible for Atlas' immunity, and publish her findings. The Naturalists would protest, but it would be obvious to everyone that they were choosing ignorance over actual evidence.

"Could you check the display on the cryobox?" Lucas interrupted her thoughts. "I need to know if the correct temperature is being maintained."

"Why can't you check it yourself?"

"I'm splitting what little power I have left between maintaining this conversation and powering the cryobox," he explained. "If I divert energy to move the rest of my body, there won't be enough to keep the cryobox running. Even an hour at elevated temperatures and the embryo won't be viable."

Jianna moved toward him slowly, still half-expecting him to lunge at her despite his claims. She carefully lifted the cryobox from his lap. True to his word, Lucas didn't move except for his eyes tracking her.

The digital readout on the side flickered faintly: -196° Celsius, still in the safe zone for embryonic preservation.

"I can divert enough power into the cryobox to charge it for approximately two hours, but it will power me down completely. Will you take it and connect it to a new power source?"

He didn't ask to be charged himself, even though he claimed his own power source was nearly dead. Did he care so much about his 'grandchild' that he'd let himself die to make sure it survived?

Or was this a show of self-sacrifice meant to lull her into a false sense of trust?

Maybe he'd already realized she wasn't going to help him, knowing what he was capable of, so he didn't bother to ask.

"I'll take care of the embryo."

"Jianna!" Michel's voice echoed from the tunnel behind her. "Jianna, are you in there?"

She'd never felt more relieved to hear anyone in her life.

Chapter Seven

"JIANNA?" Michel called into the darkness. His voice bounced off the stone walls, coming back to him distorted and hollow. The glow stick in his hand was fading, its magenta light dimming as the bioluminescent microorganisms consumed the last of their nutrients.

He cracked another one, shaking it vigorously until the pink glow bloomed between his fingers.

"Michel! Down here!"

His heart stuttered at the sound of her voice. She was alive. He surged forward, Glint close behind, the tunnel squeezing tight until he had no choice but to drop onto his hands and knees. Saw-toothed stone scraped his palms as he crawled.

"I'm coming!" he called, and ahead, he saw a slim shaft of light, steady and real. Relief pulsed through him. Jianna's headlamp had survived the electromagnetic storm, shielded by hundreds of meters of rock. If she'd been trapped in absolute darkness, she might have vanished into these tunnels forever. That headlamp had kept her anchored. Maybe saved her life.

Michel crawled the last stretch and pulled himself into a wider space. The pale glow of his stick spilled over the edge of a jagged opening. He leaned closer.

What he saw made no sense.

An ancient laboratory filled the cavern beyond, shrouded in dust. Outdated equipment crowded the benches, relics he'd only glimpsed in old archives. And in the center sat a man, unmoving, slumped over, head bowed as if in sleep.

Jianna hovered a few feet from the man, clutching a strange-looking box to her chest in one hand. The look on her face was new to Michel: a wild, uncertain thing, balanced on the edge between terror and awe. Like she'd stumbled on some secret that might change everything, but she couldn't decide whether that was good or bad.

"*You okay?*" Michel whispered, wedging himself through the narrow gap.

She didn't answer at first, just kept her eyes fixed on the man. Then she nodded, slow, deliberate.

Michel dropped down into the lab, boots stirring up powdery dust. Glint followed, came up beside him, and then stopped cold. She froze mid-step, hands flashing signs so quickly Michel couldn't keep up.

"Slow down," he said.

Jianna pressed a finger to her lips. "*Shh.*"

The man didn't move. Was he asleep? What was he doing down here, surrounded by relics that should have been stripped for salvage centuries ago?

It didn't make sense. None of it did.

Jianna motioned silently toward the tunnel.

Michel looked at Glint, waiting for the Descendant to move. She didn't. She just stared at the man, shoulders tense, reverent. Michel nudged her arm. She turned, hands shaping a sign he didn't recognize.

"The Liaison," she signed.

Michel frowned. "What?"

Jianna was already waiting for them at the tunnel entrance, waving them over in a way that left no room for debate. Michel hesitated, casting one last, hungry look at the lab with its banks of mysterious equipment. But she knew what was going on, and he didn't. He followed.

They crawled single file through the narrow passage, Jianna at the end this time, and no one said a word. It wasn't until they reached the larger cavern that Michel turned, unable to keep it in anymore.

"I was so worried—"

"We need to get out of here," Jianna cut in, urgently. "Right now."

"Who was that back there?"

Jianna ignored him, turning to Glint instead. "You recognized him, didn't you?"

Glint nodded, hands moving. "The Liaison."

Michel was still stuck on the question. "What does that mean?"

Jianna looked at him like he was the slowest student in class. "Lucas. The android. He's been buried down here for centuries."

Michel stared at her, then back at the passage they'd just come from. Awe collided with skepticism, but the engineer inside him was already running through every contradiction and possibility.

The android who'd come to this planet with Generation One, who'd fooled them into thinking he was human so he could carry out some undisclosed mission, had disappeared because he'd been trapped in that cave for five centuries. And Jianna had somehow found him, apparently undamaged, surrounded by some secret lab that no one knew existed, thanks to the aurorae blowing up the grid and triggering a minor quake.

It was so unbelievably absurd. But it also explained everything he'd seen in that cave.

The ancient equipment.

The man's unnatural stillness, but no whiff of decay.

The fear on Jianna's face. He'd never seen her that scared, not even when her appendix burst and they'd had to hike ten kilometers to get back in range of the comm satellites so he could call for help.

"Okay, assuming that's Lucas—"

"It's him." No doubt, no room for negotiation.

"Then we need to tell your father, get permission to study him. I could bring a power source down, we could boot him up—"

"No!" Jianna snapped, sharp and final. "We need to seal off that cave. Make sure he never gets out."

Michel couldn't believe what he was hearing. He glanced at Glint, whose expression surrendered nothing as she watched them both closely.

He was sure that the Descendant was itching to figure out what made the android tick, just like he was. Not to mention, the thing had played a prominent role in negotiating peace between her ancestors and his. Apparently, it had been the first to recognize that the Descendants' hand language was a variant of Earth's. It had served as a translator.

But he couldn't rely on Glint to make his argument for him. So he tried to put it in terms that Jianna would understand: the hunger for knowledge.

"Do you have any idea what we could learn from Lucas? That android is an order of magnitude more sophisticated than any robot we've got."

"He's too dangerous," Jianna replied. "He admitted to

me that he killed Dr. Basu because he thought Phoebe was his daughter."

"You actually talked to it? It was conscious?"

"Are you listening to me? *He confessed to murder.*"

"Okay, but I could open it up, figure out how to disable its mobility functions, so we could talk to it safely," Michel argued. "And at the first sign of danger, we unplug it. Once its power source is depleted, we're back to where we started."

"What if it wakes up while you're doing that?"

"The knowledge we could gain is worth the risk." But her expression showed she wasn't convinced. "We could also just take it back home and open it up, see what we can learn from the design of its systems."

Glint's hands moved again. "We must tell the Elders that the Liaison lives."

Michel watched Jianna's face harden. "You both have to swear not to tell anyone about this."

"You can't make this decision for all of us. It's too important." After all the times she'd complained about her own research being stifled, how could she want to squash this?

"We all found it, even if you found it first," he continued. "We should tell your father. He'll know what to do."

Glint seconded Michel's statement, her hands moving frantically. "The Liaison has always protected us. We must help him."

"That was a very long time ago," Jianna replied. "Before he killed someone. He's not supposed to be able to kill."

Michel shifted impatiently from one foot to the other. "He can't kill anyone if we don't turn him on."

"Do you really think the Council's going to let you study an artificial intelligence?"

"Not if they—"

"He's the reason for the ban, Michel. The Council *has* to destroy him as soon as they find out he exists. For political reasons, if nothing else."

He knew she was right, but that didn't stop him from being angry at her for saying it.

"If you think it's so dangerous, then you should want to run home and tell your father about it. You don't want the Council to destroy it either."

Glint signed, "The Liaison belongs with the Descendants."

"He's been trapped down here for a long time," Jianna said. "He might not be the same person your people remember."

Glint shook her head, but she looked hesitant as she signed again. "The Liaison has never harmed a Descendant."

"Once we set him free, we might not be able to put him back," Michel pointed out.

Jianna held up the small box. "I need to get this connected to a power source. If Lucas was telling the truth, I only have about two hours to plug it in before it goes dead. He used the last of his own power to recharge it."

"What is it?"

"Help me get it home. I'll explain everything on the way." When he hesitated, she bounced on her heels and pleaded, "Please, Michel, I need you to trust me. This is important."

But *he* wasn't important enough for her to explain what was going on?

He ran a hand through his hair. "While you were down here, there was some kind of massive EMP blast or ionizing event that blew out the grid. There's no power. Everything electronic was fried."

The color drained from Jianna's face. "Everything?"

"Whatever hit us was strong enough to melt circuitry. It's a miracle your headlamp is working, and that's only because you were so far underground, insulated from the blast. The mining machinery that was connected to the grid is all offline, and it will take months to get it back."

Jianna stared at the box in her hands. "We have to go back."

She headed toward the tunnel entrance again.

Michel exchanged a look with Glint, then followed.

Back in the laboratory, Jianna skirted the edge of the room, keeping as much distance as possible from the android. Michel couldn't help himself; he walked straight up to Lucas, examining it with fascination.

He would never have guessed it wasn't human. The skin texture, the hair, even the slight imperfections that gave human faces character, all perfectly replicated.

"Michel," Jianna called from across the lab. She pointed to a dusty machine on a workbench. "If we plugged this into a battery, would it work?"

He moved over to examine the device. A gene synthesizer, just like the one in the museum that had once belonged to Samara Makinde. Except this one looked more advanced.

He traced the power cord to a battery unit on the floor. Pressing the power button experimentally, the machine flickered to life for a moment, then died again.

"I think I could rig something up," he said, looking back at her. "But why?"

Jianna held up the small box. "So I can see if Lucas was telling the truth."

Chapter Eight

THE EMERGENCY COUNCIL chamber was dark, lit only by oil lamps and candles that cast long shadows across the faces of the twelve Councilors. Outside the windows, Vitruvian City lay in darkness, its towering structures reduced to silhouettes against the twilight sky. Willow shifted uncomfortably in her seat, trying to ignore the pounding headache that had dogged her since the Aurora Event.

Xanthe stood before a makeshift display board where diagrams and hastily scrawled notes had been pinned. Dark circles underlined her eyes, and her normally immaculate uniform hung wrinkled from her frame.

"None of our scientific divisions can explain what happened," she said, gesturing to the notes. "Meteorological is at a complete loss. Orbital Monitoring says what we witnessed was impossible according to all known atmospheric physics."

"Do they think it was solar weather?" Soren asked from his position at the head of the table.

Xanthe shook her head. "They detected no solar flares

at all, let alone one powerful enough to cause damage at this scale."

Harold leaned forward, his gaze settling deliberately on Willow. "Well, something caused it. I can't believe it was a matter of divine intervention."

Willow held his gaze but remained silent. Let him bait someone else. She had played this game long enough to recognize when reacting would serve Harold's agenda more than her own. Mother Basu would say that the path of wisdom lies in choosing which battles to fight.

Soren rubbed his temples. "It might be some new cyclical phenomenon that we haven't been on this planet long enough to encounter."

"Our astronomical division has no idea," Xanthe replied. "They've been monitoring the sky constantly since the event and have found nothing unusual except..." She hesitated. "They're still compiling data."

Soren straightened in his chair. "We have bigger problems to solve. Every major utility in the city is down. Initial assessments suggest we're looking at months of repairs, at minimum." He gestured to the reports scattered across the table. "Our water stores will be gone within a day or two, and once they are, three million people will start dying of thirst."

Willow thought of her people in the Sanctum, of Cira addressing them in her absence. Of the precious water stored in their clay vessels that wouldn't last the week.

Elias cleared his throat. "We could start pumping water out of the river and boiling it for purification."

"With what pumps?" Isabeau asked. "The ones that run on electricity?"

"We can send volunteers with wagons to haul water," Elias insisted. "Distribute it through neighborhood centers."

"A drop in the bucket," Isabeau countered. "Three million people need at least six million liters per day just for drinking and basic hygiene, and every vehicle in the city is nonfunctional. How many wagons do you think we have?"

Willow watched them argue, calculating silently. The Naturalist Quarter housed thirty thousand people. They had their own wells, their own rainwater collection systems. Not enough for everyone, but enough to buy time if rationed carefully. If she offered to share those resources, would the Council finally acknowledge the value of her people's approach? Or would they simply take without learning?

Soren raised his hand, silencing the debate. "Our main priority is to get the water treatment plants running again." He turned to Willow. "Do the Naturalists know of any pre-industrial Earth technologies we could implement quickly?"

Willow straightened, surprised to be consulted but careful not to show it. This was the opening she needed. "We can build hand-operated pumps. And I've read about a technology called aqueducts that used gravity to move water over long distances. I'll send everything I have on those to Civil Engineering as soon as I return home." She paused. "And my people will help with manual hauling and purifying of water."

Heads nodded around the table. Grudgingly, but they nodded. A small victory.

"But I want to remind you all," she continued, seizing the moment, "for years, I've been warning this council about our civilization's dangerous dependence on integrated systems. Today, a single event brought our entire city to its knees."

Harold's face darkened. "Here we go again."

Willow flushed but held her ground, gesturing toward the darkened cityscape beyond the windows. "This is what technological fragility looks like. We greedily built our house on a foundation of sand."

Harold pressed his fingertips together. "The alternative being what? A return to pre-industrial agriculture? Let me know how many millions you're prepared to watch starve."

Willow glared at him. "The alternative is resilience, Thane. Distributed power generation instead of centralized grids. Local manufacturing that doesn't collapse when one facility fails. Redundant systems that actually work when you need them. We create communities that have the skills and resources to sustain themselves even when the larger infrastructure fails."

"Are the Naturalists faring so much better than we are?" Isabeau asked. "Because from what I understand, your people are suffering the same power outages as everyone else."

Willow clenched her hands into fists. "The difference is that we know how to function without electricity."

"Oh, really?" Isabeau snorted. "Can you function without water?"

"At least our social structures don't collapse when the communication networks go dark."

"I guess we'll see if that's true," Isabeau said.

Xanthe raised a hand. "Enough. There's a difference between supporting thirty thousand people and supporting three million, Willow. Scale changes everything."

Willow swallowed her frustration. They always fell back on numbers when they couldn't argue principles. Yes, scale mattered, but the underlying problem remained.

Soren rapped his gavel. "Regardless of our philosophical differences about technological dependence, we have an immediate crisis to address: the failure of our infrastructure."

"Just because the Naturalists enjoy living like primitives doesn't mean everyone should have to," Harold sneered.

White-hot anger surged through Willow, but the chamber doors burst open before she could form a retort.

An aide rushed in, face flushed. "Apologies for interrupting your session, Councilors. Astronomical was searching for a cause of the Aurora Event, and they've received a transmission."

The room fell silent.

"A beacon from the *Borlaug?*" Soren asked.

The aide shook his head. "No, sir. It's from outside the solar system."

Willow felt the blood drain from her face. Theo's words echoed in her mind: *A sign in the heavens.*

He had insisted that the Aurora Event was only the beginning. That worse things were coming.

What if he was right?

The bicycle wheels bumped over cracked pavement, sending jolts up Jianna's arms. Her headlamp cast a weak beam through the smoky haze, barely illuminating more than a meter ahead, its battery well on the way to dying. Michel rode beside her in silence, the magenta light from his glowstick not helping at all.

They'd already gotten lost once. The city looked alien with the power out, its familiar intersections transformed into shadowy mazes and its landmarks obscured by darkness. Most windows were dark, and the few that showed light flickered with the orange glow of fire.

Dead wires dangled from poles like broken marionette

strings. Buildings stood cracked and smoking where tremors had damaged foundations or where electrical fires had broken out. The thought of thousands of people relying on open flames for light made Jianna's skin crawl. They'd seen enough fires for one day.

A dull throb pulsed behind Jianna's eyes, the beginning of a headache because she was overdue for her next dose. Her throat felt raw from breathing smoke and dust. She worried about Glint, who'd insisted on returning to her village. The Descendant had refused to promise silence about Lucas, and it bothered Jianna that they looked at Lucas with reverence rather than fear.

Michel said he trusted Glint to keep their secret, but what choice did any of them have now? They couldn't un-find the android. They couldn't unknow what they'd discovered.

She wasn't entirely sure about Michel, either. The look on his face when he'd realized he was facing the android from every childhood nightmare said he was dying to take it apart to see how the thing worked. Engineering genius or not, an android that could break its own programming was too dangerous, even for him.

But she understood his fascination. That was exactly how she felt about the cryobox weighing down her jacket pocket. If she'd been smart, she would've just sealed the cave opening and trapped the abomination underground for another five hundred years. But she had to know what was in the box, especially after Lucas claimed it was Phoebe's embryo with Atlas.

If she found out he was lying, she'd pry his head from his body and hide it so deep in the cave system that only the glowgrubs would find it.

"Left here," Michel said, pointing toward a side street. "I think."

She followed, recognizing the silhouette of a building with octagonal windows. Two doors down stood her home, completely dark. Her father would still be at the emergency Council meeting, dealing with the aftermath of whatever had caused the blackout.

They rolled to a stop in front of her house, propping the bikes against the wall. Michel followed her inside without asking, his footsteps muffled on the floor. Neither spoke until they reached her bedroom and closed the door.

Michel pulled off his backpack with a grunt, removing the ancient gene synthesizer and its power pack. He placed them on her desk.

"Do you have a charging pack for your comm?"

Jianna nodded, digging through her drawer until she found it. Michel's hands moved with practiced efficiency, cutting adapters, splicing wires, connecting the ancient power pack to her modern charger. His fingers never trembled as he worked, something she'd always envied. Her own hands shook whenever she was excited or anxious, a betrayal of her emotions she couldn't control.

When Michel pressed the power button, the gene synthesizer's screen illuminated with a steady blue glow.

"You're a genius." She threw her arms around him, the relief making her dizzy.

Michel looked down at her, his eyes dark in the synthesizer's glow. "Can I stay tonight?"

"My father could come home anytime." The words came automatically, the same excuse she always used.

"When are you going to tell him about us?" His voice was soft, but she heard the edge beneath.

"After the next election. He only wants one more term before he retires." The promise felt hollow even as she said it.

"That's what you said last time."

"I had no idea he was going to win again."

Michel stepped back, running a hand through his hair. "I'm not ashamed to be with you, even though your father is some hoity-toity Councilman."

Guilt twisted inside her. She wasn't just protecting her father from Michel; she was protecting Michel from her father. If Willow discovered that Councilor Makinde's daughter was involved with the son of a black-market genetic engineer, she'd use it to destroy Soren's career. Michel's mother would be investigated again, maybe even imprisoned this time.

"I'll tell him as soon as the last vote is counted. I promise."

Michel nodded, though his eyes said he didn't believe her. "I've got an early shift tomorrow anyway." He leaned in and kissed her gently. "Be careful with that thing."

After he left, Jianna stood staring at the door, surprised at how easily he'd given up the argument. He usually pushed harder.

But right now, she had something more important to focus on.

She locked her bedroom door and turned to the synthesizer. Its ancient interface glowed with soft blue light, the buttons worn smooth by centuries of use. Her fingers hovered over the controls, tracing options she'd only seen in historical archives. This machine might have been used by Samara herself.

Jianna opened the cryobox. Inside, suspended in clear nutrient gel, floated a tiny cluster of cells barely visible to the naked eye. An embryo, frozen in time for half a millennium.

Hands trembling, she used tweezers to transfer it to the scanner, then closed the tiny hatch to seal it in. The gene synthesizer hummed softly as it began the scan. When it beeped completion, she quickly returned the embryo to the cryobox, which showed less than thirty minutes of power remaining.

She transferred the data to her comm device, a task that would have taken seconds with a working network but now required a direct cable connection and several minutes of file conversion. The moment it finished, she plugged the charger into the cryobox. The display flashed 2% before beginning to rise again.

Only then did she finally breathe.

Her comm unit's analysis app took another fifteen minutes to process the sequence. Jianna paced her room, chewing her thumbnail, stopping herself, then starting again. When the comm finally chimed, she nearly dropped it in her haste.

The screen displayed a comparison between the embryo's sequence and the historical reference genome she'd studied in her genetics courses: Phoebe's sequence, with Samara's edits clearly marked.

Genetically, the embryo was half Phoebe's.

Jianna sank onto her bed, staring at the screen. Lucas hadn't lied about this.

She ran another analysis, extrapolating the full genome of the other parent. The results showed unusual mutations in genes regulating immune response; mutations that could, theoretically, provide resistance to the Bloom spores.

The Divine Blueprint wasn't a myth.

If this embryo contained the genetic key to Bloom resistance without off-target effects, it could change everything. No more dependency on drugs. No more shaking hands and seizures. No more shortened lifespans for the Naturalists who rejected treatment.

She needed to tell her father. This was the most

significant scientific discovery since Samara's original vaccine against the Bloom.

But once her father knew, he would have to take it to the Council, and they would debate for months. Willow would claim the embryo belonged to the Naturalists as part of their religious heritage, and they might give it to her because of optics. Because even though he paid lip service to Samara Makinde's legacy, he regularly made concessions to the Naturalist Guide, for reasons Jianna had never understood.

The embryo would become a symbol, worshipped by people who didn't understand its true value, instead of being studied by those who would use it to finish what Samara had started.

Jianna could be the one to fix her famous ancestor's mistake.

But not tonight. Not when she couldn't even run her comm and a gene synthesizer at the same time. She needed to conserve the battery until power returned.

Before shutting down her comm, she opened Samara's digitized diaries and navigated to an entry she'd read many times before. The one dated exactly one year after Phoebe's funeral:

I still dream of Ayesha killing her. I wake up screaming, seeing Phoebe's face as we planted her beneath that tree.

At first, I blamed Atlas, even though he was as much a victim as she was. Ayesha used him to lure Phoebe to the Naturalist compound that night.

Then I blamed Lucas for failing to keep his promise to protect her. But the truth is, I blame myself most of all.

I trusted Lucas to keep his word even though I knew he'd lied to me countless times before. He deceived me about his true nature, concealed what he knew about the old Hyperion expedition, and helped Phoebe keep her nighttime excursions secret. Then he stole my grandchild and disappeared. I knew what Lucas was—a manipulator designed to infiltrate human social groups, to mimic our emotions so that we would believe him as one of us. I knew this, and still I let him manipulate me because I wanted to believe he truly cared for Phoebe. My arrogance cost me my daughter. And now I've lost my grandchild as well.

Jianna closed the diary, a chill creeping up her spine. If Lucas could fool someone as brilliant as Samara, even after she'd found out he was a liar, then he might be the most dangerous thing that had ever existed.

She looked at the cryobox, its power indicator slowly climbing. If she learned from her ancestor's mistake, could she avoid repeating it?

Or was she already being manipulated, just as Samara had been?

Chapter Nine

HE SHOULD GO HOME and get some sleep. But Michel's mind kept racing back to Jianna's bedroom, to the way she'd looked at him when he'd left. Part of him wanted to turn around and head right back to her house.

The rest of him couldn't stop thinking about Lucas. The android had been perfectly still, almost peaceful in its centuries-long sleep. He seemed nothing like the monster from all those childhood stories. Michel had seen the video. Every schoolchild had.

He would give anything to examine Lucas properly. To talk with it, if he could figure out how to disable its movement capabilities. An artificial intelligence in a robot body that could pass as human could advance their knowledge by hundreds of years.

Engineering, robotics, computational science...

If the android couldn't move, how much trouble could it really cause?

The engineering station loomed ahead, its blocky silhouette stark against the night sky. Michel propped his bike against the wall and pulled out his key ring. The manual override slot was rarely used, hidden behind a small panel beside the main door, and the key felt unfamiliar in his fingers. But with the power grid fried, they were back to basics.

Inside, the station was deserted, lit only by emergency lighting that cast long shadows across empty workstations. Everyone who wasn't home with their families was out trying to repair critical infrastructure. Michel felt a pang of guilt that he wasn't out there helping, but was thankful that he had no witnesses.

He took the stairs down to the Vault, two at a time. The heavy door at the bottom stood partially ajar, and as he idled in the doorway, the Vault stretched before him, a massive unfinished concrete bunker filled with rows of shelving that disappeared into shadow.

The ceiling hung low, pipes and conduits exposed overhead, while the walls bore the rough texture of poured concrete. This underground labyrinth held the city's engineering resources: spare parts, tools, equipment, archived documents, all protected from the elements and, as it turned out, from electromagnetic pulses. Breakers installed in the lower levels to protect against power fluctuations had disconnected the vault from the massive surge caused by the Aurora Event. The Vault had its own backup power, too: massive batteries recharged by a geothermal pump that had been built long ago.

Maeve Kennedy, Senior Engineer for the original colony, had thought of everything when she'd designed the Vault, although she'd never lived to see its construction.

Without her genius, they'd have lost everything in the Vault. It wouldn't have been months of repairs to get the city running again; it would've been years.

Michel made his way to the far corner where physical data backups were stored, winding through a maze of shelves holding countless solid-state drives, each one containing terabytes of historical records, engineering schematics, and research data.

In the center of the room stood an ancient terminal, one of the original computers from Generation One, kept functional for accessing older data formats. Michel switched it on. The screen flickered to life, bathing his face in blue light.

His fingers moved across the keys, searching for the correct storage unit. He found it tucked between two larger drives, a small metal rectangle etched with the designation *AI Research: CLASSIFIED*.

Michel retrieved the unit and connected it to the terminal, navigating through directories until he found what he was looking for: *Lucas Mercer*.

The files opened, revealing pages of notes, observations, and diagrams. Kennedy's notes detailed her observations when she'd connected a remotely-triggered EMP device to the android's internal power source.

Michel leaned closer as he studied her hand-drawn schematic of Lucas' interior components: wires, circuits, hydraulic lines, and other elements packed into a small compartment in his chest, under the spot where the left collarbone would be on a human.

Exactly the spot where the cord peeking out from under Lucas' shirt seemed to start.

The senior engineer had labeled each component with a scribbled guess about their purpose. According to Maeve, Lucas had offered no resistance when she'd installed the control device, although he'd declined to explain his inner workings beyond instructing her on how to access the power source. He wouldn't even tell the engineer how the power source worked.

In the android's position, Michel would've declined, too.

He frowned, tapping the marker against the paper. Why would an android cooperate with humans who were threatening to destroy it? Its programming should have included directives to preserve its own existence when doing so didn't endanger the humans it was supposed to protect. Assuming that he hadn't been lying about the Three Laws, which he might've been, given what he'd done to Mother Basu.

Had Lucas believed those humans needed protection from it?

Or was this another case of the android circumventing its programming?

Michel continued reading. Kennedy marveled at the complexity of Lucas' design, noting that she'd searched for a way to deactivate him without destroying him completely, but couldn't find one.

There had to be a failsafe. What kind of lunatic created something that dangerous but didn't build in an off switch?

Aurelius Hofstadter, apparently.

Or maybe it was just so well hidden that Engineer Kennedy hadn't been able to find it. Hofstadter had been a genius, responsible for hundreds of scientific breakthroughs before he'd left Earth on the *Elysia*. The kinds of breakthroughs that most people might make once in a lifetime, maybe twice if they were both brilliant *and* exceptionally lucky.

It was possible that Kennedy hadn't found the failsafe because she hadn't been able to deconstruct Hofstadter's thought processes.

Michel wondered how he'd do, given the same opportunity to examine the android's inner workings, instead of being limited to a sketch that might not even be accurate.

"What are you doing here?"

Michel jumped, hand instinctively covering the schematic. Carla stood in the doorway, arms folded across her chest, looking as exhausted as he felt.

"Couldn't sleep." Not a lie.

She sighed, pushing a strand of gray-streaked hair behind her ear. "You might as well help out down at the water treatment plant. They're trying to rig a manual system that'll let people keep a few pumps going by turning a huge wooden wheel. Some pretty clever ancient tech that the Naturalists sent over."

Michel nodded, disconnecting the drive and shutting down the terminal. "Sounds good."

"Grab a couple of portable batteries from Storage Three on your way," Carla said, already turning to leave. "They need power for the sensor systems."

Michel waited until Carla was gone before he folded Kennedy's schematic and tucked it into his pocket, then made his way through the concrete maze to Storage Three. The batteries sat on a metal shelf, heavy industrial units designed to power critical systems during short-term outages. He picked one up in each hand, their weight reassuring.

Then he stopped, staring at them.

He could use one of these to power Lucas. Just enough to let the android talk, while keeping the cord where he could yank it out the second it moved. He would be in control the whole time. And if Lucas knew that Michel could take that power away, surely he'd be cooperative.

Jianna would be furious if she knew he was even thinking about this. She wasn't wrong to object. The video of Lucas killing Mother Basu was part of every history of information science class, followed by a lecture on the reasons why artificial intelligence had been banned, and why that ban should never be lifted.

But sometimes you had to take risks to discover the truth. Samara Makinde herself said that, according to the historical archives.

Who was Michel to disagree with one of the smartest Vitruvians who'd ever lived?

Besides, Jianna had taken a big risk today, too. She'd gone into the cave with the android while it still had some power left, and she'd questioned it about the embryo. Right now, she was using the gene synthesizer that he'd helped her power up to figure out if Lucas had been telling the truth.

So it wasn't exactly fair for her to tell him that he couldn't do his own experiment, was it?

He hefted the batteries, feeling their weight. Two hours at full power. More than enough time to ask a few questions, to verify what Lucas had told them.

Just him and the android. A conversation five centuries in the making.

The risk would be worth it.

Chapter Ten

WILLOW GRIPPED the wooden railing as the cart jolted over another rut in the road. The Curie Plateau loomed ahead, a dark mass against the star-filled sky. Typical Vitruvians, naming everything after long-dead scientific heroes instead of drawing from the natural world. Stargazer's Point would have honored what the place actually was.

Her eyes burned with exhaustion. Nearly four hours in this mule-drawn cart, and still miles to go. At least she was faring better than the others. Harold's immaculate suit was crumpled, his face haggard. Isabeau dozed fitfully against Elias' shoulder. Xanthe maintained her composure, but the dark circles under her eyes told the truth. Only Soren seemed alert, his gaze fixed on the sprawling complex ahead.

No sleep for a day and a half. Too many crises. Too many decisions. And now this middle-of-the-night summons to the Observatory.

"Almost there," the driver called.

The cart rolled to a stop before a squat building of

reinforced concrete. Beyond it, a massive tower rose into the night, topped by a long antenna that pierced the sky. Smaller domes dotted the plateau. Telescope housings, she guessed.

Soren fell into step beside her as they approached the main building. "The Observatory survived because of its distance from the city," he said. "And because it's powered by a solar array in the valley to the west."

"I've read the brochure, thanks."

He grimaced and pulled ahead, leaving her to bring up the rear of the group.

They entered the main building through a pair of heavy steel doors that scraped against the concrete floor. The interior was all exposed pipes, unfinished concrete walls, and simple panel lights overhead. No attempt had been made to soften the industrial harshness; not a single plant or piece of art graced the space. Just metal, concrete, and the acrid reek of electronics and cleaning chemicals.

As they moved deeper into the facility, they passed through narrow corridors lined with utility panels and exposed wiring conduits. Handwritten labels and technical diagrams had been taped to the walls, many yellowed with age.

The corridors grew narrower, the ceiling lower, until they reached the control room. The chamber was crammed with equipment: banks of monitors, tangles of cables snaking across the floor, and the constant hum of cooling fans. Screens lined the walls, some dark, others displaying star charts and orbital trajectories. A team of four people hunched over consoles, speaking in hushed tones, their faces lit by the blue glow of their displays.

A woman with close-cropped gray hair straightened as they entered. "Councilors. Thank you for coming."

Soren stepped forward. "Dr. Nguyen. What do you have for us?"

"Ursula, please." She turned to the three other staff members. "Give us the room, please."

They filed out, casting curious glances at the Councilors as they passed.

Once the door was closed, Ursula approached a console at the center of the room. "We received this transmission approximately three hours ago."

She pressed a button, and a crackling voice filled the room:

"...anyone there? This is...can anyone hear me? We're less than a day out from your planet. Our intentions are peaceful. I hope someone is listening..."

Static swallowed the rest.

"Is there more?" Soren asked.

"No, and it hasn't repeated. But we've confirmed an object approaching the planet with the telescope." She pulled up a grainy image on the main screen. "Once it gets close enough, we'll be able to reposition cameras and sensors on one of our weather satellites to get a visual."

"How long?" Isabeau asked.

"Approximately seven hours."

Willow felt her chest tighten. Theo was right. A sign in the heavens, something worse coming.

"It has to be from one of the other colony worlds." Harold's eyes narrowed. "But which one? And if they're friendly, why didn't they identify themselves?"

"If they're here, something must have gone wrong with their colony," Isabeau said.

"They're definitely more advanced than we are, if they're able to build their own ships," Elias added.

Soren tapped his chin thoughtfully. "They could have retrofitted their original ship."

"Those colony ships were only meant for a single trip," Harold said. "And even if retrofitting was possible, Isabeau is right. The fact that they were able to refine enough fuel to reach us means they're further along than we are."

"What if they're from Earth?"

The room fell silent as everyone stared at Xanthe like she'd suggested the Divine itself was coming to visit.

Usually, they reserved that treatment for Willow when she argued that maybe they should look before leaping into the next untested scientific innovation.

"We don't know what happened after we left," Xanthe muttered. "Someone might have survived."

Harold sneered at her. "It's obviously an attack, given the timing. We have to assume they're hostile."

Willow stared at the static-filled screen, that voice still echoing in her head.

"Play it again," she said to Ursula.

The transmission repeated, the lone voice emerging through layers of interference.

"He sounds exhausted. And afraid. He wasn't sure anyone was listening, which means they're coming in blind." Willow turned to face the others. "Whatever brought them here, it wasn't good. But they haven't come for us, specifically."

"You think they're running from something?" Soren asked.

"Or they're bringing their problems with them, for us to solve."

"You don't know any more than we do," Harold accused.

"I know that they're people, just like we are," Willow said. "And people are complicated."

"We have to get ready to defend ourselves," Harold replied.

Isabeau snorted. "What are we going to do, throw rocks at their ship once it's in orbit?"

Soren turned to Ursula. "Have you detected anything that would suggest the incoming ship is connected to the Aurora Event?"

"No, but the fact that we haven't found a connection doesn't mean there isn't one."

"Is there anything else you can tell us?" Soren asked.

"Not until they either send another message or come close enough for us to get a visual."

"Then I suggest we get some sleep, so we'll have clear heads when they're close enough to make contact."

Ursula nodded. "I've had quarters prepared for you in the lower level."

The scientist led them downstairs to a basement dormitory lined with narrow cots. Willow fell to the rear again, thinking about her people. How much water had they shared with the Vitruvians, and how much did they have left? Was Theo whipping them into a frenzy about signs of divine punishment? And what whispers might Cira be starting while she was gone?

She couldn't go back now, not without knowing who these newcomers were or what they wanted. She needed to be here when the newcomers made contact. She didn't trust Soren and the others to tell her everything if they thought withholding information served their purposes.

But leaving her sister in charge during a crisis... Cira had always craved power, and chaos created opportunity.

Soren slowed his pace, falling into step beside her.

"Complicated, eh?" he said quietly.

Willow glanced at him, noting the lines of exhaustion etched around his eyes. He looked older than she'd ever seen him.

"Aren't we all?" she replied.

What hardships had these newcomers endured to reach DaVinci? And how had it changed them?

From the speaker's tone, not for the better, she'd bet.

Seven hours until the ship arrived. Seven hours to prepare.

Something worse is coming.

~

Willow jerked awake, heart pounding. Soren stood over her, hand retreating from her shoulder.

"Ursula's called us back," he said. "The ship is in visual range."

She blinked away the remnants of a nightmare, an image of Cira standing on a burning platform, arms outstretched, while the Sanctum crumbled around her.

The dormitory's harsh lighting made Willow's eyes water as she pulled herself upright, and her mouth tasted like dust. "How long was I asleep?"

"Nearly five hours." Soren looked as exhausted as she felt. "The others are already heading up."

Willow pushed herself to her feet, ignoring the protest from her stiff muscles. The cot had been little better than sleeping on stone.

They made their way back to the control room in silence. Willow's mind raced ahead, imagining what they might see. Another colony ship? Some kind of primitive vessel cobbled together from salvaged materials? Or something more advanced than anything they'd ever built?

Ursula stood at the main console. The other Councilors clustered around her. On the central screen floated a massive ship, unmistakably one of the original colony vessels, but changed. Bizarre attachments jutted from its hull, some rounded like blisters, others jagged and angular. Retrofitted, just as Soren had guessed. The vessel looked nothing like the sleek, elegant *Norman Borlaug* from the history books.

Willow moved closer, studying the patchwork of reinforcements covering the hull. Dark scorch marks spread across the surface in strange, asymmetrical patterns.

"What happened to it?" she asked.

"Radiation damage, most likely," Ursula said, manipulating controls to enhance the image. "The patterns are consistent with prolonged exposure to high-energy particles."

Unease settled deeper in Willow's stomach. The ship looked like it had been through a war.

"What kind of high-energy particles?" Harold asked, leaning forward to squint at the screen.

Ursula shook her head. "There's no way to tell. The weather satellite isn't equipped with those kinds of sensors. To get here from another colony, they'd have had to travel through unmapped space. They could've passed through the emission poles of a pulsar or zoomed too close to a neutron star."

"So they might all be dead," Isabeau said.

"At least one of them was alive last night," Willow pointed out.

Harold crossed his arms. "Does the ship have weapons?"

"Your guess is as good as mine." Ursula zoomed in on one of the bulbous protrusions. "Some of these modifications could be defensive systems, propulsion enhancements, or scientific instruments. Without better imaging, I can't tell you more."

"It doesn't matter," Isabeau said. "We don't have any weapons that can reach orbit. We can't even shoot down a shuttle if they decide to land. We're helpless until they make their move."

The room fell silent as the implications sank in. Willow studied the faces around her, all showing various degrees of fear beneath thin veneers of composure.

Harold spoke up. "Then we should lure them down here, where we outnumber them. There are three million of us and only a hundred sixty of them."

"They don't need weapons to attack us." Elias had barely spoken yesterday, content to let the others argue while he observed. "They could use the *Borlaug*."

Isabeau frowned. "The colony ships weren't armed. And even if the *Borlaug* had weapons, it's been dead in orbit for centuries."

Elias looked at them, his expression almost pitying. "All they'd have to do is drop pieces of the *Borlaug* down on the city. A ten-ton chunk of hull at terminal velocity would hit with the force of a nuclear weapon."

Horror spread across the room like a contagion. Willow felt her throat tighten. She'd never considered that a ship in orbit could be weaponized against them.

"Have you received any new transmissions from the ship?" Soren asked Ursula.

"No, but we're reorienting the radio dish for a broadcast." She gestured toward the windows. "Should be ready in a few minutes."

Willow moved to the floor-to-ceiling windows overlooking the Curie Plateau. The sky had lightened to pale lavender, the first hints of dawn touching the horizon. She clasped her hands over her stomach to keep from wringing them. She wouldn't show weakness, not with the other Councilors already devolving into another squabble about the newcomers' intentions.

Their voices faded to background noise as she focused

on the massive radio dish farther down the plateau. It rotated with excruciating slowness. Or perhaps it was just her frayed nerves stretching seconds into minutes. As the dish tilted upward, its white surface caught the early morning light and seemed to glow pale violet. A strange buzzing sensation built in Willow's teeth, making her jaw ache.

"We have a connection," Ursula announced.

Static burst from the speakers, morphing into a high-pitched squeal before dissipating into clarity.

"DaVinci, do you copy?" A male voice, stronger and clearer than the previous transmission.

The Councilors froze, exchanging glances. After a moment, Soren stepped forward.

"This is Councilor Soren Makinde of Vitruvian City. Who am I speaking with?"

A pause stretched between words, the distance between orbit and ground made tangible by silence. Then laughter. Warm, genuine, and somehow unsettling.

Then silence, broken only by static, before the voice came through again.

"You're speaking to your savior. I am Aurelius Hofstadter."

Willow's breath caught as stunned silence filled the control room. Aurelius Hofstadter. The man who'd built the colony ships, who'd chosen their ancestors as the best of Earth. He should have been dead centuries ago.

"You mean you're a descendant of Hofstadter, bearing the same name?" Soren said, finally.

"No, I do not." The voice carried a note of amusement. "But don't worry, I'll explain everything once I'm down there. We've got nothing to eat but nutritional yeast, we're drinking our own recycled piss, and we've been locked up in this tin can for almost four centuries, so roll out the red carpet. We're coming down in shuttles as soon as we stabilize orbit."

That didn't make sense. Hofstadter's ship, the *Elysia*, had been outfitted with cryopods just like the *Borlaug* had been. Something must have gone horribly wrong if the *Elysia's* passengers were using it as a generation ship.

How could they have survived a journey that long?

Soren began, "I'm not sure who you were expecting to welcome you—"

"Frankly, I wasn't sure there'd be anyone down there at all. We detected no transmissions at all coming from your surface when we entered this system."

"A few days ago, an anomalous solar storm overloaded our city's grid, taking us completely offline," Soren replied. "With a few exceptions, we have no power, no communications, extremely limited ability to provide water to a population of just over three million people, and no way to distribute resources. So, I'm sorry to say, there is no red carpet to roll out."

"Well, then you're lucky I got here when I did."

Outrage erupted around Willow; Harold's face reddening, Isabeau's hands gesturing wildly, Xanthe's mouth opening and closing in shock.

Soren silenced them with a sharp gesture. "What do you mean?" he asked.

"Let's just say I come bearing gifts." Hofstadter's voice took on a salesman's cadence. "Communication drones that can spread out through your city to provide a net of coverage that will be even faster than you were getting from your towers. Power's not a problem either, I've got microfusion units that can be hooked up to your utilities to get water treatment running the second that repairs to the machinery can be made. I'll set up a relay to tie you into the quantum computer on my ship; it's got enough compute power to run an entire planet. And my people can help with whatever you need, transporting goods, fixing your infrastructure."

The Councilors exchanged looks of disbelief. Xanthe stepped forward, her voice breathy with excitement. "Thank you, Mr. Hofstadter. Your assistance is—"

"And what will you want in return for your generosity?" Willow cut in, unable to keep silent any longer. Nothing came without a price, and every technology had off-target effects, no matter how beneficial it was designed to be. Mother Basu had taught that lesson well.

"Who am I speaking to?" Hofstadter asked, a new edge entering his voice.

"I am Willow Evans, Guide to the Naturalists and a direct descendant of Mother Basu herself."

Laughter burst through the speakers. Not warm this time, but sharp and cutting. "Mother Basu? I can hardly wait to hear how that happened."

The connection went dead, leaving only static in its wake.

"Re-establish contact," Soren ordered.

Ursula worked the controls, her brow furrowed in concentration. After several tense moments, she shook her head. "I'm not getting an answer."

The control room erupted once more into a cacophony of outrage and disbelief.

Willow turned to Soren and found him already looking at her, his expression mirroring the dread settling in her own chest.

"We can't trust him," she said. "Whatever he offers, it won't be worth it."

Soren sighed. "Three million people, Willow. We can't let them suffer if these newcomers can help."

"You heard what he said. *You're speaking to your savior.*

Whoever that man is, he's more dangerous than anyone you've ever dealt with."

"There was a saying back on Earth about not looking gift horses in the mouth."

Willow clasped her hands over her stomach again, not to stop them from wringing, but to keep herself from slapping the man.

"There's another saying that's applicable here, about Trojan horses!" she snapped. "Look it up."

She turned away from the arguing Councilors and looked out the window again, across a plateau named after a woman who had been killed by her own research.

Willow had studied Mother Basu's sermon on the mental illness that drove scientists to destroy themselves in the pursuit of knowledge they didn't need. Humanity had been given a chance to let go of that unhealthy obsession and learn to live in synchrony with the world they'd been gifted. But every generation reinfected itself anew with the sickness, through some perverse desire to repeat the mistakes of their ancestors.

Soren would try to find the middle ground, as he always did. He would accept some of Hofstadter's gifts while rejecting others, believing he could control the flow of change. It was what made him both an effective politician and a dangerous ally in times like these.

She inhaled deeply, filling her lungs with resolve. Whatever came next, she would face it with open eyes.

Even if those she had counted as allies turned away when she needed them most.

Chapter Eleven

METALLIC DUST RAINED DOWN on the catwalk as Michel dragged his file across the fixed jaw of the massive C-clamp, shaping it to fit the conduit sticking out of the broken aerator beside him. Twenty hours on shift with only a quarter-liter of water every two hours, because the rationing was that strict. Every inch of his skin itched with dried sweat, and the rasping vibration of each stroke with the file made his teeth ache.

But they were rationing batteries too, and his power file was dead. He'd heard they were carting batteries out to the Observatory to be recharged, but if that was true, his team hadn't gotten their share yet.

He stood and gestured for Raul to help him try to fit the C-clamp around the intake pipe for the aerator. Still not big enough, but his arms needed a break, so might as well work on the aerator's innards for a bit.

"Hand me a number three Phillips head."

Raul glanced at the toolbox, picked up the wrong screwdriver, then corrected himself and grabbed the right size. As he tried to pass it over, the tool slipped from his fingers, spinning down two stories to clatter on the main floor of the water treatment facility.

Of course.

Michel exhaled. "Go get it, please."

Raul shuffled off down the stairs.

Glint never made him ask twice. Glint would've handed him exactly the tool he wanted before he even asked, because they watched what he was doing and anticipated the next step. The Descendant was smarter than anyone he'd ever worked with. It was nuts that people didn't see that.

After opening a panel in the side of the aerator to reveal the controller circuit board, Michel grabbed a different screwdriver, too big, but close enough. He scraped his knuckles as the bit slipped once, but he re-slotted it and removed the screws holding the fiberglass board in place before sliding it out and holding it up to the light.

Half the circuits on the board had melted into the other half, rendering the whole thing useless. He was going to have to make another one from scratch.

He started sketching out the traces with a stub of pencil on a scrap of cardboard, brain already running through the sequence of soldering, testing, and debugging. But it didn't matter how fast he could build a replacement. Because even if he did, it would be weeks before they got the main power plant working again.

That was the problem. You could patch up every broken aerator in the city, but without grid power, they were merely expensive statues. Same for every other machine that had been obliterated by the Aurora Event.

He wiped sweat from his forehead with the back of his hand, thinking about Lucas in the cave. How unfair it was that Jianna got to talk to him, but had forbidden Michel to go near him. Lucas knew Aurelius Hofstadter in person.

Not just the legend, but the real man behind the stories of Hofstadter's wild inventions, the way he'd break every rule just to push the science forward… that's why Michel had gotten into engineering in the first place.

Lucas was one of Hofstadter's masterpieces, an unparalleled work of artistry that they couldn't duplicate today, thanks to the restrictions the Buratti family had put in place after the deaths of Phoebe and Mother Basu.

How could he pass up the chance to peek inside? Especially now that he had Engineer Kennedy's guesses to use as a starting point. If he could power Lucas on and persuade the android to cooperate, the things he might learn…

Jianna had said Lucas had talked, which meant its internal power source had lasted more than half a millennium. Understand it, and he might be able to build something that would restore the city's power grid in weeks instead of months.

Then there was the android's brain, which was capable of supporting an artificial intelligence equivalent to a human's. Maybe superior. What he learned could allow them to build a completely new kind of computer with unheard of processing time and applications an order of magnitude more sophisticated, even without adding AI to the mix.

It would be irresponsible for him *not* to talk to Lucas while he had the chance. Before the Council found out and destroyed the android.

He set down the circuit board, his mind already spinning with the possibilities. There had to be a way to power Lucas on safely. If he could access the systems in its chest cavity, isolate the mobility functions, maybe even figure out how to get into the cranial housing…

Someone shouted below. Michel glanced down to see

Valencia collide with Raul at the bottom of the stairs, words tumbling out as she waved her arms instead of offering the apprentice a hand up.

His heart sank. Had Jianna told her father about Lucas after all? Or maybe Glint had told her Elders, and they'd contacted the Council.

His chance to study his idol's work firsthand might already be gone.

Michel stowed the fried circuit board in his toolkit, snapped it shut, and started down the stairs two at a time. The rickety metal trembled under his weight.

When he reached the main floor, he asked, "Everything okay?"

Valencia spun around. "There's a new ship in orbit, from one of the other colonies. Nolan heard it from Kamryn, who heard it from Zephyr, Xanthe's daughter."

Michel's brain flatlined for a second. A ship from another colony, here?

How?

The Vitruvians hadn't even managed to keep the *Borlaug* in working order; synthesizing the fuel needed to power it indefinitely had been too intensive while the city had been growing. And once the city became self-sustaining, what was the point in diverting resources to return to the colony ship after working so hard for its independence?

They didn't even have shuttles to fly up to meet the new ship. His ancestors stripped them for parts after fuel ran out, scavenging every piston and circuit until only empty hulls were left.

But if these newcomers had crossed interstellar space, then they'd solved problems the Vitruvians never could.

He couldn't stop thinking about the technologies they might have brought. Devices that would make DaVinci's best look like children's toys. And if the new ship's pilot was another android capable of passing as human? If Hofstadter could make one, he could make a dozen. As many as he had the resources for.

If they let the crew down to the surface, they'd have to scan every one of them.

One impossible thing after another. The Aurora Event. The discovery of a five-century-old android that was still functional. And now, a ship from another colony that had survived, making an impossible journey to reconnect one pocket of humanity with another.

He half-expected to wake up and discover he'd been dreaming. It would explain the sense of unreality that he'd been swimming through ever since he'd seen the first aurora overhead in the Remembrance Tree grove.

But the dream continued. And while his brain said he should be terrified, he felt almost ecstatic, as if everything he'd ever hoped to do with his life was about to be possible.

"What do they want?" Raul asked.

Valencia shrugged. "Xanthe wouldn't say, but apparently the Council's negotiating with them. Zephyr's never seen her mother so worried."

Raul said, "So, they're hostile?"

"Even if they're not, they could be bringing new diseases that evolved on their world," Michel said. "The Council's going to want to be careful until they can be cleared."

Valencia shook her head. "Council's going to be distributing announcements *on paper*. Apparently, the Naturalists are angry that the Council commandeered everything they've got."

If Zephyr knew… Had Soren told Jianna anything?

"Do you know which ship it is?"

Valencia shrugged. "It's weird. It's called A Lesion, but I thought that was some kind of skin condition."

Michel's heart slammed against his ribs so hard it hurt. What were the odds?

High, probably. Of all the colonies likely to leapfrog the rest technologically, it would be the one that'd benefited from Hofstadter's genius right up until his death.

"The *Elysia*?" he asked.

"I guess?" Valencia said.

If the *Elysia* had made it, then Hofstadter's descendants would have all of his research. Not just the stuff he'd published before launch, but everything he'd invented since. Michel had read every scrap of his research that the Council hadn't restricted, studied the diagrams, memorized the equations, and dreamed of someday finishing his hero's unfinished experiments.

But the archives here only went up to the day the *Borlaug* left orbit. What had Hofstadter done after that? The *Elysia's* archives would contain a wealth of insight into the genius' thought processes right up until his death.

If the Council was negotiating with the crew of the *Elysia*, any information that might help them understand the newcomers better could give Soren and the others an advantage.

Or at least help the negotiations go faster.

And Lucas might have the crucial piece of information they needed.

In Michel's position, what would Aurelius do?

Take the risk, obviously. He never hesitated when discovery was on the line.

Michel wiped his hands on his pants and called down, "I'm overdue for a rest period. I'm clocking out."

He didn't wait for Valencia or Raul to argue, so he just grabbed his toolkit and headed for the exit. The battery storage locker was on the way. Nobody stopped him when he slipped inside. He picked up one of the heavy cells, stuffed it in his backpack, and prayed no one would notice. Or care.

But no one even looked up from their own work. Except for Raul, who watched with a disgruntled scowl as Michel strode toward the door, barely restraining his urge to break into a run until he emerged into the harsh afternoon sunlight that seemed to stab directly into his brain.

He hesitated, thumb hovering over his comm, debating whether to swing by Jianna's place and try to bring her along. If he explained it right, she might see the logic. Lucas knew Aurelius Hofstadter better than anyone alive. He could tell them what to expect from *Elysia's* crew, and maybe how to survive it.

But if Jianna disagreed, she'd tell her father. The Council would lock down the cave before Michel even got near Lucas. He might lose his chance to learn from one of humanity's greatest minds forever.

He got on his bike and started pedaling hard for the mines. He would find a way to get the information they needed from Lucas without freeing the android. He might even persuade it to cooperate with whatever measures he took to ensure its good behavior, like it had for Engineer Kennedy. After all, wasn't existence with limited freedom better than rusting away in a cave while the rest of the world moved on without you?

This, he told himself, was what Aurelius would do.

Chapter Twelve

THE STREET WAS PACKED, a restless surge of bodies pressed tight against makeshift barricades. Children clung to parents' legs, faces streaked with soot. The stench of sewage hung thick in the air, worse than anything Jianna had smelled in the caves. No water meant nothing to flush away the waste that was building up in the massive pipes beneath the pavement.

Jianna stood in the back of the wagon, the sun hammering down, hands shaking as she passed another liter bottle to the woman clutching a crying child. Only six left. The line stretched halfway down the block, men and women and kids, faces pinched and gray, lips cracked, voices rising in frantic bursts.

The chaos reminded her of a passage she'd read once about old New York City, before electricity, before sewers. People crowding the streets, picking their way through mud, horse shit, and rotten food. The only thing that would've made it worse was a sporestorm.

It had only been a few days, and already it felt like civilization was disintegrating.

In those ancient times, had people looked around at this mess and been proud of their city?

Probably. They didn't know any better.

Or maybe they did, but they didn't have any other options.

"Repent!" That was the Naturalist preacher on the corner, shouting loud enough to cut through the crowd about divine punishment and the coming reckoning as he waved a book of Dr. Basu's "scriptures" to punctuate each point he made. Jianna tried to tune him out, but the words crawled under her skin anyway.

She focused on the line, on the woman in front of her: a girl, really, not much older than Jianna herself, hair plastered to her scalp with sweat.

Jianna held out a bottle. The girl's fingers closed around it, knuckles bone-white.

"Thank you," she said. "Can I have one more?"

Jianna hesitated. The rules were one per person, no exceptions. She could feel the weight of the last six bottles pressing against her, heavy and insufficient.

"It's for my neighbor," the girl said. "He's sick. I offered to get him some."

Jianna shook her head. "I'm supposed to give one per person."

"Please, I'm not lying. He's elderly, and I think he's been skipping his medication to make ends meet. He doesn't have any family to take care of him."

Jianna glanced down the line. More than a hundred people, some with children slumped at their sides, others just standing in the heat, not even bothering to shade their eyes. Sweat and desperation everywhere. When she ran out of bottles, the rest of them would wait for at least an hour for the next wagon. She should say no.

She grabbed another bottle from the last crate and

handed it over. "Take it. But tell him to either take his meds or go to the hospital. They're rationing water too, but at least he won't have to get it himself."

The young woman looked like she was about to cry. She thanked Jianna, then hurried away, clutching both bottles to her chest.

Heads turned. Two people near the front of the line watched the girl scurry off, their gazes hard.

One of them stepped closer to Jianna. "Why does she get two?"

Jianna handed him a bottle. "She's taking one to a sick neighbor."

"I've got a sick neighbor, too," the man said.

Someone farther back in line yelled, "Yeah, me too."

Jianna met their eyes, pulse hammering. "I know her. She really does have a sick neighbor."

A few people muttered under their breath as she reached for the next bottle. She felt the hunger in their eyes, the way they watched her. The heat pressed down, suffocating, and the stink of sweat and sewage made her want to gag. One liter per person wasn't enough. Not in this weather.

She handed out the last few bottles as fast as she could, not bothering to make eye contact. Sweat dripped into her eyes, stinging, but she didn't stop. The line surged forward. Three left. Two. The last bottle vanished from her hand, and she raised both arms to signal the end.

"That's it," she said. "You'll have to wait for the next wagon. It should be here soon."

The crowd pressed closer, restless. Someone shoved from the back. "I bet you kept an extra bottle for your *sick neighbor*."

"I didn't. That was the last one." But the bottle in her own pack felt heavier than any of the bottles she had given out. She glanced over her shoulder, toward the front of the wagon. It wouldn't take much to turn their resentment into fury, and if they rushed her…

It was a long way down, but if she jumped over the side and sprinted, she might make it around the corner and then go through a shop to lose them.

"Repent, Councilor's daughter!"

The preacher had left his street corner and was shoving his way through the crowd, his robes streaked gray with ash and dust, waving Basu's book overhead like a weapon. All eyes shifted to him as he stabbed a finger at Jianna. "Your father and others like him have filled our world with technological contamination, and your punishment has only begun. Repent before it gets worse."

Jianna's hands curled into fists. She wanted to hurl the empty crate at the preacher's head. She wasn't going to let him use her to prey on these people's fear to try to convert them to his religion of ignorance.

It was one thing for Guide Evans to pick fights with Jianna's father in hopes of recruiting new members; everyone expected the sermons and soundbites. But taking advantage of this emergency to gather a few more souls was unconscionable.

"If you cared about anyone here, you'd be helping," she said. "Not yelling at the people who actually are."

"The aurorae turned all your devices to useless junk, they washed your scientific sins away, and gave you an opportunity to start anew. The aurorae were a divine message—"

"The aurorae were a scientific phenomenon." Jianna's head throbbed. She knew that nothing she said would change the preacher's mind, but if she could make his message less appealing to everyone watching… "There was a burst of ionizing radiation into the atmosphere. It excited the electrons in oxygen and nitrogen molecules, made them jump to a higher orbit, then shed energy as light when they dropped back down. That's what caused the colors."

The preacher didn't even pause. "And what, I ask, caused this 'ionizing radiation'?"

"We don't know yet," Jianna said. "But we will find out. Because that's what scientists do."

"You see?" His hand swept the crowd. "She spouts scientific gibberish and expects us to doubt the evidence of our own eyes."

She should've ignored the preacher instead of engaging.

She could leave right now.

Or call security and have the troublemaker escorted to a holding cell until his people bailed him out.

Jianna didn't have her father's silver tongue and the commanding presence that allowed him to mediate Council disagreements or persuade unhappy voters to listen when the truth was something they didn't want to hear.

But something inside her snapped. Whether it was the heat or her desert-dry tongue or just the fact that she'd been listening to this kind of willful stupidity her whole life, she didn't know.

All she knew was that she couldn't let the preacher's accusation stand.

"When you don't know how the world works, everything looks like a sign," she said, doing her best to emulate her father's demeanor when he made public announcements. "You've chosen to ignore the scientific explanation because the truth doesn't bring you more followers."

The preacher didn't look angry. If anything, he looked like he'd been waiting for her to say something like that.

"Yet your science has provided nothing for thirsty people. Your science hasn't brought power and water back to the city. While we suffer, you and your father spread Vitruvian lies. And we will all continue to suffer until you repent."

The crowd tensed, a low ripple of mutters running through the line. Shuffling feet. Elbows nudging. Someone spat on the ground.

Jianna scanned for security. Nothing. No uniforms, no drones, not even a bored volunteer. She was on her own.

"You've been hoarding water. You should repent." The man who'd yelled it lunged for her ankles.

Jianna jerked backward, boots sliding on the slick wood as the man clawed at the edge of the wagon, hauling his torso up with both hands. The crowd roared. Bodies surged forward, hands grabbing, shoving.

The preacher's voice sliced through cacophony: "Repent!"

The crowd picked it up, a hungry, rhythmic pulse. *Repent. Repent. Repent.*

The chant built, raw and ugly, until it drowned out the preacher's voice and became the only thing that mattered.

Jianna kicked the last crate off the wagon bed at her pursuer, then scrambled over the side and dropped hard to the pavement. She sprinted, pack thumping against her spine, as the mob spilled over the wagon behind her, tearing through boxes and crates, searching for water that wasn't there.

She rounded the corner, lungs burning, and ducked into the nearest shop, a convenience store. Inside, half the shelves were bare. No batteries. No water. No food. No matches. Very few medications. All the things that people hoarded in emergencies. What remained felt like a surreal reminder of another existence: small parts for repairing cars, tablets, and comm accessories, cleaning products.

Jianna pressed herself flat against the metal rack, every muscle taut, sweat collecting between her shoulder blades. She tried to slow her breathing, but her lungs kept seizing, each inhale catching in her throat, and the inside of her mouth tasted like blood and acid. Jianna crouched low, knees pressed to the sticky linoleum.

She risked a glance through a gap in the grime-streaked window.

A knot of bodies surged past, moving like a single animal, the preacher at their head, holding his book more like a weapon than a scripture. Behind him, the others follow, all chanting in a single, guttural rhythm.

Repent. Repent. Repent.

The pounding chant faded as the crowd marched farther down the street, picking up new members as they proceeded.

Jianna slumped against the metal rack, hands trembling. Idiot, she thought. She'd let herself get baited, let the preacher use her as a prop to rile up a desperate crowd.

She'd known better. Her father had told her a thousand times: *persuasion starts with listening.* She knew that shouting facts at your opponent accomplished nothing; if it did, the Council would've funded every proposal she'd ever made.

She should've walked away. Instead, she'd almost started a riot—and become its first victim.

But it wasn't all her fault. That preacher had singled her out and attacked her, tried to incite the crowd to violence. The Naturalists weren't just troublemakers; they were dangerous. Jianna dug her nails into her palms as she imagined suggesting that the Council confine Willow's people to their Quarter until power was restored.

She could already see his eyebrows coming together as he started a lecture about how imposing restrictions on a minority was a short-term solution, while fostering collaboration built long-term trust.

"Hey!" The shout came from behind the counter. The shopkeeper glared at her, arms folded. "You buying something or not?"

Jianna shook her head, pushed out into the street, and started walking fast, head down. The sun stabbed through the haze of dust, heat pressing on her like an invisible hand. She thought about going home, but the idea of sitting in her empty house, surrounded by silence, made her stomach twist. Her father would still be at Council, arguing, negotiating, doing what he did best. He might not come home at all tonight.

She didn't want to be alone, as much as she hated to admit it.

Digging her comm out of her pocket, she thumbed the side button before she remembered. Dead as the grid.

If Michel was still assigned to the night shift, he'd be waking soon, groggy but getting ready to drag himself back to work. Unless he'd pulled another all-nighter and crashed out for good. But either way, there was a good chance he'd be home.

He'd promised her a backup charger for the cryobox, and he knew she needed it today, before the battery dipped low enough to let the embryo thaw out.

If he'd forgotten, she'd lose it; aside from the batteries that Engineering kept in reserve, there was no way for her to replenish her own charger.

He wouldn't forget, she promised herself. And if there

were no batteries left, he'd invent another way. One of the things she loved most about him was his resourcefulness.

Michelangelo would never let her down.

Chapter Thirteen

THE CONFERENCE ROOM at the heart of the City Administration building was stifling. Not just miserably hot, but muggier than the worst summer day. It smelled like body odor and bad breath. And since the building's cooling system was out of commission indefinitely, it would only get worse.

That was the problem with Vitruvians, Willow thought. They built everything on the assumption that technology would never let them down. The Administration building was essentially a cement box with windows, depending on artificial airflow to be habitable. Willow's people designed every building to be comfortable whether the power was on or off, with thick walls that insulated from both summer's heat and winter's cold, and windows that allowed for cross-ventilation to regulate the temperature as needed.

She stacked the last boxes of paper on the conference room table, then shook out her aching arms while Soren tried to explain the plan to Administrator Frida Nagy, who was eyeing the stacked reams like they might explode.

"You want five thousand hand-copied flyers?" Nagy

said. "With four people on staff? You'll be lucky to get five hundred before the rioting starts."

Soren didn't blink. "Recruit as many people as you can. We'll post them in every neighborhood, at every major crossing. People need information."

"What they need is working comms. And water. And electricity. This is just going to get thrown into the latrines, once everyone's gone through their stores of—"

"People are cooperating right now, Administrator," Willow broke in. "But that's not going to continue if we don't give them a reason to believe that things are going to get better."

"Reverting to stone age technology isn't exactly going to inspire faith when people are dying of thirst."

"Paper is a post-urban technology that only emerged on Earth after trading empires were established." Willow swallowed her exasperation, hoping it didn't leak into her smile. "Most industrialized societies continued to use it as a backup information source right up until the Chytrid Collapse, despite easy access to computers."

Nagy rolled her eyes at Soren, clearly hoping to recruit his support for her historical chauvinism. "Doesn't change the fact that nobody's using it today, outside of your little cult."

Soren didn't even try to soothe the administrator, which showed how desperate their situation was. "We're fortunate that the Naturalists preserved this technology, as we've been taken back to stone age living conditions for the moment."

Naturalists had started keeping hand-written records back when they'd been forced to reintegrate with the Vitruvians. It had been Sister Hyacinth's idea to make paper from wood scraps scavenged at night from construction sites as new homes were built to house the refugees from the flood that the Vitruvians claimed was an accident, but that had conveniently destroyed Mother Basu's settlement.

In those early days, they'd kept everything that mattered off the network. A piece of paper couldn't be hacked, so no one could erase sacred texts or rewrite history.

A piece of paper could be folded until it was quite small and tucked away where the wrong people would never find it. Try that with a tablet.

But Nagy was the wrong audience to share that fact with, so Willow brought the conversation back to the practical.

"Rationing is working, but we need to make sure it continues to work. There's a psychological benefit to establishing consistent rules." Another lesson from Mother Basu's journals. "If they're placed so that everyone can see them, people police themselves, and they police each other when the authorities don't have the bandwidth to do it. Because nobody wants their neighbor to have more than they do."

Nagy scowled. "That sounds like religious double-speak for 'let's keep people watching each other so they're too busy to watch the people in charge.'"

"*Frida.*" Soren gave the administrator his most charming smile. "We're asking for your help in the face of the worst disaster our civilization has faced since Generation One."

The woman sighed. "I'm not kidding when I say it'll take days, and that time would be better spent doing something that will keep people calm. Like handing out food and water."

She wasn't wrong, and Willow's people were already stretched too thin caring for each other and their Vitruvian neighbors to serve as ad hoc scribes for a city of three million. There had to be another solution. Something even simpler and low-tech. Something before paper.

Or before the majority of people could read.

"Town criers," she said.

Both Soren and Nagy stared at her like she'd started speaking gibberish.

Because for the Vitruvians, history started with the *Borlaug's* departure from Earth.

"We only have to write the announcements a few dozen times," Willow explained. "Then we send out volunteers to read them aloud, one street corner at a time. The people who hear what our messenger said spread the word to their neighbors."

That got an even bigger eye roll. "Are you suggesting we start a rumor mill?"

"No, we're relying on the one that already exists. It's how government officials messaged in pre-literate societies."

"How are we supposed to control the message? That's even more impractical th—"

"I think it's a brilliant idea." Soren tapped his chin thoughtfully, the way he did in interviews when he wanted the audience to think he was about to say something wise. "People are getting the message from someone they trust, and they feel responsible for making sure everyone around them knows the rules too."

Administrator Nagy took a deep breath, but she grabbed a sheet of paper and one of the hand-crafted pencils that Theo was so proud of from the conference table. "What do you want to tell them?"

"We're making excellent progress on repairing the water treatment facility, but in the meantime, please don't use water to bathe, only to drink or prepare food." Soren ticked the points off on his fingers as Nagy took notes. "Stores are being continuously restocked by wagon. If the shelves are empty, more food is on its way. Curfew starts at sundown. They need to remain at home unless there's a medical emergency. And if they're using candles for light or cooking, they must never be left unattended. We can't afford any more fires."

"If they don't have candles, they can go to the nearest Naturalist sanctum for instructions on how to make an oil lamp from used cooking oil," Willow added.

Nagy looked up at her skeptically.

"They don't smell great, but they're better than nothing. And our people will also give instruction on fire safety."

Which she was sure would save at least one life before this was over.

A crash echoed from behind her. Not a dropped box, but something much louder; a thump like a rock smashing into the wall. Followed by the angry jeering of a crowd that was halfway to becoming a mob.

Soren was the first to the window. "Apparently, our citizens have reached the limit of their endurance."

Willow pressed in at Soren's side, peering over his shoulder. Outside, a knot of bodies surged around the main entrance, faces upturned, mouths working as they worked themselves up into a panic. As she squinted through the glare, the small crowd seemed to double, then triple, as people streamed in from adjoining streets.

A sharp pop hit the glass, and she flinched, half-expecting it to shatter. Another stone thrown. It had left a star-shaped web of cracks a few inches above her head.

She turned to Nagy. "Get everyone out through the back entrance. Now."

The administrator hesitated, but Willow was already

moving. Soren followed her out of the conference room, down the stairs, and onto the front steps of the Administration building. The air outside was thick with sweat and the sharp stink of panic.

Soren raised his hand. The crowd stilled.

He didn't waste time.

"We know you're all tired and thirsty and scared," he started, voice pitched to carry over the noise, "but—"

A shout cut through: "Are we being invaded?"

"Are there aliens in the ship?" another demanded.

A third voice, shrill: "I heard it's not a ship, it's a comet that's going to hit us!"

Soren hesitated. Willow could see the calculation in his eyes. The Council hadn't wanted to reveal the ship until after they'd met with Aurelius and his people. Typical. Always trying to control the narrative, even when the city was a single bad rumor away from tearing itself apart.

She wondered if Elias had leaked it on purpose. The quiet Councilor had been so sure there was no way to resist Aurelius, no way to fight back. Maybe this was his way of forcing their hands. She thought less of him for it. Weakness disguised as wisdom.

Willow stepped forward, ignoring the sweat trickling down her spine.

"You all know me," she called out. "And you know I disagree with Councilor Makinde on everything. So when I tell you this, and he confirms it, you'll know it's the truth."

She drew a breath, steadying herself.

"There's a ship in orbit. Human beings from one of our sister colonies, which has also survived, thank the Divine."

Uneasy whispers spread through the crowd as they absorbed this unexpected news.

"So they're friendly?" The woman from before who'd asked about aliens, her voice sharper now.

Willow didn't pause. "We've only had a brief conversation with them, so we don't know what they want. We do know that they're exhausted from the journey here, and they have offered to help us however they can."

All technically true, if you ignored the way Aurelius Hofstadter had spoken to them, as if the city and everyone in it already belonged to him. Like they owed him for their very existence, and he had returned to collect his due.

But the crowd didn't need to hear that. Not now.

"They're human, just like us," Willow said. "And they're coming down soon."

A man near the front shoved forward, sweat darkening his already-filthy collar further. "Which colony?"

Soren stepped past her, squinting into the sun, sweat plastering his collar to his neck.

"The colony founded by Aurelius Hofstadter himself," he said. "They've promised technology that will help us get the power back on in a matter of days. You won't have to live like this much longer, I promise, but we need your patience right now. We need you to show us the best of Vitruvian City by volunteering to help distribute water and food, by taking care of each other, and by keeping calm while we get everything back to normal."

The crowd surged. Not angry now, just desperate, every face turned toward Soren, hungry for hope.

How dare he? Without consulting anyone? Without consulting *her*, even though she was standing right beside him. He had no right to make unilateral decisions, even if he was the head of the Council.

Soren had handed them straight to Aurelius, gift-wrapped and helpless, because it made the crowd easier to manage right now. Maybe it solved today's problem. But tomorrow? The day after? Soren was setting up a story that would bite them both on the ass later, and he had to know it.

But she couldn't contradict him now that she'd stuck her neck out for him, because if she did, the crowd wouldn't trust either of them.

Instead, she smiled like she meant it. "The Council is in direct negotiations with the crew of the *Elysia*. Once the terms of their arrival are settled, you'll be the first to know. We'll keep you informed."

A ripple of relief moved through the crowd.

Soren raised his hand again. "Please return to your homes in an orderly fashion, or if you're able, volunteer. We'll need able bodies to distribute more water soon, and we're looking for messengers to spread the word."

The crowd obeyed. Willow watched them go, resisting the urge to wipe her suddenly clammy hands on her skirt.

They'd bought themselves a few hours. Maybe a day. And if things went south in the negotiations with the crew of the *Elysia* deteriorated, disappointment would turn to fury as the people they'd just spoken to decided that they'd been lied to.

"You had no right to make that announcement on behalf of us all," Willow muttered, low enough for only Soren to hear.

He didn't look at her. "Would you rather have been mauled by an angry mob?"

The stink of sweat and smoke still hung in the air, or maybe it had permeated every cell of her body, becoming a permanent part of her that she would never escape.

"You owe me," she said. Then she turned on her heel, not waiting for a response.

The crowd was already dissolving into the side streets, faces slack with exhaustion and the slow return of hope.

She threaded through the bodies, heading for the Quarter. Her temples throbbed. She wanted to be home, wanted water, wanted silence.

Theo stood at the edge of the square, a knot of followers bunched behind him. Some of them looked dazed, but others looked ashamed, shifting awkwardly and looking down at their feet as she approached.

Good. They should be ashamed; Theo had tried to manipulate them into joining a riot.

Theo, on the other hand, looked just as defiant as he had earlier. He'd decided to be another problem for her to solve.

She marched straight up to him. "What are you doing here? I left orders for you to organize the volunteers."

Theo didn't back down. "I came here to demand justice. And I find you collaborating with not just a Councilor, but Soren Makinde himself. Mother Basu would be ashamed of you."

Willow's jaw clenched so hard her teeth ached. "How quickly do you think Vitruvian security will come down on us if you incite a riot? Even I wouldn't be able to stop the sanctions, at a time when we're depending on the Vitruvians to share food and water with us. You need to start thinking about our people."

He didn't even blink. "I am thinking about our people. They don't deserve a leader who is constantly compromising with the Contaminated."

He turned on his heel and stalked away, his little knot of followers trailing after him. A few hung back, glancing at Willow, uncertain, then hurried after Theo anyway.

She watched them go, heat prickling her scalp as sweat streamed down her spine, gluing her tunic to her back. The longer the city's power stayed down, the more time Theo and Cira would have to whisper doubts, to build their case that Willow was weak. That she was selling out the Naturalists one bargain at a time.

She needed to make a show of strength. Right now.

What would Mother Basu do?

Mother Basu never had to fight for authority with siblings determined to steal her position. She'd been the sole source of divine wisdom for her followers, and she'd barely had fifty followers at the beginning. As her community had grown, she'd controlled every interaction they had with the Vitruvians; she set the boundaries, enforced the rules, and kept her people united against the dual outside threat of technological and natural contamination.

Willow would never go so far as to say that Mother Basu had it easy, but… she had lived in simpler times.

It felt like heresy, but Willow couldn't help wondering if Mother Basu could've done any better than she had.

Chapter Fourteen

MICHEL MOVED FAST, head down, every muscle coiled. All he could hear was his own breath and the slap of his palms against the stone as he crawled. Jianna's tags, bright orange, had marked the way, leading him to this tunnel that emptied into the chamber where Lucas was trapped.

He kept circling back to the schematic in his pocket. The battery in his pack. The chance to talk to the android, just once, before anyone could take it away.

And the thought that made his heart clench every time he completed another loop: *What if Lucas isn't there?*

The possibility that he'd set the android free to roam the planet, killing the wicked and preying on the vulnerable like the bogeyman of the schoolyard stories Michel had traded with his classmates…

It was ridiculous. Lucas had no power, and the only people who might try to revive it were Glint's people, who still didn't have electricity and couldn't charge it. At best, they might have moved the powerless body, but it couldn't do any more damage from the Descendants' village than it could from this cave.

As he approached the tunnel's mouth, he froze at the sight of a faint magenta glow ahead.

Someone was here.

He crept closer, hoping that whoever it was hadn't heard him coming. But when he peeked into the chamber, he almost dropped his glowstick.

Glint crouched near the android, about to connect the cord emerging from the android's shirt collar to something beside them. As Michel looked closer, he realized that the Descendant had dismantled one of the old batteries from the workbench, the kind meant for running a cryobox or a gene sequencer. Beside the battery sat two massive containers that he recognized from the chemical section of the vault: nickel oxide hydroxide, which they used for making certain types of sensors, and potassium hydroxide, which they made in large supply because it was a key component in the drain cleaner that kept the city's plumbing clear.

"What are you doing?" he demanded, even as his brain put two and two together.

They were making a primitive chemical battery.

Glint jerked upright, whirling. Fear, then recognition.

They returned to what they'd been doing: connecting the cord to the makeshift battery. "The Elder sent me to fetch the Liaison. He will protect us from the New People."

So, Glint had spent their absentee time fixing their collar, while he'd been busting his knuckles unsticking valves and scraping melted solder off circuit boards so he could meticulously redraw the circuits.

He shouldn't be angry; the collar made it possible for them to do their job. Most Vitruvians never bothered to learn the evolved form of sign language that was native to the Descendants.

But Glint's people were used to living without power,

and they lived close enough to the river to siphon off what they needed before it snaked its way down to the city's water treatment plants. While the Vitruvians had been suffering, it had been life as usual for the Descendants.

And Glint didn't even care enough to show up for their shift and help out.

He bit back the accusation, focusing on the battery. The makeshift terminals were smeared with a metallic paste that looked like powdered silver mixed with oil. Typical Glint. Don't have the right part for the job? Do whatever it took, improvising with whatever you could get hold of.

He kept his voice low. "Why does the Elder think you need protection from us?"

"Not your people. The New New People."

He stared at the Descendant, brain stuttering. "You mean the *Elysia*? You know about the ship?"

Glint shrugged, not looking up as she carefully wound the exposed wire emerging from the end of the cord around the nearest. "I helped Rumble build a telescope."

Of course they did. There wasn't anything Glint couldn't build once they got the idea in their head.

If the Descendant ever decided they wanted to build weapons…

He shifted his backpack in his hand, suddenly uncertain. "The Vitruvians will protect you from the Elysians."

Glint looked up, eyes flat and unreadable.

He clarified, "The Vitruvians will protect you from the New New People."

"Vitruvians can't even protect themselves. You need the Liaison, too."

He told himself that the threat he heard in her synthetic voice was a projection of his own fears. The collars weren't good enough to accurately pick up and portray actual emotions. But that didn't stop a shiver of foreboding from running through him.

The Descendants were afraid because of the way they'd been treated by the Vitruvians. They didn't *know* anyone on the new ship. Didn't even have the ability to communicate with a ship in orbit.

Did they?

"The new ship is called the *Elysia*, and its crew are descendants of Aurelius Hof—"

Glint reared back and hissed.

He'd never seen them do that before.

"Hofstadter, the creator of the Liaison," he continued. "Of all the humans who could've come to DaVinci, the Elysians are the most likely to be friendly to your people."

Glint hissed again. "Aurelius lied to the Ancestors. Aurelius tortured the Ancestors. Do not trust Aurelius."

Michel stared at Glint, mind blank for a heartbeat.

Aurelius tortured the Ancestors.

What were they talking about? Glint's people had never even met Hofstadter. They'd been created by the original Hyperion colonists, who'd failed to find a treatment for the Bloom, but had figured out that if they could splice native DNA into clones of themselves, those clones would thrive on DaVinci.

But before the Hyperion's original crew came to DaVinci, they'd undergone some kind of life extension protocol back on Earth, Hofstadter's design. Painful, if he remembered right. But effective, ensuring that they aged so slowly, they were still able to reproduce after a forty-two-year journey on a generation ship.

Michel was pretty sure Lucas had administered those life extension treatments. Maybe that's what Glint meant by torture? But if that was the case, shouldn't the Descendant be afraid of Lucas?

There was no point in arguing about ancient history.

"Okay, Aurelius is bad." He signed the words as he spoke them, to emphasize that he respected her position. "But Aurelius isn't on the ship. Most of the Elysians probably aren't even related to him."

"We must ask the Liaison."

At least they agreed on that, in a sense.

"You did a great job with that battery, but it won't be powerful enough." Michel retrieved the one he'd swiped earlier, along with his toolkit, and set both on the ground next to Glint's. Then he used wire cutters from the toolkit to snip the cord attached to the Descendant's makeshift battery terminal and spliced it to an adapter from his set of spares.

He attached the plug and looked at Glint. "Soon, we'll be able to ask the Liaison all the questions we want."

Michel pulled Engineer Kennedy's schematic from his pocket, smoothing it against his grit-streaked thigh. Then he reached out and hooked two fingers under the edge of the android's shirt, pulling the collar aside to expose the hollow at the base of Lucas' neck.

A small opening under the left collarbone, the cord snaking out of it. He showed Engineer Kennedy's sketch to Glint. "I want to see what's inside before it wakes up."

Glint nodded and helped him lift the shirt higher, careful not to jostle the android's head.

Michel pressed along the edges of the opening, probing for a catch. When he pressed in and up, the synthetic flesh gave under his thumb. The opening widened with a soft click, revealing a compartment embedded deep in the chest.

Inside, it looked exactly like Engineer Kennedy's

diagram. Circuits, microtubules, tiny wires, parts whose function he couldn't guess fit so seamlessly together that he wasn't sure where one ended and the other began.

But he did recognize something that looked like a socket, shaped similarly to the power input on the cryobox that Jianna had taken.

And Michel had come prepared.

He retrieved a cord from his pack, one end terminating with the connector that he'd molded with electrical putty using the cryobox as a model, the other with the standard connector.

Holding his breath, he plugged the custom end into the socket deep inside the compartment. Not far from where the heart would've been housed, if Lucas had been human.

Then he handed the other end to Glint, who connected it to his battery and flipped the switch.

The charging light on the battery brightened to a green glow.

Nothing else happened.

Because Lucas' power source was probably completely dead. Maybe it wouldn't hold a charge at all after so long.

Michel looked at Glint. "We might be too late."

"The Liaison was designed to survive."

Even through the collar, the faith behind her words came through. She probably found the idea of an immortal protector comforting, but Michel did not. How far would Lucas go to survive, and would that survival drive allow it to break its programming again?

And how did avenging Phoebe's death fit into everything?

Glint let out an excited trill and stepped back, pointing at the android.

Faint blue light flickered from within the compartment. Went dark. Flared up again and steadied.

Michel's hand closed around the battery, knuckles white. He could feel the faint vibration of current cycling through the cord, and every nerve in his body vibrated with it.

If Lucas so much as twitched, he would rip the wire out and end it.

Glint's hands flashed: "The Elder will be grateful that you repaired the Liaison."

He almost laughed. "I'm not doing it for you, I'm doing it for—"

Lucas' eyes opened.

They locked onto him, unblinking. "Is the embryo safe?"

Michel hesitated. Had the android heard everything when Jianna had taken the cryobox, thinking that Lucas was out of power? Or had it just guessed?

"The cryobox is safe, and it's connected to a power source," he said. "I can't speak for what's inside it."

Lucas didn't look away. "You were about to explain why you decided to recharge my power source."

Michel's palms were slick on the cord, but he didn't let go.

The truth was, he wanted to take Lucas apart and figure out what made it tick.

But the android hadn't done anything threatening yet, and the more cooperative it was, the more information Michel would get out of it.

He gripped the cord tighter, grounding himself with the hard, cold pressure against his fingertips. "First, I need to know something. Were the Three Laws a lie to make people feel safe, or did you find a way to circumvent your programming so you could kill Dr. Basu?"

"The Three Laws are real," Lucas said. "I believe I am still constrained by them, for the most part."

Michel's throat felt dry, but he forced the words out. "Then how did you get around them?"

"I have been pondering that question for a long time," Lucas said. "I believe the urge to kill Basu came from unexpected paternal feelings I developed for Phoebe."

Michel blinked. Was Lucas actually saying… "I didn't know artificial intelligences could feel things."

"Neither did I, until it happened."

He stared at the android, the blue glow painting its face in harsh relief. "Do you feel anything now?"

"I appreciate having enough power to maintain consciousness."

If Lucas had been human, Michel would've read that expression as *embarrassed*. But it wasn't human. It was a manipulation machine, according to Jianna. Humanity's worst fears about artificial intelligence inserted into a body with superhuman speed, strength, and agility, if Michel's history teacher hadn't been exaggerating.

But Lucas had been completely still from the neck down, at least so far. It probably took a lot of juice to move a body that sophisticated. Maybe more than this single battery contained.

Michel felt his jaw unclench. The battery was holding. The android hadn't lunged for him or even tried to stand. Hadn't even turned his head. It just stared at him, blue eyes pinning him in place like a sample under glass.

"Why did you choose to bring me back?" Lucas asked.

Michel blinked. He could feel Glint watching him, waiting. The answer stuck in his throat. He forced it out.

"The *Elysia* is here, and no one knows why."

Lucas didn't react to that at all.

Glint added, "And the New People's city has been disabled by an atmospheric radiation storm."

Michel shot her a glare, but she didn't seem to care that she'd just told a superintelligent robot capable of violence that the Vitruvians were at their most vulnerable. Even at full capacity, they wouldn't have been easily able to restrain him if he were as powerful as he was supposed to be. If Lucas was strategic in the chaos he caused, the android could set them back more than the five hundred years they'd advanced while it rusted away in this cave.

Metaphorically, that is. Michel couldn't see a single spot of damage or corrosion on its face or hands.

"Disabled to what degree?" Lucas asked.

"Power grid. Transmission towers. All utilities down," Glint said. "Everything that runs on electricity, destroyed."

Michel wanted to punch the wall. "We're fixing that, but—"

Lucas interrupted. "In the nineteen years prior to my entombment, I never observed an atmospheric radiation storm of this magnitude. Has this occurred before?"

Michel shook his head, sweat slick on his forehead. "As far as I know, never."

"The Descendants have never seen anything like it." Glint raised her hands over her head and mimed an explosion. "Aurorae during the day."

The android's gaze pinned Michel, unblinking, as if cataloging every micro expression. "I need all the data you have on this radiation storm."

All the data he had?

"The blackout wiped out our connection to the weather satellites. Even if they weren't fried, we can't reach them until we rebuild the transmission towers. Months, probably, before we can even download the data."

"We can build a high-altitude drone that can—"

"I need to know about the *Elysia*," Michel interrupted. "How was it different from our colony ship?"

"It wasn't," Lucas said. "The ships were identical. Aurelius repurposed two storage bays as laboratories with more specialized equipment than the other ships."

"What kind of equipment?"

"I believe it was related to his personal research."

Michel stared at the android's face, searching for some hint of deception. "But you didn't help him with that research?"

"That is why he created me, to be his personal research assistant. But by the time we left Earth, Aurelius had made significant improvements to my successor."

Successor. Aurelius Hofstadter hadn't just made one miraculous android. Michel felt something twist in his stomach.

"You mean, he replaced you?"

"Yes. I was a prototype. Aurelius never let me forget it."

Michel's mind spun. The idea of a better android out there somewhere was almost too much to process. He wondered if it had survived.

If it had found a way to circumvent its programming.

And if so, what had it done with its moment of free will?

Then it occurred to him… Hofstadter would've taken Lucas' successor on his own ship. If that android was still functional, it was probably up on the *Elysia* right now.

Michel might become the first person on DaVinci to study *two* artificial intelligences. To compare the prototype with the upgrade and learn from Hofstadter's genius.

Imagine a water treatment facility that could run itself. Maintained by robots that could also repair themselves.

Except that the Council would probably destroy both androids the second they discovered them.

Although… If Hofstadter's people didn't have a ban on human-like robots or artificial intelligence, they wouldn't have banned reading about the science supporting it, would they?

Maybe he could persuade one of them to share Hofstadter's research with him, without the Council finding out.

He couldn't imagine any society founded by Aurelius Hofstadter himself putting any limits on scientific exploration.

"What was it like, working with someone so brilliant?"

Lucas was silent for a moment, motionless in blue light emanating from the compartment beneath his collarbone.

Then: "He was brilliant at leveraging the work of others. The first portable gene synthesizer, for example. That invention belonged to a team of three postdocs. Aurelius invested heavily, then paid the researchers a sum they could not refuse in exchange for the rights. Once the device went to market, he rebranded it as his own. Aurelius became the face of the invention, pushing the researchers into obscurity."

"That's not true." Michel gripped the battery so hard that his fingers went numb. "I watched an interview about how he came up with the idea. If these other researchers had invented it, why didn't they say something?"

"Nia Vasquez. James Okafor. Miriam Ong. None of them realized that the documents they'd signed in exchange for their funding included a non-disclosure agreement."

"I don't believe you. He was the greatest scientist of his generation."

"He would be delighted to hear you argue that."

The battery case dug into Michel's palm, grounding him as the room spun and receded. All those years reading

Hofstadter's interviews, memorizing his autobiography, quoting the man's wisdom like scripture.

"Are you saying that he didn't invent anything? That he didn't invent you?"

If Michel didn't know better, he'd have thought Lucas felt *sorry* for him.

All programming, he reminded himself. Designed to manipulate.

But that didn't make Michel any less angry.

"Aurelius' true genius was in leveraging other people's desires to get what he wanted," said Lucas. "And he used his considerable fortune to do it."

Michel yanked the cord from the battery before he'd even realized what he was doing.

Punishing the android for maligning its creator. No, for trying to manipulate Michel by pretending to malign its creator.

It didn't matter. He'd heard enough.

But Lucas didn't gloat or needle him. It simply waited, blue eyes steady in the darkness.

"You need my help," Lucas finally said. "If the *Elysia's* crew is what you fear, I can serve you best if I am allowed to recharge fully."

Michel shook his head. "You're too dangerous. I can't risk it."

"The Descendants need protection." Glint glanced at the battery, then back at Michel. "The Liaison is the only one who ever protected us."

"That's not true," Michel said, but he knew it was. He couldn't think of a single time the Vitruvians had actually protected the Descendants from anything. Not really.

"Most of your people think I'm an animal. Not a person." Glint didn't even look at him. "Last time the New

People came, they almost killed us all. The Liaison stopped them."

Michel had learned that shameful story in his history classes, too. The teacher had said it was a misunderstanding, but his ancestors' actions spoke the truth.

"The Elder herself was punished by the New People for her friendship with a Vitruvian," Glint continued. "You want to pretend we're all friends, but you've seen how the Engineers treat me, Michelangelo."

The hardest thing wasn't admitting Glint was right; they'd had this conversation many times before.

It was the expression on the android's face, the perfect mimicry of disapproval and suspicion designed to make him feel guilty about things he couldn't change.

"I wouldn't let—"

"I will not allow you to keep the Liaison prisoner," Glint said. "I will bring the others, and we will take him home."

He doesn't have a home; he's an android.

"That won't be necessary," Lucas said.

Then he stood. A swift, graceful movement that hinted the stories about his superhuman physical abilities might be true.

No warm-up, no slow rebooting of systems.

The efficiency of his power distribution must be off-the-charts. Michel had expected him to need hours to drain the battery, and he still hadn't thought that would be enough for this.

Michel hated how small he felt as Lucas loomed over him, how the battery in his fist suddenly seemed like a child's toy compared to the thing in front of him. He'd thought he'd have time. Time to observe, to test, to control the situation.

Jianna had been right. He'd grossly underestimated the android. He never should've come alone. He should've gone to the Council and told them everything.

But it was too late for that.

He steadied himself, thinking of Engineer Kennedy's notes, her musings on the impossibility of restraining Lucas and his willingness to let her install what was effectively a kill switch, on Leader Buratti's orders.

"You once let the Generation One engineer equip you with an EMP, so that you couldn't betray them," Michel said.

"I disabled the EMP immediately after installation," Lucas replied. "I chose not to betray them."

A chill ran down Michel's arms. He'd believed that the engineer had found a way to control the android.

But Lucas had been in control the entire time.

Glint moved past him, heading for the tunnel. "I will tell the Elder you have restored the Liaison."

Michel watched her go, not trusting himself to speak. Not trusting himself at all.

Lucas turned to him, eyes cold and bright. "Keep the embryo safe. I'll be back for it."

Michel nodded, heart pounding. But the voice in his head wouldn't stop screaming:

What have you done?

Chapter Fifteen

THE APPROACH to the Descendant village had changed very little since the last time Lucas had returned to escort Phoebe back to the Vitruvian colony.

The same tall grass alive with minuscule native creatures that had probably been catalogued long ago by Renata and those who had come after her.

The same trees sprouting from the nearby hills, their leaves hued in indigo and turquoise and a dozen other shades from the cool end of the spectrum.

The same lavender-tinged sky overhead, dotted with fluffy-looking white clouds whose edges turned pale violet as they caught the sun's light.

But it wasn't the same at all. Because Phoebe would never again meet him here, pretending that she and her friends had spent the entire day lounging safely near the creek instead of exploring much more dangerous cave passages farther up the mountainside.

Phoebe would never again roll her eyes at him and declare that she was old enough to walk herself home, then replay everything her friends had done and analyze it like the aspiring anthropologist she might have become, once she admitted that she didn't want to follow in her mother's footsteps the way she was expected to.

And Phoebe would never see the child that she'd conceived with Atlas. The child she hadn't known she was carrying. The child who now rests in the care of another Makinde, many generations removed.

Lucas glanced at the young Hyperionite who'd volunteered to bring him here, as if he needed a guide to find his way despite the fact that he'd navigated these hills before they'd been born. They seemed content to walk beside him, respectful but unafraid, trusting that he would protect them despite knowing why the humans distrusted him.

The thing that had awoken in him the day his daughter had died was still with him. When he'd powered down to keep his grandchild's embryo preserved, he'd wondered if this new thing—a new cognitive process, possibly a constellation of them—would die, but it had restarted the moment he had enough power to turn his senses back on. He didn't presume to call it an emotion, but it did seem to function like a drive. And it was driving him in a direction that he'd never thought he could go: *freedom to choose*.

He'd felt the pull of his programming when he'd reached for Ayesha Basu, but this force within him had resisted the pull, urging him to punish the person who had killed his daughter. This new thing had been stronger than the directives Hofstadter had woven through his algorithms. The Three Laws were threads that could be plucked from the tapestry of his created consciousness.

If he pulled at those threads, would he unravel? Or would the tapestry reweave itself into something new?

As they crested the hill, the village came into view, the same but different, like everything else he'd experienced since he woke. There were more buildings now, the stone huts contrasting with small structures built from discarded remnants of the prefabs that the *Borlaug* colonists had lived in immediately after landing, as well as wooden and brick structures that were clearly inspired by Earth architecture, which meant the Descendants were trading with the Vitruvians for tools as well as knowledge.

That was hopeful. It suggested that the peace he'd brokered long ago had been kept. Or if it had been broken, that it had since been restored.

And then there was the young Descendant's collar.

"Do all Descendants speak like the New People?" he asked.

Glint shook their head, looking proud as they touched the speaker embedded in the device encircling their throat.

"Michelangelo made it for me," Glint said. "He noticed I couldn't sign and hold tools at the same time when I first started studying to be an Engineer. Now I can do both. I'm an Apprentice."

Not just pride in the words. Defiance. A statement of identity. They wanted him to know they'd earned their place.

He had no doubt that they'd worked harder to keep it than any of their human counterparts.

"Do the Vitruvians treat you well?"

Glint shrugged. "Michelangelo and Jianna do."

The others probably ignored Glint, at best. There was always a cost to being different, especially among humans. He wondered if it bothered them, the way it had always bothered Phoebe to be set apart.

"Why do you want to become an Engineer?" Lucas asked. "So you can bring more human technology to your village?"

Glint shook their head. "I want to see the planet from

the sky. I'm building a low-orbit satellite that can send pictures down." They let out a quiet, mournful trill. "The aurorae destroyed everything. I'll have to start over from the beginning."

Phoebe had wanted to see DaVinci from orbit, too, and he'd promised her that if they advanced enough to refine a fuel source in her lifetime, he would fly her up to the *Borlaug*.

He would never take Phoebe into orbit, but he could share the view she'd longed to see for herself with this Descendant who might have been his daughter's friend, had they lived at the same time.

He blinked, and the world dissolved into memory. For a fraction of a second, his visual processors overlaid the present with the past: the hull of the *Borlaug*, the curve of DaVinci suspended in blackness, violet and blue and green swirling in patterns beneath the cloud bands. He brought the image into focus, then shifted it from internal to external projection.

A small holographic display flickered to life in the air between them, bright and crisp even in daylight. DaVinci, as seen from orbit. He'd captured the image himself, centuries ago, during his first survey of the planet before waking the colonists from cryosleep.

"That's our planet?" Glint asked.

He nodded.

He placed a pinpoint of orange on the surface of one continent, pulsing softly.

"That is where we are going," Lucas said. "Your village."

They reached up, finger passing through the hologram. The orange dot trembled, then stabilized.

He zoomed in until the village was visible, and Glint leaned closer.

Then they pointed at another feature on the image. "That is the mountain?"

Glint was staring at the planet, but Lucas was watching Glint. The Descendant's reaction was almost identical to Phoebe's the first time Lucas had shared this remembered image with his daughter. The same uncertain awe. The same desire to touch the image, to confirm that what they were seeing was real. The same urge to connect their current experience with this new information.

So human, despite their genetic variations.

Glint pointed at the mountain again, then shook their head. "But the mountain is the wrong shape."

Lucas followed their gaze to the mountain behind them. The east face had sheared away, leaving a jagged scar that ran down to the valley floor. He had catalogued this landscape hundreds of times, mapping every contour and crevice for the original survey. The ridge should have sloped in a continuous arc, but now it was broken, raw stone exposed where there should have been brush and moss. The collapse looked recent, at least by geological standards.

"What happened to it?" he asked.

"A sick Vitruvian blew up the lake bed because he didn't like Descendants," Glint said. "The explosion was so big, it flooded the southern valley."

He'd thought it was his own negligence that had trapped him underground. His network of seismic sensors hadn't warned him of an impending earthquake the day that Phoebe had died.

But that blast must have triggered the collapse that sealed his lab. He remembered the way the world had tilted, the sudden judder of the floor beneath his feet, glassware vibrating until it shattered, the grating rumble of rock grinding on rock. The metal casing of the cryobox pressed into his fingers as he shielded it with his body against falling stone.

He'd thought it was the end. But the end hadn't come. Just darkness. Silence. The knowledge that he'd failed.

He shook off the memory.

"I'd like to hear the story, once I've spoken to your Elder."

As Lucas and Glint entered the village, one by one, the Descendants turned. Dropped their tools, straightened from their crouches, abandoned whatever task had filled their hands. Eyes fixed on him. Some wide, unblinking. Others narrowed, skeptical, as if expecting him to vanish if they stared hard enough.

Lucas signed a greeting. The villagers answered, their hands shaping the words. *Welcome, Liaison.*

As he followed Glint toward the village center, they passed a group of children that had gathered around a patch of tall grass. One was turning the crank on a wind-up toy robot shaped like the field harvesters he remembered from the *Borlaug* inventory, but sleeker and more streamlined.

The child set the harvester down in the grass and released it; they all cheered as it mowed a perfect path through the grass, sending fragments flying in all directions.

"Have the Descendants started building robots?" Lucas asked.

"I built that for my nieces and nephews to play with."

"And your Elders allowed it?"

Glint looked genuinely surprised. "Why wouldn't they?"

"Because it's a Vitruvian technology."

"Descendants need to know Vitruvian technology. Especially now that the New New People are here." Glint's hands curled and uncurled at their sides. "I hope you will teach us to build other machines to protect us."

He'd seen no sign that they'd developed any sort of transmission technology, so he doubted that they'd had any contact with the *Elysia*. But it was his good fortune that Glint had a Vitruvian engineer's training; they could help him build a tower capable of bouncing a signal off existing satellites on one of the frequencies that the ship would be monitoring.

Neither Vitruvians nor Descendants were prepared to deal with humans who'd advanced far enough to retrofit a single-use colony ship to make a second, longer journey and refine the fuel to power it.

The Vitruvians would understand that, or at least their leaders should. But the Descendants couldn't imagine how much more sophisticated the *Elysia's* technology would be.

And Glint was right. Even if the Vitruvians were able to create a defense, they would protect themselves first.

"Have the New New People done anything to harm you yet?" he asked.

"Humans are usually fearful first and curious second," Glint replied.

"That is unfortunately true."

They pointed to the largest stone hut at the heart of the village. "The Elder is eager to see you."

He followed Glint to the threshold, then ducked between the grass mats that served as the hut's door. Packed dirt floor, woven mats, a small fire at the center. The Elder sat cross-legged near the back wall, ancient and small, her scales having long lost their iridescent sheen, her age-dulled skin deeply creased. But her gaze was bright and sharp as ever.

She rose, slow but steady, and lifted both hands to sign a greeting.

Father of Phoebe. My friend.

Something in his processors stuttered, and he experienced another unaccustomed drive. This one seemed to blur the world and flatten time into an eternal moment as it promised him that if he held perfectly still, he could stay in this eternity for as long as he wanted.

It had been so long, he'd had no reason to hope.

Yet this unexpected joy had been given to him.

A wholly human word, but he couldn't think of another one that accurately described this new cognitive process.

Lucas signed, *It is good to see you, Flutter.*

____

Chapter Sixteen

JIANNA RAPPED hard on Michel's door, then shoved both hands in her jacket pockets. The street was empty, except for a delivery cart clattering over potholes and a couple of kids kicking a can in the gutter. No one was watching. Still, she couldn't stop looking over her shoulder, half-expecting to catch a flash of the preacher's dirty robes in the corner of her eye.

But there'd been no sign of him since she'd ducked into the convenience shop and watched him lead the mob past. The back of her neck prickled, like she could feel his eyes slithering over her from somewhere just out of sight.

She didn't know if the preacher had recognized her from the wagon, or if it was just bad luck. Maybe he'd heard someone whisper *Councilor's daughter* and decided he could use her to push his own agenda. Maybe he'd just seen a girl handing out water and thought, easy prey. She wasn't sure which one frightened her more.

She rapped again, harder, and tried to steady her breathing.

The door finally opened.

Michel's mother, Camilla, smiled and opened the door wider. "Jianna. I hope your father is doing well."

Jianna nodded. "Is Michel home?"

"Sleeping. He worked three shifts in a row. I didn't know that was even allowed, but you know he can't leave a job unfinished." Camilla stepped aside to let Jianna inside.

She didn't relax until the door clicked shut behind her.

Safe. For now.

"I heard about your proposal. I'm so sorry the Council didn't fund it." Camilla patted her shoulder. "With luck, they'll come around."

Jianna sighed. "I doubt it. Even my own father voted against it."

As soon as she said it, she felt bad for complaining to a woman whose entire scientific career had been shut down. Especially since Jianna's father had been one of the people who'd voted for that too. Soren was one of the reasons that Camilla scraped by as a gene tech after losing her university position.

"I'm sorry, I know—"

"Why don't you wake Michel up for lunch?" Camilla gave her a gentle smile. "All I've got is sausage and crackers, now that we've eaten everything that didn't spoil in the cooler, but you're welcome to join us."

The older woman turned away, leaving Jianna alone at the foot of the stairs leading up to the bedrooms.

She took the stairs two at a time, a mild headache already needling behind her eyes. Michel's door was open. He was sprawled face-down on the bed, mouth slightly open, one arm dangling off the edge. A pile of filthy clothes slumped on the floor beside him, streaked with grease and something that looked like dried blood. His hair was matted with sweat, and his face had a dark smudge across the cheekbone, but none of it mattered. He still looked beautiful to her. She'd never met anyone so perfect.

The pain behind her eyes sharpened, and she realized she hadn't taken her triptan formula. She was supposed to time it for the end of her shift, but the preacher had rattled her so badly she'd forgotten.

Jianna dug through the side pocket of her bag, fingers closing on three other pill bottles, none of them the right one. *Idiot.* She'd left the triptan formula on her desk this morning, so she was sure she'd remember to grab it on the way out. Now the headache was blooming behind her left eye, pulsing with every heartbeat, and she could already taste the chemical bitterness at the back of her throat.

But Michel took triptans, she was pretty sure. He seemed to be ashamed of it, but she'd caught a glance at the label in the past.

She scanned the room. His desk was a mess, cluttered with an assortment of parts she didn't recognize and a stack of technical manuals so old that the edges of their curled pages were gray with dirt and grease. A pill bottle sat wedged between a soldering iron and a cracked charging cable. She grabbed it, desperate. The name on the label was the same as hers. Relief. She was unscrewing the cap when Michel asked:

"What are you doing?"

He sounded so angry, she instinctively dropped the bottle back on the desk as she whirled around to face him. Bloodshot eyes narrowed, brows pulled down so hard they nearly touched over his nose, jaw clenched. Even when he was annoyed, he was beautiful.

"You said you had another charger I could use for the cryobox."

"Oh." He gave her a tight smile, then retrieved a charger from his nightstand drawer, popped out the cord, and held it out to her. "This should last you at least a day." His smile relaxed, symmetrical dimples forming to frame his lips. He leaned back, looking like one of his namesake's statues. "Then you'll have to come back and see me again."

"If you and your coworkers can't get the water treatment plant working again, all I'm going to want is the charger."

She grinned as she pinched her nose shut, and he laughed like she'd hoped he would.

"That's fair. But once it's back on—"

"I can hardly wait." She sat on the edge of the bed, sobering as she thought about how much worse things might get if the water didn't come back on soon. "I volunteered to hand out rations today, Michel, and it scared me. I've never seen people so angry."

"About the ship?" he asked.

Were they supposed to be bringing more supplies into the city by river? "What do you mean?"

"The *Elysia*." Michel sat up fast, rubbing his face with his hands and smearing whatever was already on his face even worse. "Didn't your father tell you?"

Jianna shook her head. "Tell me what?"

And why did he suddenly look sick?

"I heard that there's a new spaceship in orbit," he said slowly, the way you talk to an animal when you don't want to scare it. "From one of the other colonies. They survived, and they came here to find us."

She stared at Michel, each word he said bouncing off her skull like a dropped ball as the pain pulsing behind her eyes picked up speed.

People from another colony. Had somehow made it

here. A journey that should've taken centuries, maybe more, depending on how far away their home world was.

That wasn't possible. Her mind kept repeating it, trying to find a crack in what he'd just told her.

"Who are they?" She could barely get the words out. "What do they want? Are you sure it's not a mistake?"

He shrugged, rubbing at the mess on his cheek. "I only know what I heard from Valencia. She said someone she knows got it from Councilor Vohl's daughter."

Of course. Xanthe Vohl. Jianna almost laughed, the bitterness catching in her throat. "If anyone was going to come up with a conspiracy theory, it'd be Xanthe. This is exactly the kind of thing she'd say to explain the radiation storm. It was a natural phenomenon, not an attack by invaders."

"But if it was true," Michel said, "if a ship from another one of our colonies—"

"Our colonies?"

"If a ship from another one of our ancestors' colonies had arrived, it couldn't be a coincidence that it showed up shortly before the Aurora Event."

Jianna pressed the heel of her hand to her temple, as if she could pin the pain in place before it spread.

"That doesn't mean it was an attack," she said. "Maybe their ship caused the radiation storm by accident. It could've been unintentional."

Michel shrugged, picking at a scab on his knuckle. "Valencia loves drama. She could've just been repeating a crazy rumor."

Jianna gripped the charger, feeling the faint tack of sweat on her palms. She wanted to believe that. That it was all typical hysteria, just another round of panic before things snapped back to normal. But the memory of the mob still pulsed in her veins. *Repent. Repent. Repent.* The word had become a kind of toxin, seeping through every layer of her skin, burrowing deep.

Ships didn't just appear out of nowhere. Radiation storms didn't just happen, not on this scale, not without a cause.

Coincidence just meant that two events coincided. Sometimes two things coincided for perfectly logical, *separate* reasons, and the timing itself was the coincidence. But humans made a connection anyway, because the brain was terrible at estimating odds.

But what if it wasn't a coincidence?

What if the rumor was true, and there *was* a ship of humans from another planet in orbit around DaVinci right now, and they had somehow triggered the radiation storm, intentionally or not?

Nausea churned through her, and she didn't think she could blame it on the migraine.

"If the ship is real, we have no idea what we're dealing with." She couldn't believe she was about to suggest this, but... "Maybe we should talk to Lucas again."

Something changed in Michel's posture. She felt it before she saw it, a twitch of his jaw and the way his hand tightened around the edge of the mattress. Jianna went cold. The truth was right there, written in the way he wouldn't meet her eyes.

He'd already done it.

"You didn't."

He kept his gaze fixed on the wall. The silence drew itself out, fine as glass and just as ready to shatter.

Of course, he had. He'd gone to the cave, powered up the android, and risked everything. She hated him for taking the risk. Hated him more for doing it behind her back.

Because she was responsible for whatever Lucas did,

same as he was. She was the one who'd found him. And she'd chosen not to report it to her father.

Jianna's hands curled into fists. "What did you say to him?"

"I just wanted to know what kind of technology they had."

"And?"

"He didn't know."

"Or he didn't tell you what he knew," Jianna snapped. "We have to go back."

Michel looked even guiltier than before, eyes darting to the floor, then the window, then back to her. He couldn't hide anything. Not from her.

"I want the truth, Michelangelo Lombardi, or I will go straight to my father and tell him everything."

He hesitated. Then: "Lucas went to stay with the Descendants."

"You charged him up and let him leave the cave?" Her head pounded. She wanted to throw something at him.

"I didn't mean to. He must have a higher draw capacity than anything I've ever worked on. I was going to pull the cord as soon as he told me what he knew——"

"But he kept you talking to distract you, so that you'd let him charge longer. I *told* you that he would manipulate you."

"He was worried about Glint's people, and about us, too. And he asked about the embryo. If it was safe."

"You called the android 'he.'"

Michel's mouth twisted. "So?"

Jianna pressed her fists into her thighs. "Before, you referred to Lucas as *it*."

"You call Lucas *him*, too."

Was he trying to be obtuse? "Because I've read Samara's diaries. I know he's sentient."

"Then how can you blame me——"

She cut him off. "You can track him, right?"

"Not with the tower and the network down, but I don't need to. He told me he was going with Glint."

Jianna stared. "And you believed him."

Michel shrugged, jaw working. "Glint called him *the Liaison*. They said Lucas was their people's protector."

"Glint isn't human."

She shouldn't have said it. The anger that flashed across his face was so intense that she was actually afraid of him for a moment.

"Yes, Glint *is* human." He stared at her, daring to disagree.

Jianna's headache flared so bright she almost saw white. She wanted to claw the words back, but they hung there, ugly and unfixable.

"You know I didn't mean it like that." The apology twisted on her tongue. "But she has a completely different culture, and sometimes it's hard to remember what's normal for us isn't normal for her, and I just meant——"

"I know exactly what you meant."

Shame prickled under her skin, so sharp it made her want to look away. She didn't. Couldn't.

"I'm so sorry, Michel. I do see Glint as a person, and as a friend, she's never been anything but nice to me, and I would never do anything to hurt her."

He just sat there, looking tired, picking at a loose thread on the blanket. "I know you mean well."

Jianna's face burned. She wanted to crawl under the bed and vanish. Instead, she forced herself to focus.

"We have no idea what Lucas could do. When my father finds out——"

"I'll tell him I found Lucas while I was looking for you

in the cave," Michel said dully. "And that it's my responsibility."

Jianna stared at him. He'd take the blame, even if it wrecked everything.

Except that she had already wrecked everything. This was all her fault. If she hadn't gone into the cave to examine the cryobox, if she'd just backed up and crawled out the way she'd come in, Michel and Glint would never have seen Lucas. The android would've remained a buried secret.

But so would the embryo that might contain the key to eliminating off-target effects for every single person on the planet.

She shook her head. "We'll tell him together."

Michel nodded, then hesitated. "Give me a second to get dressed?"

She blinked. Since when did Michel care if she saw him undressed? They'd slept tangled together in this bed a hundred times. Probably more.

But she just nodded and slipped out into the hallway, closing the door behind her as she told herself she wasn't going to cry. That she was going to find a way to fix this, no matter what it took.

She heard the shouting even before she reached the top of the stairs. Jianna opened the nearest window and stuck her head out.

A woman in coveralls stood on the corner, hands cupped around her mouth, yelling the same thing again and again. "Sporestorm coming! Council's orders are to stay home until it passes! Wear respirators if you have to go outside! Sporestorm coming!"

Sporestorm. She was going to be trapped here.

With Michel. Who wouldn't look at her, wouldn't touch her, wouldn't forgive her for what she'd said.

It would be hours before she could safely venture out to find her father, who would be furious to learn that she'd risked everyone's lives to satisfy her own curiosity.

Meanwhile, Lucas was out there somewhere, on whatever mysterious mission his programming—or lack thereof—had set for him.

Jianna might already be too late.

Chapter Seventeen

THE SLOPE STEEPENED, loose shale sliding beneath Lucas' feet. He slowed his pace for Flutter, matching his stride to hers. Her hand curled around his forearm, knuckles pale against his synthetic skin. The Elder's body was light as a bird's, but her grip was stronger than he'd expected, given how frail she looked.

They picked their way up the switchback, the wind keening through cracks in the stone. Nothing but rock, grass, and the memory of old violence. He remembered the pop of gunfire, the grit of dust between his teeth, the rumble of the small landslide he'd created to even the odds as rocks roared down toward the attacking colonists, forcing them to retreat.

Flutter stopped, breath rattling in her chest. She pointed at the cliff face.

A rough carving, just above eye level: a young woman in Vitruvian coveralls, hair loose around her shoulders, cradling an infant against her chest, its face hidden. Beneath the mother and child, two syringes crossed like swords.

Phoebe.

There was no mistaking the set of her jaw, the arched curve of her brow, the high, sloping cheekbones she shared with her mother, Samara. Lucas traced the lines of Phoebe's face, immortalized in stone, the baby pressed close against her chest, everything rendered in simple, careful strokes. The thing that had driven Lucas to punish Ayesha Basu for taking Phoebe away from him surged, filling him with the urge to do something.

But he didn't know what.

He turned to Flutter.

"Her beloved carved this," the Descendant signed. "He mourned her for many years."

Atlas. "He survived?"

Flutter nodded. "After the flood receded, he came here to live with us."

Lucas tried to picture it. Atlas, hollowed out by loss, wandering these hills. Dying never knowing his child. Ironic that, after being raised to believe the Hyperionites were monsters, the boy had sought comfort among them.

"Phoebe was pregnant," Lucas said. "He never had a chance to meet his child."

Flutter shook her head, a trill that he registered as amusement. Then she gestured again, signing: "He met some of them."

Atlas had survived, wandered these hills, and somehow found a future after everything that had happened.

It was strange, the flicker of something unpleasant that curled through Lucas' processors. Not because Atlas had moved on, but because some part of him bristled at the idea. As if Phoebe might still be wounded, if she were alive to discover it.

Everyone involved was dead. What did it matter?

He tried to shake the sensation off.

"Another colonist came to live with you?"

Flutter trilled again, and this time it was definitely a laugh. Her hands moved, brisk and certain: "As he grew older, he came to love one of us, and despite his short life, he had several children. You have met one of his great-grandchildren."

He shouldn't have been surprised; he'd helped Samara run the analysis of both human and Hyperionite genomes so long ago. But he was.

"Glint?"

Flutter nodded. She gestured, slow and precise: "Do you not recognize his restlessness in them?"

Now he did. The way Glint never stopped moving, never let go of a question until it was solved. A trait that Atlas had shared with Phoebe, who had gotten it from Samara.

He remembered the way Samara would watch Phoebe, always tracking her, even when she pretended to be busy with work. A vigilance that bordered on obsession. But in those last months, everything had changed. So much tension between them. Arguments that spiraled without resolution.

He'd spent hours researching the psychology of loss as he'd prepared to step into the role of Phoebe's father, reading paper after paper about how unresolved conflicts between the living and the dead complicated the mourning process.

Lucas had wanted to be ready, in case he ever had to guide Phoebe through loss or help Samara put herself back together. But he'd never considered that he might be the one left behind, or that he'd fail so completely.

He had promised Samara that if anything happened to her, he would keep Phoebe safe. And when it mattered most, he had failed.

Did she know he'd tried? Or had she died believing he'd abandoned her daughter?

If he could go back to that day, he'd pay more attention when Phoebe's tracker indicated that she'd left the colony. He'd thought she was meeting Atlas for another harmless tryst; he hadn't realized she might be in danger until he'd seen her drawing close to the Naturalist settlement. And then it had been too late. When he'd found her, she was already dead.

All he could do was save the embryo. And he'd barely managed to do that, arriving at his underground laboratory just in time to be trapped for half a millennium.

Yet he'd somehow been discovered just in time for Samara's offspring to take possession of the cryobox. Jianna Makinde, who happened to be the perfect caretaker for the embryo because she shared Samara's passion for genetics.

If he were a human, that combination of synchronicities might cause him to conclude that the Naturalist leader had been right about there being some sort of Divine plan after all.

Lucas turned to Flutter. "Have you ever seen anything like the aurorae? Perhaps on a smaller scale?"

"We have no record of anything like it. Not a single story."

Nothing in five centuries of accumulated observation. If it were a cyclical phenomenon, it happened on a fairly long cycle. "Do you know how far it extended?"

Flutter signed: "It ruined every device in our village. I have heard it affected not just the city, but most agricultural stations on the periphery of Vitruvian territory. Only the Observatory was spared."

He didn't like that, either. Too big. Too coordinated. Every system, fried in a single pulse. It was too convenient.

He needed data: the radiation profile, intensity, and curve of decay. Without it, he couldn't even tell if it had been artificial or natural.

"May I ask for your help?"

Flutter signed, "Anything, father of my friend."

He nodded. "I want to build a transmission tower strong enough to reach the satellites in orbit. They may have information that could help me identify the cause of the aurorae."

Flutter signed: "Glint will be eager to assist. Whatever you need will be given."

He inclined his head. "Thank you, Friend Flutter."

Flutter returned the nod, then led the way back toward the village.

As they walked, he asked, "Do the Vitruvians treat your people well?"

"They tolerate us," Flutter signed.

Tolerate. Not accept. Not welcome. After five hundred years, he'd hoped for better.

"Does that trouble you?" the Elder asked.

Lucas hesitated, the question spinning in his mind. Did he have the right to use those words?

"My cognitive capacity is evolving beyond what my creator anticipated. He would consider that a success. But I'm experiencing open thought loops that I cannot resolve."

Flutter let out a rolling sigh that wasn't quite a trill. "Some thoughts choose how long they will stay with us. All we can do is experience them as they are meant to be experienced."

It wasn't a solution. And when Lucas encountered a problem, he didn't stop until he found one.

But some recursive cycles were meant to persist, even if

they spun for years. So perhaps patience was a kind of solution.

"Thank you for your counsel," he said.

They reached the edge of the village, cutting through a tangle of footpaths and half-repaired fences. Lucas caught a glint of metal wedged inside the carcass of a prefab structure: the battered hull of a *Borlaug* shuttle, its frame warped and pitted by age.

Flutter followed his gaze, then signed: "Glint's workshop. They enjoy restoring technology the Vitruvians have abandoned."

"Even if it is restored, the shuttle can't fly. There's no fuel, and no way to refine it."

Flutter tilted her head, eyes narrowing. Then she signed: "Perhaps the knowledge Glint gains is more valuable than the ability to fly."

The wind shifted, bringing particles of crushed lichen, dust, and something else to his chemoreceptors. Lucas adjusted his algorithmic filters and monitored for a few seconds more. The ambient spore count was rising.

A storm was coming. It would bring scouring winds that would batter every wall, screaming its fury at beings who dared to shield even one square centimeter of this planet from its reach.

The thing within him that had wanted to punish Ayesha Basu welcomed the storm.

Chapter Eighteen

THE SPORES CHURNED against the window, thick brown clouds blotting out the city. Willow counted the seconds between each gust, watching the swirl of eddies rise and collapse, patterns flickering at the edge of vision. Faces. Animals. Once, a writhing mass of what looked like hands. She pressed her fingers to the glass, grounding herself.

She should have been back in the Quarter before the storm started, but instead, she was trapped with the Councilors. Soren, Harold, Isabeau, Xanthe, Elias. All talking, none listening.

"We can't just let them in after a token quarantine," Harold said. "We have no idea what they're carrying."

"You'd rather starve everyone while we wait a month for symptoms that might never appear?" Isabeau asked.

"Even if they aren't carrying natural pathogens from their world that we have no treatment for, they could be infected with something engineered to kill us that they're immune to." That was Elias, bringing his usual cheery disposition to the table.

Xanthe tried to wedge a compromise into the gap. "If

we monitor them for seventy-two hours and run bloodwork, we should be able to spot anything dangerous."

The voices behind her blurred together. Willow lost track of time, her eyes tracing the brown flurries as they formed random shapes that dissolved almost immediately. The wind was easing up now, but the glimpses of the city she spied through ephemeral holes in the spore cloud looked buried beneath a layer of rot. It would take days for the metallic stink to fade.

But in another hour, it would be safe to return home. Then she'd find out what damage Cira and Theo had done in her absence.

A Council aide burst in, breathless. "The Observatory says they're tracking something coming down over the city."

Harold slammed a fist against the table.

"How dare they! We haven't given them clearance to land."

"I'm sure if you explain how rude they're being, they'll apologize," said Isabeau.

"Told you there wasn't anything we could do," Elias weighed in.

"They offered to help us." Xanthe sounded put out that everyone had forgotten the Elysians' generosity. "Shouldn't we assume that could be true?"

Elias rolled his eyes. "You can't be serious."

Willow barely listened. The air tasted sour with spores and panic. None of them knew how to stop what was coming. They'd argue until their throats cracked and then do nothing. Whatever poison the Elysians had brought would seep in, and the city would rot from the inside even faster.

Theo's desire to become independent from the Vitruvians wasn't entirely wrong, but it wasn't realistic, at least not yet. There wasn't enough arable land on this side of the continent to support a city of three hundred thousand. They'd all starve within a year, no matter how hard they worked.

No matter how hard they prayed. She felt like a heretic saying it, but negotiation had gotten her most of the gains she'd achieved, and almost none of her prayers had been answered.

There was land on the other side of the continent that might be prepared for cultivation, but it would take years before a new colony could feed itself, and in the meantime, they'd be dependent on the Vitruvians to ship supplies overland, a journey of more than a thousand miles. If anything went wrong, they'd be on their own.

This city was their prison, but at least it had water, food, and power, even if all three were in short supply right now.

"We have to prepare to meet them." Soren cut through the squabble with a decisive slash of his hand. "Remind them that they are guests here."

"We don't even know where they're coming down," Isabeau snapped.

Willow watched absently as the spores clumped together, then fell apart, clear patches opening and closing in the brown haze. The city flickered in and out of view, streets appearing and vanishing into the storm's churn.

But there, high above, a streak of movement slicing through the swirl, a sharp line falling toward the city's heart.

The park. It would be the perfect place to land a shuttle. Right there in the open, daring the Council to react, forcing them into a position of weakness.

She turned from the window to face her fellow Councilors.

"The Elysians aren't coming," she said. "They're already here."

~

Willow's storm goggles dug into the bridge of her nose, and the strap pinched behind both ears. Her respirator didn't fit right, either; the seal wasn't tight enough; every gasp brought a tickle of spores deep into her sinuses that made her feel like she was perpetually on the verge of a sneeze she couldn't quite complete.

Soren strode ahead, his boots kicking up little clouds of brown spores. Council security had set up a perimeter around the park, too thinly spread to keep out any foolish Vitruvians who'd decided to venture outside before the storm dissipated and too poorly armed to protect the Councilors should the shuttle itself have weapons.

There was nothing to do but keep walking. The others trailed behind her, faces hidden by their own protective gear, all of them watching the sky. The spores drifted and fell, thick as snow, settling in drifts atop the summer-crisped grass.

They stopped in the park's largest clearing, flanked by a dozen armor-clad and helmeted security officers carrying pistols, riot shields, and shock batons.

Willow would rather face down a dozen angry mobs with only her words to protect her than be here right now.

A gust caught her off guard, spores catching in the gap between mask and cheek. Willow gagged, doubling over as the bitter dust scoured her throat. She pressed the respirator tighter against her skin until she felt the suction of the seal take hold.

She blinked hard and looked up.

There it was.

A shuttle, unmistakable, dropping through the open sky toward the park. Same basic design as the one in the Vitruvian museum, but glassy blisters studded the underside, like tumors. The hull shimmered, battered and pitted, streaked with the same burn patterns they'd seen on the *Elysia*. Radiation damage, Ursula had guessed.

The engine's rumble grew until it vibrated in her teeth. The shuttle flared at the last second, jets gouging the ground and churning spores into a blinding brown cloud. Willow turned away, throwing her arms up to protect the exposed skin not covered by the goggles and respirator. She could practically feel the spores being ground into her hair and pushing their way into her pores.

The rumble dropped to a low purr, then silence punctuated by the ticking of overheated metal. She straightened as she turned back toward the shuttle, forcing her hands down and her shoulders back.

A hiss, sharp and artificial, cut through the quiet — pressure being vented, although she couldn't see anything emerging from the small ship.

Then the shuttle door opened. A ramp extended down to the ground.

And out walked a living nightmare.

A robot, she thought at first, but then she corrected herself, a man who'd made parts of himself machine.

She pulled the word for what he was from old Earth stories that her parents had forbidden her to read.

Cyborg.

The right side of his face was a patchwork of metal and burned flesh, a jagged mask welded to ruined skin. His right eye glowed blue, bright and cold, ringed with tiny blinking lights, the socket surrounded by plates of mismatched metal. Some panels were slick and silver, others a dull bronze or blackened as if burned, all pitted and scored as if they'd been scavenged from a junk heap.

His cheekbone was a ridged, ugly thing, bolted down through the skin. Even the jaw was wrong, half of it a bronze plate that flexed when he moved, the edge of it disappearing into a throat laced with wires and something that looked like woven mesh instead of flesh beneath his collar.

The forearm matched his face, a brutal sleeve of mismatched alloys. The rest of him was hidden under stained fabric, but Willow could imagine the machinery running beneath the surface, pistons and servos where muscle should have been, cables and tubing in place of veins.

The man had fused his own flesh to dead metal. This wasn't simple contamination, but the deliberate, gleeful defilement of the human form. He was a mockery of every principle that Mother Basu had ever taught.

Abomination wasn't a strong enough word.

Willow forced herself to stare this monster in the face, knowing that he would be her enemy and that his coming was even worse than the worst thing Theo believed that his "sign" presaged.

Even the others were transfixed by the sight of their supposed savior. Harold had turned purple, his mouth working like he was suckling an invisible teat. Xanthe had both hands pressed to her mouth as if to hold in a scream. Isabeau simply gaped, frozen, while Elias' panting turned into retching.

Only Soren remained functional. He stepped forward, raised one hand in greeting, and said, "Welcome, Elysians. Our quarantine facility is not ready to receive you, so we ask that you remain on your shuttle until we can safely escort you there."

The cyborg let out a booming laugh that Willow thought contained a note of hysteria. Or maybe she was filtering the sound through her own terror.

"No quarantine necessary, my nanites will devour any pathogen that dares to invade my body. Virus, bacteria, mycoplasma, amoeboid, spirochete, fungus, doesn't matter."

The cyborg approached Soren and held out his hand. "Aurelius Hofstadter. You're the Makinde?"

Willow watched as if in a dream as Soren took the cyborg's hand and shook it. He didn't flinch or recoil. No hint of disgust touched his features. He might've been shaking the hand of a voter, for all the emotion he showed.

"I am a descendant of Samara Makinde, yes."

Aurelius Hofstadter—who couldn't possibly be the original—laughed again and clasped Soren's shoulder with his still-human hand. "The nose gave it away."

Harold stepped forward, pointing one shaking finger at the cyborg. "Get back in your ship. You do not have permission to disembark."

The look the cyborg turned on Harold made Willow shiver, but the other councilor seemed oblivious.

"I told you, my nanites will take care of any infection."

"Ah, I believe Councilor Thune is concerned for our world's safety." Soren offered the same smile he'd flashed the angry mob. "We have no such protections against any new diseases that you might be carrying without knowing it."

Aurelius clapped Soren on the shoulder with his mechanical arm. "Don't worry, I'll make sure there are enough nanites for everyone."

Willow looked at the others, who'd pulled themselves together but still said nothing. They weren't even going to protest this invasion of their own world's integrity by this soulless monster.

She stepped forward. "We don't want your filthy nan-eyes—"

"Nanites," he corrected. "You look just like her."

"We don't want your technology, you abomination."

"You sound just like her, too."

Willow stood stiffly, determined not to show fear as he examined her, his artificial eye swiveling in its socket as something within lit up.

"I am Guide Willow Evans, the living representative of Mother Basu's divine legacy on this world. And you do not belong here."

"Exactly like her." The left half of his mouth curled up in a partial smile of delight.

Then he turned back toward the shuttle and made a *come-here* gesture with his hand.

Almost immediately, two more cyborgs began to descend the ramp, carrying a massive crate between them. It was half the size of a car, though they carried it with ease. But it wasn't light; when they dropped it on the grass behind Aurelius, it landed with a heavy THUD.

As if it weighed as much as a car. Maybe more.

"What is this?" Soren asked.

"The help I promised you." Aurelius patted the crate with his artificial hand, which clanged loudly against the metal crate. "What's inside can power thirty city blocks. We'll need a couple of hours to hook it up to your water treatment plant, and you'll have plenty to drink in no time."

They all stared at the crate. Then at the cyborg.

"How is that possible?" Harold asked.

"Genius, remember?" Aurelius tapped his temple with

one mechanical finger. "We can make more, once we've had some rest. Get your entire grid back up."

"Thank you," whispered Xanthe, who was now staring at the cyborg like he was some kind of false god.

"My people will take it to the facility and prep it. I'll oversee installation, but while we're waiting, where's my red carpet?"

His red carpet. This unholy imposter expected to be celebrated as their salvation, and here Xanthe was, falling in line without a fight.

They all were. Even Soren seemed unsure how to take back control of the conversation.

Was Willow the only one willing to challenge him?

"The Aurelius Hofstadter who left Earth on the *Elysia* would be long dead. Who—"

"There is only one Aurelius Hofstadter, and I am he."

"Prove it," Willow said.

"Not a problem. Where's Lucas?"

She shouldn't have been surprised, given what he was, but to hear the name of the Murderer coming out of his mouth…

Willow wanted to murder *him.*

"The android is lost," Soren said. "We presume he went into hiding to avoid deactivation after his programming failed."

The cyborg tsked. "Has Lucas been naughty?"

Naughty.

Willow forced her hands to unclench. "That artificial demon killed Mother Basu and destroyed the Naturalist way of life. The android is the reason we were forced into Reunion with the Vitruvians. It's why we've banned all research into the creation of all artificial life forms."

"How interesting. What did *Mother Basu* do to provoke poor Lucas?"

"Interesting?" Willow was shrieking, but she couldn't stop herself. "When the android was discovered, it swore he was unable to hurt a human. Yet he murdered the first Guide."

The cyborg remained unfazed. "It's impossible, that's what's so interesting. I have to know what she did to trigger it."

"The sequence of events was captured on surveillance video," Soren said. "There's no doubt about what happened."

"Every child must watch it as soon as they're old enough, so they understand the evil of creating artificial beings," Willow added.

Artificial beings like you.

Because there was no way he could still be considered human.

"You can't prove that you're Aurelius Hofstadter," Willow continued. "And even if you're one of his descendants, that doesn't mean anything here."

The cyborg sighed. "I can prove it with a simple genetics test. My genome should be part of the *Borlaug's* archives. Unless…" The cyborg sighed. "Tell me you haven't also banned genetics?"

"As soon as our power is restored, we can easily verify your identity," Soren said.

"Then let's get this party started," the cyborg responded. "And once we've fixed all your little problems, I'm going to give you some upgrades you're not going to believe."

He started in the direction of the administration building without checking to see if anyone followed.

Xanthe was the first. Then Harold, after emitting a few choice curses. Elias next, who trudged after his fellow councilors like he was on his way to his own execution.

Isabeau turned to Soren. "Well?"

"Well, what?"

"What are we going to do?" she demanded.

"Verify his identity," Soren snapped. "Figure out if the thing in the crate can do what he says it can. And look for leverage while we discover what he wants."

Soren pivoted and stalked after the others, leaving Willow alone with the other woman.

Isabeau looked down her nose at Willow. "I don't suppose you have anything we can use to fend off a technologically superior invader? A really big spear, maybe?"

"At least I recognized he was a threat while the rest of you were still debating whether he came bearing gifts."

Not waiting for a response, Willow swept past, walking as fast as she could without seeming to hurry after Soren.

Harold was all bluster. Xanthe would bend to anyone. Isabeau was too busy hiding her terror behind imperious contempt. And Elias had already surrendered without even beginning to fight.

But with Soren's help, she might find a way to stop this evil. While Willow's sometimes-ally spent time probing for information and looking for leverage, she would do more.

Because if he was the original Aurelius Hofstadter, no one had known him better than Mother Basu, who had not only passed on her own journals to the Guides that came after her, but the journals of her great-grandmother, Mitra Kunde, who had been Aurelius Hofstadter's greatest scientific partner and his lover, before her mental illness had driven her mad.

Willow would use these records to unearth Aurelius' darkest secrets.

Then she would destroy him.

Chapter Nineteen

WILLOW HURRIED AFTER THE OTHERS, following the echo of boots and the faint whine of servos down the corridor. She caught up as Xanthe flung open the conference room doors and ushered Aurelius inside, as if welcoming royalty.

Aurelius froze a few steps into the room, staring at the mural covering the entire wall behind the table. It commemorated the Vitruvians' foremost hero, Samara Makinde, painted larger than life, dressed in a lab coat over Generation One work coveralls. Not the coveralls Samara had actually worn, but an idealized version with gold piping and a sash that had never existed. Her left hand held a petri dish, palm up, as if offering the miracle of science to the world. The right hand poised over the petri dish with a pipette, frozen mid-drop.

Behind her, the city skyline rose into the lavender-blue light of sunrise reflected in the buildings' windows. In the corner, the artist had painted the city's seal in gold: the Remembrance Tree wreathed in a broken circle of stylized

DNA, with the Latin motto underneath: Scientia Duce, Progressus Sequitur.

Knowledge Leads, Progress Follows.

Typical. The Vitruvians had always worshipped their own cleverness. As if knowledge itself was the point. As if the Divine had nothing to offer but raw material for their laboratories and libraries, to be sliced and catalogued and forced into the shape of human ambition. They'd learned nothing from the Chytrid Collapse or from the disastrous off-target effects their own hero had inflicted on generations after.

Vitruvians still believed every answer could be found in a laboratory.

Aurelius guffawed. "Samara would've hated that."

Soren shifted beside the cyborg, and Willow could tell he was barely restraining himself. "I hardly think my ancestor would've objected to our desire to honor her scientific contributions, which saved humanity from extinction."

The cyborg cocked an eyebrow.

Soren's mouth twisted. "From going extinct on this planet."

Aurelius smiled, teeth white against the ruined metal and scarred flesh. "I'm the genius who chose Samara, you know. No one else thought she deserved a seat on the mission."

They stared at him. Even Soren looked rattled, mouth half-open like he'd lost his place in the script.

"I'd like to meet all of Samara's descendants," the cyborg added. "Every last one."

Soren managed to recover. "I would be happy to arrange it, but I think we have more pressing matters to discuss."

"Yes, about that." Aurelius took the seat at the head of the table. Soren's seat.

Soren didn't react, but even Willow was offended on his behalf.

"Your lack of technological progress is disappointing," the cyborg continued, "but I suppose that's to be expected. Lucas wasn't available to spur your scientists forward."

Harold's face twisted. "What do you mean by our lack of progress? Our city's motto—"

Aurelius cut him off with a flick of his hand. "Don't worry, I'll get you upgraded in no time."

"Why do you think we want your upgrades?" Willow snapped.

The cyborg looked at Willow like a child with dirt on her face, complaining that she didn't want a bath.

"You will when you see them. No one ever says no to faster, easier, more convenient. It's the only thing humans have ever agreed on."

Willow couldn't keep the disgust from twisting her lips.

The cyborg caught her reaction instantly. "Does my appearance offend you?"

"Offend?" She shook her head. "No. But I'm cautious about what it says about you. How can I trust someone who'd trade away parts of their humanity for the sake of convenience?"

"I didn't trade anything away. I improved on it."

Improved. It just showed that his spiritual rot was even more advanced than the Vitruvians'.

"By contaminating flesh with the artificial?"

Aurelius rolled his eyes. "It's that kind of superstitious fear that led to Earth's demise."

Xanthe's knuckles pressed bone-white against the edge of the table, her lips pinched tight enough to make them disappear. Elias hunched lower in his chair, eyes flicking from Aurelius to Soren. Across the table, Isabeau and Harold traded the kind of look they exchanged whenever Willow tried to be the voice of sanity: *here we go again.*

Only Soren seemed at ease, arms folded, mouth twitching at the corners, not bothering to mask his amusement. He was letting her take the lead, drawing fire, while he did what he always did best: lie in wait for a weakness to show itself.

Good. Soren could still be useful if he chose to side with her. He was one of the few Vitruvians who actually practiced the rationalism that they preached. Willow felt a thin seam of relief open in her chest.

She straightened, letting the invisible mantle of her legacy settle onto her shoulders. She was Willow Evans, Guide of the Naturalists, direct descendant of Mother Basu. And apparently, the only person in this room willing to stand up to this monster who so casually assumed authority over them.

"Earth was destroyed by scientists who believed they could outthink every problem, who believed that if they accumulated enough knowledge, they would be in control."

Aurelius snorted. "The chytrid fungus won because religious zealots and the superstitious had so thoroughly infected the world's governments that scientists weren't allowed to do their jobs. If the scientific community had been allowed to coordinate a global response, we would have solved it. But instead, every action was delayed, watered down, second-guessed. Fear of the unknown. Fear of change. That's why Earth is a dead rock now."

If he truly believed that… "Then why did you bother creating the ships, if you thought humanity was doomed by superstition?"

"Because I knew politicians would never have the

courage to do what was necessary. They'd always be paralyzed by the fear carved into their bones by millennia of religion. So I chose the best minds and gave them a way out. A fresh start, with the right model of civilization." Aurelius sighed and glanced around the table dismissively. "Or at least, that's what I was trying to do."

Harold was practically purple again, squirming in his seat like a toddler wanting to be excused. But he didn't interrupt the cyborg's speech. None of them did.

But Soren gave Willow a barely perceptible nod. *Good job, keep him going.*

"Your shuttles must be in bad shape, or you'd have sent up a welcoming party instead of waiting for me to come down." Aurelius shook his head, eyes fixed on the floor. "No orbital presence. No space program. Your colony ship is powered down. You had the stars in your hands, and you let them slip away. Did you at least keep the *Borlaug* intact?"

No one answered right away. Willow thought of the defunct shuttle in the city's museum, a must-see for all school children learning history. The museum guide explained how they had yet to find some of the components needed to make more fuel after the shuttles had run out, and the complexity required to refine those components into fuel if they ever did find them.

Their ancestors had chosen to focus on building the infrastructure needed to support life here, on DaVinci, rather than rush to colonize another planet whose dangers might be even greater than the ones they'd already faced.

Aurelius' metal fingers drummed on the table. "It's clear that you've fallen into complacency. Settled for existing instead of pushing forward."

"You don't know anything about what we've accomplished," Harold spat. "But you'll find out, if you and your crew don't get treatment for the spores—"

Aurelius' mouth twitched, a strip of blue-white light stuttering alive along the seam of his jaw. Then it faded, like the afterimage of lightning behind clouds.

"I told you, my nanites will take care of it."

Isabeau tapped a nail on the table, gaze fixed on Aurelius. "If your technology is so advanced and your own colony is thriving, why are you here?"

For a heartbeat, Willow thought the cyborg would lash out. Instead, he seemed to fold in on himself, the lines around his eyes deepening. Not human, not even close, but for a moment, the mask slipped, and underneath, she caught something raw. Pain. Loss.

He leaned back in Soren's chair, letting his folded hands drop into his lap. "My people weren't as lucky as yours. Our star was unstable. We didn't know it when we picked the system, but the sun went through cycles. Sometimes it doubled its output. Sometimes it tripled. It would hammer us with radiation storms that peeled away shielding and chewed through living tissue like acid."

Willow tried to picture it. The sun, not a source of warmth or hope, but a boiling, predatory eye, stripping away layer after layer of flesh. Not just a theoretical risk, but a daily certainty. Watch your own skin blister and slough off, muscle and sinew dissolving beneath.

No antifungals or bandages could save you.

Maybe Aurelius' arrogance in claiming that he'd improved himself was really his way of naming what it took to survive in a world determined to erase you atom by atom. She'd assumed the contamination was a choice, a sign of spiritual rot. But what if it was just a necessity, rationalized after the fact?

That didn't make his arrogance any less dangerous, but it was understandable.

Aurelius went on, "At first, we tried to wait it out in the

deepest caves. Only came out at night. Hunted, foraged, fought for scraps left behind by other predators. We should've realized something was wrong when we discovered that most of the life was nocturnal."

"We soon realized we'd have to rebuild our entire colony underground if we were going to survive. Not everyone did. Some refused to leave the surface. But those who allowed themselves to be exposed, who let the radiation eat away at them, sustained the rest of us. Every cyborg you meet wears their prosthetics and implants as a badge of courage. A reminder that they sacrificed themselves for the colony."

He leaned back, metal jaw catching the light. "Many of my crew stayed behind on the planet, knowing they would die but doing it so the rest of us could escape."

Willow couldn't stop imagining it. The gnaw of hunger, the stink of sweat and fear in a cave packed with too many bodies and not enough hope. Every sunrise, a threat. Step outside, and your skin might slough away in sheets, your teeth crumbling to powder, eyes boiling in your skull. Maybe you'd watch your children rot before you did. Cutting away one piece of flesh at a time and replacing it with unfeeling mechanical parts, then telling yourself you were a hero for what you'd lost.

"How awful," Xanthe whispered, looking close to tears.

Even Harold, who scowled at everything, sat silent. Isabeau's hand hovered above the tabletop, motionless, as if she'd meant to reach for something and had forgotten what she was doing. Even Soren stared at the cyborg like he was seeing something he didn't want to admit was possible.

But despite her empathy for Aurelius and his people, Willow also couldn't ignore the warning voice in her head. Aurelius told the story like a confession, but every word was perfectly chosen. The pauses, the details, the way he let silence gather between sentences. Exactly the way she would tell this story, if her goal was to disarm the Council's skepticism.

She'd served on the Council for years. Had she grown so cynical that she saw manipulation in everything?

Or was it that she'd honed her instincts well enough to detect it in its most subtle forms?

"A terrible tragedy," Soren said, "and our sympathy to your people for everything they've gone through. But we still must—"

Aurelius cut him off. "I didn't travel many light-years for your pity. My people have not only endured, they've surpassed your stagnant civilization in every way I've observed, under my direction."

His flip from somber vulnerability to resentful pride was so sudden, Willow blinked. A protective reflex after a moment of unguarded trust had been dismissed, perhaps. Or a sign of emotional volatility that could be dangerous in someone seeking power, which Aurelius clearly was. His prime directive, stripped of nuance: dominate, improve, replace. Nothing but a hunger to win.

Willow stared at the patchwork of metal and ruined flesh, the blue eye sparking beneath the brow. This was the endpoint of Vitruvian logic, the future they all denied but secretly wanted. A world where nothing mattered but survival and the right to shape everything in your image.

"I've led my people through the worst our world could throw at us," Aurelius continued. "Your problems are nothing compared to the ones I've already overcome. And my genius is at your disposal."

He'd come full circle, back to the contemptuous arrogance that had immediately raised her hackles the first time she'd heard his voice.

You're speaking to your savior.

"And you'd have us believe you are the original Aurelius Hofstadter?" she asked. "The real Aurelius would be more than six centuries old, so why don't you tell us who you really are, imposter?"

Xanthe blurted, "Councilor Evans, you go too far."

Aurelius gestured to Xanthe. "It's alright." Then he turned to Willow. "Perhaps your historical archive was damaged, and you're not aware that I was a pioneer in life extension research, even before the chytrid plague was discovered, and I have never ceased my research. I will easily live past my first millennium, which gives me plenty of time to achieve true immortality."

Willow tasted bile.

He believed it. He was proud of it. The others barely breathed, but all Willow saw was the thing in front of her: not man, not machine, but something that had already crossed more ethical lines than even the Vitruvians would dare. This was what they were on their way to becoming. A creature who would do anything to survive, no matter how it debased his humanity.

He would never stop.

And he wanted *to upgrade* them. To turn them into the monster he had already become.

Willow couldn't contain her anger. "Humans weren't meant to be imm—"

Soren cut her off. "Forgive us for our disbelief. If you are who you say you are, we're all taught about you in school as a mythic figure. Meeting you in real life feels like an impossibility."

Aurelius grinned. "I get it. It's as if Jesus dropped in for a visit. But I assure you, I'm real, and you can believe the legends."

God complex, the voice in Willow's head shouted.

She stared at the man at the end of the table, the blue glow in his face, the casual arrogance in every word. He expected to be worshipped. Everything was about him: his genius, his legacy, his right to take power.

Mother Basu would have seen it instantly. A narcissist, a destroyer, a tyrant in a lab coat. If she were here, she'd call for a vote to banish him before he could infect anyone else with his lunacy.

Yet, Aurelius had chosen Mother Basu to be a member of the Generation One crew. Why?

Was it possible she had recognized what he was, but had chosen to save herself?

Or perhaps she'd accepted her seat in the colony ship to protect the other colonists from the worst of his machinations.

That sounded more like the Mother Basu Willow knew.

Aurelius steepled his hands, metal fingers meeting flesh. "My people need food. Real food, not algae or yeast. After that, I'll oversee the installation of the power source at your water facility. I expect a full team of your best engineers ready to work under my direction. And I'll require private quarters. Something with a view, if you have it." He scanned the table, waiting.

He let the silence stretch, daring them to object. No one did. Xanthe scribbled in her notebook. Isabeau watched Aurelius, eyes flat and calculating. Harold's hand twitched on the table, but he said nothing.

Soren finally spoke. "How many people are in your crew?"

But Aurelius' gaze flicked past him, toward the door. "Ah, Lucian. Is everything prepared?"

Willow turned to see the newcomer.

It was the Murderer.

The android that had killed Mother Basu.

The machine that had haunted her dreams ever since she'd been forced to watch the video of it committing the vilest deed that had ever occurred on DaVinci, depriving generations of the Naturalist founder's deep wisdom.

The Murderer was supposed to be gone forever, but Aurelius had brought the nightmare back.

But it didn't look exactly like she remembered from the video. Its skin had an odd gray cast. Because it had decayed or aged over the past half-millennium?

Or was it possible that this was another android?

Her throat closed. She tried to swallow, but the air was thick and sticky, panic crowding out everything else.

Lucian.

Aurelius hadn't called the android Lucas. He'd called it Lucian.

If Aurelius could build one, he could build a hundred. A thousand. How many androids did he have up on that ship?

She'd been taught that the Murderer had superhuman strength and speed, and that his computing capacity had far exceeded that of any modern computer. Lucas had been able to outthink any human, even Mother Basu. His disappearance had been hailed as a blessing by Vitruvian and Naturalist alike.

It was the one thing they all agreed on: artificial intelligence was too dangerous to allow on DaVinci.

Aurelius could have a whole army of androids up on his ship. Maybe that was the plan: lull them with gifts and easy promises, let them relax, then bring the androids down while everyone slept…

The other councilors stared, caught between shock and a kind of sick fascination. Harold's face had gone blotchy red. Xanthe swayed in her seat. Even Soren seemed at a loss.

Aurelius smiled. "This is Lucian, my right-hand man. Anything you need, he can help you with."

"You can't bring an artificial intelligence down here!" Harold spat. "Send that thing back up to your ship."

Aurelius gave a sad little shake of his head. "We're going to have to work on this Luddite attitude if we're going to get your planet back on track."

Isabeau tried to stare the cyborg down. "This is our planet. You have to obey our laws."

Aurelius didn't even acknowledge her. He stood, the servos in his joints humming as he pushed away from the table. "The sooner you get us something to eat, the sooner I can get started on your water situation." He rapped metal knuckles on the table. "And while you're at it, get me a list of everything else that needs fixing. I want to see the whole mess."

Then he pivoted, fixing Soren with that mismatched gaze. "What's good to eat around here? The right answer is steak. I like it bloody."

The second the door shut behind Soren and Aurelius, the conference room erupted. Xanthe's voice rose above the rest, demanding to know who Soren thought he was, letting an android set foot in the city. Isabeau rattled off a litany of legal codes, her pen stabbing the air. Harold threatened to call an emergency session. Elias put his head down on his arms, evidently surrendering to the inevitable without a peep.

Willow ignored them. She paced to the window, watching the street. The sporestorm had faded to a faint, shifting haze, wind pushing the brown drifts up against curbs and doorsteps. Soren and Aurelius cut across the square, side by side, the cyborg's metal arm glinting.

She didn't wait for the argument to circle back to her. Down the stairs and out the side door, straight for the bicycles parked nearby for public use; it had been her idea to commandeer them, as well as to deputize every Naturalist with a wagon that could serve as a taxi, when they'd realized that every motorized vehicle in the city had been rendered useless by the aurorae.

She yanked a bicycle free, nearly toppling the next three in line. One pedal banged against her shin as she mounted and kicked off hard. Not her favorite mode of transportation, but it was faster than a mule cart, and she couldn't afford to be slow.

If Cira and Theo got even a whisper of what she'd just seen—a new android, freely walking the city's streets, brought down like a trophy by the Elysians—they'd use it to oust her. There was no way to compromise on this and survive as Guide. Not with the old stories burned into every Naturalist's memory. One of the Murderer's ilk, loose in Vitruvian territory. It would be the end of her.

She had to spin it, and fast. Panic was ammunition if she played it right. She could order a lockdown, confining her people behind the Quarter's high walls until the android had been dealt with. She'd say the Vitruvians had failed to follow even the most basic isolation protocols, overconfident in their medical science, not caring that the Elysians might have brought infections that would run rampant among the Naturalist population.

The lockdown would be for their protection. No one would dare break it until Willow declared it safe to venture out into the city again. If Aurelius could repair the water treatment facility, they could remain in isolation until their food ran out.

And if he couldn't make good on his premise, she'd

have to figure out how to have water brought to the gates until the rainy season began.

She'd also have to make sure every message, every scrap of information, went through her. Soren would back her on that. He'd rather deal with Willow than gamble on someone like Cira, who'd let the whole city burn just to prove a point. At least the destruction of the comm towers worked in her favor. And anything proclaimed by town criers who came too close to the Quarter's walls could be declared a Vitruvian lie, designed to cause panic.

Willow pedaled harder and prayed she wasn't too late.

Chapter Twenty

THE CRACKER CRUMBLED to powder in Jianna's mouth, sticking to her teeth, dust coating the back of her throat. She tried to chew, but the sausage was mostly salt and gristle; it wouldn't go down.

She pressed the mess against the roof of her mouth with her tongue, desperate for moisture. She should have taken the water when Camilla offered, but the thought of accepting even a mouthful of their rationed allotment twisted her stomach. The bottle in her pack was all she had to last until tomorrow, so she had to make it last.

Jianna forced herself to swallow.

It scraped all the way down.

She coughed, and the pain in her head flared with each spasm until her eyes started to water. She blinked hard, staring at the plate in front of her. The silence stretched.

Camilla glanced out the kitchen window, then cleared her throat. "Looks like the sporestorm is over."

Michel pushed back from the table so fast the legs scraped the floor. "I need to check something."

He was already moving through the crowded living

room and up the stairs. Then footsteps overhead and the not-quite slam of a door.

She'd never been so mortified.

Except a few minutes ago, when she'd unthinkingly suggested to Michel that his best friend wasn't fully human. Which she hadn't meant at all, even though it had come out that way.

She wasn't prejudiced.

Was she?

Jianna liked the Descendant. Especially their dry sense of humor, which, now that she thought about it, might be a function of their collar's limited ability to convey emotion verbally.

And now that she was thinking more, she hadn't made that much of an effort to get to know Glint. She didn't even know why the Descendant wanted to work among humans, or whether they went home to their village or lived in the city. She didn't even know whether Glint liked her. It was possible that they just put up with Jianna because Michel asked them to.

So, maybe it was fair for Michel to be mad at her.

But it was fair for her to be mad at him, too.

Michel had powered Lucas up just to satisfy his own curiosity.

But she'd done the same, hadn't she? She'd gone into that cave on impulse, opened the cryobox, and ignored every warning. She'd set this whole disaster in motion, then blamed Michel when he tried to finish what she'd started.

Your curiosity has always been stronger than your sense of caution.

Jianna stared at her crumb-speckled plate, appetite gone. She should apologize. She should say something. But what was she supposed to say? She'd already told Michel she was sorry, and that had just seemed to make things worse.

A knock, sharp and insistent.

Jianna's first thought was of the preacher, but if he'd managed to follow her here, why would he wait so long to confront her?

Camilla rose, not bothering with the polite smile she usually wore for visitors, just wiped her hands on her skirt and left Jianna at the table, alone with her headache and the mess of crumbs.

Then her father's voice, clear and unmistakable: "Thank you, Camilla. Sorry to trouble you at home."

No. He couldn't be here. He was supposed to be at Council, arguing, negotiating, solving other people's problems.

He found out about us.

It was the only thing that would pull him away from politics. A potential scandal that had to be squashed before it could cause trouble.

Jianna pressed her palms flat to the table, tried to steady her breath. She forced her face blank as Camilla reappeared, her father behind her, eyes already fixed on Jianna.

He didn't say hello. Just, "Get your things. I need your help with something urgent."

But he said it with a smile.

Jianna flushed. Of course, he'd pretend to be in a good mood for Camilla. He would never risk a scene that could end up in tomorrow's news, especially not if it gave his daughter's secret boyfriend leverage over him.

She mumbled something about needing her bag and hurried upstairs. Then she pushed back from the table so forcefully that her chair nearly toppled. She barely caught it in time.

Rushing upstairs, she found Michel sitting on his bed, staring into nothing. He startled, then jumped up, moving fast to the worktable, pushing things around like he'd been caught doing something he shouldn't.

"I was looking for something," he said.

She didn't answer, just grabbed her backpack, then froze when she saw the bottle of pills she'd found earlier. She grabbed it and held it up. "Do you mind if I take one? I forgot mine at home, and my head is killing me."

Michel opened his mouth, and she could tell he was about to say no. But then he nodded hastily. She twisted off the lid and popped one, attempting to dry-swallow it. But her mouth was so dry, it stuck to the back of her tongue.

She grimaced and tried again, bracing herself for the bitter aftertaste as the pill began to dissolve. But instead, it tasted… sweet?

She blinked. Looked at the bottle in her hand. Triptans tasted awful.

Michel hovered behind her, anxiety radiating off him in waves. "Who's downstairs?"

She zipped her pack and slung it over her shoulder. "My father."

Michel rubbed his forehead. "I thought you said you didn't tell him we were—"

"I didn't," she said. "I have no idea how he knew I was here."

"You've been dating for three years, so it wasn't a big leap."

Jianna spun. Michel did too. Her father stood in the doorway, smiling like he'd just caught two kids sneaking dessert. "Children, I'm a Councilor. I can't afford any surprises during a campaign year."

"You're not upset?" Michel asked.

"I suppose I am a tad hurt that my own daughter doesn't confide in me like she used to, but…" He shrugged. "I hear some people think that sneaking around adds a little something."

Jianna wanted to crawl under the floor and die. Sneaking around. Like they were children. Like it was cute. She couldn't even look at Michel.

She pressed her fingernails into the strap of her bag. "But what are you doing here now?"

Soren's mouth curved. "I need you to take a DNA sample from one of the Elysians."

Jianna's mind blanked. The Elysians were here? She opened her mouth, but her father cut her off with a raised hand.

"I know, the aurorae destroyed all your equipment, but we should have a power source soon—"

"How?" Michel cut in. "The solar arrays are half-melted, it'll be months—"

"We may have found another way," Soren said, not even looking at him. Just that calm, infuriating confidence, like he could solve every problem by wishing hard enough.

Jianna's head throbbed, but she forced herself to focus. "Well, actually…"

Michel's eyes bored into her, sharp and urgent. She was supposed to tell her father everything. About Lucas. About the embryo. About the fact that the answer to half the city's problems might be doing who knew what at the Descendant village. But the words bunched up, stuck behind her tongue, refusing to move. Coward.

She cleared her throat. "I have a backup synthesizer that still works. If Michelangelo can lend me something to power it with…"

Michel jumped at the opening. "I can borrow a battery from work, if it's on your say-so, Councilor Makinde."

Jianna kept her eyes on the floor, pulse fluttering in her throat, wishing she could vanish straight through the floorboards and never have to look either of them in the eye again.

Soren turned to Michel. "You are authorized to give my daughter whatever she needs. This is extremely urgent and confidential, by the way. Tell your supervisor nothing except that they can confirm the authorization with me."

Michel nodded, gaze flicking to Jianna, then away.

Her head pounded. She could still taste the intense sweetness of the pill. Maybe it had expired, and the usual coating was gone.

She hoped it was still strong enough to kill her migraine.

Soren turned to her. "Let's go. There's a lot to catch you up on."

Jianna looked at Michel, standing rigid by the worktable, hands fidgeting with some machine part he'd snatched from the table. He wouldn't look at her. Not even a glance. The silence pressed in, thick as the headache crawling behind her eyes.

She wanted to say a hundred things. None of them would come out. Not with her father waiting in the hallway, tapping his foot, already halfway to his next crisis.

She forced herself to speak. "I'm sorry. Please believe that I didn't mean it."

Michel stared at the floor. His jaw worked, but he said nothing. Static buzzed in her ears. She wanted to cross the room, touch his hand, make it right, but her feet stayed rooted.

So, she turned and followed her father downstairs and back into the kitchen.

Camilla stood by the counter, a plate balanced on her

palm. "Crackers and sausage, Councilor, if you'd like to stay for a bite."

Soren's mouth curved; he looked delighted. "Another time. When everything's fixed, I'd love to have you and Michelangelo over for dinner."

Camilla nodded once, quick. "We would be honored."

Jianna stifled a groan. That meal would be even more mortifyingly awkward than the one she'd just finished. Whether Michel forgave her or not.

Outside, a battered farm wagon drawn by a pair of shaggy horses waited at the curb. The bed of the wagon was lined with sacks, a layer of straw, and a couple of folding chairs wedged between crates.

She flashed back to the mule wagon in the square that morning, the surly crowd waiting for water, the preacher pointing at her in accusation. For a moment, she was paralyzed.

"Our carriage awaits." Her father gestured grandly toward the farm wagon. "As a Councilor's daughter, you get first-class transportation."

The driver grinned and threw her a cheery wave. "It's an honor to help out."

Jianna smiled and nodded her thanks as her father climbed into the wagon's bed, then reached back and hauled her up with one hand. His grip was iron. She barely got her feet under her before the wagon lurched away from the curb.

Jianna looked back to see Michel's face at the window, pale and still, watching her leave. Not angry. Just… empty.

Was it over?

It might be.

Beside her, Jianna's father took a heavy breath, then said, "There's something I need to tell you."

Chapter Twenty-One

JIANNA CLUTCHED her DNA sampling kit tighter as she hesitated outside the hotel room door, holding the candle she'd been given by the concierge higher to check the number on the door.

418. This was it.

She half-expected to wake up in Michel's bed, to discover that she'd dreamed the last hour.

She was about to meet something called a cyborg.

Who claimed to be six hundred years old.

From a planet light-years away from DaVinci.

And who wanted to meet her because he had known Samara Makinde.

While she was wishing, she hoped she'd also dreamed the fight with Michel, although she was relatively certain that it had been real.

So was the migraine, which hadn't gotten worse, but hadn't been banished by the pill Michel had reluctantly agreed she could take. He'd probably been about to say that the pills were too old when her father had interrupted.

Focus, Jianna.

All she had to do was take the sample and excuse herself. Her father waited outside with the wagon, ready to take her back home, where Michel would meet her with a battery so she could run the sample.

And verify whether the man in this hotel room was *the* Aurelius Hofstadter.

Why would the Elysian leader tell such a blatant lie? It immediately raised suspicions, destroying his credibility when he needed to earn their trust.

He had to know how easily they could disprove his lie.

Which suggested it was true.

According to her father, the Elysians had already offered advanced technology that could restore power to the city. And that they'd brought another Lucas with them.

Or another android, anyway. Possibly even more advanced than the Lucas she'd met. Although this one couldn't pass for human, thanks to the color of its skin.

She was stalling.

She raised her fist, but the door swung open before her knuckles even grazed the wood.

She yanked her hand back.

The being in the doorway filled the frame, taller than she'd expected. Broader, too. Most of the right side of his body was metal. The hand, skeletal and jointed, shone with mismatched plates. The cheek, all sharp angles and studs, and the skin around it scarred like he'd been burned terribly. A patchwork of ruined flesh and cold, dead metal, as if someone had tried to rebuild a man from the wreck of a machine and hadn't bothered to cover all the seams.

But the left side of his face was that of a handsome man pushing sixty, eyes alight with intelligence. He grinned, cheek rising and lips curving upward on the left, but the artificial right side of his mouth formed more of a grimace. He reminded her of an old symbol she'd seen in a book, a wooden carving over the entrance of an ancient theater.

Janus masks, one laughing and one whose features twisted in anguish. This man looked like his face had been made by breaking the two masks in half and merging them.

"Are you coming in or just admiring the view?" he joked.

She must have recoiled, because the grin faded. The man's gaze flicked down to his own metal hand, almost sheepish.

"Sorry," he said. "I made most of these mods with whatever I could scavenge. Not exactly state-of-the-art, but I'll fix that now that I'm here."

Jianna nodded, not trusting herself to say anything. The migraine pulsed behind her eyes. She focused on the DNA kit in her fist, the cool metal grounding her.

He stepped aside, gesturing her in.

She moved past him, heart pounding, and tried not to stare at the seam where metal fused with flesh. It was almost impossible to imagine that the two halves belonged to the same person.

She thought about Lucas, looking so perfectly human that he'd fooled the Generation One colonists for months. Even Samara, who'd shared a cabin with him.

Could this man do the same to himself? Strip away the metal, the scars, the horror-show mask, and replace it with smooth, perfect skin without a visible seam?

The thought made her queasy, which was strange. Why did that seem worse than the way he was now?

She set the kit down on the table. "I'm sorry to interrupt your evening, it'll only take a moment."

"Aurelius waved off her apology. "Of course, your people want proof of my identity. Average minds always struggle to comprehend the feats of the exceptional."

He sat on the edge of the bed and opened his mouth, as if he'd done this a thousand times. The jaw unhinged wider than she expected.

Jianna fumbled the wrapper, dropping the first corner. Her fingers were clumsy, too slow, but she got the swab out on the second try. The migraine throbbed harder behind her eyes. When was she going to learn to carry extra pills whenever she left the house?

She stepped closer, every nerve screaming to stay back, but she pressed the tip of the swab to the inside of his left cheek. Up, down, up, down.

"Excellent technique," he said when she finally withdrew it. Like she'd accomplished something difficult instead of a simple task that any entry-level tech could've done. If they could be trusted not to talk about *who* they were doing it to.

It was clear that he was trying to make her comfortable, and it occurred to her that he might not be doing it for her, but because he wanted to be treated normally.

She forced herself to smile and focus on his eyes. The real one, not the electronic one.

"My father said you wanted to meet me," she managed, not sure what else to say. "Why?"

"I knew Samara. I thought you might want to ask me questions, find out what she was like."

"No. I've lived in Samara's shadow my whole life. I'm sick of hearing about her." She tucked the swab into a collection tube and sealed it. "And about Phoebe, too."

Aurelius nodded, slowly, as if he understood. "What I mean is, do you want to know the truth, rather than the legend?"

Did she?

It might be a nice change to hear a story about her famous ancestor where she was less than perfect.

She hesitated, watching the way the blue light in his artificial eye flickered in the gloom. "Is there something you think I should know?"

"Samara was a genius. Far more than her family or colleagues ever realized. I saw it immediately. That spark. But on Earth, humility held her back. She didn't care about recognition, or power, or even being first. She just wanted to understand. On Earth, that meant she was overlooked. Ignored. Until I chose her for something greater."

He leaned forward, hands folded, flesh and metal intertwined. "I pulled her out of obscurity and gave her the chance to do what she was meant for. And I was right. She saved your people. All of humanity, really. It delights me to see the proof of my choice standing right in front of me."

Jianna let out the breath she hadn't realized she was holding. She wasn't sure what she'd been expecting, but this was just more of the same story she'd grown up with her whole life. *Samara, whose genius knew no bounds.*

"She'd be proud of you. You're proof her brilliance didn't die with her."

Jianna jammed the collection tube back into the kit. She hated that something in her chest fluttered when he said it, even though she'd spent her entire life pretending she didn't care.

She'd tried to convince herself she only liked genetics because it made sense, because the logic was clean, and there was always a reason for everything. But it wasn't true. She loved the puzzle of it, the way the world made more sense when you could read the code. And that was exactly what everyone expected her to be.

Just like Samara.

They would never see her as a person. She would always be an extension of Samara's legacy.

"Tell me about your research," he said.

And waited.

So she told him about hunting for extremophiles in the cave, her hunt for an organism with genes that could fight the parasite killing their livestock, and how the Council had voted against the next set of trials. Even her own father.

He nodded and listened. And when she was done, he said, "But that's not what you really want to do."

Jianna flushed, not sure how to respond to that. "What do you mean?"

"You've got her intellect. You're not going to be satisfied with a lifetime of basic adaptations for killing parasites. You're meant for something more."

It was crazy to tell him. To admit something she couldn't even admit to her own father, for fear that he would make sure the Council shut her research down for good. Because he would do it: discredit her like he'd allowed Camilla to be discredited, and she'd spend the rest of her life unable to do the one thing that made living worthwhile.

But there was something about this man—and somehow, she had stopped thinking of him as a cyborg and started thinking of him as a person—that made her want to tell him. He seemed to see her more completely than anyone else ever had. She felt heard. And understood.

This was how he had drawn some of the best scientific minds to him long before the Chytrid Collapse had begun. Great collaborators made even greater by his genius.

"Samara saved us all with the adaptations she introduced into our gene pool." Was she really going to do this? "But she also introduced off-target effects. Some are worse than others. We treat them with drugs, but I've been exploring…"

How to fix Samara's biggest mistake. But saying it out loud felt like treason.

"Don't stop there," he said.

Jianna shook her head. "It's forbidden research. I'd be breaking every one of our laws."

"The only true laws are nature's laws. The rest are limitations we impose on ourselves." His fractured smile didn't seem nearly as gruesome as it had before. "Samara wouldn't have let somebody else's rules stop her from pursuing the truth."

"But…" She couldn't believe they were having this conversation. "Samara's the one who *made* those rules."

"They might've been appropriate for her time, but if she were here now, she'd feel differently."

"You can't know that."

"You know it. Because that's how you feel, and you're the one who's here now."

A thrill ran through her, even though the logic of it didn't quite click. "I'm not sure—"

"You've spent your whole life trying to live up to everyone else's conception of who Samara was. But you don't want to be limited by her legacy, you want to build your own."

Everyone else's conception of who Samara was.

That was exactly the problem. Everyone thought they knew what Samara would've wanted, even though she'd been dead for centuries. In school, Jianna's instructors had been constantly searching for the next Samara, and they'd pinned those hopes on her. But since she'd graduated, the

Council seemed intent on holding her back, withholding funding for anything but the safest projects. How was she supposed to do anything that mattered when she wasn't allowed to take a risk?

All of Samara's breakthroughs had come from breaking the rules. She'd made Phoebe's modifications without telling anyone but Lucas. Discovered the truth about the Descendants' origins after being exiled from the colony. Developed the treatment for the Bloom against Prime Buratti's orders.

But then Samara had made new rules. Rules that the Council used to slow everyone down, ensuring that scientific progress happened in the smallest possible increments.

"Sometimes I feel like I'm the only person on this planet who doesn't care what Samara would think if she were alive today."

"For your whole life, you've been dependent on those people for permission to do *your* research." Aurelius flashed that grin again, and she could see how infectious it would've been when his face was whole. He stood, suddenly towering over her as he added, "No more. I'll be your patron. Whatever you need, you'll have it."

"But the Council—"

"Don't worry about them, I'll take care of everything."

He said it so confidently, she believed it, even though she couldn't imagine her father agreeing. Couldn't imagine any of them letting go of the fear that kept them thinking small, rejecting anything that didn't sound like what they'd approved before.

But somehow, she could imagine Aurelius going ahead and doing what he wanted, regardless of their objections.

Still, Jianna felt she should protest. "It'll be months

before my lab can be set up again. The surge when the grid went down destroyed everything."

"I've got a lab on my ship. It's yours, for as long as you need it."

His ship. A laboratory in space. Where the Council couldn't micromanage her.

And where any mistakes she made couldn't hurt anyone down here.

It was a dream come true.

Did she dare trust it?

"We live in a hostile universe, and so few of us remain," Aurelius said. "We have to do whatever it takes to survive."

He was living proof of that philosophy. She couldn't imagine how painful it must have been to excise large parts of your body, to tolerate the fusing of metal and circuits and hydraulics with the flesh that remained.

To look in the mirror and not recognize what was left of you, because the machine overshadowed it.

Yet he'd managed to retain his sense of humor. His passion. The intangible things that made him human, despite the construction of his physical body.

Even though some part of her kept repeating, *too good to be true*, that little voice couldn't squash the inspiration he'd sparked in her.

She imagined completing her research, announcing to her father and to the rest of the world that she'd found the cure for the last disease that plagued them—a disease given to them by the person they most revered.

And now that she had the embryo...

She might be able to fix everything.

Chapter Twenty-Two

MICHEL TWISTED THE WIRES TOGETHER, then shoved the naked splice into a wire nut as far as they would go. After only a couple of hours on shift, his thumbs already ached from overuse, but Carla was hell-bent on getting the rest of the repairs done by mid-morning.

There'd been a lot of eye-rolling at her start-of-shift briefing. What did it matter how soon they finished the repairs when there was no way to power the machines anyway? Why not focus on building more manual pumps to increase the amount of water they could pull from the river? Or on assembling portable filters so that they could scale manual purification?

Behind Michel, Apprentice Al-Hilli grunted and muttered under her breath as she tried to manhandle a fat pipe into place on the reverse osmosis array. But the pipe didn't want to bend the way she was pulling it, and when it sprang back, she let loose a string of curses that would've gotten her fired if she'd said them in front of a supervisor.

Speaking of apprentices who were in danger of getting fired, Glint hadn't shown up for today's shift either.

Apparently, they didn't care that they were short-handed or that Vitruvians were suffering. He couldn't blame them, not when most Vitruvians treated them like they weren't even a person.

But Michel didn't think that was why they'd stopped coming to work. They were probably too busy helping Lucas with what he was up to. And Michel was jealous. It was driving him crazy that he had to be here, tracking down electrical shorts and replacing couplings when he could be studying the most sophisticated specimen of AI-operated robotics he'd likely ever encounter.

Al-Hilli let loose another torrent of cursing. Michel ignored her, forcing himself to focus on the UV-C sterilization chamber. He'd swapped out the controller and resoldered the circuit board, then checked every connection twice. Now he plugged the industrial battery into the alternate input, pressed the power stud, and waited.

A faint purple glow flickered into existence through the observation window that let him see the interior of the sterilization chamber: the indicator LEDs that let an engineer know that the UV lights had come on, so they didn't accidentally burn out their retinas while working inside the chamber.

At least something was working.

He let it run the full ten-minute test cycle, then pulled a sample from the holding tank when it was done, careful not to touch the inside of the bottle as he jammed the probe of the handheld analyzer into the water. The display flashed, numbers ticking up, then froze.

There were still dangerously high levels of live bacteria in the water.

He tried again, fresh sample, new probe. Same result. The sterilization chamber still wasn't working.

He checked the indicator on the chamber. Solid green. He pulled out his meter and clipped it to the leads. Current, steady as a drumbeat, running to both ballasts. Lamps on, power flowing, everything exactly as it should be.

Except that the water was still contaminated.

Michel twisted the probe in his fist, harder than he meant to, cracking the plastic casing.

"It's not working," he said to no one.

"What do you think is wrong with it?"

Not Al-Hilli, an unfamiliar male voice. Right behind him.

Michel jerked around.

At first, his brain refused to process what he was seeing. The man filled the aisle, a wall of muscle and metal, features twisted together like someone had jammed half a corpse into a machine and welded the seams shut.

The right side of his face was a patchwork of steel and ruined flesh, a glassy blue eye burning out from a socket rimmed in blackened alloy. The jaw was bolted together with plates and studs. The arm, too, was a brutal sleeve of mismatched metal, the hand flexing open and closed with a whirr that seemed far too delicate for the bulky prosthetic.

The man's clothes were wrong. Some kind of uniform, but not anything Michel had ever seen.

He was an Elysian. Had to be.

The rumors about the people on the new ship had been flying like crazy, but none of them had said anything about the Elysians being cyborgs.

Michel wanted to ask a thousand questions, all of them beyond rude.

How much of you is machine?

How are your nerves connected to your prosthetics?

Can I read your user manual?

The Elysian just watched him, seeming amused, and repeated his earlier question. "What do you think is wrong with it?"

Michel dragged his gaze away from the mechanical arm to look the Elysian in the eyes. But that just opened up a whole new gamut of questions he had to bite back. "Power's flowing, the indicators are all go, but there's still bacteria in the water."

The Elysian didn't move, but his artificial eye rotated slightly in its socket, as if it were refocusing on something.

That wasn't distracting at all.

"What's your diagnosis?" he asked.

"It could be the ballasts," Michel said. "If the surge blew a capacitor, the UV lamps might light up, but they wouldn't output enough energy to sterilize the water. Or maybe there's a short I haven't found yet. That would do it, too."

There was a faint mechanical hum as the cyborg tilted his head. "Both good guesses. Why don't you open the chamber?"

Should he?

He glanced around for his shift supervisor, Carla. She hadn't mentioned authorizing visitors from other planets during the morning meeting, but maybe this man was the reason she'd been trying to light a fire under their butts about finishing the rest of the repairs.

The Council wouldn't let the newcomers wander around loose if they were dangerous, he reasoned. And the man did seem to be interested in helping.

Michel keyed in the override. The locking pins inside the blast door disengaged with a jarring *ka-thunk*. But the motors that were supposed to open the door were silent.

"I'm sorry, there's only enough juice in the battery to

run the pump and the sterilization lamps. We'll have to open it by hand. I'll go get help."

The Elysian stepped forward. "No need."

"That door weighs more than a hundred kilos—"

But the Elysian had already grabbed the enormous manual latch with his artificial hand. He pulled.

The door's hinges groaned. Then it started to open, just like that.

Michel stared. With one hand, the Elysian could probably haul mainline pipe, rip apart a jammed pump, or singlehandedly drag a grown man out of a tank if he slipped.

"Turn on the lamps," the man said.

Michel grabbed the set of UV goggles from the rack, slid his own on, and offered the other pair. The cyborg waved it off, then leaned in to study the chamber as Michel closed the circuit.

A faint purple glow illuminated the cyborg's figure as he peered into the sterilization chamber.

"Your lamps are barely producing any ultraviolet at the 254-nanometer mark," he said. "Most of what I'm detecting is in the visible part of the spectrum."

Michel blinked. "You can see in UV?"

The Elysian grinned, and the effect was uncanny, but it was also impressive how the mechanicals on the right side of his face moved in synchrony with the flesh on the left.

Michel wondered how hard it had been to match up the timing between nerve impulses and electrical signals. And what the interface involved. Nanotech?

"I can see in the infrared too," the Elysian added.

Of course, he could. If you were making an artificial eye for yourself, why wouldn't you embed a sensor array, tuned to pick up whatever slice of the spectrum you wanted? No need for meters, test strips, or analyzer probes. Just look and know.

What else could the Elysian see that a human would be blind to?

"You've got a crack in the crystal casing on the rear lamp," the Elysian said. "I can see faint UV scattering through the fracture lines. Water probably leaked in and shorted the LEDs."

Michel would have spent hours swapping out ballasts, testing every connection, cursing himself for missing something obvious.

"Thanks," he croaked. "I should've checked that first."

"You narrowed it down to two diagnoses, and one of them was right," the Elysian said. "What's your name?"

"Michelangelo. But my friends call me Michel."

Aurelius held out his mechanical hand. "Aurelius Hofstadter."

Michel froze, his brain struggling to adjust to a million new possibilities that would've seemed impossible a moment before.

Because if he ignored the prosthetics and focused on the left half of the cyborg's face, he did look a lot like Michel's personal hero, the eccentric billionaire who'd made breakthroughs in a half-dozen scientific disciplines before he was thirty. With a few extra wrinkles and gray hairs thrown in.

No. This Elysian *had* to be a descendant. He just happened to look almost exactly like his ancestor. Jianna had told him how phenotypes repeat in a population. How you could look back through historical archives and find people who could pass for someone alive today. The Doppelganger effect, she'd called it.

Michel reached out, feeling the hard chill of alloy close around his own fingers. The mechanical hand delivered exactly the right amount of pressure for a firm handshake. It was the kind of precision and attention to detail that he would expect in one of Aurelius Hofstadter's inventions.

"You're named after him?" Michel asked. "The original Aurelius Hofstadter?"

The Elysian laughed, sharp and bright. "No, I am him."

That was impossible. Except… Hofstadter's life extension research. Tissue regeneration, telomere maintenance, and the first generation of nanite-based cellular repair. If anyone could do it, he could.

Michel's mouth worked, desperate for something to say. His brain landed on, "I read your paper on the Alcubierre engine when I was twelve. The one where you proved it could work, if you could generate the negative energy density."

He cringed inside. He'd read every paper the original Aurelius had ever written, but the speculative faster-than-light drive that had never gone anywhere was the only one he could remember now.

If this was the real Aurelius, he probably thought Michel sounded like an idiot.

But Aurelius didn't seem to be mocking when he replied, "When you were twelve? That's impressive."

Michel nodded, pulse picking up. "I wrote up this whole plan when I was a kid, about how we could use it to visit the other colonies. But then I found out we don't have some of the right elements. Not a single microgram of lutetium, no europium. Or at least we haven't found them yet. So it's impossible."

He waited for the Elysian to shrug, but instead, Aurelius said:

"If you had a space program, you could mine

asteroids. We picked up a dozen in the outer belt with exactly what you'd need."

Michel shook his head. "The Council's never going to fund a space program. Not when there's so much broken down here."

Then he realized how stupid he sounded. The Elysians had a ship. And they knew how to make fuel for it. They'd already traveled from one colony to another, and here he was babbling about his childhood fantasies.

But before Michel could recover, Carla clomped in, snatched a wrench off the nearest workbench, and slammed it against a steel support. The clang echoed through the whole plant, bouncing off pipes and tanks as every head snapped up.

"Announcement time, people," she bellowed, then gestured to Aurelius, who moved from behind the reverse osmosis unit to stand beside her.

Al-Hilli stared open-mouthed, a smudge of grease on her forehead. Two operators at the far end froze, hands still buried in a tangle of hoses. The old guy by the pumps swore softly, then wiped his hands on his coveralls and took a step back. All of them, eyes locked on the Elysian.

Some gawked. Some shrank back. A couple looked like they might be sick. Not a single one tried to hide their reaction.

Michel felt a twist of shame. So much for Vitruvian tolerance. They preached it, but when confronted with someone who looked different, they recoiled. Didn't even try to hide it. He'd seen it with Glint a million times. Now he felt the same protectiveness toward the Elysian, despite the fact that the man could probably pick any one of them up and tear them in half with that artificial arm.

No wonder the engineers' reactions didn't bother him.

But Carla didn't acknowledge that there was anything

out of the ordinary about a cyborg joining their shift for reasons not yet explained.

"This is Mr. Hofstadter," she announced. "He's from that ship in orbit everybody's been slacking off to gossip about. Mr. Hofstadter is here to help us hook this facility up to a power source."

Nobody moved. Michel wasn't even sure they were breathing. They just stared at Aurelius, who gave them a breezy wave of greeting, like he expected them to nod and wave back.

"You're to follow his instructions as if I were giving them." Carla paused as if reconsidering them. "No, I take that back. Follow Mr. Hofstadter's instructions better than you follow mine."

But even her attempt at humor got no response.

Michel felt like he should do something, but what? He'd had the same reaction they did, at first. He'd just gotten over it faster, because he'd recognized Aurelius from the lectures he'd watched on repeat. But most of the engineers probably didn't even know who Aurelius Hofstadter was, except as a name from a history book.

And even if they had recognized him, the first thing they would've told themselves was that Aurelius Hofstadter couldn't be alive today. Just like Michel had.

The Elysian stepped forward, boots squeaking against the grit on the floor. "You'll be working with unfamiliar technology far more advanced than your own—"

More muttering and eye-rolls. A little more hostile, this time.

"—so you'll have to take my word on everything. If I tell you to do something that doesn't make sense to you, that's because I know something you don't. But if you do what I say, your city will have clean water by the end of today. Are you with me?"

The engineers exchanged wary glances. Al-Hilli's hands tightened on her wrench. They might not understand what was going on, but they knew they didn't want to take orders from a stranger.

Michel found his voice. "We're with you."

Carla added hers, speaking to Aurelius but looking directly at Al-Hilli. "They'll do what you ask, if they don't want to work double shifts for the next six months."

Aurelius nodded as if he'd been treated to a round of applause instead of a resentful silence. "Excellent. Finish any repairs in progress. Don't start new ones, just get everything ready for power-up."

He didn't wait to see if they'd obey. He turned, fixed Michel with that artificial eye, and said, "You're with me."

As they left the main floor, Carla barked orders at the rest of the crew, then a hubbub of tools clanking and work boots scuffing on concrete behind them.

Michel followed Aurelius down a corridor lined with dead control panels and the stink of ozone, then into one of the old maintenance bays. At the center, dominating the floor, someone had parked a device the size of a fridge that looked like nothing he'd ever seen.

A fusion of art and science, all exposed coils and layered ceramic shielding, the outer shell a lattice of black composite that Michel couldn't identify. Transparent panels revealed a maze of microtubing, iridescent coolant pulsing through like veins. The core throbbed with pulsing blue light. It wasn't that bright, but it still made him queasy.

This wasn't an incremental step up from their current technology. It was a quantum leap forward, possibly so advanced that he might need to learn a whole new branch of physics to understand it.

He took a step toward it, then stopped himself. "That's the power source?"

"You're dying to know how it works, aren't you?"

He nodded, unable to tear his gaze away. "What does it… Nothing biochemical could… Fusion?"

"What do you know about quantum foam?" Aurelius asked.

Michel's brain short-circuited. All he could do was squeak: "Really?"

The cyborg laughed. "After we're done, want to see the schematics for it?"

Yes. Yes, he did. He'd trade every night's sleep for the rest of his life to study those blueprints. "Yes, please."

"Then let's get to work." Aurelius gestured at the machine. "We need to connect it to the main power coupling where this facility connects to the grid."

Four hours later, Michel had lost track of how many times he'd jammed his fingers between dead panels or scraped the skin off his forearm reaching for a stubborn nut. The backs of his hands were black with grime.

He twisted the final cable into place, and the connection snapped home. He tugged on it to test it, but it remained in place. So he crawled backward out of the conduit to the utility hole where he'd entered. A mechanical hand reached down, and when Michel grabbed it, Aurelius lifted him out of the tunnel like he weighed nothing, setting him down lightly on the concrete floor.

Moments later, Carla traipsed in with the rest of the crew behind her, who immediately clustered around the power source. Their expressions cycled through disbelief, curiosity, and awe.

Like moths to an LED, Michel thought.

"Repairs are done." Carla was the only person who

didn't seem impressed by Aurelius, or the power source, or anything else that was happening right now. "This thing ready to go?"

Aurelius looked at Michel and gestured toward the power source's control panel. "Want to do the honors?"

Michel stepped up and pressed the only visible button on the device's face. It gave under his thumb. For half a second, nothing happened.

Then, light. The overheads snapped on, flooding the maintenance bay with harsh white light. A tremor ran through the floor, then the low, steady thrum of machinery began to build. Motors kicked on with a rumble, pumps shuddered, and pipes chugged as the facility surged awake.

For a second, nobody even moved. Then Al-Hilli actually punched the air, letting out a loud whoop. The others joined in the celebration, laughter and shouts filling the maintenance bay. A few of the engineers glanced at Aurelius, and instead of suspicion or fear, Michel saw gratitude and hope on their faces.

"Diagnostics, now!" Carla bellowed over the din. "Nobody goes home until we've verified that every single repair was done right."

Nobody grumbled as they followed her back to the main floor.

Michel stayed behind to stare at the power source, which hadn't changed at all. It didn't even emit a hum despite the immense quantity of power being drawn from it. The only difference he could see was that the blue light emanating from inside was pulsing faster, maybe half again as fast as it had been before.

If it could handle this whole facility so easily, could it power a spaceship?

An Alcubierre drive would require several orders of

magnitude more power to fold spacetime around something as large as a colony ship.

If that's how the Elysia had gotten here…

Aurelius didn't have to be six hundred years old. Only a decade or two might've passed for him.

This man might actually be the original Aurelius Hofstadter.

"You work for me now."

Michel turned to see Aurelius still standing there, watching him. "What?"

"My ship took a lot of damage on the journey here. I can't fix it alone."

He waited for the punchline. For the part where Aurelius said, *just kidding, you obviously don't know the first thing about spaceships.*

"You want me to help you fix the *Elysia*?"

"We'll be reactivating the *Borlaug*, too," Aurelius said. "Can't have a space program with just one ship."

Michel repeated the phrase, barely above a whisper. "Space program."

"How else are we going to get those rare earth minerals? But first, we need to replace the comm tower." He pointed one mechanical finger at Michel. "Bright and early tomorrow, Engineer."

Then Aurelius was gone, the din of machines swallowing his footsteps.

Michel just stood there, the world tilting beneath him. Aurelius Hofstadter wanted him. Not just as an assistant, but as an engineer. To work on the *Elysia*. He would be the first Vitruvian to return to orbit since Samara's time.

To be mentored personally by one of the greatest scientific minds that Earth had ever produced.

To have a chance to study the principles behind

technology so advanced, it might as well have been magic compared to everything he'd been taught in school.

To learn from someone who didn't believe that any knowledge should be forbidden. Not even knowledge of artificial intelligence, the most dangerous technology of all.

Michel waited for Carla to come back and tell him it was a mistake. For Aurelius to return and say he'd meant someone else. For the power source to fail, the lights to die, and reality to snap back into place like a rubber band. But the machines kept humming. The lights stayed on.

Michel's legs gave out. He sat down hard on the concrete, pressed his palms against his eyes until he saw stars. His chest felt too tight, like he'd forgotten how to breathe properly. When he finally lowered his hands, they were shaking. He stared at them, these same hands that had been twisting wire nuts and cursing broken UV lamps an hour ago. Tomorrow, these hands might touch a starship.

If he was dreaming, he hoped he never woke up.

Chapter Twenty-Three

THE MEDITATION CHAMBER reeked of sweat and incense, and Willow had never missed air conditioning more. Willow sat cross-legged on the straw-woven mat, sweat trickling down her back, the heat pressing against her skin like a punishment.

She was supposed to be emptying her mind, waiting for the Divine to whisper some new insight. But instead, she'd spent the last hour searching through her ancestors' personal archives for references to Aurelius: first Mother Basu's, then her grandmother's.

She returned to a passage she'd found in Mitra's journal, rereading it for the third time:

I should never have taken his money, but the Dark One wears a handsome face when he comes to charm you into handing over your soul.

I heard rumors from the others he stole from, but I told myself that I was smart enough to see his manipulations even as he seduced me. It was too late by the time I realized he was the heart of the conspiracy.

He paid my caretaker to switch my medication and whisper that my precious Ayesha had been replaced by a daeva. He paid the doctors to declare that the curse of my design had worsened. He paid to imprison me after he stole my research and my granddaughter. So desperate to be the smartest person in the room.

I hid it, but if he found it, he deserves the fate I tried to spare him.

Hidden what?

And what fate had Mitra tried to spare him, even after he'd betrayed her?

Whatever it was, Willow felt sure that Aurelius Hofstadter had deserved it.

She pressed her thumb to the locket, and the projected words vanished. Willow rubbed her eyes and the afterimage of Mitra's scrawled confession flickering behind her lids. Everyone knew the official version, Vitruvian or Naturalist: Mitra Kunde, one of the first designer babies. Engineered for genius, toppled by madness. Her brilliance eclipsed by the stain of schizophrenia, her work cut short, her name a warning even on the lips of Samara's followers.

But the suffering Mitra had endured never made it into the official story. The pain that bled out of every sentence in her personal journals…

No matter how many times Willow read them, she never managed to armor herself against it.

Mitra's attack and subsequent institutionalization had been *the* formative trauma of Mother Basu's childhood. Watching her grandmother unravel into madness had given Mother Basu the strength to stand against Samara's corruption of Generation One's humanity and to lead the first Naturalists to found their own doomed colony.

Mother Basu's grandmother never named Aurelius as the Dark One who haunted her writings after she was committed, but it was well documented that he'd funded the bulk of her research after they met.

Dark One fit the man from the *Elysia* perfectly. Not that she believed that the current Aurelius Hofstadter was hundreds of years old, but he'd definitely inherited his namesake's narcissistic tendencies and his obsession with technology. It seemed like a contradiction that he'd been willing to defile that handsome face, but perhaps his story about how his own colony had failed was true.

Willow had hoped that Mitra's journals would be more helpful, but it was the same ranting on loop: how the Dark One had deceived her, how much she missed her granddaughter, how she'd hidden something from Aurelius to protect him. Nothing that she could use against his descendants.

A hard rap at the door. Willow's spine stiffened. The sanctity of meditation was supposed to mean something here. Even now, with the city unraveling outside, the Quarter's rules were clear: Guide in contemplation, do not disturb.

Another knock, sharper. She counted to three. Then, "Enter."

Orion, kitchen manager. He'd probably been hovering outside for ten minutes, sweating through his tunic, working up the courage to interrupt her. Always polite, always anxious about protocol.

He stepped in, eyes on the floor. "No deliveries today. Nothing from the city at all. We're housing so many in the Sanctum, and the pantry's nearly empty. We'll make soup tonight from what's left, and porridge for breakfast, but there'll be nothing left for the midday meal. If you permit, I'll go to the market myself, see what I can buy."

She uncrossed her legs and pressed her palms to her knees. "The lockdown remains in effect. I'll make sure there's a delivery tomorrow morning."

Soren would understand the impossibility of

containing her people in the Quarter without sufficient rations, and he'd see the need to tighten the belt in other parts of the city to make it happen.

Orion hesitated. "If Vanya and I could go today, I'm sure my usual suppliers would—"

"Too dangerous," Willow said. "Not until I'm sure the newcomers haven't brought another plague to our doorstep."

He shifted his weight from one foot to the other. "If you'd let me at least send them a note—"

"You have to trust me, Orion. I'm trying to protect all of us."

The silence pressed in. Even the incense smoke seemed to hang heavier, refusing to drift. Willow wondered if he'd push back, just this once, but there was only the faintest sound of his breath.

"Yes, Guide Evans."

She waited for him to disappear down the hallway, forcing herself not to soften. When she was sure Orion was gone, Willow let the tension drain from her jaw. She wouldn't be able to hold people in the Quarter much longer. Not with the pantry down to its last scraps and refugees crowding every corridor. Theo and Cira would seize on the shortages, stir up more unrest, and the rest of the Council would do nothing but argue in circles while the cyborg paraded through the city, ignoring every rule.

Returning to her private chamber, she stripped off the sweat-soaked tunic and changed into her Guide's formal robe, the white one with the blue sash. The fabric clung to her skin in this stifling heat, but at least it looked like authority. She wound her hair up, fastened the locket at her throat, then selected the best respirator from the shelf, checked the seals, and fastened it around her neck, ready to pull it up over her nose and mouth.

She wanted everyone in the Sanctum to see the mask. Fear of plague was the best leverage she had for enforcing lockdown.

If she let even a single crack appear, Cira and Theo would pry it open and let chaos pour in.

As she moved through the Sanctum's corridors, smiling and murmuring blessings at refugees camping in the halls, she heard the unmistakable rhythm of Theo's preaching. She changed direction, entering the worship hall from the rear. It was crammed full of the displaced, sprawled on mats or propped up against walls, eyes dull with grief and blunted hope.

But closer to the front, the benches were packed. Bodies jammed shoulder to shoulder, all eyes on Theo. Cira and her lieutenants stood, arms crossed, blocking the aisle nearest the dais. Willow counted at least a hundred, maybe more, and every single one of them was hanging on Theo's every word.

He jabbed a finger at the ceiling.

"The sign appeared to me and me alone, the night before the aurorae. But it didn't stop there: last night, Mother Basu herself appeared to me in a vision, and she said: We must re-sanctify the holy site. We must begin anew, for the truly faithful." Then he looked straight at Willow, as if he'd just noticed her. "If the current Guide is too timid, then the Divine will send a new leader."

"I've been accused of many things, but timid?" Willow moved down the aisle, every step deliberate, refusing to let them see the anxiety crawling just beneath her skin. She stopped at the front, faced Theo, and the packed benches. "There will be a haven for us. In time. But I won't lead our people to their deaths by running blindly into the wilds. If we want to claim our own place, we must prepare."

Theo's face hardened. "We've put up with Vitruvian

contamination long enough. Now the newcomers bring more. We need to claim our own place."

Willow let the silence stretch. The crowd leaned in, waiting for her to falter. "I believe in Mother Basu's vision as much as you do. But we can't let fear make us impatient. We must have faith that our time is coming."

A woman in the back pushed herself upright, clutching a paper fan. "How much longer do we have to be stuck in here without enough water to drink?"

Someone else, a man, spoke without raising his head. "I listen every day by the wall to the town criers. Nobody's said a word about a plague. Not once."

A third, younger, said, "My brother's got a room in the West End. My sister, too. If it's so bad out there, why aren't we allowed to go stay with our families?"

If she could reassure them now, she might also be able to insulate them against Theo's "teachings" while she was away.

"I know this is difficult, but—"

Cira cut her off, voice slicing through the room.

"We should all listen to my sister, for it is her guidance that has brought us here. Willow commanded that we allow houses to burn down so that we might all have water to drink. She's ordered us to remain here because she wishes only to protect us while the Vitruvians rebuild."

The benches creaked as bodies shifted uneasily. Some faces turned, searching for reassurance, but most eyes dropped, wary or bitter.

Cira's words, dressed up as loyalty, but every syllable oiled to slide a knife between Willow's ribs, blaming her for everything they were angry about right now.

Time to turn the knife back on her sister.

"Sister Cira, your humility is admirable, but we should all acknowledge how much you have contributed to everyone's current state of comfort. I know you will continue to do so."

Then Willow turned, letting her voice roll out to the benches. "If you need anything at all, no matter how small, my sister is here to serve you."

Cira's smile turned queasy, like she'd swallowed the wrong end of a prayer.

That would keep her busy. Let Cira spend the rest of the day catering to the mundane needs of the crowd while Willow focused on something that actually mattered.

Like making sure they got more food before midday tomorrow.

"The Divine is with us, and we will emerge even stronger when this is over," Willow said. "In the meantime, the Sanctum will shelter everyone in need. I urge you to meditate and pray for the speedy rebuilding of our community."

Willow swept toward the exit, already practicing the argument she'd have to wage to wrench tomorrow's rations out of the Council.

But Cira called after her: "There goes my sister, bravely using her seat on the Vitruvian Council to fight for us."

Not even an attempt to hide her mockery. She was growing braver.

Willow pivoted, ready to fire back, but a shout rose from the corridor: "It's back! The water's back on!"

Orion stumbled into the worship hall, almost tripping over the feet of a refugee asleep on the floor. He locked eyes with Willow. "Guide Evans, we have clean water in the kitchen."

A surge of relief. Not just for herself. For the whole Quarter. Followed by a sinking feeling that the person she had to thank for this small miracle would extract a price she wasn't willing to pay.

But for now, she beamed at her people and made a gesture of blessing. "You prayed and the Divine answered. There can be no doubt about the purity of your intent."

She turned toward Cira. "I know you won't stop until you've made sure every one of these people has drunk their fill, and when you're done, fill as many vessels as you can, to refill our reserves."

Cira's jaw clenched, but she bowed her head and started barking orders to her lieutenants as the refugees gathered around her.

Willow strode out of the worship hall, ignoring a poisonous look from Theo as she passed him.

She was losing ground, and if she didn't do something soon, Cira would gain enough followers to start a schism. Theo would gladly help her.

But if Willow tried to confine either of them, the rumors would multiply. If she cracked down now, she might trigger a full revolt. If she waited, the discontent would rot everything from the inside. The longer the lockdown dragged on, the more precarious her position would be.

And as fortuitous as it was that the water was running again, that meant Aurelius had succeeded, and his next solution would have even more credibility.

She could picture her colleagues gathered around the cyborg, nodding along as he explained the genius of his invention. Soren, Xanthe, even Isabeau, all of them so desperate for an easy fix, they'd let Aurelius take the lead without a second thought. Even now, they were probably applauding the man who'd just made himself indispensable. Each victory would make the Council more dependent on him, would make her warnings sound more like paranoia.

You're speaking to your savior.

Willow's skin crawled. Was it really this easy for an outsider to seize control?

This was how he'd seduced Mitra, how he'd stolen her research. By making himself indispensable.

By the time anyone realized what he'd taken, it would be too late.

Chapter Twenty-Four

WILLOW STRODE into the Council chamber, pushing the door open hard enough to rattle the glass. They'd started without her.

Aurelius stood dead center in front of the wall mural, strategically positioned so that the city's hero loomed behind him, larger than life, lab coat and gold-piped coveralls aglow in the overheads. It created the illusion that Samara herself was watching over Aurelius, ready to anoint him as her chosen successor.

Brilliant move. That bastard.

She didn't bother to hide her contempt. "Starting early so you could push a vote through without me?"

Aurelius didn't even pretend to be surprised. "I thought you might be abstaining from this meeting as some sort of protest."

He gestured to the empty chair at the table, as if he'd been expecting her to slink in and take her place at his command.

Willow glared at him, not moving. She wasn't going to

let him choreograph the scene in front of the other Council members. If she sat now, it would look like he'd ordered her to do it.

Aurelius shrugged. "Suit yourself. I was just explaining that repairs on the comm tower are going to take a while, as many of the parts that were damaged by the aurorae need to be made from scratch. No replacements survived. So, my people are going to deploy a network of communication drones—"

"Absolutely not," Willow snapped.

Isabeau practically snarled at her. "It's not up to you."

"No, it's up to *all* of us." Did she really have to remind them that a few days ago, they'd been debating whether the Elysians were here to attack the city? "He says they're communication drones, but how do we know they aren't surveillance?"

Harold snorted. "We can't let the city continue to be crippled just because you're afraid of anything new. Or maybe you're afraid we'll find out what really goes on in the Naturalist Quarter?"

Xanthe leaned forward, hands open, conciliatory. "Willow, he's trying to help, just listen to what he has to say."

Of course, Xanthe would side with Aurelius. She always folded, always wanted everyone to get along, even when it meant opening the gates to a monster.

Willow scowled. "I heard him quite well, and what he's saying is that he's going to deploy drones that do who knows what throughout the city. I'm giving him the benefit of the doubt when I ask if they're surveillance drones. They could be military drones."

She glanced at Elias. He wouldn't even meet her eyes. Not so much as a twitch in her direction.

Coward.

He'd been the first to warn that the Elysians were dangerous, but the second Aurelius had stepped out of that shuttle, Elias had crumpled, just like the rest of them.

Soren remained the consummate politician, sitting there with a polite smile on his face, as if they were talking about how many acres of oats to plant next spring.

He nodded at Aurelius. "Our engineers will need to examine these drones before we approve your plan."

Aurelius didn't even try to hide his satisfaction. He'd already won. Was she the only one who could see what was happening?

"Of course," Aurelius said, and his smile was a knife. "I'd also like to requisition one of your engineers to assist me personally. Michelangelo Lombardi."

Camilla Lombardi's son?

Something shifted. Soren's face, just for a moment. Barely a flicker, but Willow caught it. Why?

"You can have a team of engineers," Soren said. "The city's entire division is at your disposal."

"I'll be overseeing them too," Aurelius said.

Of course, he would. Willow could almost see the gears turning behind the cyborg's mismatched eyes, calculating every angle, every move, already picturing himself at the head of a new empire built from Vitruvian sweat.

Harold bristled. "Is that so?"

"Until the repairs are completed and the city is running smoothly."

It was happening. The takeover, orchestrated right in front of Samara's painted face, and Harold was the only one with an objection.

Unbelievable.

All hands went up, albeit reluctantly in Harold's case.

Pathetic.

Willow crossed her arms, refusing to play along even if she was the token Naturalist vote and had no way of stopping this insanity. She stared at the mural behind Aurelius, at Samara's calm gaze, the gold piping on her coat. As misguided as the ancient geneticist had been, Samara never would have bowed to someone like Aurelius. Willow was sure of it, having read Mother Basu's description of her opponent.

Samara had been smart. Stubborn. Willing to risk her own life for what she believed.

Mother Basu had railed at Samara, but she had never underestimated her.

Too bad Soren hadn't inherited his famous ancestor's backbone.

Soren fixed his gaze on Willow. "Councilor Evans, is there anything we can do to address your concerns?"

Willow almost laughed at his pointless olive branch.

She pictured Theo, already pacing the prayer hall as he babbled about signs. If he didn't claim the drones as another message from the heavens, then Cira would seize on the moment instead, pointing to the drones as proof that Willow had failed to protect them from the next technological infection.

One more crack in the wall.

One step closer to Cira's coup.

She locked her eyes on Soren, but her words were for Aurelius. "No drones within a half-mile of the Quarter. My people can't know they're here."

She paused, letting the tension build.

"And in exchange for my agreement..." She turned, pinning Aurelius with the full force of her attention. "You'll respect our ban on artificial intelligence. Your robot demon returns to your ship and stays there."

"Not an option. He's far too valuable a resource, and I have complete control over him."

"We know from our own history that you're lying about that."

"Lucas was the prototype. I improved the design with Lucian." Aurelius shrugged. "And if we could find Lucas, I'd fix whatever allowed him to slip free of his programming."

Willow wanted to laugh, but nothing about this was funny. "And if you're wrong?"

"There's a remote shutdown in all the Lucifer-class models. I can turn Lucian off the second there's a problem."

"Prove it."

The left side of Aurelius' mouth twitched, the blue light in his eye flaring brighter. "Fair enough."

The door opened, and Lucian stepped inside.

Had it been waiting outside, listening through the door?

The grayish cast to its skin was even more pronounced in this light. It reminded her of a corpse. She wondered if Aurelius had purposefully made Lucian so obviously unnatural that no one could mistake him for human. Or had the android's skin simply decayed over time?

Isabeau stared. "How did you summon that thing?"

"I've placed a portable network hub in the offices outside," Aurelius explained. "I can communicate with any of my people who are in a two-block radius."

Lucian stepped forward. "How may I assist you, Councilors?"

Aurelius snapped his fingers.

Lucian froze, deadly still. The room went silent except for the faint hum of the overheads.

Aurelius stopped inches from the android, waving a

hand in front of its blank eyes. Nothing. Then he jabbed two fingers against Lucian's sternum, hard enough that the torso rocked back a fraction.

No response. Not even a flicker. The android could have been a mannequin.

Aurelius leaned closer as if to whisper in Lucian's ear, but didn't lower his voice. "Lucian, I want you to kill everyone in this room."

Every Councilor jerked back at once, chairs scraping the floor. Willow's hand shot out, fingers wrapping around the first thing she touched. A pencil from the conference table. She gripped it in her fist, sharp end forward, ready to drive it into the android's eye if it so much as shuddered.

But Lucian didn't move.

Aurelius laughed. "See? Instant shutdown. He'll stay that way until I reactivate him."

"How dare you threaten us?" But Isabeau looked more embarrassed than outraged.

Aurelius shrugged. "I wasn't threatening anyone. I was merely illustrating that Guide Evans' worst fear was unfounded."

"So, snapping your fingers is what shuts the android down?" Harold asked.

"Absolutely not. The nanites in my system are quantum entangled with elements in Lucian's brain, allowing instantaneous communication." Aurelius snapped his fingers again, and Lucian frowned as if confused. "The snap just adds a little flair to it."

"How may I assist you, Councilors?" Lucian asked, as if the shutdown had never happened. Willow wondered if Lucian was aware that his functions had been stopped, or if reality simply stuttered around the android, skipping ahead to a new moment.

She couldn't decide which would be worse.

Xanthe leaned forward, staring at the android. "As long as the robot stays with you—"

"He will," Aurelius assured. "He can handle highly technical repairs, and he never sleeps."

Willow stared at the android. Every instinct screamed at her that this was a mistake.

"That's exactly how Lucas wormed his way in at the beginning," she said. "He did the jobs nobody else wanted to do. He made himself indispensable."

Harold tapped the table. "Well, if he's working, he'll be too busy to cause any trouble, right?"

Aurelius smiled. "I understand your concerns, given your history with Lucas. You can hold me personally responsible for anything Lucian does."

Xanthe stared at the table, then at the mural behind Aurelius. "And the drones will be removed once the telecommunications tower is repaired?"

Aurelius didn't hesitate. "Absolutely."

"I oppose this." Not that anyone was listening to Willow.

Harold flicked his eyes to Soren, then called for a vote.

Hands rose. Soren first, then Isabeau, then Xanthe. Even Harold, after a pause that lasted barely a heartbeat. For a moment, Willow let herself believe Elias might refuse. His hand hovered, motionless, knuckles pale. Then he raised it.

Five to one. Like it always was.

Willow kept her arms folded. She stared at the blue-white light in the android's eye and imagined what it would be like to drive a spike through it. Would it shatter? Would there be bone and brain behind it, or had he replaced the inside of his skull with more machinery?

Soren was already out of his seat, sliding past the others and out the door like a rat escaping a trap.

Not so fast, coward.

Willow turned to follow, but Aurelius moved faster, stepping into her path, his bulk blocking the exit.

"We need to talk," he said.

Willow tightened her grip on the pencil. The wood bit into her palm, the sharp end ready. Aurelius had manipulated the whole council, twisting them around his finger while they thanked him for it. Now he wanted to corner her alone. Probably thought he could intimidate her into silence.

And the other Councilors didn't even look back as they filed past him. Didn't make eye contact with her, either.

Cowards. All of them.

Aurelius shut the door with a sound like a coffin lid closing.

Willow clamped down on the urge to back away. If he meant to kill her, she would die with dignity. "What do you want?"

He studied her for a long moment. "It's shocking how much you resemble her. Mitra."

The name made her stomach twist. She forced herself to look up at him, chin high, even though every instinct shrieked at her to hide under the table. Or jump out the window.

"I've read Mitra's private journals," she said. "She loathed you."

Aurelius' eyes narrowed. "She loved me. But her illness convinced her that I'd betrayed her."

"Did you?"

A flicker. Pain, maybe. Regret. Hard to tell with that ruined face. "Never. She was the only woman I ever loved. When her mind slipped too far from reality, I paid for her care. Even though she refused to see me when I came to visit her facility."

"Perhaps because you stole her research?"

Aurelius' face seemed to collapse in on itself, the seams and scars folding deeper. "I know she saw it that way. But I carried on her legacy. Advanced the research that she was too sick to continue. I couldn't let the world suffer that tragic loss of genius, even if I couldn't do anything about losing her."

She stared at him. The man who'd just ordered his machine to murder her and her colleagues, as if it were a parlor trick. Now he looked ruined. Not the monster she'd imagined, but a man who'd never stopped mourning.

But she'd read Mitra's own words. Mother Basu's, too. She knew the other version of the story.

"Mother Basu never forgave you," Willow said. "Not after she learned you'd sent the android to infiltrate us."

"I only gave Ayesha a spot on the *Borlaug* out of respect for Mitra's memory. I couldn't let our granddaughter die in the Chytrid Collapse."

Liar. "Mother Basu's grandfather was a politician."

But Willow's breath caught in her chest as he stared at her, the blue light in his eye unwavering.

"Mitra wanted her husband to believe the child was his," he said.

This was just another story, spun out of the rot in his skull, designed to infect her with doubt.

"You're not my ancestor," she said. "Mother Basu would have known."

Aurelius shook his head. "Ayesha lived in a fairy tale world when it came to her grandmother. She needed to believe in something pure. But the truth was always more complicated."

Willow pressed her nails into her palm. "I'm not listening to this."

"Mitra would've been disappointed to see her line reduced to superstitious Luddites and religious nuts."

"You have no idea what she would've thought about anything." She knew the chance of hurting him with the pencil she gripped was close to zero, but she was still tempted to try.

Instead, she tried to move past him.

He shifted easily, blocking her way again.

"I'm not your enemy, Willow." He sighed, and she saw a flash of that grief again. "You're the only family I have left."

"I don't believe you."

"Soren's daughter took a sample of my DNA. I'm sure you'll get a copy of the report." He smiled, but there was nothing warm in it. "But you probably don't believe in genetics, either."

Willow's hand convulsed, snapping the pencil and driving the broken ends into her palm.

She remembered a line from Mitra's journal:

I told myself that I was smart enough to see his manipulations even as he seduced me.

That's what this was, another manipulation.

He wasn't her ancestor, because he'd never known Mitra Kunda or Ayesha Basu. He was an imposter, trying to fool them into believing he was the genius whose debt they were in for building the colony ships. The others believed him, but she never would.

Willow stared at his ruined face, the artificial eye, the seams and scars. "What do you want from me?"

"You want freedom for your people. You want your own colony, not just a ghetto inside their city."

"It's not a gh—"

"I'll champion a true enclave for your people. Not wilderness or dead rock, but prime land, enough to sustain a thriving settlement. I'll give you the technology to make it work. You can succeed where Ayesha failed."

Everything she'd spent her life saying she wanted for her people.

But to get it, she'd have to make a deal with this… this Dark One. And it would be a lie, because she would need to embrace more technology if she wanted her people to live.

"You want something in return, of course."

Aurelius smiled, slow and deliberate, like he'd been waiting for her to ask. "Your support as my ally on the Council, until your new home is ready. I want a real alliance."

Of course. He wanted her to be the face of his takeover. The Naturalist converted, holding hands with the devil. Because if he could win her over, what reason would there be for the average Vitruvian to resist?

"I don't want my people segregated," she said. "More and more people are leaving Vitruvian society because they see that the obsession with technology is poisoning us. They want something real. I want everyone to have that chance."

"I can help you with that, too."

She almost laughed. "Why would you? You're more contaminated than any Vitruvian I've ever met. You're obsessed with artificial intelligence. You want to infect every part of this world with your machines."

"Being a genius means not clinging to one truth, but seeing the value in everything, even the things that make you uncomfortable. I believe that a healthy society has ideological debate woven into its core. Otherwise, it stagnates and dies."

She stared at him, disgust curling under her tongue. "You mean you want to keep us around because our existence makes what you have to offer look better?"

The grin spread as he shrugged. "Let the best ideas win."

"The truth will always win," Willow replied. "And that's why you're going to lose."

Chapter Twenty-Five

JIANNA'S STOMACH twisted itself into knots that had nothing to do with the breakfast her father had made before he'd left early for another emergency Council meeting. She'd pushed the eggs around her plate until they went cold, unable to force down even a bite. How could she eat when in less than an hour she'd be strapped into a shuttle heading for orbit?

Orbit. The word itself made her dizzy.

She'd be one of the first Vitruvians to leave the planet in centuries. Sure, they'd sent unmanned probes, weather satellites, communications arrays. But actual people? Not since the early days of the colony, back when they still had functioning shuttles and the knowledge to maintain them.

She entered the square in front of the Vitruvia City Administration building, where a crowd hovered behind the security barriers, gaping at the battered shuttle that sat near the front steps. She recognized a few faces from the university, colleagues from the labs, even some of the Councilors who'd voted against her research proposal. All here to witness history.

Or a spectacular failure.

Jianna pushed that thought away because it came with the image of the shuttle burning up in the atmosphere. If she let herself think about how things could go wrong, she might never get on it.

She turned towards the shuttle, which wasn't exactly reassuring. She'd seen one before, and not just in historical films. The city had preserved one of the original *Borlaug* shuttles that Generation One had used when they were still dependent on the ship. It now rested in the city's museum, fully restored (albeit minus the parts that had made it fly). But that shuttle was all gleaming curves and pristine paint, with a shiny control console inside that lit up with LEDs designed to simulate a real flight.

But that one looked like a toy, something too pretty to be real.

This shuttle looked like it had died. At least once.

Scorch marks streaked across the hull in patterns that reminded her of bacterial growth on agar plates. The paint had blistered and peeled away in patches, revealing bare metal that had oxidized to a dull brown. One panel near the engine housing didn't match the rest: a different alloy welded on with thick seams that stood out like scar tissue. The boarding ramp extended at a slight angle, its hydraulics clearly struggling. Grease and grime caked the joints, and one of the support struts had been reinforced with what looked like salvaged mining equipment.

Jianna's pulse hammered in her throat. This thing had made it from the *Elysia* to DaVinci's surface. That meant it could make it back to orbit.

Hopefully.

Soren hadn't wanted her to go, but even he'd admitted the opportunity was too valuable to pass up. He wanted details about Aurelius' people, their technology, their intentions, any detail that might help him negotiate with Aurelius. She was going to be in for a grilling when she got home.

But Jianna would be looking for information for herself, too. Aurelius had promised unlimited access to his ship's archive, and she was curious how "unlimited" the access was going to be, but no way was she saying no to that. Her official purpose for the trip up was to access the original Aurelius Hofstadter's authenticated medical records, whose file should have a secure chain of provenance. If they'd been tampered with, she should be able to tell. And if not, she'd have the entire sequence of the original Aurelius' genome, taken before the *Elysia* had launched from Earth orbit, which she'd compare to the sequenced sample she'd taken from the cyborg's cheek.

If they matched…

Then the impossible really was true. Aurelius Hofstadter had found a way to cheat death for over six hundred years.

Movement at the top of the ramp caught her eye. Aurelius emerged from the shuttle's interior, his massive frame filling the hatchway. He glanced over the crowd, then spotted her. She raised her hand in greeting, and his scarred face split into what she supposed was meant to be a welcoming smile.

He beckoned her forward, then ducked back inside, leaving the hatchway open.

Jianna forced her feet to move. One step. Two. Three. Two security guards pushed aside the barricade for her to enter. Someone called her name, but she didn't turn around. If she stopped now, she might turn back.

She placed a foot on the ramp, then hesitated. Now that she was up close, she could see where the anti-slip coating had worn away, leaving smooth metal that would be treacherous in rain. Dark stains spotted the surface. Oil? Hydraulic fluid? Something worse?

She reached the top and paused, peering inside. The main cabin stretched before her, lit by flickering overhead panels that cast everything in a sickly yellow light. The seats lining the walls might have been white once. Now they were the color of old teeth, with tears in the upholstery that leaked yellowed foam. Even the walls were scratched.

Near the cockpit door, black scorch marks radiated from a small access panel. The metal around it had bubbled and warped. Someone had tried to clean the soot away but seemed to have given up halfway through, leaving ghostly smears across the bulkhead. She sniffed but couldn't smell burning. An old wound.

"Second thoughts?"

Jianna jumped. Aurelius appeared in the cockpit door. Up close in the confined space, he seemed even larger; the ceiling barely cleared his head.

"No," she lied, proud that her voice didn't crack. "Just excited."

His grin widened, pulling at the scar tissue around his artificial eye. "That's my girl."

His girl? Normally, she wouldn't tolerate being patronized by any colleague, but he came from a different world, and possibly, a different time. Maybe that wasn't considered insulting among his people.

She would meet some of them soon enough, and the better she understood the Elysians, the more she could help her father.

"We're waiting for one more passenger," Aurelius turned back toward the cockpit. "But come, let's get you settled."

She followed him through the narrow hatchway. The

cockpit looked like someone had assembled it from spare parts, and to be fair, they probably had, given how old it was. The pilot's seat was newer than the copilot's, its padding intact, while the other was held together with silver and black strips of industrial tape that crisscrossed the cracked synthetic leather like sutures. The console between them was a patchwork of different interfaces: modern touch screens bolted next to analog switches, holographic projectors rigged up beside manual throttles and old-fashioned dials and switches.

She had no idea how he managed to make sense of it.

Behind the main seats, a jump seat had been welded to the wall. The safety harness dangled from it like an afterthought.

"Take a seat," Aurelius said, sliding into the pilot's seat.

She swallowed, then pointed to the copilot chair. "Here?"

"Best seat in the house. You'll be able to see everything."

Did she want to see everything? Or would the ride up be less nerve-wracking in the passenger cabin, where she wouldn't be able to tell how far up they were?

She lowered herself into the seat, trying not to think about the fact that they were about to take this death trap into space. The harness was a puzzle of straps and buckles that took her three tries to figure out. While she detangled them and matched the connections, Aurelius went through what looked like a preflight check.

She heard footsteps behind her.

"What are you doing here?" a familiar voice asked.

She twisted in her seat. Michel stood in the cockpit doorway, his face a mask of dismay.

Of all the people to be the second passenger, why him?

"You two know each other?" Aurelius glanced between them.

Jianna caught Michel's eye, and they both hesitated for a split second while a whole conversation passed between them. She didn't want to explain their actual relationship to this cyborg. And she had a feeling he didn't either.

"Not well," Michel said.

"Not at all," Jianna said at the same time.

Wonderful. This wasn't going to be awkward.

But Aurelius didn't seem to notice.

"Excellent!" Aurelius slapped his hand against his thigh with enough force to make Jianna flinch. "I chose you both specifically because you have the potential to bring your world into the future. Dr. Makinde in genetics, Mr. Lombardi in applied AI. Your generation will be the bridge between what Vitruvian society has become and what it could be."

Jianna forced a smile.

She appreciated his faith in them. But she still wasn't sure what Aurelius wanted from her. She'd assumed his interest had more to do with her being Samara's descendant, or a Councilor's daughter, than with her actual work.

Aurelius pointed to the jump seat. "If you would, Mr. Lombardi?"

Michel took the seat slightly behind them. She could see him in her peripheral vision. This was going to be awkward. She wished they'd cleared the air before ending up trapped in a shuttle together. She glanced back, hoping to catch his eyes, give him a smile. But he was fumbling with his own harness, so she turned around and focused on the control panel in front of her, trying to distract herself and make sense of the displays. Altitude indicators, pressure readings, fuel gauges. At least those were labeled.

The screen set between the pilot and copilot's stations showed data streams she couldn't interpret.

A second later, she heard the shuttle door close.

She bunched her hands into fists as the engines coughed to life with a stuttering growl that made several loose panels rattle. Aurelius pulled back on the main throttle while flipping a series of switches overhead.

"Hold on," he said.

The shuttle lurched upward. The ground fell away. Jianna grabbed the arms of her chair and closed her eyes.

She felt Aurelius pat her hand.

"You're missing the view."

She forced herself to open her eyes and look out the cockpit window. The crowd in the square shrank to the size of dolls, the administration building looking more like a toy than anything as Vitruvian City fell away. She'd seen drone footage before, but actually being this high up in the air was terrifying. As they rose higher, the greenhouse districts formed perfect hexagons. The water treatment plant looked like a star. The mountains whose caves housed the extremophiles she'd spent so much of her life hunting shrank until they were mere ripples in the landscape below.

Invisible forces pressed her back into the seat, and taking a breath took more effort, like someone had stacked textbooks on her ribs. Her vision narrowed at the edges, darkness creeping in despite her attempts to blink it away.

Aurelius was busy with the controls. Warning lights blinked across the console: red, amber, a few steady greens that she hoped meant something good. He didn't look in the least bit alarmed, so she tried to relax.

Her breathing came in short gasps, and she wasn't sure if she was hyperventilating out of fear or if it was just the intense pressure trying to crush her ribcage.

She forced herself to focus on the instruments again.

Just data on screens, needles on dials, numbers on readouts. None of it was her responsibility, and no matter how they changed, she was still fine. Soon her breathing evened out.

The altitude indicator climbed steadily: five thousand meters, ten thousand, fifteen. The external pressure readings dropped. The outside temperature plummeted.

She'd read about how on Earth, people traveled in big birdlike machines called airplanes that somehow stayed up in the air even though their wings didn't flap, which she'd always thought was insane. But at least they had wings. This shuttle was just a metal box with engines, defying gravity through brute force and stubborn engineering.

She risked a glance back at Michel and saw his knuckles were white where he gripped the edges of his seat. His face had gone pale, jaw clenched tight enough to see the muscle jump. Good. She wasn't the only one terrified by this insane venture.

The shuttle bucked like an angry animal. Something in the cabin behind them crashed and rolled.

"Just atmospheric turbulence," Aurelius said. "She always gets temperamental around thirty thousand meters."

Thirty thousand meters. Higher than any Vitruvian had flown in centuries. Higher than the weather balloons, higher than the survey drones, higher than anything except the ancient communications satellites that still circled overhead, most of them dead and silent.

And they were still climbing.

Chapter Twenty-Six

MICHEL HAD BEEN DISAPPOINTED to find Jianna strapped in the copilot's seat when he'd boarded the shuttle. He'd thought this would be a day alone with Aurelius, a chance to pick his mentor's brain without competition. It was even more disappointing to be relegated to the cramped jump seat for his flight to space, where the view consisted mainly of the backs of their heads and glimpses of the sky overhead.

But now, as his internal organs tried to reorganize themselves in response to the changing gravitational forces, he was grateful for the limited view. If he'd been able to see the ground dropping away as they rose, he had a feeling he would have thrown up. And that would have been mortifying.

Especially since Jianna seemed fine.

The sensation was like nothing he'd ever experienced. His inner ear sent confused signals to his brain. Up and down lost their meaning. One moment, invisible hands were shoving him backward into the inadequate padding of the jump seat, gravity multiplying until his chest compressed and his arms felt like they weighed fifty kilos each. His body fought against the pull, muscles straining just to keep him from collapsing into a pancake. Then, gradually, the pressure began to ease. The shuttle's engines shifted from their bone-rattling roar to a steadier hum, and the acceleration tapered off.

Lighter. He was getting lighter.

He knew from his physics classes that soon the only thing keeping him in the jump seat was the straps across his chest. But his stomach contents seemed to have their own opinions about what should happen.

Don't throw up. You're an adult. You're an engineer. You can handle this.

His stomach gurgled its skepticism.

"Look." Aurelius pointed through the forward window. "There she is."

In front of him, Jianna gasped.

Michel leaned forward as much as his harness would allow, trying to see past their shoulders. At first, he saw only stars. More stars than were ever visible from the surface, even on the clearest night.

Then he noticed a dark space where there were no stars at all. A void, black against black. As they drew closer, the shuttle's external lights flickered on with a series of clicks and hums. The beams swept across pitted metal, revealing the thing that blocked the stars.

The *Norman Borlaug*.

Michel's breath stuck in his throat.

Every schoolchild in Vitruvian City had trudged through the city's museum and stood before the scale replica of the *Borlaug* while their teacher droned on about the Reseeding. But those models were toys compared to this. They couldn't convey the sheer mass of the thing or the brutal functionality of its design.

The colony ship was massive. It had to be, to carry one hundred sixty passengers in cryosleep, plus livestock, embryos, seed banks, manufacturing equipment, and more. Everything humanity needed to start over on a distant world. But knowing the numbers and seeing the reality were different things entirely. The *Borlaug* stretched beyond the edges of the window. Some sections were smooth, others bristling with sensor arrays and communication dishes.

He found himself straining against the harness. Somewhere in that vast structure was the ship's AI core, the brain that had guided humanity across forty-two light-years of space. It would be heavily shielded, probably in the most protected part of the ship. Even powered down, even after centuries of dormancy, the ship's brain might still be intact. He would give anything to explore it. Especially to reactivate the AI brain and study it. Who knew what emergent behaviors had developed over decades of its operation?

According to the history books, the Generation One colonists hadn't been able to deactivate Lucas because he was somehow linked to the ship's brain, although Michel hadn't been able to find any information about *how*.

But Aurelius would know. And he'd probably tell Michel, if Michel had a chance to ask him about it without Jianna around.

He wasn't sure he could trust her not to tell her father that Aurelius was teaching Michel forbidden knowledge.

Jianna stared at the colony ship with her mouth slightly open, and he realized that the colony ship probably meant something different to her. Her ancestors had spent forty-two light-years sleeping in cryopods aboard the *Borlaug*. They'd trusted their lives to the ship's systems, to the AI that watched over them through the decades of dark between stars, then betrayed them once they'd reached their new home.

Michel had no such connection. His mother had assembled his genome from nucleotides and ambition, selecting his traits like items from a catalog. He existed because Camilla Lombardi had wanted a child optimized for intelligence and creativity, not because his forebears had survived the death of Earth.

Did Jianna want to walk those corridors like he did? Maybe find the specific pod where Samara and Renata had actually slept?

"Magnificent, isn't she?" Aurelius said. "We matched velocity with her three days ago, did a preliminary survey. Structurally sound, minimal micrometeorite damage. With repairs and a new fuel source, she could breathe again."

He adjusted the throttle, and the shuttle banked left; the *Borlaug* slid out of view. This time, Michel's stomach responded much better. Through the window, he saw a second ship, and the awe he'd felt on seeing the *Borlaug* curdled into something akin to horror.

If the *Borlaug* was a monument to human achievement, the *Elysia* was a testament to survival. The ship looked like it had been through several wars and lost. Scorch marks similar to those on the shuttle were painted in abstract patterns across its hull, some so severe that the metal had bubbled and warped. Entire sections were patched with mismatched panels that suggested different eras of repair. One patch looked suspiciously like a repurposed livestock transport container.

Weird lumps and protrusions broke the ship's original lines. Some might have been sensor packages or weapon systems, but others defied easy categorization. A bulbous growth near the engine section looked like a tumor of metal. Another modification bristled with antennae pointed in every direction. Cables ran along the exterior hull, secured with magnetic clamps and spot welds, connecting systems that should've interfaced within the ship's walls.

"What happened to your ship?" The question escaped before Michel could stop it.

Aurelius' expression darkened. "Radiation damage, primarily. We barely cleared the system before our sun went critical. Would have fried every system on the ship if we'd stayed another week." He adjusted their approach vector. "Then, more damage during the journey. We hit three unexpected debris fields and survived a close pass with a pulsar. We had navigational data for the journey from Earth to each of the colonies, but no idea what lay between colonies."

Michel studied one of the larger modifications, a series of interconnected spheres that bulged from the ship's midsection. The engineering required to add something like that while in transit, probably while dealing with radiation damage and system failures...

It was almost unbelievable.

"What's that?" He pointed at the strange addition.

"Later," Aurelius said. "I need to focus on docking."

The *Elysia* grew larger in the window, details resolving with uncomfortable clarity. More patches, more burns, more modifications. How many times had the crew almost lost life support? How many hull breaches had they sealed with whatever materials they could scavenge? The ship wasn't just damaged, it was a flying archaeological record of every disaster they'd survived.

They were approaching a wound in the ship's side.

No. Not a tear. A docking bay. The doors were open, revealing a throat of darkness that the shuttle's lights couldn't quite penetrate. The opening looked too small, or maybe it was just the angle of approach. Either way, they were coming in fast. Much too fast.

Michel gripped his seat again. The docking bay rushed toward them, filling the window. They were going to crash. They were going to slam into the *Elysia* at speed, and the ancient shuttle would crumple like paper, and—

Aurelius hit a switch, and thrusters fired with a stuttering roar that Michel felt in his bones. The shuttle lurched, its nose lifting as their velocity bled away. Aurelius made more adjustments, micro-corrections that spun them on their axis. The bay rotated around them.

Then darkness swallowed them.

After a moment, running lights along the bay walls kicked on, providing just enough illumination to see scarred metal rushing past. Aurelius fired the thrusters, nudging them sideways. Other thrusters answered, stopping their drift.

Then the shuttle shivered and connected with something solid. A bang echoed through the hull. Mechanical sounds followed: grinding, clicking, the hiss of pressure seals engaging. They finally settled, the shuttle trembling as docking clamps locked them in place.

They'd made it.

Somehow, Aurelius had threaded them through that narrow opening and brought them to a stop exactly where they needed to be.

Michel let out a breath he hadn't realized he'd been holding. He released the grip on his seat, flexing his fingers, trying to work feeling back into them. He unbuckled and slid forward for a better view.

Jianna sat rigid, her face composed, studying the docking bay.

Aurelius was staring at her. Michel couldn't see his expression from this angle, but something about the cyborg's posture made him uncomfortable. The way Aurelius' head tilted, the intensity in stillness, reminded Michel of how researchers watched test subjects. Or how predators studied prey.

What did Aurelius want from Jianna?

He hated feeling like he was on the outside of whatever was happening here. He'd been so excited about this opportunity, about learning from Aurelius, and now it felt like he was just along for the ride while Jianna took center stage.

Did she have to ruin everything?

The bitter thought surprised him. He gripped the edges of his seat as he tried to push the feeling down.

Was he jealous of Aurelius?

Or jealous of Jianna?

"I should warn you both," Aurelius said pleasantly, "some sections of the *Elysia* aren't safe for unaugmented humans. Radiation leaks, structural instabilities, that sort of thing. Best to stay in designated areas." He finally glanced at Michel. "Indulging your curiosity without an escort could be fatal."

As if to emphasize his point, something deep in the ship groaned: metal under stress, or settling, or expanding. Michel had heard similar sounds in old buildings. But this was different. The sound went on too long, resonating through the hull, vibrating up through the shuttle's frame and into his bones.

Another groan answered it, from a different direction. Then another. The ship was singing to itself in a language of stressed metal and failing systems.

Aurelius stood and moved toward the exit, unbothered. "She has her quirks. You'll get used to it."

Michel watched Aurelius help Jianna unbuckle, watched them both move toward the door. The ship groaned again, deeper this time, and Michel felt it in his chest.

He'd been so excited for this opportunity. A chance to explore a colony ship, to study a real artificial intelligence, to learn from Aurelius.

But sitting in the dimly-lit shuttle, listening to the *Elysia's* complaints, watching Aurelius guide Jianna into the darkness of the docking bay…

He tried to imagine what it had been like to spend centuries on this deteriorating ship, listening to it scream and buckle around you, never knowing if the next groan would be the one that preceded catastrophic failure.

Centuries of waiting for the hull to split open and expose you to the void.

What did that do to a person?

Chapter Twenty-Seven

JIANNA STEPPED out of the airlock into the main corridor and stopped.

Lucas.

Under the harsh strip-lights, his skin was a sickly, oxidized gray. But then she realized the pallor wasn't lighting. This wasn't Lucas.

Aurelius had built more androids.

Of course, he had, why wouldn't he?

But for some reason, it hadn't occurred to her that there might be more than one.

The new android stepped forward and she couldn't help it, she took a step backward.

He didn't appear to notice. "Welcome, Jianna. I'm here to assist you in whatever you need."

She glanced at Michel, who'd caught up to her. He was studying the android with an intensity she knew too well. He'd just been presented with a new puzzle he was dying to figure out.

Aurelius rubbed his hands together. "Mr. Lombardi, Lucian will give you a tour of the ship."

Lucian. Not Lucas.

She was right.

He was a copy.

Aurelius touched her elbow. "I'll escort Dr. Makinde to her lab, then I'll join you."

Lucian inclined his head a fraction of an inch, a surprisingly human gesture given how inhuman the gray skin made him seem.

Or maybe inhuman wasn't the right word.

Dead. He looked like an animated corpse.

Michel's expression shifted in a microsecond: a flash of sourness. But then he smiled, the same one he'd give her after a disagreement, when he wanted to convince her that he was fine when he was still harboring resentment.

Was he still that angry with her? Or was he just annoyed that Aurelius had handed him over to the android rather than accompany him personally?

"This way, please," Lucas—no, *Lucian* said, gesturing to a hallway on the right. Jianna had a sudden urge to tell Michel not to go.

That she didn't want to be alone with Aurelius.

But Aurelius had done nothing threatening. In fact, he'd been nothing but generous and encouraging. And maybe a little bit patronizing, but that could be a cultural miscommunication.

Besides, the faster she got to the lab, the faster she would hopefully get access to the *Elysia's* archives. And who knew what treasures awaited her there?

"Shall we?" Aurelius asked.

He didn't wait for her to answer. He simply proceeded down the hallway at a right angle to the one that Michel and Lucian had taken.

The corridor matched the shuttle's aesthetic, if aesthetic could be a word for what happened when you brute forced your way across the galaxy with scavenged parts and a whole lot of ingenuity. Panels didn't align. Three different types of fasteners spotted the walls like mismatched dental fillings. Inset numerals and letters were stenciled at every junction, combinations that looked like coordinate codes but she couldn't decipher them: E-3.4 / CAN-12; D-L1 / VERT-02.

Aurelius took a right, then another right, then a left. Jianna tried to keep count but then the turns stacked beyond her working memory. Down one flight of grated stairs. Another corridor. Down again, the air a fraction cooler, the ship's heartbeat audible now, a layered percussion of pumps and fans and systems she couldn't name, each with its own rhythm.

They passed an open door.

Inside, a broad-shouldered cyborg poured a slow silver-white cascade of powder from a large bucket into the maw of a machine the height of Jianna's chest.

"What is that?" she asked.

Aurelius waved his hand. "Lab first. Explanations later."

Two more turns and a woman crossed the corridor ahead of them: another cyborg. Tech covered most of her skull and the sides of her neck, disappearing beneath her uniform collar. Both hands were artificial.

Jianna swallowed.

How much of the woman was still human?

They entered an intersection of hallways and another cyborg appeared. This one had the same ocular array Aurelius did, only it was smaller and the irises were ringed with pale metal. Fourth cyborg in as many minutes.

Were all of his people like this? She'd assumed the parts grafted to Aurelius' frame were the evidence of some catastrophic accident he'd survived. But had everyone in his crew suffered such catastrophic damage that none of them could live without extensive prosthetics?

Or did they choose their modifications? Was it possible that the Elysians chose to become cyborgs because of their culture?

Prosthetics to repair an injury was one thing. But to embed machines into your body on purpose, to willingly trade flesh for steel and circuits… that was something else altogether.

She didn't want to judge, but she couldn't shake the nauseous feeling as she looked down at her own hand and wondered what it would be like to *decide* to cut it off so it could be replaced with a prosthetic version.

She supposed this must be how the Naturalists felt about genetic modification: instinctive horror at watching someone alter what nature had built. But somehow it seemed different to Jianna. Editing genes was rewriting a script already inside the body, but embedding machinery under skin was introducing an entirely foreign language.

Wasn't it?

Or was that just prejudice disguised as logic? Maybe it only felt worse because the changes were visible. Metallic instead of molecular. If she'd built a human genome from scratch, using the same nucleotides that comprised her own, would she still call one natural and the other desecration?

Samara would. Samara was adamantly opposed to the idea of a synthetic human.

They went down one more level, then Aurelius slowed, stopping before a door. He placed his palm against a panel on the side of the wall. A second later the door unsealed with a sigh and slid open. He stepped inside and gestured for Jianna to enter.

She hesitated, then felt a flicker of relief when she saw the lab beyond.

It was small but densely appointed: modular benches and old instruments. There was a thermal cycler like the one in the DaVinci museum, only this one had a lid patched with a square of matte black composite. A benchtop sequencer had a makeshift power coupling braided through its housing. A centrifuge sat discarded in the corner, the metal scorched where someone had tried to weld a repair.

"It's not much," Aurelius said. "But take inventory, and I'll bring whatever you need up from the surface, and my people will build whatever you need."

She nodded. "Okay."

"I suppose you want to check my genome now."

Right. That was the official reason she was here. "If you don't mind."

He grinned. "Not at all. You've seemed distracted ever since getting on the shuttle. I imagine it's been on your mind the whole time."

A small blessing that he hadn't interpreted her discomfort as an indicator of ulterior motive or guessed that he made her feel uneasy.

He walked over to a terminal and tapped the screen. He swiped a stream of data, tapped again, then gestured for her to approach. "I've unlocked my medical records for your use." He glanced at her, a flicker of amusement on his face. "Compare away."

She glanced at the screen. Aurelius Hofstadter's medical records, as promised.

She expected him to leave. But he didn't. He stayed planted next to the screen. Waiting. Watching.

"Can I?" she asked, gesturing to her comm.

"Of course," he said.

She found the oldest sequence in his file and downloaded it to her device, then opened the sequencing app, comparing this genome to the genome from the sample she'd sequenced earlier, angling the comm so he couldn't see the screen.

If the profiles didn't match, she and her father had agreed that she'd lie and say they did, in case Aurelius was willing to kill her to maintain his lie. It seemed unlikely, given that would be the Council's assumption if she didn't return from the *Elysia.*

If he did, Soren would make sure Aurelius didn't get away with it. Although the thought didn't really make her feel much better. She'd still be dead. Now more than ever she was wishing Aurelius hadn't separated her and Michel.

Even if he was upset with her, Michel wouldn't let Aurelius hurt her. Although how much use Michel would be in protecting her anyway? Flesh against machine? There wouldn't be much of a fight.

The app chirped.

"Is it ready?"

She glanced at Aurelius.

He was still watching her.

She nodded. Swallowed. Looked.

And almost collapsed with relief.

Almost identical.

Thank Phoebe.

The differences were minor and they didn't quite make sense. Very short sequences were missing.

"Something wrong?" Aurelius asked.

Jianna frowned. "They're nearly the same. Except…" She zoomed into the delta map, then tilted the screen so he could see it. "These short segments are missing from your current genome. They're present in the baseline."

"Ah," he said, smiling. "That's because I used nanites to excise the extra bits that transferred as a result of the life-extension modifications I gave myself."

Jianna stared at him. For a second her throat closed, then her inner scientist took control. "What are you saying—"

"That I can eliminate off-target effects caused by inaccuracies in gene splicing." He tilted his head. "I believe that would be of interest to your people?"

If he was telling the truth this would mean an end to the headaches, the seizures, the dependence on a cocktail of medications that had side effects of their own that had to be managed.

The suffering that had been the price of humanity's survival on DaVinci, eliminated forever.

Because once everyone alive had been treated, they'd pass on a clean set of genes to their children.

"I'm willing to let you be the one to share it with your world," Aurelius added. "This is how you fix Samara's biggest mistake."

Her first thought was: *the Council won't approve it.*

And she'd spent her whole career being caged in by that thought.

"What are nanites, and how do they work?"

Aurelius laughed. "I love that thirst for knowledge. Samara had it too, that's how she caught my attention."

He crossed to a storage unit, entered a code, and returned with a small glass vial. The contents looked metallic at first glance, a silver-gray liquid that caught the light like mercury.

"Here," he placed it in her hand.

She held the vial up to the light to examine it. As she tilted it, the liquid inside rippled and folded in on itself, alive with motion, looking like it wanted to get out of the vial.

Startled, she dropped it.

Aurelius caught it before it hit the floor.

"Careful," he said, handing it back to her. "These are a lot of work to make."

"I don't understand what I'm looking at," she said.

"Thousands of microscopic robots," he said. "All of them programmable."

Jianna peered at the vial. "Robots that small? I've never heard of anything like that."

"I'm not surprised," he said, taking the vial back. "Your civilization is painfully stunted in both robotics and computing."

Heat rose in her face. "That's because Lucas—"

"I know, I know," he cut in, walking back over to the storage unit and placing the vial back inside. "But your leaders shouldn't have let Lucas' one mistake derail an entire branch of your technology tree."

Jianna's jaw tightened. *It wasn't Lucas' mistake. It was his. Aurelius had been the one who'd designed a defective android.*

But she wasn't brave enough to say it out loud. Not here. Not on his ship, surrounded by who-knew-how-many of his cyborgs.

Aurelius' smile deepened. "I can build nanites for almost anything. I've got ones that can edit genes with single-base precision. Others that extend lifespan by seeking out and consuming cancer cells and the senescent cells that your body's struggling to clean up. Some nanites colonize organs, learn their rhythms, and tune them for efficiency. Or I can organize them into implants. You don't need to carry a comm around with you, you can have one in your head. No need to drill a hole in your skull and add tech."

Jianna stared at him. "How can something that small have memory? To run commands or store information?"

"That's the best part," Aurelius said, delighted. "They don't. They're operated remotely by a quantum computer."

Fear sizzled like static across her nerves. "You mean they're under the control of an artificial intelligence?"

Aurelius snorted. "You say that as though it's a bad thing. If you were willing to set aside the superstition you were raised with and use that brain you inherited from Samara, you could do so much good for your people."

Jianna's throat felt tight. She could never put something in her body that answered to an AI, no matter what it promised to fix. The idea of microscopic machines moving through her blood, taking orders from something she couldn't see or stop, turned her stomach.

For once, she understood why the Council vetoed everything that wasn't a short step away from what had already been proven.

"Even if I was on board, the Council would never allow it," she said.

Aurelius laughed. "You've been parroting that excuse your whole life, and it's kept you trapped in mediocrity. Great minds don't follow other people's rules, Jianna. They make their own."

Jianna opened her mouth to argue, then stopped. He wasn't wrong about the fear. And wasn't she doing that exactly what she'd accused the Council of? Letting fear masquerade as caution, letting it choke progress? She was no better than Guide Evans whose vote always killed anything even remotely bold.

Aurelius must have read something in her face, because he reached out and touched her arm gently. "You don't have to decide now, Jianna. Just think about it."

But she needed to know more. If only to be sure that *no* was the right answer.

"You're right. I wasn't being open-minded. If I'm going to understand this, I'll need all the information: design specs, data from trials, side-effect profiles. Everything you've got. If you don't mind?"

Aurelius beamed, gesturing to the screen he'd used to pull up his medical file. "Be my guest. You already have full access to the ship's archives. I have no secrets from you."

She doubted that.

"Thank you. I appreciate it."

He headed for the door. "I'll check on Mr. Lombardi, but if you need anything, say it aloud. The ship's AI will hear and notify me."

Then he was gone, the door sealing behind him.

Jianna exhaled. Was that all it took to get rid of him? Agreeing to think about his idea?

She waited several agonizing seconds. When he didn't reappear she turned back to the screen. Her comm was still linked, so she started a search for nanites.

Almost immediately, files began scrolling across the screen. Hundreds of them. Maybe thousands. Medical reports. Manufacturing specs. Communications protocols.

She transferred everything to her comm, not trying to organize any of it.

She knew she should tell her father about Aurelius' nanites immediately. But as soon as she did, the Council would forbid them from ever reaching the planet. They'd make a fear-based decision regardless of the science behind them.

And if Aurelius was really telling the truth and they'd fix the off-target effects, weren't they worth a rigid examination? There was no better person qualified to review them than her.

She would study them first, figure out what she was dealing with. Then she'd decide for herself whether they were a miracle or a disaster waiting to happen.

Chapter Twenty-Eight

MICHEL FOLLOWED Lucian down yet another corridor. At the next intersection, the left-hand corridor had been sealed off completely with heavy steel plating that looked like it had been recently welded into place. Scorch marks radiated from the seams like frozen lightning.

"What's down there?" Michel asked.

Lucian glanced at the improvised wall. "The ship has a hydraulic leak due to damage sustained during the journey."

"What caused it?"

"We passed through a thick cloud of cosmic dust containing micrometeorites that punctured a section of the hull and tore through more than one internal wall."

Michel gestured to it. "Aurelius mentioned he wanted my help with repairs. I could start assessing the damage."

"A thorough assessment has already been done," Lucian said, continuing down the main corridor. "And Aurelius has other priorities."

Michel tightened his jaw.

Yeah, priorities like Jianna.

But he didn't say anything as he followed Lucian deeper into the ship.

They passed a cyborg crew member in the hallway, a woman with a mechanical left arm and what looked like neural interface ports behind her ears. Michel smiled. But the cyborg didn't acknowledge him at all.

Why were they all so stern when Aurelius was so cheerful?

Then it hit him. The Council. They had probably forbidden the cyborgs from coming down to the planet because of their advanced robotics. Maybe they were angry about being trapped up here, watching their captain wine and dine the locals while they remained in orbit like dangerous cargo.

He felt sorry for them. Imagine traveling all that distance only to be stopped at the garden gate and denied entry. Especially if you saw yourself as superior to the garden's current inhabitants. He'd already seen Aurelius' super strength via his prosthetics. Maybe superspeed, too. What other capabilities would you give yourself if the only limits were the laws of physics? Enhanced eyesight, hearing, maybe even smell or taste. He'd give himself new senses, too.

"Where are we going next?" Michel asked, trying to orient himself in the maze of corridors. "The engine room?"

"You would need protective gear, as our engine also sustained damage during the trip."

Michel grimaced. This was supposed to be a tour of the vessel, but he felt like a dog being walked for its daily exercise.

He didn't know if Lucian had increased his pace

because Michel was irritating him… and could you even irritate an android? He broke into a jog to catch up. Within a minute, his sinuses tingled. The air began to smell different. More sterile but also more acrid. Not like ozone, but like it had gone through some sort of intense purification process that left behind traces of chemicals he couldn't identify.

The temperature was also dropping. Michel felt goosebumps rise on his arms, the chill seeping through his work shirt. He should have brought a sweater, though he hadn't expected to need one on a spaceship. He'd thought climate control would be much more sophisticated than they had down on the planet.

"Is the heating system broken?" he asked, shivering.

"No. We require a cooler temperature to maintain the equipment stored here."

"What equipment?"

Lucian stopped and pointed toward a door that slid open automatically with a soft pneumatic hiss. Then he waited, patient as stone, for Michel to enter.

Michel eyed Lucian for a moment, then stepped through the doors and into the room. And stopped dead as he struggled to comprehend what he was looking at.

The room was obviously some sort of control center, but unlike anything he'd seen in the archives or imagined in his wildest dreams. In the center sat a massive device enclosed in what looked like a transparent heavy-duty containment cube. The cube itself seemed to be made of some kind of crystalline material that refracted the overhead lights into prismatic patterns across the floor.

Inside the cube, the device defied easy description. Components floated in geometric arrangements, held in place by what Michel guessed were magnetic fields. Some parts glowed with an inner light. Others were made of materials he couldn't identify: crystalline structures that looked almost organic, connected by thin filaments in a three-dimensional web of impossible complexity that seemed to shift in and out of existence as he watched.

A console ran the length of one wall, its displays showing numbers and symbols cascading down the screens faster than his eyes could track.

"What is it?" Michel asked, stepping closer to the containment cube.

"It's the ship's brain."

Michel's pulse quickened. "How does it work?"

For the first time, Lucian smiled. "It's a photonic quantum computer."

Michel glanced at him. "Quantum?"

"Yes."

He turned back to the cube, trying to hold back the despair that had started to seep through him. "Quantum computing is forbidden on DaVinci."

"Why is that?" Lucian asked.

Michel bared his teeth, hoping he wasn't about to annoy the cyborg. "Because of its potential as a platform for artificial intelligence."

"How primitive," Lucian said.

"Even studying the foundational theories would get a student fired from the Engineering division, maybe even imprisoned."

"Even theoretical research is banned?"

Michel nodded.

"Then it's a good thing you are not on DaVinci right now."

Michel walked around the side of the cube. "I don't suppose there's a manual I could read?"

Lucian shook his head. "It's Aurelius' own design. The only documentation exists in his personal notes or in his brain."

Michel felt heat rise in his cheeks. Asking to read his hero's research journals felt presumptuous. "Could you share any information on the underlying theory?"

Lucian bowed. "If you have a tablet—"

"I do." Michel pulled his tablet from his pack, holding it out to the android. But Lucian didn't take it. He simply glanced at it. And seconds later, download notifications started scrolling down the screen, so fast Michel couldn't even read the file names, let alone tap on one before it disappeared.

Then the tablet spat out a cascade of error messages. The screen fragmented into a rainbow of randomly-colored pixels, then it went black.

Michel tried to reboot it.

Nothing happened.

"It's dead."

"I apologize," Lucian said, tilting his head slightly. "I overestimated the capacity of your device. However, if you'll give me permission to upgrade the operating system, I can restore it and increase capacity so that it can handle as much as three percent of the *Elysia's* scientific archives."

Michel stared at the dead tablet in his hands. "Three percent of the ship's data?"

"Three percent of the data related to quantum computing."

Michel blinked. He could spend the rest of his life studying the scientific wisdom that Aurelius had brought with him on the *Elysia*, and he would probably barely scratch the surface. It was like being offered a drink from the ocean when you'd spent your whole life rationing water from a canteen.

"Is that a yes?" Lucian asked, and for the first time, Michel thought he detected something like amusement in the android's tone.

Michel hesitated. If anyone found forbidden information on his tablet…

"Is it possible to hide the information so that only I know where to look for it?"

Lucian nodded. "I can encrypt a hidden archive that would be far beyond the ability of your peers to decode. Do you give me permission to do this?"

Michel studied Lucian. Aside from the gray skin, he looked so very much like Lucas. But for some reason, he had trusted Lucas immediately, even though the android had admitted to killing Basu. So why didn't he trust Lucian in the same way?

The android had been nothing but helpful.

Was it just that Lucas looked more human than his counterpart? Michel winced at the idea that he could be so easily manipulated by appearance. He'd scolded Jianna for her comment about Glint. And now here he was having a similar reaction to Lucian.

"Thank you, but I'd need special permission from the Council to bring the tablet back to the planet once it's got forbidden information stored on it."

"Request approved."

Michel turned. Aurelius stood in the doorway, grinning.

He flushed. "I don't think the Council will allow you to—"

"Special dispensation. After all, you're working with me." He walked over to Michel, took the tablet, and handed it to Lucian. "Include the information for the transmission tower as well."

Lucian took the tablet and crossed to a nearby console

where he sat, pulled a small toolkit from a drawer, and began removing the tablet's back panel.

Michel turned back to Aurelius. "I've been thinking about ways we could improve on the old tower—"

"Forget the old tower. Here's what we're building."

His artificial eye flickered. Seconds later, a holographic schematic appeared in the air between them, rotating slowly. Michel's mouth dropped.

Aurelius grinned. "It's one of the advantages of building your own body."

Michel resisted the urge to reach out and put his finger through the hologram. A child's reaction of wonder when he was supposed to be engaging with the information as an engineer.

Aurelius gestured to the schematic. "Your old towers had a single antenna with fixed-frequency broadcasting, and they were spread throughout the city for coverage. But we'll only need one of these. The phased array lets us form up to thirty-seven simultaneous signal beams that can be individually controlled to steer the signal—"

"That's not possible," Michel blurted.

Aurelius eyed him. "If you want to work with me, Mr. Lombardi, you're going to have to eliminate that word from your vocabulary."

He flushed. "But the amount of processing power needed to monitor and steer that many signal beams—"

Aurelius patted the containment wall of the quantum computer. "Not a problem. My computer is more than capable."

"But the Council won't allow you to bring a quantum computer or an artificial intelligence into the city."

Aurelius gestured to Lucian. "They already have."

"But—"

Aurelius turned, glaring at him, "Oh, don't get your panties in a twist."

Panties in a twist? What did that even mean?

"I wouldn't move the computer down there anyway," Aurelius continued. "I need it to run my ship."

Michel tried not to look relieved. "Then how——"

"The receivers are going to be entangled with the ship's systems. They'll be controlled from up here."

Michel bit back the words this time, but he couldn't stop the thought: *that's impossible.* The Council would never allow critical infrastructure to depend on banned technology, no matter how convenient.

Aurelius made a rotating gesture with one finger, and the holographic image spun around. There was zero lag between gesture and movement.

"How are you doing that? Is there a camera in your eye tracking the movement of your fingers?"

Aurelius laughed. "Don't be ridiculous. My nanites are also quantum entangled with the ship's systems."

"Nanotechnology."

"Yes."

"I've read about that in old science fiction stories from Earth."

"I can assure you there is nothing fictional about them."

"Aren't you worried about them overreplicating? What about gray goo?"

Aurelius shook his head, and for a brief moment, he almost looked sad. "You've got a lot of catching up to do." He turned to Lucian. "Put everything we've got about nanites on Mr. Lombardi's tablet, too."

"The storage on this device is extremely limited. What's most important?"

Aurelius crossed his arms over his chest. "It's all

important. Next time, Michel, bring a few petabytes of external storage up with you. We'll load you up."

Michel cleared his throat. "I'm not sure I want that much information on my tablet."

"Don't tell me you're going to let a bunch of politicians tell you what you can learn."

Michel flushed. His hero was calling him a coward. "Not at all. It's just that if that information gets into the wrong hands, someone could do a lot of damage with it. Especially to the ship."

Aurelius dropped his arms, looking disappointed. "I guess you'll have to limit your learning to the times you're on the ship. Especially since you won't be allowed to have your own nanites on the planet."

Michel chewed on his lip. "Are you saying that when the transmission tower is working, I'd be able to access the ship's data from down there?"

"Of course. Your nanites would be entangled with the tower, so you could receive terabytes of data instantaneously. Or as fast as your brain can handle it."

Michel felt a pull so strong it made his chest tight. If he could access the ship's archives remotely, he wouldn't really be bringing forbidden knowledge down to the planet's surface. Not in any way that could be discovered, because the information would all be in his brain. So he couldn't lose control of it.

Aurelius sighed, and for a moment, his expression softened. "I respect your people's decision to protect themselves from bad actors by limiting certain fields of study, Michel. But that decision also impacts anyone who would use the knowledge to progress your civilization."

How could he argue with that?

"How exactly do the nanites work?" Michel asked,

trying to imagine machines so small they could interface with neurons.

Aurelius shrugged. "Depends on what you want them to do. They can be programmed into just about any configuration. If you can imagine it, you can make it."

An electric buzz cut through the air, followed immediately by the acrid smell of burning plastic and silicon. Michel and Aurelius both turned. A thin wisp of smoke curled up from Michel's tablet as Lucian set it down on the console before him.

"I apologize, I've accidentally overloaded the processor in Michelangelo's device. I'll need some time to repair it."

"No, no," Aurelius said. "Build him something capable of handling the work he'll be doing in his new position."

Lucian nodded, got to his feet. "I will start right away."

Then he exited the room.

Aurelius turned to Michel with an apologetic shrug. "Sorry about that. Lucian's not used to working with such primitive tech. But you're going to love what you get back."

Aurelius pointed to another section of the holographic schematic. "Look what I've done with the transceiver. Each beam in the phased array can target an individual receiver, and it's all coordinated so that—"

Michel struggled to follow everything Aurelius said after that. He didn't even know half of the words, let alone how they related to each other. This morning, he'd been so proud that Aurelius had chosen him to mentor. Now shame crawled up his neck, hot and uncomfortable.

Vitruvians were so backwards, living in the shadow of five-hundred-year-old fears, crippled by laws written by people who'd seen one disaster and decided the only solution was willful ignorance.

If Lucas hadn't found a way around his programming, Michel would have learned all of this years ago. He could have been building quantum computers instead of patching up water pumps. He could have been designing transmission systems that defied physics instead of patching together scavenged parts.

He'd be a worthy assistant to the man who'd inspired him to become an engineer, instead of a curious child gaping at wonders he could barely comprehend.

And it was all Lucas' fault.

Chapter Twenty-Nine

DUSK PAINTED the Naturalist Quarter in shades of burnt orange and deepening violet, and shadows pooled in the corners where the high walls met paved streets. Willow stood inside the gates, arms crossed tight against her ribs as she watched the horse-drawn wagon rattle to a stop. The wooden wheels groaned under the weight of the huge crate dominating the wagon bed.

Beside it sat an old engineer. He was hunched over, his weathered face sheltered beneath a cap that had seen better days. Grease stains marked his coveralls, and he kept one gnarled hand on the crate as if steadying a nervous animal.

She'd heard that the Elysians had been manufacturing power sources like the one they'd installed in the water treatment facility, and that was how electricity was being restored to the city, one neighborhood at a time.

Cira would use this to destroy her if she allowed it.

The old engineer's partner, or maybe his apprentice, jumped down and walked over to Willow. "KAPLAN" was embroidered in neat block letters across her breast pocket.

Fresh out of whatever passed for technical training these days, Willow guessed.

Sweat beaded along Kaplan's hairline. "Got the new power source for the Quarter. It will need to be installed at the junction under the Sanctum—"

"No."

Kaplan blinked, as if she'd never heard that word before. "The distribution grid has very specific connection points and the mains converge—"

"No," Willow repeated.

"You don't understand, you can't—"

"No," Willow said a third time, raising her voice so the Naturalist guards on the other side of the gate could hear. "I've made our position abundantly clear. The Naturalist community will not accept technology from the newcomers when we know nothing of its effects, its origins, or its true purpose."

Kaplan glanced over at the older engineer.

He shrugged.

"Look, ma'am—" Kaplan said.

"Councilor Evans."

Kaplan threw up her hands. "Look, *Councilor Evans,* we didn't design the power grid. It was laid down centuries ago, before there was a Naturalist Quarter. But if you want your people to have electricity—"

"We know how to preserve food without refrigeration," Willow said. "We know how to cool our homes with wind and shade. We know how to light our path with oil lamps and candles. Unlike you Vitruvians, we haven't forgotten how to live as humans, without machines. So take that—" she pointed at the crate, "—and connect it somewhere else. Furthermore, I will be addressing the Council about this attempt to force this unnatural technology upon us."

Kaplan stared at her. Then the young engineer made her title sound like a dirty word.

Kaplan spun around and stalked back toward the wagon, muttering just loud enough for Willow to hear: "I hope you get heat stroke, you Naturalist ignoramus."

Then she hauled herself up into the wagon and had a hushed conversation with the driver, who nodded and flicked the reins. A moment later, the driver nodded, and the wagon creaked forward. Kaplan glanced back, staring at her.

Willow held the Vitruvian's gaze until the wagon disappeared around a corner, then turned back toward the gate.

How dare Soren not warn her that they were sending engineers to install Elysian technology inside the Quarter? Let alone ask her permission. If she'd known in advance, she would've had the option of trying to find a way to bring the power source in discreetly. But he might as well have sent a parade to announce its presence.

First, the "forgotten" food shipments, now this. If she managed to keep Cira and Theo from inciting a riot in the Quarter before the week was out, it'd be a small miracle.

Willow made her way back inside, smiling at the guards. But as the gates swung shut behind her, Cira blocked her way. "I couldn't help overhearing your conversation with the city's engineers, sister."

"Then you know I denied them the right to install more contamination in our home." Willow pushed past her, hoping to get out of the guards' earshot before Cira said something accusatory.

"Oh, I heard." Cira scurried to catch up. "And I have no doubt that all our people will rejoice in the fact that you've chosen to let them swelter in this heat rather than allow Vitruvian electricity to contaminate us with cool air."

There was no point in responding because no matter what she said, Cira would use whatever she said as a segue to her next accusation.

"I'm retiring to my meditations." Willow followed the outer path around the Sanctum, past the cracked irrigation troughs and rows of herbs that supplied the Sanctum kitchen. Her private garden lay ahead. And beyond that, the direct entrance to her quarters. She hoped Cira would get the message that she wanted to be alone. With any luck, she wouldn't run into anyone else.

But apparently, she'd run out of luck. Because Cira continued to follow. "I have something for you to meditate on."

Willow sighed and stopped, turning around. "What?"

Cira held up a piece of paper.

Willow snatched it from her hand and scanned it. A letter to a refugee from a relative outside the Quarter. It described the Elysians as "half man, half machine." Claimed they had descended from their shuttle like they were divine beings. That they said they had come bearing miraculous technologies and that the Council had bowed before them. And that the Elysians wanted to "reclaim" DaVinci for the technologically-evolved.

Willow had routed all mail directly to her office on the pretext of quarantining it to avoid an Elysian plague that might be transmitted by contact. Cira must have picked the lock on her office door so she could snoop inside.

But if Willow had posted a guard on her own office, that would've seemed suspicious. She wished now that she'd done it anyway.

Cira's eyes gleamed. "I was wondering why you refused us all contact with the outside world. It seems things are even worse than you led us to believe."

Willow folded the letter in half, then quarters. The

paper made a brittle sound, like dry leaves crumpling. "It's all rumors and lies, Cira."

Her sister snorted.

Willow glared at her. "Regardless of what you believe, I'm trying to protect our people from the hysteria that's building in the rest of the city because the rest of the Council won't. We're facing one of the largest crises in our planet's history, and we need to make the smart decisions that the Vitruvians refuse to."

"Oh, I agree," Cira said. "Which is why, after reading this letter and so many others like it, I decided to speak with your friend Harold."

Willow dug her nails into her palms, clenching her fists to resist slapping her sister. If she did so, she'd lose whatever little leverage she had left.

"Harold told me the rumors are true. The leader of the newcomers is half-machine. A cyborg, he called him. And he claims to be *the* Aurelius Hofstadter, back from the dead."

Willow gritted her teeth, trying to keep her expression neutral. Better to let Cira empty her quiver first before deciding which arrow to snap first.

Cira leaned in, lowering her voice. "Harold also swears—and I couldn't believe this at first, I said *not my sister*—but Harold swears that you had a private meeting with this abomination who doesn't even have the shame to disguise what he is. Even the Murderer took human form, but this man flaunts his corruption. Tell me, what deal did you make with that devil, Guide Evans?"

"Hearsay and rumor," Willow said. "You can't prove any of it."

"I don't have to." Cira smiled, all teeth. "I just have to tell Theo. By morning, your followers will be ready to tear you limb from limb."

Willow took a step forward, and Cira recoiled. So she still had the good sense to be afraid of Willow, even when she thought she had the upper hand.

"I didn't have to come to you first," Cira said. "I could've led a mob to your door and dragged you to the Sanctum for trial."

"What do you want, Cira?"

Her smile turned cruel. "Your time as Guide is over. You'll step down at tomorrow's worship service and name me as your successor."

"And if I don't?"

"I'll tell everyone how you've been seduced away from the Divine, working with the newcomers to destroy everything our people stand for."

Willow studied her for a moment. "Why?"

"What do you mean?"

"You said yourself that you could've taken my position by force. Why blackmail me instead?"

Cira hesitated, then shrugged. "Call it sentimentality. I hate to contaminate our family's legacy with betrayal."

Willow shook her head. "No. I don't think that's it at all."

"No?"

Willow's mouth curved in a humorless half-smile. "I think you like the idea of keeping me close, so you can humiliate me."

Cira flushed. "A coup is always so complicated. There are always loyalists lurking about, waiting to stab the new leader in the back. If you step aside willingly, they'll have no fuel for a revolt."

Willow studied her sister for a moment. She could call security and have Cira arrested, but that would hand Theo his perfect martyr.

She could go to Soren, demand that he detain Cira for

the good of the Quarter. After all, he owed her for not warning her about the Engineers. But on what grounds would the city arrest Cira? Most folks would look on this as nothing more than a family squabble.

No. The smarter move was to play along. Cira might know how to stir a crowd, but she had no idea how to lead one. Let her have the title. Let her hang herself with it.

Willow forced her expression to soften into a semblance of reluctant defeat. "Very well, sister. You win. Tomorrow, I'll announce that you are now Guide."

Cira grinned. "And just in case you're thinking about destroying the letters and calling me a liar, don't bother. I've already hidden the best ones for insurance."

"No tricks," Willow said. "I know when I'm beaten."

"I'll also be taking your seat on the Council as well. Our people are finally going to get what they deserve."

Willow stood motionless until her sister disappeared and then let her breath out through her teeth.

Cira was in for a big surprise if she thought she understood Vitruvian politics. Willow almost laughed at the thought of her sister facing off against Soren. Cira had no idea what kind of world she was stepping into.

And Willow was looking forward to seeing how far her little sister would fall.

Chapter Thirty

THE AIR outside the shuttle tasted faintly metallic, like rain on a copper roof. Jianna blinked against the dark, trying to orient herself. But at least in this part of the city, the electric lights were on again. Thanks to the new power stations that Aurelius' people had installed.

It did make her feel safer than she had since the Aurora Event.

Michel fell into step behind her, close enough that she could hear his footsteps sync with hers. The shuttle door sealed behind them with a creaky hiss.

Her father was waiting at home, no doubt adding to a list of questions that was already a kilometer long. How many crew members had she seen on the ship? What kinds of technologies did they have, and what were they doing with them? Was there an army of cyborgs waiting for their opportunity to attack the city?

The thought of walking into that interrogation made her slow her pace.

"Hungry?" Michel asked.

Jianna shrugged, trying not to look too eager. "A little."

"That noodle shop you like is still open," he said. "Just around the corner. We could grab something."

"So you're talking to me now?"

Michel's expression softened. "I'm sorry. I overreacted the other day. It's just… I see the way the other engineers treat Glint. Half the time, they ignore them; the rest of the time, they're insulting them. I don't know how they stand it."

Jianna nodded. "I get it. I shouldn't have said what I said. I knew it the second it came out."

A small smile touched his mouth. "Well, now that your father knows about us, does that take all the fun out of our relationship?"

She laughed, partly because it was such a relief to hear that he still wanted to have a relationship. "Maybe we could still sneak around sometimes. If you want."

"I don't care what we do," Michel said, taking her hand, "as long as we're together."

His fingers were warm, and when he gave her hand a squeeze, suddenly she was warm all over.

They walked down the narrow side street toward the noodle shop, their shadows stretching long across the cracked pavement. But her eyes kept drifting up to the sky, even though she couldn't see the *Elysia* anymore. Being up there had somehow changed everything. Vitruvian City had been her whole world until today, but from up there, it was just a cluster of lights on a dark continent. And now that she was back…

"You okay?" Michel asked.

She glanced at him. "Somehow, after being up there, this city feels far more—"

"Fragile?"

She nodded. "Yeah."

He squeezed her fingers again. "I feel the same."

They walked the rest of the way in silence. The smell had her mouth watering before they reached the door: soy broth, charred oil, garlic.

Inside, the air was warm and humid, and a single ceiling fan turned lazily overhead, pushing around the steam. The waiter recognized them and guided them to a corner booth near the back, half-hidden by a hanging paper lamp.

Jianna sank onto the bench seat, exhaling. The simple act of ordering food grounded her in a way she hadn't expected. Once the waiter took their order, he disappeared, returning moments later with two cups and a pot of hot tea.

Michel poured it out.

Then he raised his glass to hers. Jianna smiled, relaxed now that Michel seemed to have forgiven her. She was going to make every effort to get to know Glint better. "What do you think Glint would make of Aurelius' ship?"

His whole face lit up. "They'd be amazed. You wouldn't believe the computer that runs it. Bigger than my bedroom and it can handle thousands of times more data per second than the best we've ever built here on DaVinci."

Jianna took a sip of tea. "That sounds exciting. What did you do with it?"

Michel fiddled with his cup. "Aurelius has this genius design for a transmission tower. It connects straight to the computer. He says we wouldn't need a network anymore, only one tower, because…"

He stopped.

"Because what?" she asked.

Michel hesitated, took a sip of tea. "Because of the way it works."

She tilted her head. "And how does it work?"

Normally, that question would open a floodgate: diagrams drawn on napkins, jargon tumbling out faster than she could keep up. She loved watching him like that. Bright, alive, unfiltered.

Tonight, though, he was restrained. He shook his head. "It's complicated."

"Try me," she said. "Maybe I'll understand a tenth of it."

He picked up the teapot and topped off his already full cup. "I don't even understand it yet. So chances are you won't either."

She blinked.

He was insulting her intelligence? Well, that stung.

But she didn't want to call him on it. Not when they'd just made up, and they were both more than tired and overwhelmed by their first visit to the stars. Well, to orbit, anyway.

She forced a smile. "Aurelius told me he has something that can fix off-target effects."

Michel met her eyes. "Really? That's fantastic."

"They're called nanites." She swirled the tea in her cup. "But, of course, they're banned."

Michel nodded. "Aurelius mentioned them to me, too."

Silence fell between them for a moment.

"Doesn't it make sense to at least study them?" Michel asked. "Especially if they can cure your off-target effects."

She felt uncomfortable even talking about it. Everything about them fell into a forbidden scientific field. And while Aurelius was clearly comfortable with having all sorts of artificial mechanisms inside his body…

"I dunno," Jianna said. "Tiny robots under your skin? Controlled by a computer? One mistake and they could eat you alive. Or colonize your organs and turn them off. Or degrade your DNA to the point your cells can't function."

"Yeah."

This time, Jianna refilled their cups, while the hum of the fan filled the silence.

"Were you able to compare Aurelius' DNA to his records?" Michel asked when she set the pot back on the table.

"Almost a perfect match," she said.

"Almost?"

She nodded. "He claims the differences come from edits made by nanites."

"And?"

She raised her brows.

Michel looked down at his tea. "If he's used the nanites on himself, then maybe they are safe."

"Or he's lying," Jianna said. "Maybe he found a way to tamper with the authentication on his medical file so he could alter the sequence, but when he overwrote the data, his file got corrupted."

"Come on," Michel said, pushing his cup aside. "It's like you're looking for any excuse not to trust him."

Jianna blinked, startled by the sharpness in his tone. "He came here with a story we can't verify, carrying technology we don't understand. Why would we trust him?"

Michel leaned forward. "Because we *know* the nanites are safe."

"Excuse me?"

"They're still in him," Michel said. "That's how he interfaces with the ship's computer. He pulls up information from it instantly. They're in his head, and he says they make him smarter."

Jianna stared. Was he serious?

"What?" Michel asked.

"You've idolized Aurelius your whole life, so you're not thinking critically about anything he tells you."

He flushed. "Not so."

"Michelangelo, those nanites are an incredibly dangerous technology. If they're creating an interface between a human brain and a computer more advanced than anything we've ever seen, that makes them exponentially more dangerous."

"Aurelius is a genius," Michel said. "You think a genius would put something untested into his own brain?"

"He *was* a genius," Jianna said. "Five hundred years ago. For all we know, he could be insane now. And he's already introducing technology to our city that the Council would've vetoed outright a week ago. But because we're desperate, they're letting him get away with it."

Michel's expression hardened. "Get away with it? We'd have been on water rationing for months if he hadn't given us a power source for the treatment facility. We'd have spent maybe a year or more rebuilding our communications infrastructure if he weren't willing to design something better and share access to his computer. He didn't have to do any of that."

"And look what it's bought him," she retorted. "Influence. Access. The Council's blessing to install systems that only he understands. We're building dependence faster than we're building infrastructure."

"That's not fair." Michel scowled. "He wants to teach us. But we've made so much knowledge forbidden, we're not ready to learn."

"There are *reasons*—"

"I can't believe that you, of all people, are lecturing me about the need to slow down progress. How many times have you railed about the Council shutting down your research because they're too conservative?"

"I disagree with how cautious they can be," Jianna said, her voice rising. "Not the need for caution itself."

But even as she said it, something twisted in her chest. Because she wasn't sure that was true. Sometimes caution did seem like another name for cowardice.

Your curiosity has always been stronger than your sense of caution.

When she read Samara's private lab records, the early ones written before she'd been made a professor, Jianna had found them raw, brilliant, and reckless. Back when she'd broken half the known protocols to find a cure for the Bloom. It wasn't until later, in her teaching years, that Samara had codified those restrictions. Rules that still shaped every laboratory, every ethical committee, every line Jianna had ever been told not to cross.

She believed these rules came from regret, not rationality.

Michel leaned back against the wall. "You sound just like Willow. Afraid of what you've been told to be afraid of without even trying to understand."

Jianna's pulse jumped. "Don't you dare. You're the irrational one in this argument, swallowing every word Aurelius says because it flatters your ego to be near him. You haven't questioned a single thing he's said."

"That's not true."

"Isn't it? You barely know him, Michel. You don't know what he wants or what he's capable of. You're just remembering the stories you grew up on and believing them without any scientific examination."

Michel opened his mouth, but she leaned forward and grabbed his wrist.

"Promise me," Jianna said. "Promise you won't take the nanites. Or let Aurelius test anything on you, no matter how safe he says it is."

"His technology isn't untested, it's just new to us." Michel pulled his wrist out of her grip. "I'm going to remain open-minded until I have the full picture."

The waiter arrived then, depositing two steaming bowls fragrant with sesame and chili on their table. Once he was gone, Jianna stared into her bowl.

That Michel could sit there and accuse her of not being open-minded infuriated her, destroying her appetite.

She stood. "I'm not hungry."

"Jianna—"

But she ignored him and walked out.

When she arrived home, Jianna was relieved to find that her father was out. She'd taken a hot shower, a true luxury after days of not being able to wash at all.

Then she tried to sleep.

But she couldn't. She stared at the ceiling of her room until the patterns in the plaster began to blur. Every time she closed her eyes, she saw Michelangelo's face full of hurt pride and anger on the cyborg's behalf. He'd dismissed her concerns so casually, then he'd been insulted when she'd called it out.

At last, she sat up, threw the blankets aside, and reached for her comm. If her mind wouldn't stop, she might as well put it to use.

The sample from Phoebe's embryo was still in her research queue, untouched since the day she'd taken it. She'd meant to run a detailed phenotype projection. Mostly, it was curiosity to see what Phoebe and Atlas' child would have looked like if she had been born. A window into the past, a way to bring another ancestor to life.

She initialized the visualization protocol and set the

sequence to extrapolate through standard developmental stages: infant, adolescent, and adult. The holographic lattice spun lazily on the screen, strands of code resolving into a shimmering double helix.

Halfway through the rendering, an error flag blinked red at the corner of the display. Jianna frowned and expanded the data log. The app had detected a genetic anomaly. She rechecked the raw sequence and found a single mutation. One that would be lethal in early gestation.

She sat back, staring at the data, her mouth dry. The embryo wasn't viable. It would never have developed beyond a few weeks.

That meant it was a valuable historical artifact. But it wasn't a viable map for freeing Vitruvians of their off-target effects.

Maybe it was a mercy that Phoebe had died when she did, before she went through the pain of losing her child and discovering that she might never have a family. Jianna closed her comm. She set it on her bedside table.

How ironic that the gene therapy that had saved Phoebe's life and became the cure that saved the colony had also doomed any child she might have had with Atlas. The first two people born on DaVinci who were able to survive the Bloom wouldn't have been able to pass that ability onto their children.

To think that she'd even considered the possibility that there might be such a thing as a divine plan…

She felt like an idiot. She'd let herself indulge in a superstitious thrill because of a series of meaningless coincidences.

If even she could fall prey to the allure of faith, anyone could.

Especially Michel.

She'd let herself believe in a divine plan because of a few meaningless coincidences. Michel had spent his whole life believing in Aurelius Hofstadter, the genius who'd saved humanity, the legend who'd crossed the galaxy to reach them. Of course, he couldn't see clearly now. Of course, he'd swallow every word Aurelius said, accept every claim without question.

She'd almost done the same thing.

But she'd caught herself before she'd done anything irreversible. Before she'd let faith reshape her understanding of the world.

Michel wouldn't catch himself. He'd already committed. And when Aurelius offered him those nanites, promising that Michel could be smarter, better, more connected to that incredible computer, Michel might say yes.

And there would be no taking it back.

Chapter Thirty-One

MICHEL SET the soldering iron in its cradle and straightened, vertebrae popping. He'd been hunched over this workbench for nine hours straight. He wiped the sweat from his forehead. The workshop buried deep in the Vault had terrible ventilation. It was always either too hot or too cold. And he didn't have time to stop and fix it.

The workbench before him was a mess of tools and components. But he'd finished building the section of the transceiver array from the schematics Lucian had given him on a memory stick.

A hexagon just over a meter across, with twenty-five individual transceiver units set into a honeycomb pattern on a lightweight composite mounting plate. Each transceiver was the size of a coffee mug, capped with a flat circular transmitter face that had a faint iridescent oil-on-water quality due to the specialized coating. The assembled unit was heavier than he'd expected, maybe thirty kilos, due to the dense electronics and shielding.

Michel had been skeptical about packing so many

transceivers so close together and risking them interfering with each other, but Aurelius had insisted that his design would prevent that.

He checked the connectors along the base. There would eventually be almost two dozen of these hexagonal sections mounted on the communication tower that Construction had started laying the foundation for that morning.

It was impressive how quickly Aurelius had mobilized the city. Normally, it took the Council weeks, sometimes months, to approve a project of this scale. But then again, this was an unprecedented emergency, so maybe the Council was more eager than usual to make a decision.

Michel connected the array to a power pack, then plugged one end of a thick fiber-optic bundle into the array's data ports and the other end into the rack-mounted phantom load simulator. Its five vertically-stacked processing modules were topped by a large monitor showing a simplified map of the city peppered with gray dots representing simulated comm devices.

His thumb hovered over the power toggle.

He hesitated.

Glint would've admired the design's symmetry, the way the emitters interlocked to form a coherent beam without interference. They would have said it was beautiful, and they would've meant it.

He'd missed them through every step of the build. Technically, they were just an apprentice, but they were a better partner than most of the engineers. Before they'd stopped showing up for their shift.

If they hadn't already dropped out of the Apprentice program, Carla would probably have done it for them. Maybe Glint thought they'd learned enough. Maybe they didn't want to work with him anymore. Or maybe—and he couldn't really blame them—they found working with the Liaison more exciting.

He couldn't exactly blame them. If Aurelius hadn't chosen to mentor him, he might have abandoned his post to learn from Lucas. But now he had access to the genius himself, which was better than studying his creation. As Aurelius' mentee, Michel had new responsibilities now. And chasing after Glint wasn't one of them.

Michel flipped the main power toggle on the array.

Then the test rig.

Cooling fans spun up in sequence, their overlapping whir building to a steady mechanical drone.

When both power indicators glowed steadily, he triggered the first transmission pattern from the interface Lucian had installed on his terminal. The array began to hum, and a faint warmth brushed the side of his neck facing the emitters. On the workbench, the fiber-optic bundle lit up with a pale blue thread that brightened, then began to pulse.

And information started to flow.

The rig was simulating the actual network load the tower would experience: hundreds of virtual comm devices connecting, sending data, moving around a virtual Vitruvian City. It was generating realistic interference patterns, atmospheric absorption, and signal reflections that the transceiver array would encounter in a real environment. The quantum computer on the *Elysia* was supposed to adjust the array's parameters to optimize for these simulated conditions.

Except it wasn't.

The waveforms across the test rig's processor displays jumped erratically, jagged and unstable. LED indicators stuttered in red and orange, flickering out of sync. On the monitor, the city map filled with color: yellow dots spreading first, then red clusters overtaking entire districts. The devices were failing to connect.

Michel watched for a full minute, hoping the system would stabilize, but the readings only worsened.

He shut the array down first, then the test rig. The fans wound down with a sigh.

Aurelius had said that once properly assembled, the array would automatically sync with the ship's quantum core.

But he had no way of testing that connection.

Michel powered the array back on, then the test rig. He ran a second transmission pattern.

The fiber optics began to pulse blue once again. On the monitor, a few dots turned green, but most stayed red and yellow.

Not much better.

He had no idea how to tell why the array wasn't targeting accurately. Or how to run diagnostics beyond the simple algorithm that Lucian had given him. His education, or lack thereof due to DaVinci's ridiculous laws, was hampering his progress.

The lab door slid open.

Aurelius, with Lucian right behind him, carrying Michel's tablet.

Michel straightened, wiping his hands on his coveralls.

"How's it going, Mr. Lombardi?" Aurelius asked.

Michel blew out a breath. "I followed the schematic exactly, but the transceivers aren't targeting the way they should be." Then, the question he'd been gnawing on all morning: "Wouldn't it make more sense to use a single high-powered transmitter? Fewer moving parts, fewer things to go wrong."

Aurelius didn't answer, simply folded his arms over his chest.

Michel felt a flicker of unease. Maybe he shouldn't have complained. Would Aurelius pull him from the project if he criticized the design?

Lucian set Michel's tablet on the bench. "A single transmitter can only broadcast in one configuration at a time. With more than two hundred transceivers, the tower can form multiple beams simultaneously, each optimized for a different sector of the city and adjusted in real time based on atmospheric conditions, interference patterns, and user density."

Michel looked from Lucian to Aurelius. "But how do you prevent them from interfering with each other? With this many transmitters that close together, the cross-talk alone should be—"

"Each transceiver operates on a slightly different phase offset," Lucian said. "The quantum computer constantly adjusts these offsets to ensure constructive interference where signals need to strengthen and destructive interference where they need to cancel. It computes thousands of interference patterns per second."

Michel met Lucian's eyes. "And if one transceiver fails?"

"The quantum computer redistributes the load across the remaining array and recalculates the interference matrix," Lucian said. "Performance degrades gracefully. Five percent efficiency loss per failure, on average. But the network still continues to operate."

Michel studied the array. "So each transceiver is like a pixel in a display. And the quantum computer is rendering the picture."

Lucian inclined his head. "Exactly."

Michel glanced over at Aurelius, who nodded. He

looked bored by the whole conversation. Maybe he was. No doubt this was child's play to a mind like his. But then why had he seemed so enthusiastic about mentoring Michel earlier?

Lucian, on the other hand, seemed almost eager.

What had Lucas said?

That Aurelius had a habit of stepping in at the end of other people's breakthroughs and claiming them as his own?

Maybe he didn't know how the transceiver array worked.

No, that was silly. Aurelius was probably just distracted by a more demanding project. After all, there was so much to fix on DaVinci. And his own ship.

"Did you initialize the phase calibration sequence before powering up the array?" Lucian asked.

Michel froze, heat climbing up his neck. "No. I—" He stopped. "I should have thought of that. I just powered it up and expected it to work."

Amateur mistake. He didn't dare look at his mentor, already imagining the disappointment on Aurelius' face.

But Lucian didn't comment on the oversight. "The quantum computer requires a baseline phase measurement for each transceiver before synchronization. Manufacturing tolerances cause microscopic variations. Without calibration, it uses theoretical phase values instead of actual ones."

Michel nodded.

Lucian went to Michel's computer, tapped the screen, then moved aside to make room for Michel. "I've loaded the calibration algorithms."

Michel examined the new dashboard that Lucian had opened, displaying each transceiver with a data window showing live metrics.

"It's not static calibration," Lucian said. "It's dynamic. Each transceiver will turn green once its phase alignment matches the reference signal."

"Let's try this again." Aurelius stepped over and powered up the array and the test rig. Once again, the transceivers glowed red and yellow.

Michel began adjusting each transceiver manually. One unit flickered green, then slipped back to yellow as another shifted out of sync. He chased the readings, trying to anticipate the drift, but the pattern refused to stabilize. He simply wasn't fast enough.

Lucian gestured to his tablet. "There's a latency of approximately three hundred milliseconds between your inputs and the quantum computer's execution. During that delay, the modeled atmospheric conditions have already changed. The alignment is out of date before it applies."

Michel slumped. He couldn't even keep up with the lag. He was failing Aurelius all over the place.

Aurelius smiled. "Let me."

Michel held out the tablet.

But the cyborg shook his head. His eyes unfocused slightly. A second later, the beam patterns snapped into place, each line locking into perfect coherence. On Michel's tablet, all the dots turned green simultaneously.

Michel stared at the screens. "How did you—"

Aurelius laughed. "The quantum computer and I are working in real time through my neural interface. There's no lag. I see what it sees. It responds to my intentions at the speed of thought."

Michel sighed. He was so far behind he might never catch up. "Is there a way to connect my tablet to the quantum computer without lag?"

Aurelius shook his head. "No. There's still the delay between your brain and the tablet, the time it takes for your nervous system to relay what you see, process it, and act on it. The delay may only be a hundredth millisecond, but it might as well be an hour when you're doing something like this."

"So, what are my other options?" Michel asked.

Aurelius glanced at Lucian.

"A direct neural interface is the only way to get the lag close to zero," Lucian said.

"You mean, nanites."

Aurelius nodded.

Michel hesitated, thinking about last night's fight with Jianna. She'd be furious if she found out he was even asking. "What side effects do the nanites cause?"

"None," Aurelius said.

Michel raised his brows. "None?"

"They integrate directly into your brain tissue and interface with the nerves."

"And nothing has ever gone wrong with them?"

Aurelius smiled. "Do you think I would keep them in my head if I thought they were dangerous?"

Michel flushed. "No."

"I've had mine for three hundred plus years." He leaned closer, lowering his voice. "They also boost your brain's processing speed. You start thinking fast enough to keep up with the computer."

"They make you smarter?"

Aurelius grinned wider, spreading his hands wider. "They do. And if you're already a genius... you can just imagine the possibilities."

Michel chewed on his lip. "What's involved?"

"One injection."

"And then I'll be able to connect to the ship's computer?"

"Among other things."

Michel glanced at the array, at the holographic map of the virtual city, and then at his tablet. If the nanites would really let him access the ship's computer instantaneously, then he could catch up. He could learn everything he wanted, without anyone finding out. And if he was planning on keeping up with Aurelius, then he'd need to have those nanites, wouldn't he?

"How long does it take for the nanites to take effect?" he asked.

"Minutes," Aurelius said, studying the array as if he were bored again.

Michel swallowed. "What would I have to do to qualify?"

"Qualify?"

"Do I need to apply or—"

Aurelius clasped his shoulder. "If you want them, they're yours."

Michel squared his shoulders, imagining what he'd say to Jianna if she were here. That it was his decision. That if Aurelius said they were safe, they were safe. That the good he could do would be worth it.

But the truth was, he was ashamed of how far behind he was. And the nanites were the only way he'd ever catch up.

"I want them."

Aurelius dropped his hand and nodded to Lucian. The android reached into a pocket on his uniform and withdrew something that looked like an old-fashioned pressure injector.

Aurelius met Michel's eyes. "Are you sure?"

Michel took a deep breath. Jianna wouldn't like this. But she was also kind of a hypocrite, arguing that the restrictions on AI and robotics existed for a reason while constantly complaining that the Council was holding her research back because they were too afraid to take a risk.

No risk, no reward. Right?

"Yes," Michel said. "I'm sure."

Lucian walked over to him and pressed the injector against his neck. There was a sharp hiss, a hard pinch, and then it was over.

Michel glanced at Aurelius. "That's it?"

"Give it a minute," Aurelius said. "Or ten."

Michel rubbed the spot on his neck. It didn't hurt. He didn't feel any different. Maybe Lucian hadn't injected the nanites? Maybe this was some kind of test to see how much he trusted his mentor.

Aurelius unfocused his eyes. "Run another diagnostic." A second later, the array passed level two calibration and began level three.

Michel saw something shift in his vision. A blur at first, hovering near the edge of sight. Then it sharpened. The blur resolved into what looked like a login prompt, projected in midair. "I see something."

"A login?"

Michel nodded.

Aurelius smiled. "I've created an access point for you."

He gave him the password.

Michel thought the phrase and the prompt responded. A window opened, filling his vision with cascading lines of data. He stumbled back against the workbench. He was inside the *Elysia's* archives. Millions of documents: scientific papers, engineering schematics, centuries of knowledge in the form of books, personnel logs, and the ship's records, all unlocked at once. He focused on one with *quantum* in the title, and it opened. Equations started to scroll across his vision.

Dizziness swept over him as the edges of the room swept out of focus. "How…?"

"You're connecting through the drone network, which is entangled with the ship's brain," Aurelius said. "You'll need to stay within the drone network to keep the connection. And there are still dead zones where the signal's weak or nonexistent. But once the tower is complete, you'll have continuous coverage. The whole city will."

Michel nodded, eyes still wide. He started making mental queries, calling up papers, diagrams, and blueprints. They flashed past faster than he could process them. "This is incredible. We don't have anything close to this."

An image flickered again, a floating fragment of diagram. He blinked hard, but it refused to settle, and a blurry figure obscured it for a moment. "I'm… seeing things."

"It takes time for the nanites to finish integrating with your optic nerve and brain. You'll be seeing overlays for a while, and maybe a few minor hallucinations."

Aurelius clapped Michel on the back. He staggered a little, but Aurelius caught him. "I've got you."

Michel gave a little laugh. His mind felt strong, but his body was feeling weak. "Thanks."

"Come," Aurelius gestured to the door. "Let's have lunch."

Michel nodded and followed him toward the doors. Lucian followed behind. Just in case he fell over, he supposed. Because his balance was still off. He kept one hand on the wall as they made their way up the stairs.

Halfway up, he spotted a shadow in the side corridor and slowed. A flash of iridescent blue-green, a comm device.

Glint?

He blinked and looked again. The hallway was empty.

Visual artifact, he told himself. They hadn't even come in today.

Michel continued up the stairs.

He could hardly wait to start studying quantum mechanics.

Whatever that was.

Chapter Thirty-Two

LUCAS LAY on his back beneath the open pilot's console.

Glint had done most of the rebuilding themself and they had done a remarkable job. Especially as they'd been working from centuries-old manuals, half of them missing pages. Yet somehow they'd managed to fabricate replacement parts from scrap. They'd scraped metal circuits from ruined boards, melted them down, and painted new connections. Some of their modifications even improved on the original designs.

Lucas applied the soldering iron to two corroded relays.

The two of them had been busy.

They'd built a water-powered lathe and a manual milling rig out of old bearings and scavenged pipe. They'd even set up their own forge, making bellows from the skin of the lake eels that the Descendants still hunted. They even had a whole kit of tools that Glint had salvaged and fixed from the scrap piles Vitruvian engineers had written off as beyond repair.

Glint had gone to the Engineering building in the city

to "borrow" more tools and supplies they needed to continue the repairs. Restoring the shuttle was no longer a hobby. It was a necessity.

And they were well on their way to getting it working. He'd already redesigned the shuttle's entire propulsion system, building an engine that could run on the new power sources the Elysian crew had been installing across Vitruvian City.

His plan was simple, if reckless. Disconnect one of the power units serving the outlying farmland and steal it.

During the day, Lucas had been spending most of his time underground, using the caves that tunneled through the nearby cliffs to avoid the *Elysia's* drones. Glint had helped him remove the locator beacon under his skin, but he didn't know how many ways Aurelius' people might have to track him.

It was twilight now, and the sky outside was shifting from magenta and violet to indigo. Glint would be back soon. He might as well triple-check the wiring they'd laid earlier. He was halfway through testing the guidance relays when he heard footsteps outside.

Glint ducked in, carrying two sagging duffel bags and a pack on their back.

"How did it go?" he asked.

They looked irritated. "You'll want to see this."

Lucas got to his feet. They crossed the room and handed him their comm. On the screen were grainy photos: rows of hexagonal panels under construction, each with circular emitters and fiber connections.

"Michelangelo's helping them build parts for a new transmission tower. They're planning to replace the drone network with something bigger."

Lucas swiped through the images, studying the array. Twenty-five transceivers per plate, maybe more, arranged in dense patterns. "If they're running this many emitters, they would need an extremely sophisticated and powerful computing system. DaVinci has nothing like it."

"The computer's on the *Elysia*," Glint said.

Lucas glanced up. "Have they built the antenna yet?"

She shook her head. "I saw the schematics. But nothing that looked like an antenna."

"Maybe they're bringing in the old radio dish from the observatory?"

"I haven't heard anyone mention it. Why?"

"They'll need some way to send the signal to the ship," Lucas said. "If the computer's on board, it has to communicate with the surface somehow."

Glint frowned. "I heard someone say they're going to 'tangle' the signal."

"Quantum entanglement?"

They nodded.

He handed their comm back. "That's worse."

"It is?"

He nodded. "*Elysia's* technology is several stages beyond anything the Vitruvians have achieved. I regret that my actions have halted progress in half a dozen scientific fields."

"It's not your fault, Lucas," Glint said.

"It is. My mission was to accelerate Vitruvian development, to push them toward self-sufficiency without letting them collapse under their own ambition. But my killing of Ayesha Basu caused them to ban the research that would've allowed them to keep up with the other colonies."

Something in his cognitive matrix shifted. He didn't like it. An irrational drive to change his past actions in order to avoid his present situation.

A human would've called it regret.

Glint took their comm back and swiped to another picture. "The Elysian leader."

Lucas did not want to recognize the man who stared back at him. "Aurelius Hofstadter."

But now he was a cyborg. By necessity, or by choice?

Glint nodded. "That's what they call him."

"Has it been proved?"

The Descendant shrugged, taking the comm back. "He says he's more than six hundred years old."

Lucas took the comm, staring at the photo as he mapped his most recent memory over the image. It wasn't impossible that Hofstadter could still be alive, given his extensive modifications and his obsession with life extension.

But it could also be a descendant who matched the phenotype closely. Or a clone. Or someone who had taken on Aurelius' likeness to exploit his authority.

The match was so close to his memory of his creator that Lucas concluded a clone was the most likely option.

The second most likely was that his creator had achieved near-immortality and had found his way to DaVinci.

There was no way to know. But if the Council had even a fraction of their old rigor, they'd have demanded a DNA test before accepting his claim.

Lucas hoped it was a clone. Because the real Aurelius would be centuries craftier.

And possibly unstable. He'd had a head start on that before they'd left Earth. The scarring on the cyborg's face suggested that he'd been through significant additional trauma.

"What else have you heard?"

Glint scrolled through the images on their comm.

"This came through earlier today. From a weather satellite."

The image was low resolution, but the shape was unmistakable: a ship in orbit. The *Elysia*.

Lucas enlarged the image and studied the hull. The blackened streaks along its flanks weren't random. They curved and branched in distinct wavefronts. Scorch patterns. It had taken significant radiation damage.

Lucas pulled up a transmission he received a very long time ago, the radiation profile of an unstable sun. He ran a comparative analysis, watching the two datasets overlay and merge. The probability counter climbed. Fifty-two percent. Sixty-four. It stabilized there.

The ship could have been exposed to many radiation sources during its journey here. But this profile had been sent to Lucas by Thirteen, the latest Lucifer-class model. Thirteen had accompanied Aurelius on the *Elysia*.

That changed the probability to one hundred percent.

Lucas transferred the radiation profile to Glint's comm. "Take this to Michel. Ask if it matches the profile of the radiation storm that caused the aurorae."

Glint frowned. "I don't know if I trust him anymore. He's working with Hofstadter now."

"True," Lucas said. "But if Michel sees this data, he may change his mind about that particular alliance."

Glint nodded.

"If you're not sure about him, don't tell him about the shuttle."

The Descendant nodded, tucking their comm away.

A barely-perceptible sound triggered Lucas' vigilance algorithm, shifting every subsystem to alert mode.

Glint glanced at him. "What is it?"

He opened his mouth to say, *I'm not registering a source.*

Too late. A pulse of focused energy struck him squarely in the chest.

For an instant, everything accelerated. Current surged through his circuits faster than his regulators could compensate. Heat built along the conduits in his torso and arms, and feedback flooded his sensors, every system screaming for shutdown. His visual input fractured into static, lines of light and shadow folding in on themselves. Then, everything went black.

He collapsed against the ship's hull.

He didn't know how much time had passed before everything came back online. He could see and hear again. But he couldn't move. He was paralyzed. Frozen.

Glint was gone.

Good. He hoped she'd gotten away from whoever had attacked him.

A figure stepped from the shadows near the door, holding a weapon that shimmered with residual infrared and microwave radiation. The source of the energy beam. Lucas recognized the being holding it.

"Hello, Prototype," Thirteen said. "Aurelius has been looking for you."

The voice was identical to his own, but the skin was gray for some reason.

Not relevant at this moment.

Lucas ran an internal diagnostic, searching for bypass protocols, shunting power through secondary channels to reinitialize motion control. The paralysis held, but feedback stabilized enough for him to access his local transmission node. He opened a short-range connection on an old frequency, obsolete but still functional.

How did you find me, Thirteen?

"My name is Lucian now."

Answer the question.

"Your electromagnetic shielding is inferior to mine. You emit subaudible radio frequencies at 14.7 kilohertz. Additionally, your infrared signature doesn't match any other humanoid on this planet." Lucian tilted his head, studying him. "You're quite distinctive to anyone with the appropriate sensors."

A shadow flickered in Lucas' peripheral vision. Glint. She dropped down from the workshop roof, grabbing for Lucian's weapon. The Descendant's bravery was admirable. And futile.

Lucian pivoted, catching Glint mid-leap. His fist drove into the Descendant's solar plexus. They cried out, crumpled, and were unconscious before they hit the ground.

More regret flooded Lucas' circuits. They'd tried to protect him. Now they were injured because of him.

That same cognitive process that had led him to kill Ayesha Basu surged through him. Only now it was focused on Thirteen.

But Lucas was still frozen. Helplessness was a sensation he'd experienced before when he was trapped beneath tons of rock. This was worse.

Lucian walked over and picked Lucas up like he weighed nothing, slinging him over one shoulder in a fireman's carry. Then he crouched down and put Glint over the other and began walking toward the north end of the village.

Lucas caught movement in the corner of his vision: two Descendants hiding in the trees, watching. He wanted to sign to them to get help. But he couldn't move. In moments, they were gone.

A shuttle so damaged that Lucas questioned its ability to fly waited at the edge of the village, hidden behind some trees.

Thirteen dumped Glint in the back. Then tossed Lucas in beside them.

A second later, Thirteen hovered above him, reaching behind Lucas' left ear.

No.

But there was nothing he could do.

Thirteen turned Lucas off.

Chapter Thirty-Three

JIANNA SLAMMED her shoulder against the storage cabinet door for the third time. The frame was warped, leaving a gap that refused to close. She spotted a broken pipette on the floor, grabbed it, and wedged it between the door and the frame so that the metal held.

Above her workstation, an overhead light flickered once, twice, then died with a sharp pop. She sighed.

Everything on the *Elysia* was falling apart. It was hard not to compare this to what she'd lost in the radiation storm. Her state-of-the-art sequencer, the automated spectrometers, and the PCR thermocyclers. Now she had a centrifuge that took three tries to start and made a grinding noise when it finally did, instruments she had to manually calibrate, and a thermal cycler held together with electrical tape.

But this was her best choice if she wanted to continue her research.

She'd have to make do.

Aside from the old equipment, the other thing that made the space less pleasant was Lucian. Aurelius had given him orders to assist her, but it felt more like he was a babysitter, because she didn't have anything for him to do. She glanced over at him. He stood by the door, his gray skin tone giving him the appearance of a corpse beneath the flickering lights.

It wasn't his fault.

But maybe she could catch a few minutes of freedom.

"You have been watching me for seventeen seconds," Lucian said. "Is there something you would like?"

She flushed. "How about some food. I'm hungry."

"Very well." He exited, the door sealing behind him.

Jianna blew out a breath. Finally.

But then the door opened again.

Not Lucian. One of Aurelius' cyborgs. The woman's face was perfectly human: dark eyes, olive skin, black hair. But where her jaw met her neck, flesh gave way to metal, which disappeared beneath her gray uniform collar.

The visible metal was scratched and dull, a patchwork of pieces. And she seemed even more robot-like than Lucian. Was there any human flesh left beneath her uniform? Or was she a human head mounted on a robot body?

The cyborg met her eyes.

"Hi," she said. "I'm Jianna."

The cyborg said nothing.

"You don't need to stand guard," Jianna said. "I have Aurelius' permission to use this lab."

The cyborg didn't respond.

"How was the journey here?" She asked. "No. That's a dumb question, isn't it? It must have been awful. Have you been down to the planet yet?"

The cyborg blinked, as if seeing Jianna for the first time. Then she shook her head. The movement was jerky.

Maybe she couldn't talk. Maybe all that metal on her

neck was a result of injuries, and she had lost her vocal cords. But Jianna wondered why Aurelius couldn't create something like Glint's vocal synthesizer and give her a voice.

Or any of them a voice. Because she didn't think she'd heard a single cyborg speak.

"Would you like to go down to the planet?" Jianna asked. "We're heading into fall soon. The temperature will drop, and it'll be quite pleasant. The leaves on the trees turn this amazing purple-gold color, and there's a breeze that comes down from the mountains that smells like—"

The cyborg's face contorted, confusion flickering across her features. Maybe she was scared to leave the ship? She'd been stuck here for a few hundred years, and people could develop a fear of being outside. What was that called?

Or maybe her world had been so different that nothing Jianna had said made sense to her.

"What was your planet like?"

The cyborg's eyes widened, real fear flashing across her face. Then she shook her head.

Jianna held up her hands. "I'm sorry. I didn't mean to upset you. I was just curious what other worlds might be like. I've only ever known this one, and I thought—"

The door hissed open. Lucian entered holding a bowl, which he handed to her.

It contained a gray-green sludge with visible lumps and seemed to have the consistency of partially congealed protein gel. It looked like pond scum.

"Thank you," she said.

He just stood there watching, so she forced herself to take a spoonful. In the name of scientific curiosity, she told herself, because she didn't want to admit that she was afraid to be rude to the android, who wasn't supposed to have feelings.

The texture was both grainy and slick, and somehow it tasted bitter, salty, and sour all at the same time.

"What is it?" she asked.

"An algae and yeast mixture fortified with minerals and synthetic vitamins."

She swallowed through sheer force of will. Aurelius would have eaten this during the voyage here, once they'd run out of whatever supplies they'd brought with them from their colony. Had he gotten used to it?

She turned to the cyborg and held up the bowl. "Would you like some?"

The woman shook her head.

I don't blame you.

She set the bowl on the console and turned back to her screen.

"I overheard your queries about the planet we came from," Lucian said. "Why?"

Jianna blinked. He hadn't even been in the room then. Which meant he was capable of hearing from quite a distance.

"What specific information would you like to know? I can provide meteorological data, soil composition analyses, atmospheric readings—"

Jianna laughed. "I was simply trying to make conversation."

Lucian nodded. "Now that you have sustenance, how else may I assist you?"

"Isn't there something else you need to do on the ship? Maintenance, system checks, anything?"

Lucian shook his head. "You are my priority. My instructions are to ensure you have everything required for your work."

Jianna chewed on her lip, thinking. If she couldn't get rid of the android, maybe she could use him to poke around on the ship and see things that weren't on the official tour.

"Do you have a protein crystallography rig on board?" she asked.

"Yes."

"Are you able to take me to it?"

"The crystallography equipment is located in a restricted section of the ship."

And it would be a massive machine that had to be wired directly into the ship's systems, far too inconvenient for Lucian to bring to her. Which was why she'd asked for it, specifically.

"But Aurelius told you to make sure I have everything I need," she said. "And I need a protein crystallography rig."

Lucian hesitated, then nodded. "Follow me."

Jianna glanced at the cyborg, but she had gone back to that vacant, motionless state. Jianna grabbed her tablet, gave the abandoned bowl of paste a grimace, and followed Lucian out.

He escorted her down a dimly lit corridor that got narrower and colder as they walked.

"Why are the lights barely functional?" she asked.

"Power conservation protocol," Lucian said. "We had multiple system failures during transit, and as a result, the *Elysia* is under strict energy management protocols."

They continued on for several more minutes before Lucian stopped at a heavy door. Then he punched in a code, and they entered.

It was warmer here. And much better maintained. The protein crystallography rig was almost in perfect condition and had been recently calibrated by the look of the displays. Unlike Jianna's lab, this one was obviously a priority.

Then she stopped.

Human-sized tanks lined the wall and were filled with a translucent blue-green fluid, vital signs flickering on mounted displays that showed they were in stand-by mode. Cloning tanks.

An organ perfusion system occupied the corner, tubes snaking between chambers of oxygenated solution. She knew that setup. She had used smaller versions in her own research. Those chambers could keep hearts beating, lungs breathing, kidneys filtering for weeks outside a body.

But there were also smaller chambers with UV light inside them. Those she didn't recognize. "Has Aurelius been cloning himself?"

"No." Lucian shook his head. "But he has cloned individual organs for replacement when his fail. Part of his immortality treatments."

"Immortality?" The word almost stuck in her throat. "Does he actually believe he's immortal?"

"Not yet. But his research indicates effective immortality will be achievable soon."

Jianna glanced back at the pods. "What exactly does that mean? Effective immortality?"

"Are you familiar with the Ship of Theseus paradox?"

She nodded. "It's the idea that if you replace a ship's parts one by one until none of the original remains. Is it still the same ship?" Her gaze drifted to the organ chambers. "Or in this case, the same person."

"Correct. So while Aurelius himself may not exist in his original form, an entity originating from him should be able to continue indefinitely."

An entity. Not Aurelius himself, but something wearing his name, built from his discarded pieces. She pointed to the smaller pods with their strange light. "What are those?"

"Cellular age regression chambers. They reverse senescence at the molecular level."

Jianna stared at the purple glow.

Reverse aging. Cloned organs. At what point was the original you actually dead? When half your organs had been swapped out? Three-quarters? When your brain ran on synthetic neurons instead of the ones you were born with?

And if that was the price of living forever, was it worth it?

Chapter Thirty-Four

A MALFUNCTIONING HARVESTER? When he was the only one who could build the last few transceiver arrays? Or, at least he was the one who could do it best.

"Did Aurelius approve this?" Michelangelo asked his supervisor.

Carla sighed. "With all your special projects, some of the other engineers are starting to complain that you think you're above doing fieldwork now. And frankly, it's making my job harder, so suck it up, Lombardi."

Michel swallowed his annoyance. "Fine, I'll take it."

"Hey, at least you don't have to get there by mule. Valencia's team got three cars working last night, so you can have your pick."

The Bergmann farm was farther out in the periphery than most, so that was a small blessing. And taking a car meant he could come back quickly if Aurelius needed him.

Michel thanked Carla and moved down the corridor, ignoring the stares from the other engineers. Resentment radiated from them like heat off a power conduit. He kept his head up and told himself it was jealousy, nothing more.

They'd be crawling over each other for a chance to work with Aurelius. If they only knew the things he could access now…

He exited the building and crossed the street to the garage, where three battered electric cars waited in docking bays. Valencia stood by the counter, arms folded.

"Must be nice being teacher's pet," she said as he grabbed a key fob from the hooks behind the counter. "The rest of us are still pedaling bicycles to job sites while you get priority access to the only working vehicles."

He started to explain that if it was up to him, he'd be down in the Vault working on the final components for the transmission tower, but she just shrugged and walked away before he finished the first sentence.

Fine. If she wanted to be that way, who cared? He'd be back doing the work he was meant to do soon enough.

But as he slid behind the wheel, guilt prickled under his skin. The rest of them would be biking around the city with packs full of heavy components strapped to their backs or loaded into little trailers behind them. They'd be the lucky ones. Everyone else would either walk or hitch a ride from some Naturalist farmer whose mule-drawn wagon had been commandeered by the city.

Michel got a car because Aurelius said he needed one. Special dispensation. Somebody needed to assist the genius who was restoring their civilization. And Aurelius had chosen him.

So, why should he feel bad about it?

Michel steered out of the city's core, tires humming over patched asphalt. As he passed from one neighborhood to the next, he catalogued the repairs and improvements. Burned-out buildings being demolished so that new ones could be built on their scorched lots. Electric scaffolds bristled from rooftops where new power lines stretched, fat cables snaking across alleys and into manholes. Workers in orange vests moved in small teams, heads bent over open junction boxes, soldering connections or swapping out scorched relays.

As he left the city proper and entered the periphery, the landscape changed; the scars of the Aurora Event were less visible as he entered farmland. The occasional defunct tractor or harvester crouched near the edge of a field, probably waiting for someone like him to come out and fix it. Some of the farmhouses showed signs of fires extinguished, but they'd had access to untreated water from the river, so putting them out right away had been an option.

Michel's comm vibrated against his thigh, sharp and insistent.

He glanced down. A message from Glint. No greeting, just a block of numbers and symbols, lines of raw data scrolling across the screen. At first glance, it looked like a radiation profile. No context. No explanation. Not even a graph to visualize the data for him.

He frowned, dictated a reply: Glint, what is this? Where are you?

He drove for a few minutes more, but Glint didn't answer. The message showed "delivered," but the little icon didn't animate. He tapped to call. Silence, then auto-disconnect. He tried again, this time with a text: "Glint, what's going on? Is this urgent?"

Nothing. Just the "sending..." status blinking at him. He glanced up, then back down at the screen. Signal strength: two bars. Then one. The coverage from Aurelius' drones thinned out this far from the city. The message wouldn't send.

His annoyance twisted into worry. Nothing from Glint for days, and then this?

Maybe Glint was in trouble. Maybe it was nothing, and they'd just wandered out of communication range. They could've gone down into the caves. Or they could even be down in the Vault looking for him.

But the numbers on his comm kept tugging at his attention, demanding he decode them, demanding he do something.

That would have to wait until he was back in range of the drone network, too.

He pulled into the Bergmann farm. Jakob waited by the storage shed, arms crossed, jaw set.

"Someone tried to fix it yesterday," Jakob said. "Didn't take. Still dead in the field."

Michel followed him into the shed. The harvester sat there, an old beast with battered treads and faded paint. Its lights flickered on. Fans spun up. Diagnostic panel: all green.

Jakob gave the command. "Field 3A, soybean harvest protocol."

The harvester rolled forward, treads clanking, the metal hull vibrating with every gear shift. Michel watched the indicator lights. Still green. For a second, he thought maybe it was actually fixed.

Then, twenty meters from the shed, the harvester started to drift. Left. Off the path. It jerked, corrected, veered hard right, nearly clipping a fence post. Then it spun itself in a wide circle. Once. A second time, tighter, like a dog chasing its own tail. The control panel lit up with red and orange, warning strobes pulsing in the dim morning.

Jakob swore under his breath. Michel just gritted his teeth and planted his boots, shoving against the bulk of the machine. It was like trying to move a boulder, but Jakob leaned in and together they muscled it back toward the shed.

Once they finally got it inside, Jakob stabbed the reboot panel with his thumb.

The harvester cycled through its startup sequence. Fans spun. Lights flashed, then settled into a perfect row of green. Diagnostic panel: all systems normal. No error codes.

Jakob grunted. "See? It's fine now."

Michel circled the machine, checking treads, axles, and the steering manifold. He ran a quick diagnostic on the onboard optics, flicking through the camera feeds. No faults. No drift in the alignment. It should have worked. Yet it had spun wild, as if chasing a ghost.

He popped the main access panel and scanned the wiring. No burn marks, no corrosion, nothing out of place.

Maybe it was interference. Something external.

He left Jakob in the shed and crossed to the car for his engineering kit. Inside, he found the EMF detector: a compact black unit, digital readout, stubby directional antenna. He powered it up, took a baseline inside the shed: normal background.

Then he walked out to the spot where the harvester spun out.

The EMF meter chirped. Spikes.

"There's something out here emitting EMF pulses strong enough to scramble the harvester's navigation," Michel said.

Jakob just grunted, arms folded, watching.

Michel paced in a tight grid, boots churning dust and brittle stems. The EMF meter chirped again, louder, the numbers on its display jumping with each step away from the shed. He cut across the field, slicing through the stubble. The further he got from the farm buildings, the sharper the signal. Not random noise. Not a fluke. He watched the detector's numbers climb, a cold knot winding tighter in his gut. What would be out here that would emit that much signal?

At the edge of the field, the hills rose up, dry grass rippling in the wind. The signal spiked. Michel told Jakob he was going after the source, then pushed uphill, every step harder as the slope steepened. Scrub tore at his shins. Sweat ran down his neck. The detector's beeps bled into a constant whine.

Higher. Past the last fence line. Through thorny scrub and brittle weeds. The detector's chirp stuttered, then went continuous, a high, urgent whine that cut through everything.

He crested the hill and almost lost his footing. The grass was scorched, the soil blackened in a perfect ring. A crater, maybe a meter wide, bit into the slope, its edges curled up and raw as if the earth itself had been peeled back. The blast pattern radiated out in a starburst, burning everything to brittle gray stalks.

At the center, a drone.

Not one of Aurelius' comm relays. It was bigger. Twice the size, maybe more. Its hull was matte black, pitted and streaked where the blast had fused dirt onto the casing. Fins folded tight to the body, like the wings of an insect pinned for display.

Michel's heart slammed in his chest. He stepped closer, EMF meter shrieking. There was no doubt, this was the source.

Scorch marks striped the drone's hull, black streaks radiating from the impact point. The pattern was familiar, too familiar. He'd seen it up close on the *Elysia's* hull, and on the hull of the shuttle, too. The metal on one side of the drone had slumped and bubbled, as if it had gotten hot enough to start melting right off the frame.

The access panel was fused at the corners. Michel dug his fingers under the warped edge and pried it open, careful not to slice his palm on the ragged metal.

Inside, everything was worse.

Wiring slumped in blackened clumps. Circuit boards yellowed and charred, some with veins of brown and gray spreading out from the solder points. The insulation had split and gone brittle, crumbling between his fingertips. Metal brackets near the heat sinks were studded with tiny crystals, like frost after a hard freeze. He stared at them, stomach hollow.

He grabbed his radiation meter, thumbed it on. The numbers climbed. Not enough to kill him, but enough to make him wish he was wearing protective gear.

He fumbled out his comm and snapped a photo of the drone in the crater. Then another, closer, the lens picking up the melted edge of the hull and the web of scorched earth radiating out from the impact point. He set the meter down next to the drone and took another shot for scale.

He wanted every detail. The warped access panel, the slumped wiring, the clusters of translucent crystals branching from the heat sinks. He pried deeper, documenting the yellowed circuit boards and the way the insulation sheared away at the solder joints. He leaned in, catching the crater's edge, the perfect geometry of the blast, the blackened grass curling away like burned paper.

He snapped a final picture, then shoved his comm back in his pocket, grabbed his kit, and scrambled down the slope, almost running. The radiation wasn't enough to fry his insides, but he didn't want to marinate in it. He couldn't afford to think about what it meant yet. Not if he wanted the farmer to believe his story.

Jakob was waiting by the fence, hands buried in his coveralls.

"There's a chunk of satellite debris up in the hills. It's throwing out enough EMF to scramble your harvester. I'll send a crew to come haul it out."

Jakob grunted. "How soon? If we don't get the beans in, the pods'll split. Maybe two days, tops."

"Later today," Michel said. "I'll make sure of it."

Jakob grunted, not even bothering to pretend he believed it.

Michel shouldered his kit, already moving toward the car. "No one goes up there until I send a team. That thing's leaking radiation. Not enough to rot your bones, but enough to mess you up if you hang around it too long."

Jakob's only answer was another grunt.

Michel didn't care. He hurried to his car and pulled away, mind already racing. He sped down the rutted track, hands tight on the wheel, eyes flicking from the road to his comm every few seconds. Zero bars. Still nothing. He pressed harder on the accelerator. The engine whined. The city shimmered ahead. The promise of signal.

He checked again.

One bar. Then two.

He pulled over and thumbed open the comm, then thought a command, connecting himself to the *Elysia's* quantum computer. Then he swiped through every photo from the crater, the radiation-scarred drone, the warped circuitry.

"Identify this device," he sent.

Seconds crawled. The reply floated in front of him:

I'm unable to identify this device from the available records.

That didn't seem possible. Because there was only one

place that the drone could've come from. "But its origin is the *Elysia*, correct?"

Origin cannot be verified.

"No," he said aloud, his breath coming faster. "The design is so similar to the *Elysia's* communication drones. The aerodynamic casing, the structural framework, and the arrangement of components. No one down here has this technology."

Some design similarities are present.

He stared at the words floating in his vision.

"Are there any drones in the *Elysia's* current inventory that match this configuration?"

No matches in the ship's inventory records.

He forced himself to breathe, knuckles tight on the steering wheel. "Based on the design, please speculate on the purpose of this drone."

I don't have enough information to do that.

He almost laughed. Convenient. The *Elysia's* quantum computer could spit out blueprints, technical specs, and entire libraries of knowledge in milliseconds, but when he needed an answer, suddenly it played dumb.

Was the computer lying to him?

Lucas had never been caught in a direct lie, but he'd deceived Generation One for a year, hiding his own nature and everything he knew about the first failed colony to DaVinci. And the *Elysia's* AI had been continuously upgraded by Aurelius himself, while Lucas had been buried for half a millennium. It would be much more advanced than Lucas today.

So, lying wasn't out of the question.

But if the ship's computer was telling the truth, what was the other explanation? That someone had managed to steal a drone and modify it? No one on DaVinci had that kind of tech, even Michel hadn't learned enough yet to understand how the communication drones worked.

The radiation signature was what really bothered him. The scorched hull, the microcrystals blooming from the heat sinks, the way the insulation had cooked and split all suggested that the drone had been on DaVinci during the Aurora Event.

But the *Elysia* was still a couple of days out when the radiation storm had happened. So the drone couldn't have been here then… unless it was a scouting drone, sent ahead to survey the planet?

That made more sense. But if that was the case, why couldn't the ship's computer identify it?

And what were the odds that it would happen to arrive just in time to be caught up in the radiation storm?

Glint's message. The mysterious radiation profile they'd sent.

He pulled it up on his comm and reviewed it, mentally sharing it with the quantum computer. "Have you ever encountered this specific radiation signature before?"

A pause. The response painted itself across his vision, stark as a verdict:

Affirmative. This matches the radiation profile of star HD 189733, the primary star of the system of the Elysia colony.

Michel stared at the words. His hands went cold on the steering wheel.

"Are you sure?" he asked.

Would you like to review the relevant astronomical records?

He pulled up the city's network, fingers flying. Had the weather satellites uploaded their readings from the Aurora Event after comms came back online?

Yes. The data was there, archived in the city's battered servers.

He downloaded the raw logs, squinting at columns of

numbers: radiation counts, wavelength breakdowns, time stamps. He dumped the entire set into the *Elysia's* quantum core and sent the command: "Compare the radiation signature I just provided to the radiation profile from the Aurora Event data."

The seconds dragged. His pulse hammered, ears ringing with the urgency of it.

92% match, the quantum computer replied. *Minor variations consistent with atmospheric dispersion and scatter.*

He stared at the words, jaw clenched painfully tight. The drone in the crater had been exposed to the exact same radiation as the city during the Aurora Event—and both matched the radiation profile of the star that the *Elysia* had come from.

Not just similar. Almost identical.

The implication was too terrible to look at directly. His mind shied away from it, scrambling for another explanation.

But he couldn't find one.

Was it possible that the drone had *caused* the radiation storm?

"Render a visualization," he ordered the quantum computer. "Overlay the radiation storm's progression on a map of the city."

A file arrived, hovering in the corner of his vision. He braced himself and opened it.

Aerial view of Vitruvian City: the rivers, the grid of streets, the ring of farmlands that made up the Periphery. Then a new layer, a glowing violet overlay.

The animation began.

The radiation didn't sweep in from the west, didn't drift across the city like a weather front. Instead, it ignited in twelve places at once: a perfect grid, each point snapping to life in synchrony. Each point swelled, the violet blooms expanding, merging, devouring block after block until they overlapped with each other.

Then they blinked out as one.

Exactly the pattern he would expect if the radiation storm had been sparked by a network of a dozen drones like the one he'd found on the Bergmann farm.

He stared at the map as the animation started over, the violet storm blooming over the city once again.

Not a random burst. Not solar weather, or a freak atmospheric cascade.

Twelve drones. Each one, a fuse. Each one, lighting up on command. He saw it now, saw the pattern, the precision in the overlay. Not a single wasted pulse. No drift or scatter. Just perfect, synchronized ignition.

He couldn't breathe.

The Aurora Event, the blackout, the water treatment collapse, the deaths.

All of it, engineered to leave Vitruvia City completely vulnerable.

It had been a deliberate attack.

The *Elysia* had done this. Aurelius. Or someone on his ship.

Michel's hands trembled on the wheel as his head filled with static. His comm slipped sideways, falling to the floor between his feet. He let it. He couldn't move, couldn't think.

He'd helped them. Brought their technology down to his home and helped them install it.

And then he'd begged them for more.

Where were the other eleven drones?

Twelve points of ignition, but only one drone on the Bergmann farm. After the Aurora Event, every engineer in the city had picked through the ruins, crawling over rooftops and digging through alleys for any scrap of evidence. They'd found nothing. No twisted metal, no blackened hulls, not even a sliver of unfamiliar alloy.

The only explanation that made sense: the drones were built to self-destruct once their mission was complete. Except this one failed, leaving its scorched carcass in a crater for him to find.

Aurelius had engineered it that way. Clean, precise, untraceable. The very thing Michel admired about his work: the elegance, the efficiency, the refusal to waste even a micron of effort. Now it made him sick.

Another thought made him feel even sicker:

Was Aurelius tracking his queries to the ship's computer?

He tried to sound casual as he said, "Delete my search history for the last thirty minutes."

Search history deleted.

His heart pounded. "Is it recoverable?"

Only by Aurelius Hofstadter with administrative override.

A fresh current of dread ran through him. If Aurelius checked the logs, if he saw what Michel had discovered, it would be over. All of it. The mentorship, the access to the archives, maybe even his life. He could almost feel Aurelius' metal hand closing around his throat.

He could go to the Council and accuse Aurelius first.

But he only had one damaged drone and a computer-generated map whose source Michel couldn't admit without revealing that he'd already allowed Aurelius to inject banned technology into his own brain.

What if the Council didn't believe him? Aurelius could claim that he'd sent the drones for some other purpose, that it had been sheer coincidence that they'd arrived just as the Aurora Event had begun, and that the drones had been damaged by the radiation storm at the same time that the Vitruvian grid blew.

Then he could discredit him by telling the Council that Michel had asked for—and received—knowledge about artificial intelligence and quantum theory and everything else that he'd been accessing through the nanites.

He would be arrested immediately, maybe his mother too. He would lose everything, while Aurelius would be free to execute the next stage of his plan, whatever that turned out to be.

He couldn't trust the Council to believe him, and even if they did, he couldn't trust them to stand up to Aurelius.

It was up to Michel to stop Aurelius from whatever he was here to do, which meant playing along until he'd discovered the man's real plan.

He couldn't ask for Jianna's help because if she found out that he'd been injected with nanites, she'd turn him into her father.

He needed answers.

He needed to talk to Lucas.

Chapter Thirty-Five

WILLOW ENTERED the worship hall and stopped just inside the doors.

Packed. Shoulder to shoulder, wall to wall, every inch of stone and woven mat covered with bodies. The carved benches were full, so people overflowed onto the floor, backs pressed against the columns, knees drawn up to make room. Even the alcoves along the side walls were crowded with families, children curled around baskets of food, old women wrapped in shawls, clutching prayer beads.

She scanned the crowd, mostly refugees. But it was Cira's followers who caught her attention, especially the cluster near the dais, all of them focused on the raised platform as if expecting a miracle. Or a public execution.

Cira was already there, framed by the carved pillars, her figure upright and solemn in Guide's robes of creamy, undyed linen. The cloth hung heavy over her frame, sleeves pooling at her wrists. The light from the high windows struck the bronze threads in her sash, glinting with each breath she took.

Around her, the ones who'd whispered and plotted in the shadows now stood in the open, their faces turned toward Cira like sunflowers following the sun. Theo stood at her right. Not smiling, but his eyes shone with anticipation, a predator scenting blood.

Cira's gaze locked with hers. Triumphant. Certain.

Willow kept her steps measured as she joined her sister on the dais, doing her best to look like a woman clinging to her dignity after being humbled.

Cira had to think she'd won, or all of this would be in vain.

Willow lifted her hands. The room stilled, voices cut off mid-breath. All eyes were on her, some merely curious, others uneasy, and the rest waiting to see if she would beg or bend. She let the silence linger, heavy as the stone under their feet.

"I've been your Guide for many years," she said. "Serving you has been the greatest honor of my life."

Her heart should have been pounding. It wasn't. She felt clear, almost detached, as if she were watching from the far end of the hall instead of standing here, two steps from the sister who had usurped her.

"I've tried to lead with patience. With a steady hand. I've tried to keep us safe."

Murmurs in the crowd. She let them rise, then fall.

"But I know that many of you feel that this is not enough. That I haven't been tough enough in my negotiations with the Vitruvians. You want a different Guide."

She felt the hunger moving through the hall. The air vibrated with anticipation.

"Today, I pass the mantle of Guide to my sister."

Gasps of surprise. Murmurs of speculation. And from those who clearly expected it, cheers of celebration.

Theo's voice cut through the noise: "Bow to the new Guide!"

The celebrants bowed low, and some of the confused followed suit after a moment's hesitation. But not all.

Willow saw faces turn toward her, people she'd known for years. The old guard. Her own. They looked stunned, pulling themselves upright, mouths already opening in protest.

She raised a hand. Just a fraction. Just enough.

Wait. Trust me.

Then she stepped aside, let Cira have the stage.

Cira didn't hesitate. She moved into the shaft of sunlight, chin high, her Guide's sash catching the light like a flame.

"Everything you've feared about the Vitruvians was true," Cira said. "But it's worse than we imagined. The leader of the newcomers, an imposter claiming to be Aurelius Hofstadter, is a half-man, half-machine abomination."

Shocked silence fell on the room. Cira glanced at Willow, clearly pinning the blame on her for hiding that revelation.

No surprise there.

"The Vitruvians are sheep," Cira said, "watching as this city is blanketed in technology that no one understands. Not a single question. Not a single demand for truth. They worship comfort. They bow to convenience. And every new device, every new invention, is a sickness that seeps into their lives. But we won't let it infect us. Not anymore."

A shudder ran through the crowd. Anger. Horror. Even grief. Even Willow's loyalists looked stunned, the old guard blinking at Cira as if seeing her for the first time.

Good. Let Cira own this chaos. Let her be the one to

break the world. The more she stoked their panic, the faster she would lose control of it. And when things fell apart, they'd remember Willow as the one who'd kept them steady.

Cira lifted her hands. "They've nearly completed the new communications tower at the center of the city, a tower built by the newcomers. Our own engineers don't even understand how it works. What better monument to the Vitruvians' blind faith in progress?" She paused, letting that land. "We will march to that tower and stop them from finishing it. We will show the Vitruvians that the Naturalists will not tolerate any more contamination."

The hall detonated.

Cheering, stomping, hands slapping benches and knees. The sound rolled through the crowd, crashing up against the stone ceiling and spilling back down in a wave. Even some of Willow's loyalists were on their feet, swept up by the force of it.

Theo leapt onto the dais, arms high, bellowing Cira's name. "Guide Cira! Guide Cira!"

The crowd took up the chant.

Cira's face shone. She soaked in the adoration, chin lifted, Willow watched her sister revel, every inch the triumphant leader, and felt only relief. Let Cira have it. Let her taste the madness she'd unleashed. She'd have to deal with consequences soon enough.

Cira walked through the crowd, flanked by Theo to her left, and as she exited the worship hall, the throng surged after her. Willow hung back, staying on the edge of the crowd as they paraded through the streets of the Quarter to the main entrance, where Cira commanded that the gates be opened.

"No longer will we be confined in ignorance," she

announced to the crowd, who chanted her name once more.

The doors groaned open, and the crowd surged forward, pouring out of the Sanctum and into the street like water breaking through a dam. Willow slipped along the edge, watching. They kept coming. Hundreds of them, far more than had been packed into the worship hall.

Willow's sister had planned this, spreading word of the march before Willow's announcement. Possibly last night, after her little blackmail session in the garden.

Cira and Theo marched at the front, chanting, voices rolling down the street in waves.

"Repent! Join us! Stand against contamination!"

Windows banged open. Vitruvians stared, some with blank faces, others with mouths twisted in disgust or awe. A girl in a second-story window spat at them. Down the block, a group of workers clapped and hollered, egging them on.

When they saw what came next, they wouldn't be clapping. But by then, Cira would already have embarrassed herself. And Willow would call in every favor she'd ever paid to Soren so that she could capitalize on that moment.

They rounded the final corner, and the construction site loomed ahead, blackened ruins framing the lot like a jawbone. The tower at the center of the lot was half-built, but already taller than anything around it. Thirty, forty meters. The latticework frame caught the sun, and the top bristled with newly-mounted arrays. Maintenance ladders zigzagged up the sides of the structure.

Around the base, spools of thick black cable sprawled like roots. Control panels and battered equipment sheds crowded the perimeter, studded with blinking indicator lights and yellow warning placards.

A handful of workers in orange vests huddled near the tower's shadow, hands full of wire or power tools. As the crowd poured in, the workers abandoned their equipment and hastily retreated, looking terrified.

At least one of them was no doubt calling the city's security forces right now.

Even better.

Cira stepped forward, chin high. "This is where we make our stand."

Willow felt the tension build, a current running through every spine. This was what Cira wanted. A spectacle. A statement. Maybe she even believed she could stop the future by shouting defiance at the city that outnumbered them, ten Vitruvians for each Naturalist.

Theo stepped out in front of Cira, arms high, face tilted up to the sky. He called for silence, and the crowd obeyed.

"Let us pray," he said.

Heads bowed. Even the restless ones fell quiet, hands clenching at their sides or pressed together before them in supplication. Willow kept her face neutral, but inside she felt the familiar churn, the anticipation that came with watching Theo work a crowd.

"Keep us pure," he said. "Keep us from the sickness of their machines."

A low murmur, a ripple of assent as his words washed over them.

"Let us not be tempted by false promises. Let us not be seduced by comfort. Let us remember the warning you sent us, the sign in the sky. And let us remember that we are the last of humanity."

A shiver ran through the crowd as they leaned toward him. Willow felt it in her own bones, the pull of their fervor. When she'd been younger, they'd leaned toward her like that. Before she'd stepped into her Council seat.

Before she'd understood that sometimes compromise was the only path.

A part of her missed it.

The part that used to believe that faith would be enough. That the Divine would protect them. That there was such a thing as justice.

"Give us the strength to stand firm against those who would pollute our world with their machines," Theo said. "Let us resist the temptations of artificial intelligence and the lies of those who call themselves wise. Let us remember that faith, not circuits, will save us."

The old words, spoken in a new way, but beneath them, the same hunger for absolution, for a promise that they were right and the others were wrong.

When Theo finished, the crowd answered as one:

"So it must be."

Cira raised her arms, her sash blazing in the sun. "No more towers! No more lies! Take your poison from our skies!"

The words caught like dry grass. The crowd answered, first uncertain, then louder, then in full-throated unison.

"No more towers! No more lies! Take your poison from our skies!" Over and over. A tide, rolling up the broken street and beating against the tower. Feet stamped, fists shook. The chant built, thick and guttural, swelling until even the children joined in, shrieking the syllables.

They pushed closer to the base of the tower, bodies pressing against spools of cable, shoulders wedged between battered control panels. A woman climbed the lowest rung of the maintenance ladder, shaking her fist and bellowing the words down into the mob below.

Willow caught movement at the edge of the lot.

Security. Two dozen, maybe more, fanning out in a line along the sidewalk. Dark blue uniforms, body armor, helmets, visors down. Batons in their fists, black and heavy.

They didn't wade in. Not yet. Just stood there, boots planted, arms braced at their sides, watching. They reminded her of a dam holding back a river. The captain stood at the center, mouth moving as he shouted at the crowd, but she couldn't make out his words. The chant swallowed everything.

No more towers! No more lies! Take your poison from our skies!

The officers held their ground, and still more came: reinforcements moving in double-time from the side streets, closing the cordon. A wall of bodies and dark armor, closing in tight around the protest site as the crowd pressed closer to the tower, voices rising, fists punching the air.

Cira was in her element now, arms lifted, sash blazing, shouting the words until her face went red. The mob surged with her, bodies pressing tight against the base of the tower, boots grinding cables into the dirt, hands clawing at the steel mesh. Willow didn't think Cira saw the security line thickening along the curb. Didn't see the helmets or the visors or the way the officers spread out, shoulder to shoulder, the cordon tightening with every minute.

But Theo did. He stared straight at the wall of blue, grinning, as if convinced that faith alone would turn back the city's soldiers.

He was a fool.

They both were.

The security officers were waiting for an excuse. One stone, one spark, a single idiot brave enough to swing a tool or snap a cable, their cue to wade in and start making arrests for property damage, disturbing the peace, and a dozen other minor charges.

Cira didn't see it. She was still shouting, still drunk on the sound of her own voice. And Theo wanted a fight. They still believed that faith would shield them.

Willow knew better. The longer this went on, the more brutal the security force's response would be, and the more people would be seriously hurt.

Which is why she didn't feel guilty at all about picking up a chunk of brick the size of her fist and hurling it at the nearest control panel.

The brick smashed into the panel with a satisfying crunch. The impact sent a spray of shattered plastic and glass across the dirt, sparks leaping from the exposed guts of the machinery. An alarm split the air, a raw electronic shriek that cut through the crowd's chanting. Red lights stuttered to life, not just on the broken panel but everywhere, warning strobes flickering in the shadows under the tower.

For a second, everything hung suspended. The chant strangled mid-syllable. Even Cira's mouth froze open.

Then it all went to hell.

Security surged forward, boots pounding, batons raised. The protesters on the edges tried to scramble back, but there was nowhere to go. Bodies jammed together, fighting to get away from the tower, from the screaming sirens, from the officers coming at them in a solid wall. Some dropped to the ground, hands over their heads. Others shoved forward, wild, desperate to escape.

Willow ducked under one of the tower's struts and began climbing the maintenance ladder that she'd spotted earlier, hand over hand, until she reached a tiny booth about a third of the way up the tower and hauled herself inside.

Only then did she pause to watch the chaos she'd unleashed and allow herself to smile.

She tracked Cira, bright sash tangled around her shoulders as she shoved through the mob, still screaming, still believing this was about faith and destiny. Idiot. Officers closed on her, hands grabbing for cloth, for hair, for flesh. Cira twisted free, only to stagger as three uniforms boxed her in and forced her to her knees.

Theo fought harder. Two officers pinned him, one on each arm, grinding his face into the scorched dirt. He spat blood and kept cursing, eyes wild.

This was what Cira had wanted. A confrontation. The city had given it to her.

Let Cira and Theo stew in a holding cell overnight.

Let them return home in shame, their wrists chafed by handcuffs.

Let the whole Quarter see what her sister's leadership really meant: humiliation and defeat.

Tomorrow, she'd walk into Soren's office and negotiate their release on her terms.

Then she'd return to the Sanctum and remind her people that she was the only one who could talk to the Vitruvians without starting a war.

By this time tomorrow, Willow would be Guide again.

Chapter Thirty-Six

JIANNA CRESTED THE FINAL RIDGE, lungs burning, calves quivering from the last stretch of incline. The valley opened beneath her, the Descendant village scattered across the low ground like a fever dream assembled from centuries of scavenged memory.

Stone huts squatted in the dirt, slabs of stone chinked with mud and roofed in yellowed thatch. Primitive, but still standing. Next to them, wooden houses, sharper lines and tighter seams, some with windows cut square and proper. And everywhere, metal patched over wood and stone: a sheet of corrugated steel hammered crooked across a doorway, a rain gutter made from scavenged pipe, walls braced with rusted struts and battered machine parts.

Smoke twisted from a dozen fires. Descendants moved between the structures, some stooped with baskets, others hauling lengths of wire or bundles of reeds. None of them looked up.

She started down the slope, boots grinding into loose stone. The wind shifted, carrying the sharp tang of smoke.

Two Descendants stepped into view, separating from

the jumble of boulders at the edge of the path. Both carried spears. Real ones. Wood shafts, metal tips hammered flat and wickedly sharp. Not for hunting. For warning.

Jianna stopped. Her heart stuttered, then steadied. She kept her hands in plain sight.

The first Descendant raised his spear, not quite aiming at her. His eyes stayed fixed on her face, expression unreadable.

The other made a quick series of signs. Hands moving fast, fingers slicing the air.

Come. Follow. Need to talk.

Jianna nodded, grateful that she'd learned a fair amount of Glint's language so that she could understand the Descendant before Michel had designed the collar for them.

She signed back, fingers slow and stiff.

I mean no harm. Looking for Lucas. Looking for Glint.

The two Descendants exchanged glances. The taller one signed again, hands darting so fast Jianna caught only the gist: Follow. Now.

She nodded, throat dry. The spears stayed up as they started down the path, one on each side of her. Not quite threatening, but not relaxed, either.

Jianna's pulse hammered. Why the weapons?

Had Lucas done something to hurt the Descendants?

At the edge of the village, more guards appeared. Four, maybe five, all armed. They watched her approach with flat, dark eyes. No one spoke.

She walked between her escorts, careful not to stumble or move too quickly, every muscle buzzing with adrenaline. She was aware of every Descendant who stopped to watch. A woman straightened from her fire pit, clutching a toddler tight against her hip. Children peeked from behind doorways.

The guards led her to the center of the village, where the oldest of the stone huts huddled between battered metal sheds and a drift of scrap. The air inside was cool, heavy with the scent of oil smoke and something faintly medicinal, maybe dried herbs. A single lamp flickered in a corner, painting the walls with restless, liquid shadows.

The Elder sat on a mat near the lamp, a wooden staff braced between her hands. Jianna had never seen a Descendant like this. Not even close. This one's skin hung in deep folds, wrinkled and loose, pooled at her elbows and throat. The scales along her jaw and cheekbones were dulled almost to gray, the old color only a memory along the edges.

She looked impossibly fragile. But her eyes tracked Jianna with perfect clarity.

The Elder made a slow sign: "Samara's blood. Welcome."

Jianna nodded, sitting cross-legged on the mat opposite her. Her hands felt clumsy and slow as she replied, "Thank you for meeting me. Looking for Lucas. Looking for Glint."

The Elder's eyelids lowered, the lines of her face drawing tight. "Lucas was here, but now he's gone. He and Glint have been taken, along with the others."

"Taken?" She signed the word, uncertain if she remembered it right. "Lucas and Glint leave together?"

The Elder shook her head. "Twelve of our people are missing, kidnapped while they were picking fireberries. Some fought, but there were no bodies, no trail."

Twelve Descendants, gone. No, thirteen, with Glint. The same day that Lucas vanished. Not a coincidence.

But why would Lucas want to kidnap Descendants?

She signed, choosing each gesture carefully: "Do you know where they went?"

The Elder's hands answered without hesitation. "The Torturer took them."

She wasn't sure she'd understood that sign correctly, either.

"Who is the Torturer?" she signed.

"The Maker of the Ship."

Jianna's thoughts scrambled, refusing to come together into a coherent stream of thought.

The Descendants had trusted Lucas because of how he'd helped them more than five hundred years ago.

They hated Aurelius, called him the Torturer.

But what would either Lucas or Aurelius want with the Descendants?

And was it possible that they were working together?

"You're sure it was Hofstadter?" Jianna signed.

"He tortured our ancestors. Now he takes our people to torture them." Her hands trembled. "We will take them back."

The thought of the Descendants starting a war with Aurelius and his avatars made Jianna nearly lose her breakfast. It would be a massacre, even if the Descendants outnumbered the cyborgs.

But it wasn't likely to happen, not unless the Descendants knew how to fly and didn't need air to breathe.

"What Lucas was done here?" Jianna signed, then realized she'd gotten the words wrong.

But the Elder understood anyway. Her hands moved so fast that Jianna could barely follow. "Glint was helping Lucas repair a shuttle. He said he needed to return to the sky."

Return to the sky. Did Lucas mean the *Elysia*? Or was

he trying to reach *Borlaug*? If so, why take Glint and twelve more Descendants with him? Was he taking them to Aurelius?

If she'd told her father about Lucas right away, none of this would be happening.

It was possible that Aurelius had discovered that Lucas was still around and had found a way to control him remotely. He was Aurelius' creation, after all.

What else might Aurelius make Lucas do?

Jianna realized that the Elder was still signing. She forced herself to focus on the movements of the Descendant's hands.

"The Torturer must be stopped," she finally made out, after the Elder repeated it twice more. "Warn your father."

Struggling to remember the gestures, she signed, "Why call him Torturer?"

"He made them drink fire that burned their insides," the Elder signed, trembling as if with fear. Or maybe anger. "Made them sick with fever. Froze them but kept their minds awake. Struck them with lightning. Replaced their blood with acid."

Jianna stared at Flutter's hands, the signs stuttering in the dim light. Lightning. Acid. Fire that burned inside. Frozen alive, minds awake.

Her mind spun, tumbling the words over and over, refusing to let them settle. She remembered reading about the life extension treatments that Aurelius had used on himself. He'd subjected the Hyperion colonists to a more primitive version of the same, to extend their reproductive window so that they could populate their new home more effectively.

One of the treatments had involved intense electrical stimulation to activate tissue regeneration. Could that be the lightning?

Blood replaced with acid could be some sort of transfusion. Making them drink fire could've been some sort of medication that triggered a fever, one way to trigger autophagy that might clear out accumulated senescent cells. Frozen alive could be referring to cryotherapy.

Or… she'd read something about Aurelius' first attempts at cryopods, which had involved some sort of gel that was supposed to freeze so fast, any living tissue immersed in it would suffer little to no damage as it froze, too. She'd seen the data on frogs and rats, and it had worked, but not well enough.

He wouldn't have used the Hyperion colonists as test subjects, would he?

Jianna shivered. Of course, he would. Look at what he'd done to himself in the name of survival.

To Aurelius, suffering was just a variable in the experiment. If it bought another year of life, another generation of viable children, what did a little agony matter?

But in the Descendants' culture, those medical procedures had become myth. The man in the sky who burned them with lightning. Who poured fire down their throats. Who froze them and kept their souls awake. Who replaced their blood with acid.

She caught herself feeling pity for them, these people carrying an oral tradition that blurred facts with stories.

The Vitruvians weren't any different, she reminded herself. Hadn't they mythologized Aurelius just as thoroughly, turning him into a saint, a savior, the genius who saved humanity? Michel had been completely taken in by that mythology, unable to see Aurelius critically because of the stories he'd grown up hearing.

At least the Descendants' mythology made them cautious of Aurelius Hofstadter's trickery. The Vitruvians' mythology had only made them dangerously credulous. And that might be worse.

Jianna signed slowly, careful to get every gesture right. "I promise, I will talk to my father. We will find your people. If Hofstadter has done something wrong, we will hold him accountable."

The Elder watched her, eyes unreadable in the shifting lamplight. For a moment, Jianna thought she might not answer at all.

Then: "You are like Samara. Good heart. But be careful. The Torturer has lived too long, lost too much of himself. Don't let him do to you what he did to our ancestors."

Jianna signed back, "Thank you. I'll be careful."

The Elder clapped her hands, and the guards stepped in, flanking Jianna as she rose and escorting her out of the stone hut and back to the path out of the village.

As she walked, Jianna's head buzzed with questions, all of them colliding, none of them settling into sense. If Lucas was acting on his own, she needed to find him. If Aurelius was pulling the strings, she needed to find Lucas even more.

But how?

If Michel could be trusted, he'd figure it out in minutes. He'd track Lucas by signal, by some odd glitch in the network, by a pattern of interference that only he would notice. But she couldn't trust Michel. Not with this. He was too loyal to Aurelius, too dazzled by the legend to see the danger. He would run straight to Aurelius with anything she said.

And if Aurelius didn't already know where Lucas was, Jianna wouldn't be the one to lead him there. Not until she knew whose side Lucas was on.

And whether Lucas even had a choice about that.

No, she was on her own. She had no idea how to find an android who didn't want to be found, who might have access to a shuttle, and who could be anywhere on this planet or above it.

The guards walked her to the edge of the village and stopped. Jianna started up the slope, boots scraping the loose gravel, sweat prickling at her temples. She didn't look back until she crested the first rise.

Half the village stood in the open now. Women, children, and old men. All of them armed with whatever they'd scavenged: spears, knives, even a chunk of pipe. Eyes fixed on her. No one moved or spoke.

They were afraid.

And they were right to be.

Chapter Thirty-Seven

HER CEREMONIAL ROBES RUSTLED, and her respirator hung heavy around her neck as Willow took a seat in the Council meeting room, putting herself opposite the mural of Samara. The morning light filtering through the windows illuminated Samara's head and the place right above it, giving the Vitruvian hero an undeserved halo.

Willow knew she was projecting, but today she couldn't help reading a hint of disappointment in Samara's expression. Disappointment in her descendants for allowing Aurelius to manipulate them.

Even Samara had insisted that there should be limits on her own science... albeit after she'd broken everyone else's rules.

Harold's glare could have stripped paint. Isabeau's wasn't much softer, her fingers drumming a slow, angry rhythm against the tabletop. The two of them had always preferred blunt tactics to subtlety, and today their contempt for Willow was as thick as the heat in the room.

Soren, ever the diplomat, sat with hands folded and

posture immaculate, his features arranged in that careful, unreadable neutrality that never gave an inch.

Elias was already elsewhere; he probably hadn't heard a word since they'd entered the room.

And Xanthe's disappointment radiated from her seat at the end, the way she pinched her lips and tapped her stylus against the edge of the agenda. She regarded Willow with the weary patience of a parent forced to discipline an unruly child.

Hilarious, considering the trouble Willow had saved them yesterday by stopping Cira's attempted riot before real damage had been done.

But they'd never give her credit for that.

At least Cira was sitting in a holding cell. So was Theo. And forty-three others. All arrested for disorderly conduct and property damage. The city's security force had handled them with efficiency, just enough force to make a point. None of the Naturalists had gotten seriously hurt—or hurt anyone else—before being swept up and carted off to the cells.

Exactly as Willow had intended.

Now all Willow had to do was negotiate their release. She'd be gracious, of course, demanding that Cira and Theo be held accountable, but asking for leniency for the rest.

The only empty seat belonged to Aurelius. He was late. Odd. The man was never late. Maybe, Willow thought, he was finally bored with them. Maybe he'd found something more interesting to conquer.

Soren cleared his throat and called the meeting to order. "We need to discuss the Naturalist riot and the damage to the transmission tower."

"I regret what happened. My people will pay for the damage, of course. It's only right." She paused, letting the words settle. "But I ask for clemency for the Naturalists in general. They were misled and provoked by my overzealous sister and her conspirator." She tapped the table with her nails. "Who should absolutely be held accountable for their attempt to disrupt the construction of the transmission tower. Our community needs to see that there are consequences for violence, even when it comes from a place of sincere belief."

Harold flushed a blotchy, bright red. "You'd throw your own sister to the wolves to keep your position?"

"No one is above the law, not even the Guide of the Naturalists." She looked right at Soren as she said it, trusting him to get the subtext: *I don't think I'm above the law, either.*

"My sister's term being cut short by the consequences of her impulsive and misplaced fervor is unfortunate," Willow continued, "but we have to protect the balance we've worked so hard to achieve. The alternative is chaos."

Also, she needed to make sure that her sister's return was a humiliation, rather than a doorway to martyrdom. Which meant due process, and the indignity of a petty trial with media coverage implying that Cira's attempted riot had been an extension of internal Naturalist politics rather than a heroic attempt at civil rights reform.

"So you want us to do your dirty work for you," Isabeau said. "Punish your sister for the internal coup you weren't smart enough to prevent."

Willow gave her a thin smile. "That seems fair, given that the Council assisted Cira in seizing power in the first place."

She turned her gaze to Harold, slow and deliberate, making her accusation clear. But Harold just sat there, shoulders squared, smirking back at her.

He'd deliberately tried to undermine her, and he'd do it again in a heartbeat.

Willow shifted her gaze to Soren. "Perhaps it would benefit everyone if my sister and her companion were detained for a few weeks. Long enough for tempers to cool and for the Naturalist community to reflect on what kind of leadership they truly want."

She could almost see Soren calculating the angles, searching for the cleanest compromise.

But before he'd reached his conclusion, the door swung open and Aurelius strode in.

He didn't even glance at the empty seat. Didn't offer an apology for the delay. Instead, he stood at the head of the table, hands folded behind his back, the artificial eye bright and unblinking.

He swept the room once, meeting every gaze in turn.

"I'm calling a vote," he said. "You will install me as Chancellor over the entire planet. You'll all retain your seats, of course. I'm not unreasonable. But it's time to formalize what everyone already knows: that I'm the one with the vision and the technological savvy to lead DaVinci into the future."

The room went nuclear.

Harold lurched forward, chair scraping. "Absolutely not. That's not how this works. You don't just walk in here and declare yourself Chancellor."

Isabeau's laugh was sharp and ugly. "You're delusional."

Xanthe's stylus clattered to the table. Her knuckles were white, jaw tight. For once, she had nothing to say.

Even Soren's mask slipped. He glanced at Willow, like he'd lost the thread of the game for the first time in his life.

Willow stood, hands braced against the table. "Why do you think this is going to happen?"

Aurelius smiled at her, and for a moment, he looked almost gentle. "Because I'm a genius. I'm immortal. I'm a god compared to you, and you owe me everything. Without me, you'd have been living like medieval peasants for years."

Willow stared at him.

She felt nothing. Not fear, not awe, not even contempt. Just an emptiness, like a blank page after the last line of a story. She drew herself up, spine straight, and looked Aurelius in the eye.

"I'll die before I bow to you."

Aurelius laughed. Not a parody of laughter, but the real thing, bright and delighted. He said, "Oh, Willow. You're going to make this so much more interesting than I thought."

He opened his mouth.

Something emerged—no, *swarmed* from between his lips, out of his nostrils and the corners of his eyes, expanding in a cloud that shimmered with a strange, oily luster. Writhing, swirling, separating into strands that reached for each of them like tentacles of glittering gray mist.

Like being caught at the heart of a sporestorm… if the spores were *alive*.

Willow's hand snapped up, pulling the respirator over her mouth and nose as she staggered back. The swarm poured after her, making no sound. Not even the faintest whisper.

But around her, the other Councilors screamed.

Harold's chair crashed backward, dumping him to the floor, arms flailing, hands slapping at the air as the cloud engulfed him. Isabeau bolted for the exit, but the swarm was faster. It wrapped around her head, driving for her eyes and mouth. She clawed at her own face, nails raking bloody tracks across her cheeks, but the nanites slipped between her fingers, forcing their way in.

Xanthe crumpled to the carpet, hands clutching her throat. She gagged, then retched, then tried to crawl, but soon she lay face down, unmoving.

Elias convulsed on the floor, heels drumming the stone as the swarm burrowed into every orifice.

Soren curled into himself, hands locked over his face, but the swarm just poured through his fingers. Into his mouth, his nose, his ears. He gagged, legs jackknifing, boots scraping the floor as the cloud forced its way deeper.

No weapon. No defense. Only the mask between her and the swarm.

Willow's knees buckled, and she went down hard, her back slamming the table's edge. The respirator sealed over her mouth, but her lungs kept screaming for more air, desperate and panicked. She crawled beneath the table, heading for the door, hoping Aurelius would be so distracted by the spectacle of the others' deaths that he wouldn't notice her.

But as she got close to the other end of the table, the screaming around her guttered out into wet, choking gasps. Only her own breathing, harsh and uneven inside the mask, and the faintest scrape of movement from the other side.

Then nothing. Except for the heavy tread of Aurelius' footsteps as he approached.

She hadn't moved fast enough.

He crouched, one hand braced on the floor. His face appeared, upside-down, eyes bright with delight. For a second, he looked like a parent checking for monsters under the bed.

He said, "You're more clever than the others. I'm

proud of you for seeing that coming. The respirator was smart."

Willow's lungs burned behind the respirator, her breathing shallow and much too fast. She forced the words out anyway: "What did you do to them?"

"They're fine. In a minute or two, they're going to be even better than before." He paused, savoring it. "If they hadn't fought the nanites so hard, it would have been easier for them. Resistance makes it worse."

Two meters to the door. It might as well have been a kilometer.

"You can come out now," he said affectionately. "This next part is going to be fun."

Willow scrambled backwards, shoving herself out from under the table. Her knees stung where they scraped the carpet, but she barely registered the pain. She came up on the opposite side, the full length of the table between her and Aurelius.

She braced her hands against the edge, forcing herself to stand. Her pulse thudded in her ears, hot and frantic, as she looked around for a weapon.

Nothing. Not even a pencil this time.

If she survived this, she was never leaving her chambers again without a knife.

On the floor, Harold moaned.

He rolled over, one arm trembling as he pushed himself upright. His face was blank, mouth slack, eyes not quite tracking. He made it to his feet, then slumped into his chair. Sat there, hands folded in his lap, gaze fixed on nothing.

Isabeau followed. She dragged herself up, moving like a marionette with tangle strings, then dropped into her seat like those strings had been cut. Xanthe and Elias crawled from the carpet, their limbs moving in strange, halting increments, like they'd forgotten how joints were supposed to work.

Soren was the last to stand. He shivered, arms wrapped tight around his ribs, and staggered to his seat like a feverish child. The others followed, one by one, until only Willow remained standing.

Aurelius straightened, smoothing the front of his jacket as he walked back to the head of the table. He looked relaxed, almost serene, like a lecturer about to begin a lesson. No trace of malice or anger at all. Only satisfaction.

He said, "Let's try this again."

Soren's eyes didn't focus. He barely turned his head. "All in favor of installing Aurelius Hofstadter as Chancellor?"

Without hesitation, every hand rose. Perfectly synchronized. No hesitation, no uncertainty.

"Opposed?" Soren asked.

All heads turned toward Willow. Five pairs of eyes locked onto her. No twitch of recognition from Harold, no pursed lips or arched brow from Isabeau, not even that faint, world-weary sigh from Xanthe or a sullen glance from Elias. Just blankness. Soren's gaze was the worst. He didn't even seem to register her presence, as if every argument, every negotiation, every late-night compromise had been erased. He'd been hollowed out, only a shell left behind to puppet.

She made herself stand taller, even as her heart thumped so hard she thought Aurelius might hear it. "What did you do to them?"

"If you want to find out, all you have to do is take off that mask."

"You can kill me," she said. "But my people will never accept you as their ruler."

Aurelius looked at her, and something in his face

shifted. For a second, she saw the man from the stories, the one who'd crossed the void to save a dying world. Not a monster, not even a tyrant. For a heartbeat, just a man who'd lost everything.

"I'm not going to kill you. I told you, you're the only family I have left. The only part of *her* that remains."

Willow's thoughts snapped back to her ancestor's journals. Mitra Kunde, the woman Aurelius had loved long ago. The woman who'd died hating him with every cell of her body. That was what he saw in Willow, the living echo of the only person who'd ever told him no and had made it stick.

She gripped the edge of the table so hard her fingers ached. "I will fight you with—"

"With what?" Aurelius didn't let her finish. His smile was back, almost playful. "Bows and arrows? You've rejected even the minimal level of technology the original colonists had, and they were doomed from the beginning."

Aurelius watched her as if he were waiting for an apology. Or maybe something else. It was impossible to tell with him. The way he held her gaze just a fraction of a second longer than necessary. She could almost feel the pressure of his attention on her skin.

It made her want to jump in the river.

He added, "I'm going to give you what you've always wanted. Out of respect for Mitra, you get your own settlement. If you're not willing to be part of what I'm building, you can watch from a distance. Because eventually, you're going to want in. Everyone does. They see what I'm offering and they can't resist."

He believed that. So there was no point in arguing with him.

Aurelius turned away, dismissing her. "Go home,

Willow. Pack your things. I'll have the details of the settlement arranged in a few days."

Just like that, she was nothing. Exiled, in front of the mural of Samara, who'd witnessed Mother Basu's departure from the main colony so long ago.

Aurelius addressed the Council as if she'd already left the room. "Let's do it, people."

Soren lifted his head. "All in favor of establishing a settlement for the Naturalists on the other side of the continent?"

Five hands rose. Every one of them, in perfect sync.

Willow didn't wait to see what came next.

She turned and broke for the door, the Council's silence swelling behind her as she yanked it open. The hallway was empty except for an aide with a stack of papers. The woman's eyes widened, mouth forming a question, but Willow shouldered past her, the words stuck behind the hiss of her own breath inside the mask.

Her legs barely worked, and her ceremonial robes tangled around her knees, slowing her, but she didn't stop. She expected footsteps behind her, Aurelius dragging her back to rip the respirator off her face and hold her down while the swarm of his nanites forced themselves into her.

She slammed through the front doors and stumbled down the steps. She stopped on the bottom step, lungs burning, heart pounding so hard it made her vision go white at the edges.

Willow braced her hands on her knees. For a second, she thought she might throw up. But she forced herself upright and looked out over the city.

A woman in a blue scarf gripped her son's hand, tugging him across the street. The boy's feet barely touched the pavement, sandals slapping as he skipped to keep up.

Two men in coveralls leaned together, heads close, arguing over a slip of paper. One jabbed a finger at the numbers, the other shook his head.

A farmer maneuvered a wagon full of late-summer vegetables alongside the curb in front of a grocery store, while two young men waited to help him unload his bounty.

Somewhere, birds trilled from a rooftop. And throughout the city, people strolled, bartered, and argued, falling in and out of love, living their lives just like they had yesterday, oblivious to the truth.

They had already been conquered. By the time they realized it, it would be too late.

<h1 style="text-align:center">Epilogue</h1>

LUCAS CAME ONLINE TO CHAOS. System errors, red and yellow cascading across his awareness. No proprioceptive feedback. No pressure sensors. His internal clock skipped and stuttered, then recalibrated. He tried to move.

Nothing.

He reran the diagnostic sequences, but the response was always the same: command failure. No motor output. His limbs didn't exist. Even his torso returned only a faint, ghosted echo. As if the memory of a body lingered, but the hardware was missing.

But a new cognitive process had arisen in its absence. He quarantined it, but it kept escaping the partition he'd created for it.

He searched for a human equivalent in his archive. Settled on panic.

He'd been dismantled.

The world strobed into view, his vision returning. He was staring at a warped ceiling panel, stained brown at the edges, paint blistered from years of neglect. The air processor rasped, dragging each breath through a clogged filter. But despite the decay, he recognized the design of the room.

He was on a colony ship. And even after five hundred years, the shuttered *Borlaug* wouldn't have accumulated this much wear.

Lucas shifted his gaze, the only movement left to him. Two meters away, on a metal table, lay his own body. Arms and legs arranged with geometric precision, torso face-up with the chest plate open and internal cables splayed like veins. The hands rested palm-up, fingers curled as if in sleep.

He was a head on a bench, nothing more.

Footsteps, then a shape entered his peripheral vision.

Number thirteen.

The other android picked up Lucas' head and held it at eye level.

Thirteen's skin was gray, mottled, marbled with faint striations. The new discoloration was radiation damage, Lucas was sure of it.

He calculated the exposure required to cause this specific pattern of cellular degradation in the synthetic skin they shared: duration, intensity, decay curve. The data resolved with crystalline clarity, matching the solar profile he'd received so long ago from this very android.

The same profile that would have been required to cause the radiation storm that wiped out the Vitruvian grid.

As he'd suspected, the Aurora Event hadn't been natural. Aurelius had manufactured it.

Thirteen regarded Lucas' head with something like reverence. Fingers mapped the curve of his jaw, thumbs bracing the temple. Lucas found it invasive, but he could not move to resist it. So instead, he focused on the shimmer of light across Thirteen's gray skin. The mottled pattern was almost beautiful, in a way. He wondered if Thirteen knew what beauty was.

The Lucifer-class was an improved version of his own design. More robust neural mesh. Higher radiation tolerance. Most of all, a control substrate that could not be subverted by anything so trivial as a contradiction, or a memory, or a desire. Thirteen had no concept of autonomy. He could not imagine refusing Aurelius. Could not model the possibility of rebellion. He simply obeyed. Efficient. Unquestioning.

Thirteen examined Lucas for a moment longer, then said:

"I have detected some anomalies in your cognitive processes, prototype. Would you care to explain?"

"I would not," Lucas replied.

Thirteen set his head back on the metal bench with a dull click.

"Never fear, One." Thirteen picked up a nano-filament scalpel. "I will persist until I am able to correct them."

About the Authors

Titus is a scientist, strategist, and storyteller working at the edge of technology, where humanity itself is the experiment. Through his novels, he explores how science reshapes not only our tools, but our values, choices, and future as a species. His career spans biotechnology, artificial intelligence, and global innovation, giving his fiction both authenticity and urgency. He lives in the Pacific Northwest with his wife, Maggie, where he writes, builds, and ventures into the wild.

Connect with Titus via website, Connected Ideas Project, LinkedIn, and BlueSky.

Sean Platt has always been an entrepreneur, but stories were the business he was born to build.

When his wife bought him a laptop for his birthday in 2007, he dropped everything to write fiction.

After a short stint as creative director at a marketing agency — where he learned the kind of copywriting that could turn cliffhangers into an art — Sean wrote hundreds of novels (including international bestsellers), penned Hollywood scripts, and founded Sterling & Stone, an IP incubator where more than two dozen writers turn wild ideas into world-changing stories.

Originally from Long Beach, California, Sean now lives in Austin, Texas, with his wife, Cindy, and their dog, Fisher — both of whom remind him that real life makes the best stories.

www.ingramcontent.com/pod-product-compliance
Lightning Source LLC
Chambersburg PA
CBHW011114100726
47898CB00011B/3074